PRIZE SURPRISE SWEEPSTAKES!

This month's prize:

A FABULOUS SHARP VIEWCAM!

This month, as a special surprise, we're giving away a Sharp ViewCam**, the big-screen camcorder that has revolutionized home videos!

This is the camcorder everyone's talking about! Sharp's new ViewCam has a big 3" full-color viewing screen with 180° swivel action that lets you control everything you record—and watch it at the same time! Features include a remote control (so you can get into the picture yourself), 8 power zoom, full-range auto focus, battery pack, recharger and more!

The next page contains two Entry Coupons (as does every book you received this shipment). Complete and return *all* the entry coupons; **the more times you enter, the better your chances of winning!**

Then keep your fingers crossed, because you'll find out by November 15, 1995 if you're the winner!

Remember: The more times you enter, the better your chances of winning!*

*NO PURCHASE OR OBLIGATION TO CONTINUE BEING A SUBSCRIBER NECESSARY TO ENTER. SEE THE BACK PAGE FOR ALTERNATE MEANS OF ENTRY, AND RULES.

**THE PROPRIETORS OF THE TRADEMARK ARE NOT ASSOCIATED WITH THIS PROMOTION.

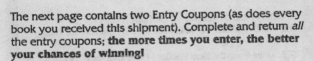

W9-DEJ-415

PRIZE SURPRISE
SWEEPSTAKES

OFFICIAL ENTRY COUPON

This entry must be received by: OCTOBER 30, 1995
This month's winner will be notified by: NOVEMBER 15, 1995

YES, I want to win the Sharp ViewCam! Please enter me in the drawing and
let me know if I've won!

Name_____

Address _____ Apt. _____

City   State/Prov.   Zip/Postal Code

Account #_____

Return entry with invoice in reply envelope.

© 1995 HARLEQUIN ENTERPRISES LTD.   CVC KAL

PRIZE SURPRISE
SWEEPSTAKES

OFFICIAL ENTRY COUPON

This entry must be received by: OCTOBER 30, 1995
This month's winner will be notified by: NOVEMBER 15, 1995

YES, I want to win the Sharp ViewCam! Please enter me in the drawing and
let me know if I've won!

Name_____

Address _____ Apt. _____

City   State/Prov.   Zip/Postal Code

Account #_____

Return entry with invoice in reply envelope.

© 1995 HARLEQUIN ENTERPRISES LTD.   CVC KAL

The ghost transformed itself into Ian MacLaurin.

Elizabeth's spine melted to jelly with relief.

"Oh, it's you!" she breathed, light-headed. She attempted to straighten herself against the door, but her knees were not working.

She could see MacLaurin was experiencing no similar relief. In fact, he looked extremely irritated.

He stopped a few feet from her and the door. "What are you doing here?"

Elizabeth straightened. "What am *I* doing here?"

"I'm in no mood for absurdity," he growled, "and we might not have much time to repair this disaster! I didn't want any missteps, and now already this evening's plan is ruined. Not to mention the possibility that we may have advertised to the entire castle that we are up to our necks in intrigue!"

Dear Reader,

The Scottish Highlands, an ancient enchanted castle, a steamy romance and an intriguing mystery— *MacLaurin's Lady* has it all, and more! This delightful story by one of Harlequin Historical's most popular authors, Julie Tetel, tells the tale of an honorable, but dispossessed, nobleman and a reclusive spinster who fall under the spell of a magical castle, with the help of his father's ghost. Don't miss this award-winning author's extraordinary book.

If you are looking for Westerns, this month's Women of the West title, Cheryl St. John's *Saint or Sinner,* is a warmhearted story about a man who is determined to right the wrongs of his past and win the trust of a reluctant spinster.

You are in for a treat with *Moonrise,* Ana Seymour's tale of a beautiful highway bandit who finds herself falling in love with the very man sent by the king to capture her. And, with this month's *Besieged,* Laurel Ames once again sets her unique characters against the rich backdrop of Regency England to tell the story of an ex-soldier who must overcome his past before he can accept the promise of a future with the woman he loves.

Whatever your taste in historical reading, we hope you'll keep a lookout for all four of these delightful titles, available wherever Harlequin Historicals are sold.

Sincerely,

Tracy Farrell
Senior Editor

Please address questions and book requests to:
Harlequin Reader Service
U.S.: 3010 Walden Ave., P.O. Box 1325, Buffalo, NY 14269
Canadian: P.O. Box 609, Fort Erie, Ont. L2A 5X3

JULIE TETEL

MacLAURIN'S LADY

Harlequin Books

TORONTO • NEW YORK • LONDON
AMSTERDAM • PARIS • SYDNEY • HAMBURG
STOCKHOLM • ATHENS • TOKYO • MILAN
MADRID • WARSAW • BUDAPEST • AUCKLAND

ISBN 0-373-28887-5

MACLAURIN'S LADY

Copyright © 1995 by Julie Tetel Andresen.

Books by Julie Tetel

Harlequin Historicals

Sweet Suspicions #128
*Sweet Seduction #167
*Sweet Sensations #182
Simon's Lady #229
*Sweet Surrender #255
MacLaurin's Lady #287

*The North Point Series

Harlequin Regency
The Temporary Bride

JULIE TETEL

has always loved both history and romance, making it easy for her to love reading and writing historical romances. She is from a suburb of Chicago and currently lives in Durham, North Carolina. She has two sons, two careers, at least two points of view and one husband.

Chapter One

The Scottish Highlands
July 1720

When Elizabeth Cameron stepped down from her carriage and into the shadow of the ancient dwelling looming before her, she let her fancy roam free.

Castle Cairn was a monstrously large pile of lichened stone, with wings rambling at every odd angle and massive turrets uniting them at unlikely junctures. Even on this sunny day, gloom crouched in the crooks and crevices of the immense facade, which seemed to frown under the weight of a crowd of crow-stepped gables and a steep-pitched slate roof. Her active imagination had no difficulty transforming this ungainly structure into a mythical beast turned to stone by a powerful wizard. It slumbered unpeacefully, she could tell, impatient to sleep off its enchantment.

Greatly satisfied by her extravagant whimsy, she turned away from the sleeping monster and sought out her host—Robert MacLaurin, Lord Mure. She spied a patchwork of familiar plaids across the courtyard and identified his lordship by his kilt of green MacLaurin tartan atop which he wore a coat of brown velvet. She began to move toward him.

When his lordship saw her, he loosed himself from the knot of his other guests. "Well, well, Mistress Elizabeth!" the laird of Castle Cairn exclaimed, meeting her halfway. "Ye're not the first to arrive, nor the last, neither. I'm happy to see ye!" He kissed her soundly on both cheeks. "I'm a wee bit surprised to see ye, as well, for ye've disappointed me too many times by refusing my fine invitations!"

She smiled. "I've been far more disappointed than you to have regretted all your fine invitations. However, this time, I was determined to attend the summer gathering of our society, and so here I am!"

"Och, ye're telling me ye've lacked until now the proper determination to attend our humble meetings?" his lordship teased.

"You know for a fact," she returned, "that I've lacked the proper parental approval."

"Yer father's changed his mind, then, and thinks that his daughter's membership in the Royal Historical Society is no longer a shame and disgrace to the Clan Cameron?"

"My father," she said with a mischievous wink, "left ten days ago for business in Glasgow and won't be back until next week."

"Ye've come against yer father's wishes?" his lordship demanded with mock disapproval.

"How would I know what his wishes are?" she defended herself with answering mock innocence. "For all I know, he *has* changed his mind and is now proud that I'm writing the history of his beloved clan."

His lordship dropped his teasing manner. His brow creased. "Yer father does not know ye're here?"

She conceded that he did not, but she was prepared for this moment. "I have an extraordinarily good reason for having come," she told him with a mysterious smile, "which I'll be happy to tell you about now or later, at your leisure!"

"Will yer father approve of it?" his lordship demanded, still frowning.

Her smile remained mysterious. "I don't know," she replied, "but you certainly will."

His lordship's brow cleared, his curiosity plainly piqued. "Tell me about it later, then, Mistress Elizabeth, when my guests are settled." His expansive gesture encompassed the great bulk of his ancestral castle. "I've room enough and to spare for any unexpected arrivals, and I'm glad ye've decided to come!"

Elizabeth was relieved that his lordship had so easily accepted her unusual decision to attend the summer meeting. "I'm more than glad I've come," she said, with a touch of awe as she once again surveyed the forbidding facade. "Castle Cairn is every bit as gloomy as you've described it, and I can hardly wait for the tour."

"We've ghosts to entertain ye, too, Mistress Elizabeth. A castle full of them!" his lordship replied with great good humor. "But speaking of unexpected arrivals, I cannot be lingering here, as much as I'd like to, for His Grace, the Duke of Devonshire, arrived some moments ago, eager to attend our meeting himself."

"The Duke of Devonshire?" she echoed. She knew very little of this distinguished peer of the realm beyond the fact that he was a patron of the historical society. "He's never chosen to attend one of our meetings before."

His lordship cleared his throat uncomfortably. "He's come to Scotland to execute some family business in

Edinburgh and said that he saw no reason not to attend our meeting."

"Then we should feel very honored," Elizabeth commented.

"Oh, indeed! And so, I'm thinking, 'tis fortunate that Lady Michael agreed to bring me my latest shipment of books from London so that she can provide His Grace London-style company for as long as he chooses to stay. And so I told His Grace."

Elizabeth smiled, imagining what such an august personage as the Duke of Devonshire would make of the week's activities. "It might be very dreary for His Grace to be shut up with a lot of boring historians over the next few days."

His lordship laughed. "And so I should think, but even the news that Lady Michael is bringing no less than four boxes of volumes I ordered from the best presses did not scare him off!"

"His Grace either has unusual fortitude or an imperfect idea of what the summer meeting of the Royal Historical Society entails."

His lordship winked and said amiably, "Well, well, enough of the chatter. I must be off to see to His Grace's comforts. And here is Mrs. Barrow, our housekeeper, who will be at your service. Ye came with no abigail, I see. Until later, then, Mistress Elizabeth, and Mrs. Barrow will tell ye all ye need to know."

Mrs. Barrow came to help Elizabeth sort out her baggage and to inform her which room would be hers. Elizabeth declined the offer of an escort to her chamber and assured the housekeeper that she could find it on her own, if given explicit directions. She noticed that some of the guests had already gone inside several minutes before, in the wake of Lord Mure. Others remained outside, milling about. She decided to seize her chance to enjoy alone her first impressions of the castle interior.

At the moment she was completely satisfied with her impulsive decision to come to Castle Cairn without her father's consent, and she welcomed her week of freedom. From guilt. From the strictures of her father's narrow notions of propriety. From the daily cares of raising her much-loved young ward, Allegra. Then, as if the very prospect of freedom freed her thoughts, she entertained the odd, self-justifying idea that she had been punished long enough for the wayward behavior of her cousin Fiona.

With a flutter of excitement she left the warmth of the sunshine behind and slipped under the main portal and into the mouth of the stone beast. Once inside, she took a good ten steps into the hall. Because her eyes had not yet adjusted to the sudden dark, she felt, more than saw, the vast proportions of the space she had entered. She breathed in the dankness. She let her skin absorb the coolness. She leaned her head back. With her eyes open, the vaults of the ceiling slowly resolved themselves into shadowed recesses.

Able to see now, she looked eagerly about. What she perceived far exceeded her expectations. She felt engulfed, swallowed whole in a space of spooky, unspoken history and ancient secrets. She shivered delightedly.

The main entry hall was a good thirty feet square, with a smooth flooring of huge stone flags. In front of her, to her right, was a wide and massive stone staircase, squared at its half-story landing, rather than curved. Its age-worn steps were weakly illuminated by a vertical row of three small, high, stained-glass windows. Evidently the wall of the staircase gave onto the outside, no doubt to one of the

dozen interior courtyards that Lord Mure had described
to her.

Farther to her right was a long hallway that vanished
into impenetrable gloom. Directly in front of her, to the
immediate left of the staircase, was another, similarly
disappearing hallway. To her far left was both another
grand hallway and a staircase, this one narrower though
no less massive than the main staircase.

Elizabeth saw that Lord Mure had not—as too many
another Highland laird had—tried to modernize such an
ancient dwelling. Instead, he had set about bringing the
history of Castle Cairn to life. Modern sconces did not
grace the walls; rather, primitive torches were cinched to
the stones with leather straps. Nor were rugs placed on
the floor as a sop to modern tastes but, in keeping with
the old tradition, several tapestries of great antiquity
hung on the wall behind her.

In addition, his lordship had stationed around the hall
several old-fashioned floor candelabra of wrought iron.
They were man-sized and wicked looking and spiked with
dozens of candles. Elizabeth inspected the candelabra
behind her, which stood not more than a foot away. She
saw that the branches were formed in the shapes of fan-
tastical reptiles whose claws held the candles and over
which wax had dripped yellow warts that disfigured their
already hideous faces and bodies. One she identified as
the legendary basilisk, whose breath was fatal and whose
gaze could drive men mad. Another shiver skittered up
her spine.

She tore her eyes away from the candelabra and focused on the more reassuring figures of several suits of
armor propped in various corners of the hall. Probably
retrieved from a long-unused armory, these stern steel
men glowed satin with age and dim light. Suddenly one

of the suits of armor across the hall began to move, and her heart twisted in fear and anticipation to see the ghost of a long-dead knight coming toward her.

She noted first that his hair was an unghostly black. It was pulled back at the nape and disordered in a way to suggest that he had just traveled a long distance. As he approached, his features came into focus. To her basilisk-struck eye, she found him unimaginably handsome, nearly beautiful, just as she would expect a knight to be. His eyes looked keen and intelligent under winged black brows. His nose was straight. His jaw was lean and wore a day's growth of beard. His lips were shapely. He was broad shouldered and muscular and strode across the hall with command.

This was no ghost coming toward her, but a man in the flesh and blood. Her fancy, already freed, took flight. She reasoned that to have merited a return from the dead, the man in armor must have embodied the full catalog of knightly virtues in his past life. He would have been gentle with the weak and fierce with his enemies. He would have been loyal and true, virtuous and strong. Above all, he would have been chivalrous to the ladies. She was sure that a man like this would be able to see past the plainness of her exterior and into the beauty of her soul. Had he come to rescue her? Bemused, she had not known she was in danger.

When he was standing in front of her, he looked her up and down and inquired, "Are you new?"

His accent was not that of a Highland knight of yore but held an English intonation. "New?" she repeated curiously, still under the spell. She supposed she must appear new to his centuries-old perceptions, although she judged him to be not too many years older than herself.

"I mean, are you new here?" he clarified.

"In a way I suppose I am," she replied. She gave herself over to the enchantment of the moment. Dozens of questions crowded her head. She asked the most practical one first. "How did you get here, sir?"

"On my horse."

But of course! "How long did that take?"

"Less than a week."

"Oh!"

His eyes narrowed. "Since I haven't been here in a while," he said, "I'm wondering whether you were one of the newer lassies."

"You're from Castle Cairn, then?"

"Yes."

"How long have you been gone?"

"Ten years."

Ten years? She had thought it would have been more like five hundred.

"And given that absence," he continued with an air of slight puzzlement, "you can see why I don't know whether you are new here or not. You're the first one among the retainers that I haven't recognized."

She blinked once, twice. Her vision cleared, and she was able to register the significance of the man's comment and of his clothing. He wore no armor or even a knightly tunic. His jacket was modern, dark and well cut. His unfrilled white shirt was open at the neck. His vest was of black leather as were his breeches, which were stuffed into polished knee boots. His clothes were unfashionably plain, but he wore them with dash.

She gave herself a mental shake and decided that her impression of knight-come-to-life had been a trick of the poor light and the fact that he had come from the hallway directly opposite. She looked beyond his shoulder and saw the suit of armor still standing at attention, immobile and utterly useless. The spell began to break, and she realized that she had been living too long in her history books.

"You mean, do I work here?" she asked, feeling a self-conscious flush crawl up her cheeks. "No, sir, I do not."

He scrutinized her again. "Are you here to apply for a position?"

So much for his ability to see beyond her plain exterior and into the beauty of her soul! Thoroughly disillusioned and now embarrassed, Elizabeth cursed her overactive imagination. She gathered the little dignity left her and said, "I'm here to attend the summer meeting of the Royal Historical Society."

He looked mildly interested by this. "I heard about the society in London, but I didn't realize that this was called the summer meeting."

"Lord Mure is kind enough to make Castle Cairn available to the society one week every summer," she informed him. "In the winter months of October through March, we meet once a month in Edinburgh, weather permitting."

"Are there other women in the society?"

"I'm the only one."

He looked her up and down a third time and smiled. Now that her mental haze had cleared, she saw that he was far from beautiful and not even conventionally handsome.

He said slowly, "So, you're one of my uncle's guests."

Now she doubted not her eyes but her ears, for she thought she heard him refer to his uncle. Could it be, then, that this man was Lord Mure's nephew? The long-lost one who had scandalized the neighborhood then disappeared? The catalog of his possible knightly virtues shrank dramatically. Lord Mure's nephew was not known for having been loyal or true; his reputation certainly did not hold him to be virtuous; and nothing about the present encounter thus far made her think him chivalrous. However, one part of his unknightly revival was, oddly, appropriate: Lord Mure thought his nephew was surely dead by now.

She said the first thing that came to mind. "I don't think your uncle is expecting you."

His reply was forestalled when Lord Mure himself reentered the hall from the outside and called, "Mistress Elizabeth! Are ye in here, Mistress Elizabeth?"

"Over here, your lordship," she called back, relieved by the interruption.

"Ye've found yer way in, then," his lordship said, stepping briskly in her direction. "I've just seen Mrs. Barrow, and she told me that she's already spoken to ye about sending Mary to wait on yer pleasures. I can tell ye that wee Jonathan is toting yer baggage up to yer chamber, so that ye'll be ready to—"

When his lordship was close enough to recognize her companion, he broke off abruptly, visibly astonished. In accents of dramatic disbelief he breathed, "Upon my soul! 'Tis Ian MacLaurin!"

"Greetings, Uncle," the younger MacLaurin replied with no answering drama. "Since my decision to travel north was a sudden one, I had no opportunity to write and warn you of my visit."

His lordship's recovery was rapid. His brow lowered. "Nor had any opportunity to write during these past ten years!"

"Behold me returned," the younger MacLaurin stated and offered no further explanation.

"To make amends?" his lordship demanded. His tone was half hopeful, half accusatory.

"To see you, Uncle," the younger MacLaurin said, "and your fellow historians. I heard in London that you were hosting a house party, and I thought the occasion suitable to pay you a long-overdue visit."

"Ye wish to attend the meeting of our society?" his lordship asked, reverting to his tones of astonishment.

"The summer meeting, yes. Is that so extraordinary?"

"Aye, 'tis most extraordinary!" his lordship expostulated.

"I shall take that as permission to stay," Ian MacLaurin said, "and since I know you've housed your guests in the main wing above, I shall choose a chamber in the east wing."

"*Ye* shall choose a chamber?" his lordship demanded darkly. "Do ye think to be running the place after all?"

"I think to be sparing you the trouble of another guest," his nephew replied easily, "and I know the old place well enough."

His lordship harrumphed. Then, because civility demanded it, he introduced Elizabeth to his nephew. His manner was reluctant, as if he performed the introduction against his better judgment.

"I've already made Mistress Cameron's acquaintance," his nephew informed him, with a half bow toward Elizabeth, "and paid her my compliments."

Elizabeth had recovered enough of her wits to venture a face-saving remark. "Yes, we have met," she confirmed, "but I was not aware that you had complimented me."

MacLaurin's black brows rose. He seemed about to reply when everyone's attention was diverted.

Some of the guests lingering in the courtyard had come inside in the meantime, along with footmen carrying the

baggage, and excited whispers of "'Tis Ian Mac-
Laurin!" had been circulating among them. The news of
the notorious nephew's return had also traveled
throughout the entire castle, bringing retainers from all
corners to converge on the entry hall. The news had sped
just as quickly around the outside of the castle to the
front courtyard where it created a stir among the hands
still dealing with the horses and the coaches.

At that very moment a clumsy stablehand ran in from
the outside, to see what he could see, but in fact could see
nothing because his eyes had not adjusted to the sudden
dark of the hall. Thus it happened that he stumbled
against a footman who, dominolike, stumbled against
one of the guests at the back of the crowd who sent a
wave of reaction to the front of the crowd. One of those
frontmost onlookers fell forward, sprawling against a suit
of armor. This hollow man clattered to the floor, spilling his gutless contents in every direction and with such
force that the mace secured in one metal glove slid and
caught the foot of the candelabra that stood behind
Elizabeth. The candelabra tipped precariously and at
such an angle that it was sure to clip Elizabeth at her heels
and send her reeling.

Someone uttered a strangled oath. The assembled
company gasped and held its collective breath, horrified
by what it was about to witness but was powerless to
prevent.

Almost before she knew what was happening, Elizabeth was swept, breathless, into MacLaurin's protective
embrace. With his right arm he caught her behind her
waist and prevented her from falling flat on her back.
With his left hand he clinched the candelabra and kept it
from toppling upon her. For the space of a heartbeat her

back was arched, her head flung back, and she felt the seductive force of a lover's impassioned hold.

MacLaurin nodded at what he held in his left hand. "To spare you the bite of the lizards, mistress," he explained matter-of-factly.

She glanced at the iron creatures, then back at him, and found herself looking straight into a pair of eyes that she had not realized were as deep and blue as the Highland sky in summer. They sparkled with such roguish masculinity that she lost her breath all over again. Locked in his embrace, she realized that whatever other virtues Ian MacLaurin may have lacked, he was very strong, and he had surely saved her from being knocked over by fifty hefty pounds of iron.

"Thank you, sir," she managed.

Despite his nephew's quick work, his lordship shook a disapproving head. "Since ye caused a riot upon yer departure," he grumbled, "I suppose 'tis only fitting that ye cause a riot upon yer return." He demanded testily, "How long are ye planning to stay, Ian MacLaurin?"

MacLaurin steadied Elizabeth on her feet, withdrew his arm from her waist and set the candelabra upright next to her. He turned to his uncle and replied audaciously, "That will depend on the quality of the food you're offering, Uncle. What time is supper set?"

His lordship looked mightily displeased but answered, grumbling, "Seven o'clock." With a scowl he added, "And wear something respectable!"

MacLaurin bowed to the assembled company, not one of whom was disappointed by the spectacular drama of the notorious nephew's return. To his uncle he intoned ceremoniously, "Until seven o'clock." Then he strode through the crowd, which parted like the seas at his passing.

Watching his nephew's back, his lordship muttered to himself, "'Twas not what I was expecting for the summer meeting!"

Elizabeth privately agreed. For the barest flash of a moment her guard had been down, her flesh had been raised and her fantasy had been unleashed. She had been held in the arms not of a ghost, not of a knight, but of a very real man who had more vital presence than seemed fair.

She caught the eye of the naughtiest of the wrought-iron reptiles. It winked at her.

And warned her of danger.

Chapter Two

Once Ian MacLaurin escaped the hall, he indulged his cynicism. *Just like old times!*

He made his way to the hallway at the right of the entry. Each step took him farther into the gloom. Each step took him farther into a past he had considered long dead. That past came vividly to life when he negotiated the turnings in the unlit hallway, when he breathed in the ancient air, when he encountered the wisps of the many ghosts that inhabited Castle Cairn. He was not afraid of them. However, a new one was among them that had not been there when he had left. It insisted that they had unfinished business. He denied that any business between them was unsettled.

He found the odd corkscrew of a staircase well hidden around several corners and in a shadowy cranny. He took the stairs two by two. With his right hand against the wall for support, he felt the familiar recesses in the wall stones, tracing the pattern that he had known since his earliest boyhood. He resisted the pull of the air and the stair and the pattern beneath his hand, for the combination struck him as satisfying as setting the mainspring of a delicate watch.

At the first landing he left the stairs and made a tricky series of right turns until he arrived at a particular door, which was open. He looked in and saw an old man at the windows fussing with the shutters at the moment they yielded creakily to the flood of day. The old man's thinning hair spidered red around his head in the sunlight.

MacLaurin walked in and around the baggage heaped in the center of the chamber. "Barrow," he said, "I give you good day."

The old man turned slowly and nodded his head. "Master Ian," he said simply. "Ye see, sir, that I have taken the liberty of airing the chamber, knowing yer preferences as I do."

MacLaurin's smile was lightly ironic. "Which means that you missed the most affecting meeting between me and my uncle."

The old man ignored the comment and looked about the room with evident distaste. "'Tis a rumpled disorder, but young Mary will set it to rights. In the meantime, I'll be tending to yer baggage, which I had brought up."

"I thank you for the consideration."

"'Tis right and proper that ye thank me," the old man said, walking from the window to the pile of baggage and shaking his head sorrowfully, "for ye've done no better at packing this time than at any other."

"I packed in haste," MacLaurin explained, "and consoled myself during the ride north that you would be able to bring my wardrobe up to my uncle's standards."

The old man eyed the younger man's plain dress with unconcealed disapproval. "'Tis a miracle ye expect, if what's in the bags is as miserable as what's on yer back."

"It is," MacLaurin replied easily, feeling as if only the ten feet and not the past ten years separated him from his old friend. "And I've faith in your miracle working."

Barrow shook his head and scolded, "The only thing more disreputable than yer dress, lad, is yer speech."

MacLaurin smiled. "So many years among the Sassenachs must have softened the burr."

The old man made a Scots noise of disgust deep in his throat, then bent to fiddle with the straps and clasps in the tangle of leather and tapestry at his feet.

MacLaurin strolled to the open window and planted his hands on the sill. He relished, in spite of himself, standing at this precise spot, where the east wing butted against the main hall, giving a sweeping view of the Grampians rising mist blue in the distance. His gaze raked the ridges of the mountaintops. He knew them to be, in truth, either pebbled playthings of ancient dragons or a necklace of pearls washed inland on mermaids' tears.

He felt the sweet breeze and breathed in the scent of summer. It was easier to resist being here if he could persuade himself that he was missing something. He chose to be sorry not to feel the winds of autumn whipping around the haughs or breathe in the sour, sweet odors of the upland tarns. He heightened his sense of deprivation by imagining drifts of snow outside, wrapping the castle in winter mystery, and vast frosted fields of clouds muffling it from above. He was glad he had come in summer, when it would be easier to leave.

He bathed a moment in the sunshine before turning and leaning his backside against the sill. His gaze lingered a moment to study the secrets of the carved walnut paneling that surrounded the capacious stone fireplace, then traced the gargoylish faces leering at him from the stone mantelpiece. He had almost forgotten his fireplace demons, the ones who had encouraged every outrageous act, the ones who had lured him into every trap. He stared at his stone demons, daring them to comment upon his unexpected return, but they were unusually silent. He shifted his gaze from the fireplace and watched Barrow engaged in his labors.

The old man was shaking out various articles of clothing. He laid them atop the grandiose four-poster bed covered in summer with white twill. From there he transferred the clothes to the armoire against the wall opposite the window. "I'm unpacking just enough for the day and the night," he said without looking up.

MacLaurin did not mistake the old man's implication. "Uncle has accepted my presence here, more or less, and won't be throwing me out on the morrow."

Barrow nodded solemnly. "Ye've come to apologize, then, and do right as I always knew ye would."

MacLaurin said without hesitation, "I've no apologies to make."

The old man's pale blue eyes were dour. "Well, then, ye've learned naught of value in the meantime."

"I've not learned to tell lies, if that's what you mean."

The old man regarded him at length. "Nay, then," he replied, "'tis not what I meant."

Whatever else he had not learned in the past decade, Ian MacLaurin had learned to control his responses to mention of the old injustice. His deep voice cut evenly. "I'm here to attend a meeting of the Royal Historical Society. That, and nothing more."

Barrow frowned. "Ye ran away before, so it comes as no surprise that ye plan to run away again."

MacLaurin was astonished to feel the sting of that remark, for cowardice had never motivated him. Old, impassioned words of self-defense sprang to his tongue, but he quickly swallowed them. He was spared the necessity of reply by the arrival of Mary, who had come to dust and clean.

Mary was a comely Highland lass with ripe curves, and she had arranged her blouse and skirt to show them off. She had heard of the infamous Ian MacLaurin's return and, mighty curious, had come straightaway to his chamber before attending to the other rooms to which she had been assigned. She was not disappointed by the tall, dark, well-formed man leaning against the sill and sunlight. His face was shadowed, but she was easily able to imagine what had set the older serving women to whispering for the past hour. And she was sorry to have missed the scene in the entry hall.

Mary affected surprise to have intruded upon master and man. She formed her lips into a pretty O and managed a curtsy that she hoped was proper from Barrow's point of view but that issued a coy invitation to the young master.

Barrow saw her ploy and dismissed her summarily, telling her to return in an hour. When the lusty lass withdrew, Barrow snapped, "If ye've not learned to control yer tongue, Master Ian, 'tis the least to expect that ye've learned to control other of yer parts."

Just like old times! "I've learned to control more than you can imagine," MacLaurin said, "and if you want to reprimand me for what I haven't done, you'll find good company with my uncle. He was inclined to blame me just now for someone else's clumsiness."

Barrow regarded his master balefully.

"What, no further reproach?" he goaded. To Barrow's silence, he said, "Well, then, tell me what you can of Mistress Cameron."

Barrow returned to the unpacking, and his expression was as oppressive as his tone. "She's a proper young lady from an upstanding clan and one of his lordship's favorites."

"I don't doubt it," MacLaurin replied carelessly, "but she's the first of my uncle's fellow historians whom I've met, and I'm wanting to make proper conversation at supper tonight."

At that, Barrow unbent enough to inform his master that Mistress Cameron lived a secluded life on her father's estate. He had heard from Mrs. Barrow that, despite all the sheltering by her protective father, Mistress Cameron harbored an independent spirit. She had not only persuaded her father to let her live in her own cottage on the Cameron lands, she had also persuaded him to make her the guardian of a poor orphaned cousin.

"Did the cousin accompany her here?" MacLaurin asked idly.

"Nay, then," Barrow answered. "'Tis still a bairn, a wee girl child." He opened his mouth to say something more, then apparently thought the better of it.

"Well?" MacLaurin prompted.

"'Tis naught."

MacLaurin smiled a charming smile that had never failed to have an effect on Barrow. "You've tantalized me with the two simple words ''Tis naught.' You may as well open the budget before I either disgrace myself or embarrass Mistress Cameron by asking her outright about her cousin."

Barrow scowled. "Wild stories circulated about the birth of the bairn, but I never believed more than the half of them!" He added ferociously, "'Twas a scandal, nevertheless, that marred the good name of Cameron, but not as horrid as the scandal ye perpetrated, Master Ian!"

"If it involves a bastard child," MacLaurin said off-handedly, shoving himself away from the window frame, "it sounds remarkably similar." He strolled toward the armoire and peered into it. "You've done estimable work with my miserable wardrobe. A miracle, in fact, as I predicted."

Barrow said begrudgingly, "Yer linens are fine."

"I'm glad, since I paid a good deal of silver for them."

Far from pleased by this rejoinder, the old man muttered darkly about the consequences of extravagance. "I shall leave ye to yer own devices," he scolded, turning to go, "and recommend that ye try to do yer uncle credit over the next few days!"

MacLaurin stopped the old man with a sudden question. "How old is the child?"

At the door to the hallway Barrow turned back, puzzled.

"How old is Mistress Cameron's cousin?" MacLaurin repeated.

"Four, almost five years, by my reckoning, she must be."

"And the child's name?"

"'Tis a strange name, I vow," Barrow said. "Electra? Nay, Aurora, mayhap?" He shook his head. Then his brow cleared. "Ah, 'tis Allegra. Aye, then, the bairn's name is Allegra."

Barrow left MacLaurin then to entertain some mighty interesting questions, the first being how many five-year-old girls named Allegra could live in the neighborhood, and the second turning on the possible relationship between Elizabeth Cameron and his old friend, Gabriel Beverly. However, because MacLaurin had always admired Bev's eye for soft and sensuous women, the most intriguing possibility was also the most improbable, and so MacLaurin dismissed it out of hand. Nevertheless, the presence of Allegra's guardian at Castle Cairn was a potential complication not to be overlooked, and he perceived the need to become better acquainted with Mistress Cameron.

He had his opportunity much sooner than he expected and got more than he bargained for.

Since it was still the early afternoon, MacLaurin saddled up again in order to escape the castle hubbub provoked by his return. Although he was here only to perform a signal service for Gabriel Beverly and not to seek vindication, he chose to travel to a particular destination out beyond MacLaurin lands—just to satisfy his curiosity. When the sun was sinking he rode back, feeling as good as he had any time during these past ten years. He was eager to get on with his mission here and then to return to London.

Drifting through the back ways of the castle, he came upon the entrance to a secluded pleasance that had been conjured from the improbable intersection of three sides of the main keep. The archway in the fourth wall, through which one entered the garden from the maze of interior courtyards, was crumbling gracefully. The sun was falling on the secret corner just so, mellowing the old stones and ripening the odors, both fair and foul, that emanated from the new growth and old decay within. The particular mix was instantly familiar to him and reminded him that the pleasance had enchanted him as a lad. He was lured to enter for a moment's diversion.

He passed under the archway and beheld a garden that had gone long untended. In the center, the old well was still set off on either side by two curved stone benches, like smile lines around a mouth, but they were cracked and black streaked. The herb garden, just beyond, had mostly gone to seed and to weed. The flower beds that lined the pathways were nearly empty, with only a few hearty pansies blooming. To his left, in the full sun, were rows of what were once berry bushes, now mostly naked sticks. To his right, in the shadows, stood a woman with her back toward him, contemplating a scraggly rosebush crawling up a derelict trellis.

Making the most of his opportunity, he took a step toward the well. The sound of crunching gravel beneath his foot brought the woman's head around.

His second impression of Elizabeth Cameron was much like his first, when he had mistaken her for a serving girl. She was still wearing her unattractive traveling habit and had not redressed her hair, which was a mousy brown whose style unfortunately matched her dress. Her features were unremarkable, and her expression—

Her expression was far different from the muddleheaded one she had worn upon first meeting him. Now it was clear and sharp and revealed that she could read what he was thinking. He saw the wisdom of making his thoughts less readable. He smiled and moved toward her. "Mistress Cameron, it is a pleasure to see you again."

She folded her hands in front of her skirts. "Yes, sir," she agreed neutrally, "a pleasure."

When he was before her, he bowed. "Would it be disagreeable to permit me a few moments of your time, mistress, so that I may amend your opinion of my bad manners when we met?"

"Were your manners at fault, sir?"

He inclined his head. "I am afraid that I offended you."

She did not deny that he had insulted her but said, "You made up for it by saving me from the candelabra."

"And for that I should be rewarded," he answered easily. "A turn in the gardens, perhaps?" He extended his arm.

She did not take it. "As your reward?"

"I'd like to get to know you better."

She hesitated.

His smile was persuasive. "I mean you no harm."

Her answering smile was wry and seemed to acknowledge the unlikeliness of the idea that he had evil designs on her person. She asked directly, "What would you like to know about me?"

She was apparently not one for flirtatious banter, so he said just as directly, "You might begin by telling me about your ward."

She slanted him a curious, cautious glance before she accepted his arm. "How do you know about my ward?"

They started to stroll in the direction of the well. "My man, Barrow, mentioned it," he replied, "and I thought you might like to discuss such a subject."

"In truth," she said evenly, "there are few subjects I love more. My ward, Allegra, is a delightful girl."

So far so good. "I invite you to tell me all about her."

She slanted him another curious, cautious glance. They had come to stand in front of one of the benches by the well. He offered her a seat, but she did not immediately take it. She said a little stiffly, "Allegra is the daughter of my late cousin Fiona Cameron and her late husband Donald MacDonald. Allegra's life started out rather sadly, I'm afraid. Fiona died the day after she was born, while Donald had died some months before in a riding accident." She paused. "Perhaps you knew my ward's parents—?"

She had, he noted, an expressive face, and her cheeks had flushed a pale pink. He tried to determine the source of her discomfort. Or was it embarrassment?

"I knew MacDonald only distantly," he admitted, "but I left Scotland before his marriage, so I never met his wife. I heard nothing of him since."

"I see," she said and fell silent.

After a moment he prompted, "And you have nothing to tell me about her beyond the sad beginning of her life?"

"Of course, after that there is nothing to tell, because her life has been quite uneventful. I took over her guardianship within a week of Fiona's death."

He found his opening. "But it is most unusual, is it not, that you, an unmarried woman, should be her guardian?"

She closed it. "Yes, it is most unusual, but I fail to see why this is of interest to you."

He could not decide whether her constraint covered shyness or whether she was hiding something. "I've been gone a good many years, as you know," he said pleasantly, "and am eager to learn all the news of the neighborhood."

"You have quite a lot to catch up on, in that case," she replied, "and the story of Allegra's young life is hardly the most compelling event to have occurred during your absence."

"But I must start somewhere, and I don't have to catch up on every detail, because friends of mine who have traveled to Scotland have kept me somewhat up-to-date over the years."

She turned fine gray eyes on him. "Would those be friends from London?"

The quiver at the corner of her mouth made him suspicious. So did her reluctance to discuss the one subject she claimed to love above all others. He decided on a bold move.

"Yes, friends," he replied. "Did you, by chance, cross paths with Gabriel Beverly? He is a friend of mine who was in the neighborhood five years ago or more."

Elizabeth's eyes widened, then lowered, and he saw a complex blend of emotions shift across her expressive face. When she raised her eyes again, he was both surprised and impressed by what he saw in their gray depths. What she said surprised and impressed him even more.

"You must not be afraid to be frank."

He chose caution. "Mistress?"

At last she sat on the bench. She looked up at him and said bluntly, "I know very little about you, sir, except that you left ten years ago and have returned today, unexpectedly. I don't know why you have returned, but I don't believe it is to attend the meeting of the Royal Historical Society, as you told your uncle."

He did not know what to say in response.

"I think, furthermore," she continued, "that you have some particular reason to be interested in my ward and that you have not introduced the name of Gabriel Beverly into our conversation at random." Her cheeks were pale, but her voice was composed. "To answer your question, yes, I met Gabriel Beverly—he was a lieutenant in the army, was he not?—when he was in Scotland five years ago." She swallowed hard. "I also know that Lieutenant Beverly is Allegra's father."

But *how* did she know? Bev had assured him that only the child's mother knew the identity of the child's father. Looking down at Mistress Cameron, the absurd possibility that she had been Bev's paramour flitted into his brain and danced out again. She would have been too ordinary for Bev's flamboyant taste.

"You have just told me," he replied, "that your ward is the offspring of your cousin and her husband."

"I have told you only what the world knows," she said. "Please understand, sir, that I care about Allegra more than anything in the world." She added, quietly and calmly, "I pray you tell me what is amiss—for I know that something is."

The determined look on her face told him that she would not move until he told her. Given that her motive to protect the child was as strong as his to repay his debt to Bev, he decided that she might prove useful to him. A stray memory of the moment he had held her in his arms drifted into his brain and lingered. *Could* she have been the woman who had flamed Bev's passion five years before?

He propped one booted foot on the bench next to her and began. "Not quite a week ago, Bev involved himself in a card game at the home of the very dashing Lady Michael."

Elizabeth's heart caught at the name. "Lady Michael is to be one of your uncle's guests," she informed him as calmly as she could. "She is on her way now to Castle Cairn."

When he had propped his boot on the bench, she had called a hasty truce between the emotions battling for supremacy in her breast. Melting relief that he was going to tell her what she needed to know warred with freezing fear of what he was going to tell her. She had suspected that something was wrong from the moment MacLaurin had stepped into the garden, taken her measure and invited her to stroll with him. The afternoon long, she had been distracted by the notion that trouble was brewing, but she could not guess from which direction it would come. It did not take many minutes in MacLaurin's company for the needle of her internal compass to align that trouble with Gabriel Beverly.

"I know," MacLaurin replied, "and that, in short, accounts for why I'm here. The longer version will require me telling you that Bev chose a gaming table where sat several notable peers of the realm, including one Rupert Warenne."

"Were you in attendance, sir?"

"No," he replied. "I have the whole of the story from Bev."

"I see. And Rupert Warenne? That is not a name I know."

"He's a sly character, never to be trusted. One of London's most unscrupulous."

Elizabeth was trying to keep her wits about her, but they were tumbling chaotically. To begin with, she had to adjust to the idea that Gabriel Beverly was truly Allegra's father. She had long suspected—no, she had always *known*—that Allegra was a love child and, in particular, Lieutenant Beverly's. Nevertheless, the gulf was great between her deeply buried knowledge and this sudden articulation of the truth. The gulf was especially difficult to bridge when the truth appeared to have such grave consequences. Then, too, she was trying to judge the reliability of a story told by such an unconventional character as Ian MacLaurin.

She did not want to divert him from the story at hand by asking irrelevant questions about the unscrupulous Warenne, so she took a deep breath and said simply, "This does not sound good."

"It isn't," he replied frankly, and continued. "The play was deep and Warenne was losing badly. Down twenty thousand or more. At one point, no doubt thinking that Bev was holding the winning hand, Warenne tossed a document on the table that he claimed would be worth a lot of money to a certain gentleman at the table. He insinuated that the document concerned the illegitimate birth of a young lady who resides in central Scotland."

Elizabeth's distress leaped into her eyes, which flew to his.

"Yes, mistress, the Grampians," he confirmed. "Warenne could have hardly made the location more precise."

"And the nature of the document?"

He shrugged. "It was probably one letter from an exchange of love letters between Bev and the girl's mother—according to Bev, that is. Even one letter could be very revealing."

Elizabeth thought of the last months of Fiona's life and could well imagine Fiona carrying on a secret-but-not-discreet correspondence with her lover. She blushed. "And what is the fate of the document?"

"I'm coming to that," he said. "First I must tell you that Bev was not holding the winning hand when Warenne tossed his document onto the table. However, because Bev believed Warenne had discovered Allegra's parentage and because he wished to protect his daughter's good name, he decided to cheat—nobly, to hear him tell it. So he won the round, claimed the stakes in the center of the table and pocketed the document."

"That is all to the good, then, no?"

"No. Unfortunately, another gentleman at the table, the one who was holding the winning hand, detected Bev's ruse and accused him of cheating. Feigning grave offense, Bev denied it, and as a measure of good faith, pushed all the money and vouchers back into the center of the table.''

''But not the document?''

''No, he slipped that into his coat. However, his opponent was unimpressed and demanded immediate satisfaction. One thing led to the next, the seconds were named, and the field of combat chosen was Lady Michael's library.''

Elizabeth felt the blood leave her cheeks.

MacLaurin must have seen her blanch, for he continued dryly, ''Although Bev's sword arm was not the equal of his opponent's, I would not be here now unless Bev had lived to tell me the tale.''

Elizabeth felt the blood return to her cheeks. She hated to think that Allegra's father had been alive all these years only to learn that he had just been killed in a duel. ''So the lieutenant did not die?''

MacLaurin's assessment was callous. ''Bev lacked the good grace to die after being caught at cheating! He was badly wounded, but it was only what he deserved. He had me fetched to his bedside within hours of the incident and begged me to retrieve the document for him.''

''Retrieve it?'' she asked. ''Where is the document now?''

''In a box of books on its way to Castle Cairn.''

Elizabeth paused a moment, then produced a questioning ''Ah?'' when a wild scenario unfolded itself in her imaginative brain.

MacLaurin nodded. ''What you are thinking is entirely correct. Bev was carrying the document in his coat when they entered the library. He slipped it into a book in one of the boxes that Lady Michael had packed to take with her on her trip to Scotland. As you have just confirmed, her destination is Castle Cairn.''

The scenario was so wild, however, that Elizabeth felt her reason reassert itself. "This is utterly nonsensical, sir!" she said. "I followed your story through the card game, the cheating and up to the part where the seconds were named and the field of combat chosen was Lady Michael's library. But why *on earth* would the lieutenant slip the document into a book in a box?"

"Bev realized that death was one of the likely outcomes of his duel with Devonshire, and he did not want the document to fall back into Warenne's hands if he died."

Elizabeth's blood ran cold. "Who?"

"I beg your pardon?"

"Who was the lieutenant's dueling opponent?"

"Devonshire," he replied.

"The Duke of Devonshire?"

"The very one, but his identity is of no moment."

The Duke of Devonshire. The coincidence was extraordinary. From the moment she had stepped out of her carriage and into the shadow of Castle Cairn, she had set her fancy free. Now she found it being taken into a realm beyond her control.

Pronouncing each word like a powerful magic formula whose effect she could not predict, she said, "The Duke of Devonshire arrived at Castle Cairn this afternoon."

MacLaurin's black brows shot up with justifiable surprise. "Devonshire?" His brows lowered. "Was he invited?"

"I don't know. Perhaps he has a standing invitation to our meetings, since he is a patron of the Royal Historical Society. However, I can tell you that your uncle was not expecting him."

"Has Devonshire ever attended one of your society meetings before?"

She shook her head. "No, but his interest in our society is no doubt due to the fact that he is connected to the Clan MacPherson through his mother, as you no doubt know—"

"I do," he said, as if he took no pleasure in the knowledge.

"And came north to attend to family business in Edinburgh, at which point, according to your uncle, he decided to stop by Castle Cairn to visit our society."

MacLaurin grunted. "The question remains. Is there a relationship between his presence here and his duel with Bev? More specifically, is there some reason why Devonshire would be interested in Bev's document?"

Clinging to doubt, Elizabeth countered, "Are you sure there *is* a document?"

MacLaurin's smile was both charming and chilling. "If there is no document, Mistress Cameron," he said, "I shall finish the work that Devonshire's sword began. I did not come all this way and to this place—" he looked around him "—for the rare amusements of a wild-goose chase!"

His ruthless assessment dispelled her doubts about his reliability, and it was as if a switch was thrown in her brain. The cogs—Lieutenant Beverly, the document, the duel with the Duke of Devonshire, Lady Michael's boxes of books, Ian MacLaurin's unexpected presence—meshed, and the gears of her historian's analytical skills began to grind.

"Do you know if Lady Michael is aware that the document is in the box of books?"

MacLaurin answered that she was not. "Talk of Warenne's ploy with the document apparently did not leave the table and, according to Bev, no one but himself and Warenne would have cared about it. As far as the other guests were concerned, the duel with Devonshire was over cheating.''

''Did the lieutenant have a chance to read the document before he slipped it into the book?''

''No, he told me that he had only time enough to hide it.''

''I see,'' she said. ''You said that the lieutenant chose a second. Did this man, perhaps, see him slip the document into a book?''

MacLaurin shook his head.

''Anyone else?''

Again MacLaurin shook his head.

''The lieutenant must have shed his coat in order to duel. Did that unscrupulous man . . . Warenne . . . did he, perhaps, have a chance to riffle through the lieutenant's coat in order to discover that the document was no longer there?''

MacLaurin shook his head a third time. ''No, and you have asked me the very questions I asked Bev.''

''They are the obvious ones, I suppose,'' she replied, then added slowly, ''So no one, besides you, the lieutenant, and now me, knows that the document is in the box of books.''

''Correct,'' he replied, ''unless, of course, Devonshire is involved, although how he could be, I cannot guess.''

''His Grace knows the books are coming,'' she offered.

MacLaurin looked interested. ''He does?''

She recalled the conversation with his lordship in the courtyard. ''That is to say that your uncle mentioned to me that he had told His Grace that Lady Michael was bringing four boxes of books. However, that does not mean that His Grace did or did not know about them before arriving.''

MacLaurin shrugged, evidently losing interest.

''Although His Grace might not have known that Lady Michael was bringing a lot of books,'' she continued, ''you did. Why, sir, do you not already have the document in hand? Lady Michael is due to arrive late this afternoon, which means that she has been traveling a good many days now. Why have you let her come so far? Why did you not—not—''

''Why did I not hold her up in the fashion of a highwayman and rob her of her books?'' MacLaurin suggested, somewhat sardonically.

''Well, perhaps not hold her up,'' she conceded, ''but some other clever ploy might have served the purpose.''

''It seemed far more clever to me,'' he said, ''to appear at my ancestral castle under the guise of a long-overdue visit than it would have been to have arrived, unannounced, at the doorstep of some friend of Lady Michael's whom I hardly know.''

''A plan that involves arriving unannounced at the doorstep of someone you hardly know is not as unreasonable as it sounds,'' she said. ''It is a question of devising the proper explanation for your presence.''

''Which explanation failed me,'' he returned readily.

Without putting a guard on her tongue, she said, ''Or perhaps having the proper entrée to the finest houses.''

''Which also failed me.'' His tone was cool, and he looked deliberately away.

''Well, in that case . . .'' she began, but trailed off.

She had become distracted by his leg, layered with seasoned leather, propped not two feet from her. She had also become aware of the balance of his body as he leaned into the arm resting on the shelf of his raised thigh. His face was in profile to her, for he was looking ahead, regarding the far wall of the garden over which old roses rambled. She studied the cut of his unshaven chin and the lines of character beginning to sculpt his mouth and cheekbones. She caught the color of his eye, just a chip of blue from where she sat.

She resolutely returned her thoughts to her main concern. "In that case," she began again, "we are faced with retrieving the document now." That prospect naturally filled her with some agitation, and so her voice quavered a little when she said, "I confess that it is unsettling to think that such an important document is lying so innocently in a box of books but is yet so very far from being safe in our hands!"

"You shall not have to worry much longer," he replied.

Her spirits picked up. "Oh, do you have a plan for us?"

He looked down at her. "Us, mistress?"

"You cannot expect me to stand idly by, sir, when so important a task lies before us."

"I shall let you know if I need you to do anything," he said briefly. He removed his leg from the bench and stood straight.

Elizabeth stood, too, and wished that the top of her head reached higher than the bottom of his chin. "You'll let me know if you need my help?" she echoed.

"I shall."

It came to her then that knowing the worst was easier to bear than fearing the worst. Now that the problem had been laid out and the objective was clear, she was feeling better than she had all afternoon. She looked up at Ian MacLaurin and saw a conspirator, a colleague of sorts, a man she could treat like one of her fellow historians. Feeling freed of the usual constraints she felt in company with eligible young men, her natural playfulness surfaced.

She smiled and said provocatively, "Perhaps that is rather more for me to say."

"Indeed, Mistress Cameron?" He favored her with a dismissive look that reminded her strongly of the one he had given her when he had asked her if she worked at Castle Cairn.

She already knew that he could not see into the beauty of her soul, so she did not waste time being offended. Her playful mood expanded. "Indeed, sir. The document is in a book. The book is in one of four boxes. The boxes, I believe, must be destined for his lordship's library. Let me see, now. You have not been here in a while and may not remember, or may not know, that his lordship keeps the library—"

"Locked," he said in unison with her. "I remember. I was planning to break in to the library tonight."

"Break in?" she said, amused. "How original! However, I doubt you'll need to go to such lengths, because I'm sure that my fellow historians and I will be spending the evening in the library unpacking the boxes of books that Lady Michael is bringing." She paused for effect, then added innocently, "I don't suppose you'd care to join us for an evening of books and fine discussion?"

She could tell by his expression that a tame session in the library in company with a group of historians was not how he had planned to spend his evening.

"Well, then," she chirped along, quite happy with herself, "since I plan to make a special point of searching through every book tonight, I shall show you the document tomorrow morning, and we can decide what to do with it after that."

MacLaurin did not immediately reply. "We shall simply have to wait to see how events sort themselves out," he said at last, "before we decide on a course of action."

She liked his use of "we" and nodded in agreement. "Perhaps we shall have an opportunity to speak again, before or after supper." She kept her face straight but could not keep the teasing note out of her voice. "In the meantime, I shall let you know if I need *you* to do anything."

His blue eyes focused on her, as if for the first time, and she glimpsed a twinkle of the roguish masculinity that had lit their depths earlier when he had saved her from being crushed by the candelabra. Then he smiled in a way that made his far-from-beautiful-not-even-handsome rugged features recompose themselves into a very attractive whole.

He bowed again and warned pleasantly, "Don't push me, Mistress Cameron."

Elizabeth smiled broadly. "I'll be a great help," she assured him cheerfully. "You'll see!" But she did not promise not to push him.

Chapter Three

After leaving the gardens, Elizabeth had more than enough to consider. Her ruminations looped in Fiona's behavior of five years before and around the document in Lady Michael's possession. She recalled Fiona's estrangement from her husband, Donald MacDonald, and accepted the fact that the charming wastrel Gabriel Beverly was, indeed, Allegra's father. She imagined the extraordinary scene at the gaming table at Lady Michael's home and pondered the sober truth that her historian's delight in discovering old documents was far different from the urgency she felt to recover one particular document now.

While she dressed for the evening, her agitation returned. It was, indeed, most unsettling, as she had said to MacLaurin, to think that a document so potentially vital to Allegra's well-being should be hovering in such a curious limbo: out of harm's way, but not within her grasp. She itched to get the document in her hands, to know that Allegra's good name was safe. She had loved and cared for her young cousin these past four years as she would a cherished sister or even a daughter, for she could not deny that she felt fiercely, maternally protective of Allegra.

Elizabeth's hand went automatically to her breast. She touched the locket she never took off in silent tribute to her own mother whom she had never known. It made her blood run hot with mortification to think of Allegra ever having to suffer the shame of—

An odd thought occurred to her. She recalled that when Fiona was dying of childbed fever the day after Allegra's birth, Fiona had had a secretive discussion with her serving woman, who later went on an errand. At the time Elizabeth had not paid much attention to that interaction, but now she saw that Fiona had probably sent a final letter to her lover informing him of his daughter's birth and the child's name. That much made sense to her. However, other parts of MacLaurin's story did not make as much sense, and a series of vexing questions occurred to her busy brain and she was suddenly eager for a private audience with MacLaurin.

Before her curiosity could be satisfied, however, Elizabeth had to attend to the details of her evening's toilette. While Mary pinned her mistress's hair, she prattled of the old scandal surrounding Ian MacLaurin. Elizabeth had been too young to have heard about the scandal when it was fresh, so she had no way of knowing that the serving girl's version was a fractured rendering of the inaccurate tales that had been tripping off servants' tongues throughout the afternoon. She listened eagerly to the vivid account of MacLaurin's past, torn between horrified delight in the details and self-disgust at such delight.

Because it was getting late, Elizabeth finished pinning her hair while Mary shook out the wrinkles in the dress Elizabeth had made in secret, never thinking that she would have such a special place to wear it. It was her most daring gown, which was to say that the neckline dipped a bit. It distinguished itself in her wardrobe by being both well cut to the figure and of a color other than the usual muddy grays her father insisted that she wear. The pretty mauve of the silk enhanced her quiet coloring, but she had chosen it primarily to complement the Cameron tartan. She had brought a sash of the vivid red and black to drape over her left shoulder and affix to her right hip with a silver heirloom brooch.

When her chemise and underskirts were in place and her dress properly laced, she dismissed Mary. She preferred putting the finishing touches on for herself. First she arranged the pretty locket she always wore on her bodice neckline. Then she stood before the cheval glass next to the bed by the open window in order to experiment with the placement of the tartan sash. At one moment her attention was caught by the odd shape of the room reflected in the mirror.

She turned to survey her surroundings. The wall opposite her bed was completely covered with heavily carved paneling. Its focal point was a large fireplace whose stone exterior was carved with curious creatures that seemed to resemble sea nymphs. To the left of the fireplace stood the wardrobe that matched her bed. Farther down the wall was an alcove that made the room oddly shaped, almost a pentagon. It was an eccentric room and no doubt entirely typical of the castle's chambers.

She returned to fiddle with her sash, slipped her room key through the clip of the brooch at her hip and left her chamber without thinking to take a candle to light her way. The moment she stepped into the hallway she realized that she had forgotten the direction of the main staircase. She turned to her right and felt her way along the wall, passing one door before she bumped into a wall that seemed to angle off from the main corridor, suggesting another hallway. It seemed that no two walls in this sprawling structure fit together at right angles.

Since she did not recall taking such a sharp turn when she came to her chamber from the main staircase, she decided that she had taken the wrong direction. So she retraced her steps, passing the one door and continuing straight on beyond her own door. She walked along the main hallway for so long that she felt a quiver of panic that she would be lost forever in the enormous maze of hallways. So it was with a rush of relief that she ran, almost literally, into a group of her fellow historians clustered at the head of the main staircase.

Happy to escort her down the stairs were Douglas MacKinnon, Godfrey MacQuarie, Patrick Grant, Donald Graham and his cousin Ganon, Robert MacDuff and the society's principal genealogist, Brian Sinclair. During the long and complicated walk to the banquet hall, they regaled her with stories of castle ghosts and trapdoors and secret passageways. Their manner with her was kindly and avuncular if not, in fact, grandfatherly, for there was not a man among them who was under five-and-fifty. Elizabeth put her opportunity to good use by convincing them that they should spend the evening after supper in the library unpacking the boxes of books that Lady Michael was bringing.

The banquet hall was large, with vaults overhead and parquet underfoot, and well lit by torches whose flames seemed to lick the cold stones of the walls. The atmosphere was festive and raised her optimism about her prospects for retrieving the document this evening. She was, furthermore, pleased that her dress drew praise all around. Her sash, predictably, inspired discussion of the various tartans, since each man was kilted as was the society's custom, while the laird, Robert MacLaurin, was in full Highland dress.

His lordship accosted her immediately and, after the opening pleasantries concerning her comfort, he said, "Now, tell me, Mistress Elizabeth, what extraordinarily good reason you have to have disobeyed your father in coming to Castle Cairn!"

She was more than happy to tell him and felt doubly glad now for the coincidence that had brought her here. "I recently came across some rare historical documents," she said, without bothering to note that they had been sent to her in the mail, "which promise to be so fascinating that I decided that I just had to come and share them."

His lordship's face lit with interest. "Rare historical documents? Ones that concern clan history?"

"Yes," she said, "but I'm not sure which clans yet, for the documents aren't signed, nor even dated. So, you see, I couldn't stay away knowing that the finest historical minds in all of Scotland were assembling here at Castle Cairn."

"And the nature of the documents?"

"They seem to be one half of an exchange of letters."

"And the contents?"

She smiled playfully. "I don't want to spoil my surprise by telling you now."

His lordship scolded, "Are ye fabricating this tale, then, Mistress Elizabeth?"

She laughed and assured him that she was not. "There's not much I *can* tell you about the contents, for I haven't had an opportunity to read through all of the letters. I came across them only a few days ago, and since deciding to come to the meeting, I've had to spend my time preparing my treatise, if I'm to participate in the program.''

That made sense to his lordship, so he said, "Well, then, I'm thinking that ye can introduce yer mysterious letters as an item of new business at the society's inaugural sitting tomorrow morning.''

She nodded and teased, "Does that mean, then, that even if my father would object to my presence here, you do not?''

His lordship pinched her cheek affectionately. "Well, well, what yer father doesn't know won't hurt him.''

A deep and cultured English voice at Elizabeth's side interposed. "My, my, Robbie. Are you leading this young lady astray?''

Elizabeth turned and saw a distinguished man in the prime of his middle years, elegant in a fine knotted wig and ice blue silk dress suit. He wore a sprig of the red whortleberry bush, the badge of the Clan MacPherson, on the lapel of his jacket.

His lordship flushed and said, "Och, now, I'd never do that! Permit me to introduce Yer Grace to Mistress Elizabeth Cameron. Mistress Cameron, I have the honor to present ye to His Grace, Edmund Francis Havinghurst, Earl of Avon and Duke of Devonshire. I'm sure ye'll be wishing to get to know one another." So saying, Lord Mure moved away from them to entertain other guests.

Upon coming face to face with His Grace, Elizabeth had a hazy recollection of having met him briefly on her father's estate when she was about ten. Before dropping a curtsy to his correct bow, she thought she saw a spark of recognition flicker in the depths of his fine, rather cold gray eyes as they focused on her. However, when she straightened and glanced up at His Grace again, she saw that his expression was bland. She decided that he could not possibly remember such an insignificant encounter when she had been but a girl.

"Are you, too, a historian, Mistress Cameron?" His Grace inquired. His fine gray eyes were focused on her again, but only politely so.

"Yes," she answered, "and to prove it, I shall point out that Your Grace is connected to the Clan Mac-Pherson through your mother."

"Very good, Mistress Cameron," His Grace said approvingly, then asked, "But can you detail the connection, I wonder?"

Thus challenged, she outlined His Grace's mother's family history with precision and efficiency. She smiled with counterchallenge. "I hope you will not find your stay at Castle Cairn too tiresome, Your Grace, with all of us eager to answer any question concerning Highland genealogy and history."

"The only tiresome prospect I can imagine," His Grace said with a slight bow, "is that of having to profess my sincere interest in Highland history to everyone I meet. I am not as dull, I assure you, as one is apparently inclined to think." Before she could demur, he continued smoothly, "I confess to having overheard the end of your conversation just now with my old friend Robbie, who was inclined to think that what your father does not know will not hurt him."

She smiled wryly and replied, "My father does not know, Your Grace, that I have come to Castle Cairn for the summer meeting."

"I see. Have you been a member of the Royal Historical Society for very long?"

"Five years, Your Grace."

His Grace's gray eyes widened a trifle. "Five years already, and you are such a young lady."

She did not miss the inflection of question in his state-ment, and she knew what he was asking. His manner was that of a man whose questions were never denied. "I am four-and-twenty, Your Grace."

"And still disobedient to your father," he commented mildly.

"It is a question of interpretation, Your Grace. He does not know that I am here, as I have said."

"But I take it that he might object, were he to dis-cover it."

"He has come to accept my membership in the soci-ety, Your Grace, and will not prevent me from attending the winter meetings, which last no longer than one after-noon at a time. However, he feels—or, at least, he felt as recently as last year—that it is bad for my character to spend an extended time satisfying what he considers to be my unbecoming curiosity."

"Are you curious, Mistress Cameron?"

"About historical matters, yes."

"You do not agree with your father, then, that satis-fying your curiosity is bad for your character?"

She paused, then said with aplomb, "I am here at Castle Cairn, am I not, Your Grace?"

His Grace bent his head to signal appreciation of her slight impertinence. "Yes, Mistress Cameron, you are, and I am inclined to think that your father is fighting a losing battle. Perhaps you could tell me his name."

"Joseph Cameron, Your Grace."

"Joseph Cameron. He is known to me, distantly." His Grace glanced away, as if to search a memory. "He mar-ried a certain Mary MacDonald, did he not, of the Glen-coe MacDonalds?" He glanced back at her. "Mary MacDonald died some years ago, if I recall correctly the branchings of the Clan MacDonald that intersect with the Clan MacPherson.''

"That is correct, Your Grace. My mother died from complications at my birth."

His Grace nodded. "You see, then, Mistress Cameron, that my interest in Highland history is genuine and that my patronage of your society is not for nothing." He bowed. "I am sure that we shall have occasion over the next few days to discuss the intertwined histories of your mother's clan and mine."

"Yes, Your Grace, I shall look forward to it," she said.

His Grace's brow rose slightly. "Will you, Mistress Cameron? I have received the distinct impression that you think me overbold in my inquisitiveness."

His Grace was exactly right, but Elizabeth had taken his measure by now and chose to respond with a boldness of her own. "Indeed, I am surprised that you did not reprimand me for my daughterly disobedience."

His Grace's brow rose higher. "Now that you have given me such a fine opening, Mistress Cameron, I cannot resist taking up the cause—in loco parentis—of saying that a young lady can never be too careful with her reputation. Daughterly disobedience and a too-keen curiosity can often contribute to a questionable reputation."

"I shall remember that, Your Grace."

"Very good, Mistress Cameron." His Grace made her an elegant leg and ran an admiring eye over her toilette. "By the way, the sash adds the right touch of color, my child, without overpowering."

Elizabeth would have thanked him if he had not immediately turned away and spoken to the man next to him. She fell into conversation with her neighbor. When she glanced back at His Grace a few moments later, she was not at all sure that she liked him.

It was only when they were called to the table set for twelve that MacLaurin made his entrance. Elizabeth's eyes widened to see the difference a few hours could make in a man's appearance. With a fresh shave and his black hair brought to order, she fully believed Mary's assertion that, ten years before, he had seduced every lass and lady under the age of fifty within one hundred miles. He was dressed to perfection, though not with the extravagance of His Grace. His linen shirt had few frills but was obviously fine, his stockings were without a fault and his dress suit of cobalt buff wool suited his coloring. He wore no mark of the Clan MacLaurin.

Elizabeth was seated to the right of his lordship at the head of the table. His Grace was escorted to the position of honor at the foot of the table. The other eight men had less carefully chosen places, with Ian MacLaurin in the middle of the table on the side opposite her. The place to the left of his lordship was conspicuously empty. It had been set for Lady Michael who, his lordship was sorry to inform his guests, must have been seriously delayed en route, for she had not yet arrived at Castle Cairn.

Elizabeth dared a discreet glance at MacLaurin. He nodded minimally, a signal for her to probe further.

It took some doing—most of the supper, in fact—for Elizabeth to bring her host around to the topic uppermost on her mind and MacLaurin's. During that time she was aware that this was the most unusual supper of the Royal Historical Society that she had ever attended. On the surface, all was normal. However, this evening's supper was different.

It was not because she was the only woman at the table, because she was often the only woman at such a supper. She was, furthermore, seated next to his lordship, a jovial bachelor and a good friend whose benevolent affection for her was evident. So she should have been at ease, but she was not—or, rather, it was more accurate to say that the conditions of her comfort did not obscure from her the darker undercurrents at the table.

She kept her conversation correctly confined to his lordship on her left and Godfrey MacQuarie on her right. Yet she was somehow aware of His Grace at the other end of the table, although she was sure that he did not once glance in her direction. It was as if His Grace were an unnatural force in himself, generating his own mysterious energy, like that given off by doors to vaults or lids to reliquaries.

She kept her gaze averted from MacLaurin. Here again, it seemed that she could not help but be aware of him and of the tension that stretched between him and His Grace, a line as thin and taut as the stuffed sheep gut of the haggis. At one moment she glanced at His Grace and saw him discussing, very amiably, some topic of interest that included all the men at that end of the table, including MacLaurin. Straining to maintain her own discussion, she discerned that their topic was dueling. She knew that MacLaurin would not be so foolish as to introduce the name of Gabriel Beverly into the discussion, so she guessed that His Grace's own recent involvement in a duel could not be the cause of the tension at the table. Perhaps it was the very absence of mention of Gabriel Beverly that produced the tension.

Later she caught whisper of the name Elspeth Mac-Millan passing between Patrick Grant and Donald Graham, who were seated just beyond Godfrey MacQuarie on her right. Elizabeth recalled that Mary's tattling tongue had clucked the name of that "puir fallen lassie" and strewn it on the littered trail of MacLaurin's amorous infamies. Perhaps it was only to be expected that MacLaurin's past should be present tonight after his absence of ten years. However, the specter of Ian MacLaurin's past seemed to haunt the table, and for some reason Elizabeth had the eerie feeling that His Grace did not wish to see that particular castle ghost dispelled.

At last Elizabeth was able to steer the conversation around to Lady Michael and her boxes of books. Hardly had she engaged the topic with his lordship than the conversation at the other end of the table seemed to quiet to a murmur, then stop.

"The sweet is almost upon us," his lordship said, "and even if Lady Michael were to arrive on the instant, she could not hope to get herself refreshed quick enough to find her way here and to take a bite of shortbread and berries with us, don't you know!"

"Oh, indeed," Elizabeth agreed readily, aware that she was suddenly the focus of attention at the table. She composed herself and said brightly, "And how disappointing it is for us! Why, we were all saying on the way to supper that we should devote this evening to unpacking the boxes of books her ladyship is bringing!" She turned to Godfrey MacQuarie. "Isn't that so, sir?"

Godfrey MacQuarie obliged her. "Aye, 'tis the latest edition of Locke's philosophical treatise Robbie has ordered for us that I've been wanting to get between my hands."

Elizabeth allowed each of her fellow members to pronounce which of his lordship's books he was most keen to see before she added, "Since we're all so eager, do you think that we could make this evening a special occasion by holding a library festivity at whatever hour Lady Michael arrives?"

His lordship considered this suggestion but rejected it on the grounds that the library was in the central tower, making access to it cumbersome, especially at night.

"The clock struck nine a while ago, Mistress Elizabeth, and I reckon 'twill strike ten soon!" his lordship told her with a smile. "The rest of us are not as young as ye are, my dear. Better that we have a good night's sleep and an early start on it tomorrow."

Just then Mrs. Barrow approached his lordship to inform him that Lady Michael had arrived and was being escorted to her chamber. She added that all her ladyship's affairs were being carried there as well, including four boxes of books. It seemed that her ladyship had not had time to properly pack in London and so had put personal articles into the boxes, which she needed to sort out. The housekeeper conveyed the further message that her ladyship had had a difficult journey and was very tired.

"'Tis only to be expected!" his lordship replied with good nature. "Pray, wait a moment, Mrs. Barrow, and I shall accompany ye to her ladyship's chamber to welcome her and to wish her good-night. She can meet the others of us in the morning." He turned to Elizabeth. "Ye see, then, that yer fine idea of a late-night library festivity was not practical, for her ladyship will spend the night with the boxes. You'll be close enough to the books, however, Mistress Elizabeth, for I've put her ladyship next to ye."

"Next to me?" Elizabeth queried with polite interest.

"Aye, in the chamber just beyond the one I chose for ye."

His lordship rose from the table, and his guests followed suit. "I'll offer ye gentlemen whiskey in what we call the receiving hall where I shall join ye after I make my graces to her ladyship.''

Elizabeth recognized her cue and stated her intention to retire. She declined the offer of an escort, saying that she relished the challenge of finding her chamber again, but requested a candle to chase away the shadows.

The seven historians, along with MacLaurin, chose to repair to the receiving hall. Godfrey MacQuarie proposed that a thorough discussion of Locke's treatise would go uncommonly well with Scots whiskey, and Patrick Grant readily seconded the idea. His Grace, who perhaps had little interest in philosophic subtleties, declared himself ready to retire. Observing that he was not as adventuresome as Mistress Cameron and did not fancy losing himself in the fascinations of Castle Cairn's hallways, he requested an escort to his chamber.

His Grace's escort was summoned, along with a taper for Mistress Elizabeth, and the two of them set out for their respective chambers. They walked together a way, exchanging only the blandest of conventionalities. At the main hall, ablaze with the light of the reptilian candelabra, His Grace was led toward the left-hand staircase. Elizabeth turned toward the main staircase. His Grace bid her a gentle good-night. She returned it prettily, she hoped.

With taper in hand, Elizabeth swung up the first steps, and her candlelight threw monstrous shadow stairs up the walls. At the top she turned left, toward her chamber. This time, safe within the miniature moon of her protective light, she was not afraid to walk the long hallway. In fact, she felt rather grand, pondering the importance of her mission, considering the best way to approach Lady Michael and help her sort out her personal articles.

She was so focused on spinning her plans that she was unprepared when a muscular arm darted out from the shadows and clasped about her waist. Her heart leaped to her throat, and she had time only to breathe a startled, "By St. Angus!" before a hand clamped over her mouth and her candle was extinguished from her sudden movement.

The next thing she heard was a soft shushing of wood against wood, and the next thing she perceived was utter darkness. She was no longer in the main hallway but was standing in some sort of alcove, caught in a strong embrace.

Chapter Four

MacLaurin was amused. "By St. Angus?" he whispered in Elizabeth Cameron's ear.

She jerked her head away from his hand. "The patron saint of Scottish historians, I'll have you know! Now, just what do you think you are about, sir?"

He put a finger to her lips. "The passageways carry every sound, and we're next to the main hallway," he whispered, still holding her against him. "I'm here to prevent you from doing something foolish."

She whispered back, "What makes you think I was going to do something foolish?"

"Anyone who thinks that a late-night library festivity is a clever plan needs to be restrained from further foolishness."

He could feel her quiver of indignation.

"It was worth a try," she said, "and I couldn't think of anything else."

"Apparently not," he said, "which leads me to believe that you were intending to go to Lady Michael's chamber now with some equally foolish plan in mind."

She was still and silent.

His amusement grew. "I thought so."

She quivered again with indignation. "What's so foolish about going to greet Lady Michael?" she countered. "It would be very natural for me to see her now, since her room is next to mine. If I arrive while your uncle is still there, he would introduce me, and then—"

"My uncle's there now," he interrupted, "with Mrs. Barrow, getting her settled."

"Well, you see, then," she said, "the stage is set for my entrance."

It was rather pleasant holding her against him, with one hand on her shoulder, the other behind her back holding her two wrists in the circle of his fingers. Of necessity, his lips were bent to her ear, while her lips were raised to his. Unable to see her in the intimate darkness, he had a heightened perception of her voice. It was musical, he realized, and as expressive as her face. It hummed now with her indignation and determination. She smelled good, too. Fresh but not too sweet. He pictured her as he had seen her in the pleasance and thought of the pansies there, untended and tenacious.

"I see nothing," he replied. "You were going to wait for my uncle to leave, then kindly help Lady Michael unpack the boxes, I suppose. Were you planning on flipping through the books, then and there, in front of her?"

"I was going to suggest to her that, while I was going about helping her with her things, I may as well look for a particular volume that interested me. Then I would start thumbing through the books, shaking them of dust."

MacLaurin was beginning to think that she was as muddleheaded as he had first thought. "What if she decided to help *you?*" he asked. "I suppose you would have to give her the title of the book you were looking for. But what if she came across it first? She would give it to you, and you would be obliged to leave. Or what if she decided to dust the books off, too, and a strange document fell out of one? Were you planning to say, 'Oh, that must be mine!'?"

"I had considered those contingencies," she lied. Not very convincingly.

"If you had, you would have abandoned the plan," he said. After a moment he commented, "And you said that you were going to be of help."

Again that quiver of indignation. "While you, sir," she replied, "were planning on breaking in to the library tonight, which is not a workable plan, either, given that the boxes are in Lady Michael's chamber."

"Very true," he admitted. "Please keep in mind that we can not afford even the slightest misstep, and we do not, above all, want to reveal any suspicious interest in those boxes."

She paused. "You have a better plan?"

"That's why I'm here."

She turned in the circle of his arms, as if trying to get her bearings. "And just how did you get here? I thought you went to the receiving hall with the others."

At her movement, he released her. "I did."

She stepped away from him. "But His Grace and I were the next ones to follow your uncle out of the banquet hall, while the others—you among them—went in the opposite direction."

"I came the back way, to head you off."

"Where are we, anyway?"

"In one of the secret passageways."

Her voice held amazement. "But how can that be? I was not aware of any door opening onto the hallways or closing just now."

"It slides."

Her amazement shaded into apprehension. "I heard there are trapdoors in Castle Cairn."

"As well as walls that move."

"Dear me!"

"Bogles and kelpies, too."

She scoffed, "I'm not afraid of *them*." Then, dryly, "So you needn't go out of your way to try and scare me."

"I wasn't trying to scare you, mistress, only to reassure you."

Her voice carried softly and sweetly. "Why is it, sir, that I don't believe you?"

"I wouldn't know." He turned away from her. "Come."

He heard her little gasp of dismay when he moved away, so he reached out and grasped her hand. Her fingers convulsed gratefully over his, and he had to remind himself that traveling a dark and unknown passageway might be a frightening experience for someone unused to the peculiarities of Castle Cairn.

Sure enough, her next question was, "You know how to avoid the trapdoors, I hope?"

"I do."

After a few more steps she asked, "Where are we going?"

"To Lady Michael's chamber."

"I thought we weren't going there."

"No, I wasn't going to let you go there alone."

"But isn't it the other direction?"

"This is a shortcut."

After several odd turns she sighed and said, "I wish I could see."

"You'll be able to in a— Ah, here we are."

He turned the corner. They had reached the intersection of two passageways. The alcove was graced with a small, leaded-glass window through which penetrated the light cast by the generous smile of an almost-full moon. He looked out the window and nodded at the round tower across the courtyard, imposing and night shadowed.

"The library," he informed her.

While Elizabeth contemplated the library, he considered their next move.

"Are we lost?" she asked on a betraying note of anxiety.

He turned toward her and dropped her hand. "It's only a question of how close to Lady Michael's chamber I want to end up."

"Oh, I see," she said, unable to contain her relief either in her voice or on her face, which glowed faintly blue.

"We were told at supper that her chamber is the one just beyond yours," he said. "I'm assuming you've been put somewhere in the middle of this end of the hall, so if you could describe the main color of your room, I can determine which is Lady Michael's and decide which passage to take."

Elizabeth did not honor his request directly but said, "My chamber is the second to last one on this end of the hall."

He was so surprised by this that his thoughts were diverted from the color of her room. "The second to last one?"

"Yes."

"On the main hall?"

"Why, yes."

"Are you *quite* sure that yours is the second to last one?"

She explained to him how, when she had left her room this evening, she had taken a wrong turn and had passed another doorway beyond her room before arriving at the adjacent hallway. "Is it important?"

He could not believe his luck. "It's perfect," he replied, but declined to elaborate further.

"Does this mean that we can retrieve the document tonight?"

"It means that my plans have changed," he said, then mused, as if to himself, "I wouldn't have expected that my uncle would put guests at the very end of the main hall." He considered this. "Then again, he wasn't expecting me to show up, either, which might explain his choice."

Elizabeth had put her hands on her hips and was regarding him with a critical eye. "Now that you have your new plan in mind—and I suppose you will tell me about it in your own good time—I would rather like, sir, to have some vexing questions answered."

Extremely pleased with the turn of events, MacLaurin was happy to indulge her. "Certainly, Mistress Cameron."

"Well, I was wondering," she began, "how it happened that the lieutenant knew that Allegra lives with me. After all, she does not bear the surname Cameron, but rather MacDonald after—" here she faltered "—after Fiona's dead husband, and it is not as if the lieutenant could have guessed that I would be raising Allegra."

That was easy enough to answer. "I don't think that Bev knows that Allegra lives with you or, if he does, he did not tell me. Neither did he specify her surname, since my goal is to find the document and not the child."

"So you only knew about Allegra because your man, Barrow, mentioned her name in connection with me?"

"That's right."

"And you simply assumed that my Allegra was *the* Allegra?"

"That's right."

She gasped. "But what if you had been wrong?"

"Then I would have known the moment I mentioned Bev's name and you did not react."

"Yes, but— Oh, never mind that!" She drew a deep breath. "I confess that this is all very strange to me, and I admit that I am afraid for the disaster that may be visited upon Allegra and—and the Clan Cameron!" She caught her breath, then said on a whisper, "I am sorry if I am speaking too loudly."

"No one can hear us here," he said calmly.

She regarded him frankly. He returned her regard just as frankly. She chose her words with care. "Although I am pleased to think that the lieutenant is wanting to protect his . . . his daughter from public . . . shame, I cannot help but wonder why he comes so belatedly to her rescue."

"Warenne only now introduced the damaging document."

"I know that," she said. "What I mean is, the lieutenant's desire to protect his daughter—his willingness to fight a *duel* over her—seems quite extraordinary, even a little inexplicable, considering that he has not made one effort during these past five years to discover the whereabouts or fate of his daughter."

That, too, was easy enough to answer. "Bev has just contracted a very respectable alliance."

"Oh, did his first wife die?"

"His first wife?"

She paused at length, and he could see that she was assimilating an unpleasant truth. Obviously Bev had claimed to be already married. MacLaurin recognized the usefulness of the strategy and thought the ploy justifiable only when dealing with women who were, or claimed to be, already married, as well. He was inclined to think the worse of Bev for it and regretted now not having asked Bev for the name of the mother of his child. Of course, it had not occurred to him to ask, for he had not expected to meet her—and was not quite sure if he *had* met her.

Elizabeth's response was direct and vehement. "My father said he was a scoundrel, and I believe it now more than ever!"

"Bev wants this marriage—his only marriage—to start off well. Continue well, too, I suppose."

She raised her brows. "You defend him?"

"It's never a bad turn when a man takes responsibility—whatever the reason and however belated—for a child he has brought into the world."

Her soft "Ahh" was knowing and ended on a quizzical, skeptical note.

He knew exactly how to interpret that. "What's the count up to now?" he inquired pleasantly.

Elizabeth blinked. "I don't know what you mean."

"When I left, I had not one but two illegitimate children to my name."

She paused and said, "Twelve." It was small comfort to him to hear that her tone was apologetic.

"Twelve?" he repeated, mightily impressed. "An additional one for each year I've been gone. I should be proud of myself." He would not now, or ever, declare his innocence. "Now, we can remain here and discuss my fascinating life, or we can concentrate on our immediate plan. Your choice, Mistress Cameron."

She choked a little. "It is more productive to concentrate on our plan, I think."

"Much more productive," he agreed.

"And the plan?"

He took her hand again and pulled her into the darkness of the passage on the left. "You will find a way to draw Lady Michael from her chamber, while I go in and search the boxes."

"Aren't you worried about being seen either entering or leaving her chamber?"

"No."

"How long do you think you need for me to divert her?"

"A half an hour should do it, I think."

"And what am I to propose to her ladyship that will take her from her chamber at this hour?" she asked.

"I haven't thought of that yet," he replied, "but am open to suggestions."

After traveling a distance in the darkness, she said, "I have it!"

At that very moment he slowed his steps and hushed her softly. He bent his head toward her ear, bumping his nose against her forehead in the process. "You can tell me later," he whispered. "We're almost at the end, and sounds from the passage echo through the wall at this point."

She nodded, her hair brushing against his cheek. He was put in mind of pansies.

Because the passage was so narrow, he had to plan what to do to position their two bodies for best access to the main hallway. After some awkward maneuvering, he placed her so that she stood in front of him. Then he slipped his arms around her at her waist and patted the wood in front of her until he found the catches to the sliding door. He turned them until he felt the satisfactory slide of wood against wood. A faint waft of fresh air curled around them. He was just able to perceive the crack of the opening, because the denser dark of the passageway contrasted with the lighter dark of the main hallway.

He pulled her against him, so that her back was to his front, with his back against the side wall of the passageway. He had chosen to stand like this, instead of side by side, so that they could both see through the opening onto the main hall. He rested his hands lightly on her shoulders, ready to guide her out when necessary.

"We'll wait here a moment, before we move," he breathed into her ear.

She nodded, the back of her head brushing his neck. He was distracted again with thoughts of pansies, unassuming and velvety.

After a moment he reached over her shoulder and caught a handful of her skirts. He twitched them toward the passageway, for he worried that a portion of her hem might have drifted into the main hallway on the sucking draft caused by the opening of the passage door. When he drew his arm up again, his fingers inadvertently caught the sash across her bosom, and his hand stumbled against her breast.

He bent to murmur a quiet "Sorry" into her ear, but his lips met instead the nape of her pansy neck. He was never able to get the word out. And he did not immediately remove his hand.

With her back molded against his front, he felt the quiver that coursed down her spine and determined that it held little in common with her earlier quiver of indignation. For the space of a heartbeat he let his hand rest against her full breast, then he lifted it, but only to her sash so that he could finger the warm and whisper-light Cameron plaid. He felt a quick and unexpected flash of desire. What had been merely pleasant at the other end of the passageway had turned provocative at this end.

He began to feel a little more sympathy for his deceitful friend, Bev. Perhaps Bev had been caught in a darkened passageway with Elizabeth Cameron. Perhaps Bev had held her intimately, his hand near her heart, breathing as she breathed, quickly and shallowly. Perhaps Bev had been surrounded by her scent and had felt the promise of her passion and had not been willing to deny himself such a charming opportunity. MacLaurin reflected that the only difference between the situation he imagined for Bev and his present one was that his opportunity was about to be spoiled because someone was coming down the main hallway.

This perception jolted him out of his sensual reverie. He quickly returned his hand to its original position and squeezed her shoulder in warning. He listened acutely, and when he was able to discern who was coming, he whispered, "Only my uncle and Mrs. Barrow." He carefully avoided contact with her neck.

A few moments later the voices of Robert MacLaurin and Mrs. Barrow floated into the passageway. After their footsteps died away, he did not move or speak until he thought they were absolutely safe from detection. Then he dropped his hands from her shoulders and said, "Let's get out of here."

"Oh, yes," she agreed. Her voice throbbed.

He did his best to clear his head. "All right, then," he said, still taking the precaution of whispering, "before we move out into the hallway, tell me your good idea for luring Lady Michael from her chamber."

She turned her head enough to whisper back, "I thought I might ask her to my room to learn her opinion of the dress I am going to wear tomorrow."

"Not good enough. Such a request could easily wait until the morning, when she was rested after her long journey."

She suggested another excuse that he rejected as "transparent, even suspicious."

"I could say that I had suddenly taken sick," she tried again, "and wished for her to go and call Mrs. Barrow back to my chamber."

He drew a deep breath. "I was hoping for something better," he said, "but that just might have to do."

He put his hands on her shoulders again, ready to propel them both out into the main hallway. Instead of moving forward, however, he drew her back against the side wall and put a warning finger to her lips. All his senses were on alert.

Chapter Five

Elizabeth's senses were completely disordered. Erratic tingles were coursing up and down her back, crossing her shoulders, tumbling down her bodice and colliding in her belly. Her heart was galloping, and her entire body was flushed. She did not know if she was frightened of the darkness, of the situation or of MacLaurin. She did not even know if she was frightened at all.

However, she did know that his senses were better attuned than hers. She had not heard the approach of his lordship and Mrs. Barrow until several seconds after he had warned her of them; and just now, when they had been about to move out into the hallway, she heard nothing more than the occasional odd shift and moan of an old structure. Then, slowly, a faint pattern of noises resolved itself into the identifiable rhythm of footsteps. A person was coming down the hall, not from the end with her chamber, but from the other end. Perhaps it was his lordship or Mrs. Barrow returning with some item for Lady Michael.

She had thought that the footsteps were very far away until a figure passed right in front of the crack in the wall, his face clearly visible in the circle of golden light shed by his single candle. She suppressed a gasp to have recognized His Grace, the Duke of Devonshire. And he had been walking very, very softly.

After seeing His Grace, neither she nor MacLaurin moved for so long that she became unable to distinguish between the rise and fall of her chest and his. She wanted desperately to put some healthy distance between them, but she knew they could not risk exposure.

They were rewarded for their patience when footsteps could be heard again, returning, this time accompanied by soft voices. As the footsteps and voices approached the crack in the wall, Elizabeth recognized the duke's smooth tones and a woman's low, responsive laugh. When the couple passed in front of the crack, Elizabeth caught only the glimpse of the backs of their heads illuminated in the aureole of golden candlelight, but it was enough to see that their heads were bent intimately toward one another.

MacLaurin did not allow much time to elapse after that before he moved. When he seemed ready to leave their hiding place, she protested that it was too soon.

"The duke and her ladyship are fully engaged with one another," he replied, taking her hand, "for the moment, anyway, and I don't want to waste any time."

"Any guesses about where they are headed?"

He drew her out into the hallway and kept his voice low. "The duke has been given the royal chambers at the extreme end of the hall, not far from where the other historians have been placed. Of course, I don't know whether he is escorting her ladyship there—nor can I know whether he intends to keep her occupied the night long. I've heard talk in London that the duke had a liaison with her ladyship. I've also heard talk that he broke it off rather recently."

Suddenly the door to an unknown world of romance and intrigue opened up to Elizabeth, and she caught a tantalizing glimpse. She must have caught her breath.

MacLaurin stopped and looked down at her. She could just discern the cast of his deeply shadowed features. His expression was searching, and his voice held a questioning note when he said, "I beg your pardon, if my reference was improper."

Her thoughts flashed first to her unmaidenly acknowledgment in the gardens that Gabriel Beverly was Allegra's father and then to her recent outrageous and erroneous reference to MacLaurin's twelve—*twelve!*—illegitimate children. She let out her breath on a rush and said, "I think we've gone too far now to be worried about *that!*"

The moment the words left her mouth, she wished she could recall them. He made nothing of them, merely nodded and said, "Right," and left it at that. He adjusted his clasp on her hand. "Follow my footsteps. I know the boards that don't creak."

She did as he bade her and was emboldened to ask, "Now what?"

"Another change in plans, once again for the better."

He said nothing more until they had traveled a good way, far enough that she imagined she was close to her chamber. Eventually he stopped, dropped her hand, fiddled with something on the wall, and she heard the slide of wood against wood. He had, apparently, found the entrance to another secret passageway.

He said, "Your chamber is one more door down. Do you think you can find it? Good. Now, all you have to do is go in your room and keep your ear to the hallway door. If you hear Devonshire and Lady Michael return, be prepared to go into the hallway and engage them in a story of suffering. Choose whatever ailment you find most suitable. And be sure to make sufficient noise. Talk loudly. Open and close your door loudly. That sort of thing, so that I can hear you."

"You'll be in Lady Michael's chamber, then?"

"Yes," he answered, "and I shall need a few seconds' warning to clear out."

She did not ask him how he was to manage the problem of getting in and out of Lady Michael's chamber with only a few seconds' warning. She was more concerned with her own part. "What if Lady Michael is alone? Should I send her to fetch Mrs. Barrow?"

He pondered the point, then said, "Perhaps it would be more natural to ask her only to help you get comfortable in bed."

She nodded. "I'll make as much noise as I can, of course. However, if His Grace is with her, I shall send him to Mrs. Barrow, is that it?"

"That's it," he confirmed. He made a move away from her, then a thought apparently occurred to him. "And don't forget to change into your nightclothes." As if to excuse himself yet another indelicate suggestion, he explained, "Given that you retired a while ago, it would look very odd to be still dressed at this hour, claiming illness."

She agreed and decided privately that her delicate sensibilities, if she had ever had any, were long gone.

Before he left her, he added, "If I'm successful before they return, I shall stop by your door and tap three times."

"Very well."

The next moment she was staring at a blank wall.

Elizabeth hurried on to her room in the darkness, sorry that she had lost her candle when MacLaurin had pulled her into the passageway. She panicked when her key did not fit the first door she came to, then felt a rush of relief when it opened the second. Upon entering her room, she was glad that she had not closed her curtains. Enough moonlight was filtering in to give her light to undress by, and she did not wish to waste time lighting a candle. With no difficulty she shed her dress, corset and underskirts, floated her night-shift over her head and shrugged into her night jacket, without taking time to tie the ribbons. She proceeded to unpin her hair, comb it out with her fingers and palm the pins, all on her way to the hallway door.

She cracked it a fraction and stood there a moment listening intently. She reckoned that not more than five minutes had passed since MacLaurin had left her in the hallway. She was satisfied to hear nothing suspicious in the hallway and then realized that she needed to cast back the covers on her bed and rumple them, in case she needed to make it look as if she had been in bed.

She was never able to move from the door to her bed, because the very next second a grinding scream of inhuman proportions rent the silence of her chamber. She whirled and clutched her heart, scattering her hairpins. She flattened her back against the door. To her ears it seemed that the monstrous scream had come from within her very room and that the wall next to the fireplace was writhing in pain.

Completely terrified, she suffered the experience of the teeth-clenching, bone-jarring scream a second time and imagined that a rusted metal monster was chewing another rusted metal monster. To compound her terror, she saw, for the second time that day, a ghost step through the screaming wall and stride toward her. It was a very substantial ghost, not at all ethereal, and it looked menacing. She did not know why her heart did not simply stop on the spot.

Then, again for the second time that day, the ghost transformed itself into Ian MacLaurin. Her spine melted to jelly with relief.

"Oh, it's you!" she breathed, light-headed. She attempted to straighten herself against the door, but her knees were not working. She hoped that her heart would return to its accustomed place in her breast. She was finding it hard to breathe with her heart in her throat.

MacLaurin had come close enough to her that she could see that he was experiencing no similar relief. In fact, he looked extremely irritated.

He stopped a few feet from her and the door. "Good God, woman! What are you doing here?"

His tone was very bracing. She straightened. "What am *I* doing here?" Since he saw no reason to speak quietly, neither did she.

"I'm in no mood for absurdity," he growled, "and we might not have much time to repair this disaster! I didn't want any missteps, and now already this evening's plan is ruined. Not to mention the possibility that we may have advertised to the entire castle that we are up to our necks in intrigue!"

Elizabeth was becoming accustomed to abrupt changes of mood in his presence and moved easily from sheer fright to lively self-defense. "I cannot be held responsible for the poor mechanical condition of that...that contraption," she fired back, "which is, if I am not mistaken, another of the special features of Castle Cairn."

"It's a secret panel," he informed her curtly, "whose internal mechanism has apparently not been oiled in a very long time."

"And you're blaming me for that? It seems to me that you should have guessed that it would be in poor condition!"

"How was I to guess, given that the wood catches in the passageways were all working?"

"Metal is different," she argued, quite reasonably.

"Ah, yes, but the wood could have warped and it wasn't, so it didn't occur to me that— Don't change the subject!" he snapped. "Just how did you get into the *rose* room? Not to mention, just how are you to get *out* of it?"

"I don't have to get out of it," she answered, thinking to gain the upper hand in this pointless argument, "because this is my room."

MacLaurin did not look mollified by this admission. "I asked you earlier for the color of your room," he reminded her, "and you told me that you were in the second to last room on this hallway. Need I tell you now that the rose room is the *last* room on the hallway?"

She held her ground. "It can't be. Lady Michael's is the one just beyond mine. I'm sure of it."

"The next room—the one you are referring to—stands at the beginning of the next hallway."

"It cannot, because I did not bump into the wall until after the next chamber. You must be mis—"

"I can hardly be mistaken," he interrupted testily. "The proof being that I just left my room, which is the last one on the east wing, and entered this room, which is the last one on the main hall. The hallway ends just beyond your room. It's not a sharp-angled joining of the two hallways, I admit, but rather proceeds along a curve. A *discernible* curve."

"Well, it comes to a *sharp-angled* end beyond Lady Michael's room," she told him loftily. "I ran into a wall this evening on my way to supper when I turned right out of my room rather than left, and it was after the next door down.''

"What you ran into," he told her, his irritation still flaring, "was not a wall but a pillar.''

"A pillar? Well, how was I to know that? It was dark.''

"You would have known it if you had taken a candle with you, which I assume you did not.''

In a small voice she admitted, "Which I, in fact, did not.'' She held up her hand in the fencer's gesture acknowledging a hit. "I know! I said that I was going to be of help. Well, maybe I still can be.''

He looked at her with hard, angry eyes and said, "I would be very surprised at this point if you could be.''

She gestured to the alcove behind him. "I wonder, can you get to Lady Michael's chamber through there, perhaps? It's a very curious corner, I think, and I'm guessing now that it must line up with the curve of the hallway.'' She asked, not unhopefully, "Do you know of another secret panel there?''

He was apparently not in a generous mood. "No, and given the fact that I grew up here, I would know it, if there was one.''

"Oh,'' was her rather deflated response. She glanced at the wall he had just walked through and asked uncertainly, "There's a secret panel that adjoins your room directly to mine, then?''

"Yes, and two sets of peepholes in the wall, as well,'' he informed her unkindly, but he was enough in control of himself by now to have lowered his voice. "So, you see, the setup would have been perfect if this had been Lady Michael's chamber. I would have been able to monitor her movements—if necessary.''

"I was not responsible for the assigning of the rooms," she said, "and it's not as if my mistake about who had what room has prevented you from getting into Lady Michael's chamber. The lack of access was there from the moment your uncle chose our respective chambers."

"Very true," he agreed, "but because of your mistake, we now have to see whether the metallic roar of the secret panel has given us away and brings my uncle down upon us. All for nothing."

That was true, and Elizabeth felt awful. Watching him watching her, she imagined that she must look pretty awful, too. Since his back was to the window and his face was mostly in shadows, she could only guess at what he was thinking.

She guessed wrong. He was thinking, with amazement, that she looked surprisingly attractive, standing there with her hair tumbling around her shoulders, her dressing gown untied and her nightdress lacy and low cut. The wink of a thin chain around her neck caught his eye, and his gaze followed the trail down until the glimpse of gold was lost between her breasts. He became aware of her uncorseted figure, but its outlines were only a suggestion because he was standing between her and the moonlight. The promise of the fullness and beauty of her body matched his experiences of it in the passageway. Her pansy scent floated all around him, as if freed from the constriction of clothes and hairpins.

MacLaurin's healthy irritation mutated into a healthy pique of the sort that had come over him in the passageway, and a curtain drew open across his mind. He thought back on everything she had said concerning Bev, Allegra and the events of five years ago. He no longer doubted the relationship that must have existed between Elizabeth Cameron and Gabriel Beverly. He now understood it as the logical explanation for all her reactions since he had brought up the subject. Barrow had told him that wild rumors had circulated about the child's birth. What was more, she had not said anything to make him think that she was not Allegra's mother.

He wondered why he had not seen it from the beginning. He supposed it was because, when he had first set eyes on her, she had hidden her beautiful body beneath an ugly dress, had screwed her hair around her head and was lost in some kind of haze. Seeing her like this—with her figure unbound, her lips parted, her fine eyes wide, her expressive face adorably expressive—he recalled that he had always admired Bev's taste for soft and sensual women. He was even inclined to credit his old army buddy with a subtler eye than he had previously realized.

He would have felt sorry that Bev had shamelessly ruined her, but he suddenly realized that her radiant temperament and her sneak-up-and-stun sensuality made her the most dangerous sort of woman. His ardor cooled instantly.

She whispered, "I'm sorry."

He forgot why she was excusing herself and thought it was on account of her having seduced Bev. He was about to air his opinion of that when a fateful tap came from the other side of the door.

He met her wide eyes and marshaled his wandering wits. He motioned for her to wait several moments. Fortunately, the door hinged on the side where he was standing, so that he would be in position to hear everything without being seen.

When the right amount of time had elapsed, he gestured Elizabeth to open the door. Muddleheaded as she was, he was not hopeful for the outcome.

Chapter Six

Elizabeth's evening was going from bad to worse. Inside her chamber was Ian MacLaurin, her accomplice, who was not very happy with her performance thus far. Outside her chamber door stood—

She opened it a crack and looked out to see none other than the Duke of Devonshire. He was in company with a woman who stood just outside the circle of light from the candle he held. That would be Lady Michael. Elizabeth had seen her only from the back, through the crack in the passageway door. From the front, her ladyship was very beautiful.

"My child," His Grace said, "we—the Lady Michael and I—were worried about you."

She exerted herself to affect credible, even sleepy surprise, and she properly kept her improperly clad body behind the door. She suppressed her squirm of realization that MacLaurin had an unobstructed view of her state of undress.

"Were you, Your Grace?" she replied. Then, as if remembering her manners, she bobbed a little curtsy. "Lady Michael. We haven't met yet."

Lady Michael murmured something, it mattered not what, given these unusual circumstances. Elizabeth could not read her ladyship's expression, but it seemed to blend delicate interest and demure discretion.

"Yes, we were concerned," His Grace pursued. He glanced down at the threshold, then back up at her. "You see, her ladyship and I were taking a turn in the castle just now...."

Elizabeth attempted an expression that conveyed both polite acknowledgment and obvious incomprehension of the reason for such a late-night activity.

"Robbie, our host," His Grace continued smoothly, "informed me of her ladyship's desire to stretch her legs after the long coach ride. We attempted to find one of the gardens that Robbie directed us toward but became hopelessly lost, I am afraid."

Still affecting grogginess, Elizabeth said that she had no difficulty understanding how that could happen.

"Yes, you see, then, that it hardly mattered whether we found the garden or not," His Grace continued, "for the goal was accomplished. After walking the castle hallways, Lady Michael found herself relaxed enough to retire."

"Oh, yes," Elizabeth said and repeated mechanically, "Relaxed enough to retire. May I wish both of you a good night, then?"

"Ah, but you see, my child," His Grace said, "as I was escorting Lady Michael back to her room, we heard—or so we thought—the most extraordinary noise."

Elizabeth aimed for an expression that betrayed little more than befuddled interest. "Indeed, Your Grace?" She stifled a yawn.

"Indeed," His Grace answered, with a note in his voice that caused Elizabeth's ears to prick up. "The noise sounded as if it came from this end of the hallway."

Elizabeth puzzled over this statement in a dull-witted way. "Could you describe the noise, if you please, Your Grace?"

His Grace's laugh was low and chilling, carrying an ill-defined threat. "No, I am not sure that I can, my child. It was quite an unusual noise, I would say, and very loud. Very loud, indeed."

This time Elizabeth affected a yawn that she was not quite able to stifle. She said, widening dreamy eyes, as if enlightened, "Oh, then that might have been what awakened me. Just before you knocked, I felt myself on the verge of waking. Otherwise, I might not have heard you." She smiled with sleepy satisfaction, as if pleased by the explanation.

She was less pleased when His Grace glanced over her shoulder into her room.

"Perhaps," His Grace allowed in his most soothing voice. "Lady Michael and I were wondering if you were in trouble of some sort, and have come to offer you help. I thought you might need, perhaps, the strong arm of a man to look around your room for you, if you were frightened—or otherwise disturbed by the cause of the noise."

Elizabeth could feel MacLaurin's reaction to that, willing her to deny His Grace entrance. However, she had already discovered that, with His Grace, a bold approach was better than timidity.

"Should you like to come in and look around to satisfy yourself, Your Grace?" she said. Her tone suggested she was willing to accommodate any odd quirk of his. She made a small gesture as if to open the door to allow him passage into her room, then checked it. With confusion she said, "But I am not properly dressed." She bit her lip. "Should you like to come back in the morning, Your Grace, to assure yourself that I am all right?"

The suggestion was completely idiotic, but she intended for her idiocy to serve a purpose.

It did. His Grace replied, "That will not be necessary, my child." He glanced down at the threshold again. "If you have not been seriously disturbed, then I need not worry for you."

Making it look as if she had initiated this pointless encounter, she said, "I am sorry to have troubled you, Your Grace." She bobbed him a curtsy, once again from behind the door, then dropped a second one for his companion. "Lady Michael."

Good-nights were said all around at least twice, and Elizabeth closed the door.

Holding her breath, she turned toward MacLaurin, and their eyes held. He looked ready to speak, but she put one index finger to her lips and pointed with the other to the bottom of the door. To judge from the faint glow of light that wedged under it, the two people on the other side had not moved. Several moments later the wedge of light disappeared. It seemed that His Grace and Lady Michael returned to Lady Michael's chamber.

MacLaurin whispered, "That went well."

"Not well enough, I think." She bent and began to pat the floorboards. She stood again and gestured him away from the door, hastily tying the ribbons on her dressing gown when his back was turned.

She followed him to the center of the room. When they were at the foot of the bed, she held out her hand, opened palm up. "I had ten pins in my hair," she said, keeping her voice low. "I've found only nine."

"And so?"

"When you startled me by walking through the wall," she explained, "I scattered the pins in my hand. I believe one must have skittered under the door into the hallway. I noticed that His Grace looked down at the threshold once or twice."

"Are you saying that he remained outside the door just now to pick it up?"

She shrugged. "I don't know. He may or may not wish to draw Lady Michael's attention to an odd circumstance. I would open the door now and look for the pin myself, but His Grace may just well be on his return trip down the hallway. That is, *if* he is returning to his—"

She caught her breath and could have sworn she heard a faint noise outside her chamber. No candle glow was visible under the door, but His Grace would surely not betray himself so obviously. Had he stopped to retrieve a telltale pin?

MacLaurin looked thoughtful. After a moment he whispered, "I'm not sure that a scattered hairpin gives us away."

"Perhaps not, but any detail out of place becomes suspicious in conjunction with the hideous noise," she replied. "A scattered hairpin becomes another clue to add to the fact that I was not asleep when His Grace came knocking."

"Your performance was rather convincing."

She looked at him and challenged, "Surprised?"

He replied frankly, "Yes."

She nodded at her bed. "No matter how good my performance, I will not have convinced him of anything if he noticed that my bed was not unmade."

"And you think he saw it?"

"He looked over my shoulder once."

She watched MacLaurin studying the angle of the
opening of the door with respect to the bed. After some
deliberation he said, "I see your point."

"Yes," she said, "and the fact that he was willing to
play along with my performance suggests to me that Lady
Michael is not in his confidence—whatever that may be!"
She looked at him. "What do you think His Grace's stake
in all of this is?"

He returned her regard. "I have no idea," he said,
"but I'm sure that he's in it up to his neck."

Elizabeth took a deep breath. "I think so, too. But
what a strange, incomprehensible puzzle! What could His
Grace possibly have to do or *want* with a document concerning Allegra's parentage? At least we know that he has
had no time to go through the boxes in Lady Michael's
chamber tonight."

When she received no response to that, she noticed that
MacLaurin's attention had wandered. She did not flatter herself that her particular charms had caused his
mental lapse, and with her dressing gown tied, she did not
feel so exposed to him. In fact, the peculiar effect of this
late-night episode in her bedchamber had resulted in her
feeling more comfortable in his presence rather than less.

His irritation upon finding her in the rose room had
wiped out the highly uncomfortable feelings she had experienced when they had been pressed together in the
passageway. His approval of her handling of the exchange at the door with His Grace—despite the mis-
placed hairpin and made bed—had acquitted her of her
earlier mistakes. She thought he accepted her now as a
competent partner, and she could see that the problem of
retrieving the document was going to be a bigger one than
she had initially thought. It was going to take the two of
them working together to do it.

"Well," she said at last, "we've exhausted the possibilities for action this night. The only thing to do now, I suppose, is to figure out when it's safe for you to leave my room. I don't think you should try the secret panel again."

His wandering attention seemed to return. "I don't think I should," he agreed with a short laugh. He glanced over his shoulder. "I'll go through the window."

"The window?" she echoed.

"Our rooms are next to one another, and I left my window open, too."

"Do you think it's a good idea?"

"There's only one way to find out."

Elizabeth followed him toward the window, past the crumpled clothing she had hastily stashed behind the bed. Over the edge of the cheval glass trailed the red Cameron sash, bleached to moonglow blue in the silver darkness.

She peered over the sill and down into the courtyard a good fifteen feet below. She judged the width of the exterior ledge to be not more than six inches. She noted the sharp turn he would have to make to get from her window to his, which was presumably around the corner and out of her sight.

"I think we've found out that this is not a good idea," she pronounced.

He disagreed. "I shall be all right and even better without these." He stripped off his coat and handed it to her. Then he unbuckled his shoes and slipped them off, unbuttoned the lower edges of his knee breeches and rolled down his white stockings. He left these items on the floor. "Hide my things for now. I'll get them later."

She nodded, holding his coat in one hand.

He was standing in profile to the moon. White light lit one side of his body, leaving the other side in darkness. His well-defined features were etched sharp and clean, creating a compelling masculine geometry. She had already noted that his black hair and blue eyes made a remarkably attractive combination. By night, the combination was reversed and even more dramatic: his eyes were black and his hair shone blue, like liquid midnight. Fascinated, she followed the curve of his hair to the cords of his neck until they joined the slope of his shoulder, broad beneath his shirt. She imagined the glide of arm muscles and chest that lay beneath the soft folds of white linen.

He turned and put both hands on the sill, readying himself for the climb out her window. Nothing could have been more romantic than a handsome young man leaving her bedchamber by such means, but romance was far from her thoughts. His daring put her in mind of yet another vexing question that had occurred to her while she was dressing for dinner.

"You know," she said, "I can't help but think that you're taking a big risk here, perhaps bigger than it is worth to you."

"The window, you mean?" he replied, unconcerned. He flexed and limbered muscles. "It'll be all right."

"The window, yes, but that's not all," she said. "Coming here in the first place was a risk, no? And for what? To retrieve a document that is more valuable to someone else than to you."

He was about to spring up on the sill, but stopped. "Why is coming here a risk to me?"

"I wouldn't know! I mention it only because your sudden return seems odd, given the fact that you have been gone for ten years, without a word to anyone."

"It seems odd to you that I would perform a service for a man who is not presently capable of performing it for himself?"

"But to have come here, of all places!" she insisted.

"Who better than I?"

Almost anyone, she thought, but his cool tones prevented her from voicing that thought. She puzzled through the motives of a man whose scandalous behavior had chased him from his home ten years earlier. She arrived at only one explanation. "Were you in the army with Lieutenant Beverly?"

He returned his attention to the sill and prepared to jump up on it. "Very good, Mistress Cameron."

"Which means, I suppose, that you owe the lieutenant some extraordinary debt."

He did not respond to that, but said instead, with a whoosh of effort, "A person's motives are always mysterious." When he established his footing on the narrow stone loaf outside her window, he rose to his full height, with his back against the wall. From his perch he looked down at her. "Take Devonshire's, for instance. Or yours."

"Mine?" she echoed. "Mine are hardly mysterious."

"Tell me about the events surrounding Allegra's birth."

Highly distracted by the sight of his muscled calf, which was right at her eye level, she answered, "I was living quite retired at the time, so it was natural that Fiona would come and live with me before her confinement."

"Ah," he said, "so that's how it was."

"How else could it have been?" she returned, finding this turn in conversation very odd. "Fiona was alone, since her husband had died some months before in a riding accident, as I told you."

She did not mention that Donald MacDonald had died almost exactly nine months before Allegra was born—or say that his fatal riding accident had most likely been precipitated by the knowledge of his wife's infidelity. Neither did she mention that she was the one who had devised the plan for Fiona to come live with her in the cottage on her father's estate, so that no one save herself and Fiona's serving woman would know the exact date of Allegra's birth. Nor did she say that Allegra was a child who had fallen from the sky, her soul a star whose last star rays may have sunk into Fiona's womb but into Elizabeth's heart.

"How was it that you were living quite retired, as you say?"

"I persuaded my father to let me live in the cottage," she said. "He was against it, of course, but I was determined to see my plan through."

"Ah, yes, I had a taste of your determination in the gardens," he commented. He began to inch his way along the ledge, away from her window. "And then?"

"And then Fiona died."

"From what?"

"Fever," she said, not thinking it necessary to elaborate.

"And you kept Allegra."

"Yes."

"It's not the customary arrangement for an unmarried young woman to raise a child."

"We agreed earlier in the gardens that it is not, but what would you have had me do otherwise?"

"I suppose you could have had the child raised by the MacDonalds, since you were claiming that kinship for

Allegra. And we are back where we started in our discussion of motives."

"How so?"

He had edged himself about five feet away from her, his footing confident and agile and showing no signs of hesitation. "You wonder at my daring to be on a ledge high above the ground in search of a document that means little to me. I wonder at your willingness to pay for one mistake for the rest of your life when you had an alternative."

"Pay? For the rest of my life?" she echoed, puzzled. "You make my guardianship of Allegra sound like a punishment. I do not consider myself punished, but rather blessed."

He looked down at her, his face and body beautiful when bathed in moonlight. "I admire your fortitude." Then he disappeared around the sharp corner.

She was about to call out to him to explain himself, but the words sat back unspoken on her tongue. An astonishing, unthinkable, unmistakable pattern unfolded in her brain and was as vivid to her mind's eye as the Cameron tartan.

He thinks that I am Allegra's mother!

Chapter Seven

Shock kept Elizabeth at the windowsill for a good ten minutes. Amazement kept her awake most of the night. Exhaustion finally claimed her, and she slept like the baby she was supposed to have had. When she came to half-consciousness the next morning, she was a different person. She stretched luxuriously and wondered who she might be. She smiled dreamily. Fiona, perhaps. And if not Fiona herself, then at least she was now Allegra's mother.

She should have been offended but, in truth, she was absurdly flattered. In the space of a few hours in one day she had been transformed in MacLaurin's mind from a serving girl at Castle Cairn to the passionate paramour of the very handsome Gabriel Beverly.

She had closed the window the night before but not drawn the curtains. Dawn's light tickled her lids, teasing them open, and the first thing she saw was MacLaurin's coat in a heap upon his shoes and stockings by the window. Grateful for the opportunity to hide them before Mary came to tend to her, she hopped out of bed, feeling well rested and clearheaded. She was eager to continue the adventure begun the night before. However, she did not wish to begin by contriving a likely explanation for why a man's jacket was in her bedchamber.

She picked up the jacket and inspected it. She wondered whether all of Mary's gossip had been exaggerated, or only the part about MacLaurin's dozen bastard children, which she had narrowed, in reality, to one. The gossip and the years had garbled the point whether his father, Gavin MacLaurin, the previous Lord Mure, had thrown his son out or whether his son had left on his own. However, the gossip was clear that Ian MacLaurin had gone without a penny after he had refused to marry the woman of his father's choice and after his father, a harsh and uncompromising man, had cut him out of his will. The title and castle went to Gavin's brother, Robert, when Gavin had died, bitter and broken, within a few months of his son's disgraceful departure.

The material of MacLaurin's jacket was fine to her eye and to her touch. The tailoring was equally expensive. It did not seem to be the jacket of a disinherited Scot, particularly one who had lately earned his living in the army, and she felt as if she was holding a mystery. She knew that she was not going to solve it by looking at the jacket, but while she was looking at it, she indulged her admiration of his broad shoulders.

After a pleasant moment of speculation she went to her wardrobe, which stood to the left of the fireplace. She rummaged among her clothes until she decided that the perfect place to hide MacLaurin's jacket was under her ugly traveling dress. His shoes and stockings she stashed next to the packet containing the rare historical documents she had mentioned to Lord Mure.

She had completely forgotten them. A few days before, she had received this packet of neatly bundled old letters in the mail. No accompanying note. No return address. She had read enough to know that they were love letters, and she had been intrigued enough to have come to Castle Cairn to find help in interpreting them.

She had been too busy in the past several days to begin to worry about who had sent them to her and why, and those questions were of secondary interest now, as well. Instead, she seized on the possibility that *these* represented the correspondence from which one letter had fallen into the hands of Rupert Warenne and over which Lieutenant Beverly had dueled. She had not read them through in their entirety, so she seated herself on the floor before the wardrobe, opened the packet and began to read.

She was quickly engrossed in a tale of tragic love told through the letters of an ardent young man to his ladylove. Soon enough she realized that they could not have been written by Lieutenant Beverly to Fiona. She began to piece together a very different and pathetic story from what she presumed was only half the correspondence. From that half, she gathered that the ardent lover was a widower with a young child who burned with a passion for a woman who was promised to a powerful rival from a neighboring clan. His poetic descriptions of that love were so moving that they wrenched Elizabeth's heart.

She lost herself in the prose and the emotion. Her goal of scanning for clues to the origin of these letters hummed faintly at the edges of her attention. Of course, she would have an easier time determining who had written them and when if she could get her hands on the other half of the correspondence, namely those letters written by the ladylove, to which the ardent lover consistently referred. But where to begin looking for those letters—if they still existed—defeated her imagination.

As she read, she culled what she thought might be a poetic reference to Loch Ossian, a landmark just beyond the eastern edge of Cameron lands. It was also not far from Castle Cairn and, in fact, lay between the two properties. Otherwise, the ardent lover scrupulously avoided the use of specific names and places. This meant that Elizabeth's trail began and ended at Loch Ossian, and she had no assurance that the ardent lover or his ladylove had even lived in the immediate vicinity. The ardent lover's powerful rival was always apostrophized as the evil one.

As she progressed through the letters, she lost interest in historical detective work and focused on The Kiss, which was how she labeled the passionate passages that spanned three different letters. Each of these passages opened up for her a forbidden scene, like the panels of a triptych upon a heathen altar, to reveal a different and tantalizing view of the art and interest of "two pairs of lips breathing nectar."

Her eyes floated over the ardent lover's phrases: balm of love, the seal of bliss, the melting sip. She grew hungry for his references to the nape of his ladylove's neck, the swerve of her jaw, the lobe of her ear, the ivory lace at her breast. She grew breathless for his hints of lovelier ivory below the lace and, even more daring, the two roses that tipped the ivory. She imagined what he must mean by the honeyed seal of soft affections and desired for herself love's first snowdrop, virgin kiss.

All the ardent lover's attention was devoted to the production of the "aromatic breeze." Yet the ardent lover wrote, even more daringly, that these pledges of future bliss, these dearest ties of young connections, were just the prelude to love that would be fulfilled for them in the Fleurise Garden.

The Fleurise Garden. Elizabeth's heart soared. She yearned for such a kiss, for such an opening, for such a garden. Certainly the ardent lover's most extravagant poetic conceit, as well as his most poignant. It was an enchanted place with thick green bushes, winking red and blue, full ripe, where the lovers would one day meet to feed one another plump berries and kiss the berry juice away. It was a fragrant place with herbs and flowers and climbing roses caressing the walls, which would ultimately entwine with the lovers' own future embraces. It was a fecund place with a charming well, from which the lovers would drink and lick the drops that lingered on the loved one's lips. It was a mysterious place of stamens rising and pistils swelling in moist and fragrant ground.

The story was too melancholy, too heartbreaking. Judging from the pitch of fevered emotion on which the correspondence abruptly ended, she imagined that the ardent lover had died for love—with or without having consummated it. Or perhaps he had killed the evil one and had been sent to prison. Or been banished, if he were noble. Or been killed in revenge by the evil one's clan. But which clan?

She looked up from her letters, and her eye fell on the fireplace nymphs. Oddly, charmingly, they seemed to sigh in sympathy. She returned her attention to the letters and guessed that several dark allusions to the ardent lover's rival clan could be tracked down in the genealogies of the Castle Cairn library, and this thought put her in mind of the more pressing matter for the day. However, before she could think about the new day's strategy, her attention darted again in a new direction.

She went to the panel beside the fireplace and smoothed her hand over the heavy carvings, feeling for seams or signs that it could slide aside. She found nothing. She stepped back and contemplated the ornate wall, seemingly so heavy and unyielding. She reminded herself that MacLaurin's bedchamber lay just on the other side of that movable panel. Without further reflection she returned to the wardrobe and began tossing her clothing onto the bed, leaving only her traveling dress with MacLaurin's jacket underneath still hanging. She covered his shoes and stockings with the packet of letters.

With needle and thread in hand, she set about her work, her brain as busy as her hands. Of all the extraordinary events of the past several days, her receipt of the old love letters was surely the most important. If she had not received the packet, she might not have been prompted to disobey her father and come to Castle Cairn. If she had not come to Castle Cairn, she would not now be in position to safeguard Allegra's future.

Today she would retrieve the document from the book in the box. She was sure of it. She had not been so providentially guided to Castle Cairn only to leave it empty-handed.

MacLaurin slept later than Elizabeth, but not much past the dawn. He dreamed a dream of chill beauty, of mermaids and of winter when the sky was like iron and when the wind was endless and hostile. Only then was it possible to catch the rare splendor of a ray of sunlight blossoming through the hard lace of gray clouds. Just before catching that ray, his eyes opened. He was at first confused with being inside another dream that had transported him to his old room at Castle Cairn.

He assembled his half-waking perceptions to take stock of his whereabouts, whereupon he became aware of a blinding headache, the kind one would have with a heavy hangover. The night before, however, he had not drunk a drop beyond a glass of whiskey served with the haggis. He closed his eyes again to recapture the mermaids and the ray of winter sunlight, but they eluded him.

He opened his eyes again. He propped himself on his elbows and found himself looking straight into the faces of the demons trapped in the fireplace frieze. They had been silent the day before, but this morning they were laughing and carrying on.

MacLaurin squinted at them. He attempted to make sense of what they were saying above the banging of blood at his temples and ears. He caught the cadence of an insolent "Such a clever lad!" He grunted.

"Think you haven't been caught in the trap?" they scorned.

"Not yet," he assured them.

This brought on a raucous round of merriment.

"Think I came unprepared?" he retorted.

"The traps are everywhere!" they informed him gleefully.

"I know, and I know how to avoid them—*all* of them."

The demons jeered, "You're talking to us, aren't you?"

Disgusted, MacLaurin threw back the covers and swung his legs over the side of the bed. He rose and stretched. He cracked his knuckles and extended long fingers toward the ceiling. Because he slept naked—mermaids and women preferring him that way—he had little more to do than tie himself into his drawers, ease into his breeches, don his white shirt, leather vest and jacket. He pulled on stockings and boots. As an afterthought he combed his fingers through his hair and retrieved from his pillow the black ribbon that a mermaid had teased from his queue during the night.

With relative efficiency, he left the castle. By the time he stepped out into the warm and sunny morning, the fists pounding inside his head had subsided to a milder pummeling. He negotiated a series of walls and headed for the barn at the near edge of the west fields. Before him, Cairn o' Mount towered upward and carried down the currents of wind that filtered through the Grampian passes. The mountain was in its summer dress, impossible in purple, and MacLaurin relished the sight of this flamboyant flaunting of nature that came for one month of the year. High above, white clouds billowed and nestled to pearl gray in the shadows of other clouds. One cloud curved and curled elegantly, reminding him of Devonshire's wig.

MacLaurin frowned, not at all pleased that Devonshire was here, but at the same time pleased that he was not anywhere else. MacLaurin's thoughts drifted along, like the clouds above, and touched on the subject of Elizabeth Cameron. It was not until his attention alighted on her that he realized that he had been avoiding thinking about her. He had nowhere to go with that observation, so he cast it idly from his mind as he would a pebble palmed in his pocket to be worried as an aid to deep reflection.

Inside the barn, his fears were confirmed—or, rather, once again, he did not realize that he had been fearing what he would find there until he confronted it. The day before, he had seen that the stables had been worse for the wear of the past ten years, although the horseflesh was still prime. However, the structure of the stables themselves, which had already been suffering under his father's stewardship, had evidently not been improved since. When he had ridden out yesterday afternoon he had noted that the east fields were in bad heart, looking scraggly and unproductive. A bit better than the castle garden, but only just.

Thus was he grimly satisfied by the decrepit state of the barn and by the age and state of the implements within. Not to mention the fact that the harrows and spades were cobwebbed in the corners and not out in the fields as they should have been in prime summer weather. Although most of the equipment was wood, several pieces had been modernized with iron, and one large plow was of sorely rusted steel. It lay atop a makeshift worktable. Next to it squatted an open crock of dark oil and some rags. MacLaurin read the composition as a lazy, ever-hopeful appeal to the fairies.

He hallooed until he roused a boy who shuffled out from behind a pile of hay, pitchfork in hand. The boy was a grandson to Rud Shaw, judging by the color of his hair and the hook to his nose. MacLaurin inquired whether the overseer was about. The boy pondered the question, then replied in Gaelic that he did not know but would ask his granddad. He went to fetch him.

MacLaurin was happy to learn that the overseer, Rud Shaw, was still alive. When Rud Shaw set his ancient eyes upon MacLaurin, the old man's expression did not suggest that he reciprocated the sentiment.

MacLaurin greeted the old man in Gaelic, but if he thought that would win him approval, he was widely mistaken. MacLaurin's Gaelic was as rusty as the farm equipment. As he attempted to engage the old man in conversation, Rud Shaw looked at once suspicious and unforgiving of MacLaurin's hesitations.

MacLaurin cast about for a topic that would draw from Rud Shaw more than a syllable of response. After exploring sheep and shooting to the extent that his limited vocabulary allowed, he backed into the subject of the local grain supply, about which Rud Shaw had a deal to say. MacLaurin learned that Rud Shaw had identified the root of all evil to lie in the dependence on local grain supplies, which inhabitants of a country with a treacherous climate like that of the Highlands of Scotland could ill afford.

MacLaurin stopped hearing the old man's words and began listening to the music of the Gaelic. He realized that he must have sung his opening remarks off-key and offended Rud Shaw's ears. He caught the rhythm and reached back for old melodies. Then, for the pure pleasure of hearing himself speak, he spun out a whimsical plan for the improvement of Castle Cairn's chronic short supply of grain. This involved increasing the number of black cattle raised in the summer rather than decreasing it, and selling them on the English market in the autumn where they would buy their grain.

Rud Shaw wondered what they would do for milk, butter and cheese, leather for brogues and harnesses, and horn for spoons if they were to sell all their cattle to the Sassenachs.

Inspired by his own eloquence, MacLaurin replied that only so many spoons could ever be used at once, and one thousand head of cattle would yield two thousand horns.

Rud Shaw's mouth twitched. He launched into discussion of grouse moor and low ground pasture that took MacLaurin out of his depths. Yet one point came through: there was no longer enough acreage to triple Cairn stock.

"No longer?" MacLaurin questioned.

The old man shrugged. "Five years ago, maybe, it would have been possible. Or even as recently as last month."

"Do you mean that Uncle has sold land?"

Rud Shaw's reply was as short and potent as a curse. "Clan Chattan."

Clan Chattan. Gaelic for MacPherson. The Duke of Devonshire again. MacLaurin glanced away and saw a long snake slither into the high grass at the edge of the field. In his mind's eye the snake molted to become a thick piece of rope that wrapped around his ankle, attempting to bind him to the earth of Castle Cairn. He realized that his fireplace demons had been right. The traps were everywhere. Before the snaking snare closed around his ankle, he sidestepped it. *This isn't my problem now!*

MacLaurin kept his sights set on the matter at hand, which was the possibility that Devonshire's presence had nothing to do with his recent duel with Bev and more to do with continuing what the MacPhersons had begun decades ago. It was worth MacLaurin's while to understand Devonshire's motivations.

"My uncle sold land to the Clan Chattan?" MacLaurin asked.

"Did sell and is now selling," Rud Shaw told him. "The papers on this second transaction have not yet been finalized."

"How much land?"

Rud Shaw bridled slightly. "I have not been informed."

A very bad sign. His uncle was selling a lot. "But why is Uncle selling land, of all things? Are the MacPhersons pressuring him?"

Rud Shaw's regard was as remote as the tip of Cairn o' Mount. "I understand that his lordship's books come very dear."

MacLaurin assumed the role of the practical Scot. "A body can't eat books."

"Worms can."

Chapter Eight

Elizabeth found her way through the castle with only three false turns. This meant that it took her under half an hour to go from her chamber to the banquet hall, which was now laid out for an elaborate breakfast.

The morning's trek helped raise her appetite. She tucked into oats and eggs and discussed the plans for the morning with her fellow historians at the breakfast table. They assured her that the day would be devoted entirely to the opening meeting of the Royal Historical Society. Since this was to take place in the library, her confidence in the day's success rose.

Her confidence ebbed when she discovered that the Duke of Devonshire had seated himself next to her. This put him at the foot of the table where he had sat the night before. With delicate distaste, His Grace waved away proffered platters of smoked fish and barley bannocks. He contented himself with a buttered scone.

When His Grace was settled, he opened the conversation on a surprising and unusual topic. "You have not yet told me, Mistress Cameron, how it is that your speech is singularly clean of the Scottish brogue."

His Grace's eyes were steady upon her. His expression was perfectly neutral, neither ironic nor vulgarly curious. He had simply made an observation that called for an explanation.

She might have answered, *I have not yet told you because you have not asked,* but decided against it on the grounds that the response was both impudent and obvious. She told herself that she did not truly care what His Grace thought of her, but she never wanted to be insipid.

She steeled herself and smiled. "Clean?"

He nodded deferentially. "From my point of view, of course." He invited her response to his request with a small but commanding gesture.

She answered, "I was raised by an English nurse."

His brows prompted her to continue.

She obliged. "My father insisted, for no reason that I ever discovered, because his brogue is as thick as the Highland mists and has never done him any harm! Nevertheless, when I was first learning to speak, I can remember having my knuckles rapped with a switch by my Nana and being corrected every other word for my singing vowels."

"And did you resent that treatment, Mistress Cameron?"

She had never thought about it. "Why, no, I did not resent it," she said slowly. "It was only—"

"Only?" His Grace prompted.

"It was only normal," she replied.

"And why do you suppose that your father raised you by an English nurse?"

Better to be bold! she reminded herself. "I fancied his reason was that I would make a better match when I grew up."

"And do you have such a match on the horizon?"

She was taken aback by the question. His Grace should have guessed that her advanced age, which she had divulged to him the day before, put her safely on the shelf. "Why, no," she answered.

"And yet with your fine speech . . ." His Grace began, but did not finish.

Elizabeth found this remark rather touching. She felt that he had just complimented more than her speech.

"I must tell Your Grace," she said evenly, "that when I became guardian to my cousin Allegra, I also became ineligible."

His Grace's brows rose delicately. "Your cousin Allegra."

His Grace had an uncanny ability to utter statements that veiled questions that could not be denied. She explained, "I was raised with Allegra's mother, Fiona, so that she was like a sister to me. When Fiona's husband died and she discovered that she was carrying a child, I had her move into the cottage where I live on my father's estate. Unfortunately, Fiona died the day after giving birth to Allegra." Recalling the outrageous conclusion MacLaurin had drawn the night before, she added, "And that's the absolute truth."

His Grace's gray eyes widened slightly. "Have I said anything to make you think I doubt you, my child?"

Elizabeth blushed. "No, Your Grace."

"I am relieved to hear it," His Grace said. "When did these most tragic events take place?"

"Almost five years ago."

"I see. And how was it, Mistress Cameron, that you became guardian to your cousin?"

"I insisted."

His Grace's eyes narrowed. "Insisted? Do I gather that your father—that is, Joseph Cameron—was against it?"

"Yes."

His Grace smoothed an invisible wrinkle in the table-cloth. "I fail to see, however, the precise connection between your quite honorable guardianship and your ineligibility as a respectable *partie*."

It was nearly impossible for Elizabeth to put the precise connection into words. Her father had been willing to maintain the pretense that Fiona was carrying her husband's child. However, once Elizabeth had chosen her course of action, her father had ever after put her in an impossible situation by treating her, paradoxically, both as the one with the stain on her virtue as well as the one who was the bastard child. But of course, she had no intention of putting such a thought into words for His Grace's ears.

Instead, she tried to guess how much digging His Grace would do into her past, which was pretty much of an open book. Since it was bad strategy to get caught in a lie, she admitted, "Just at the time of Fiona's confinement, my father was entertaining a proposal of marriage for me."

His Grace wondered if she would, perhaps, divulge the name of the man who might have made that proposal.

"Walter MacPhee," she said, unable to think of a clever way to avoid the request, "and when Fiona died, he made it clear that he would not take me with the child."

His Grace's regard was inscrutable. "The Clan Dhubhie," he remarked, visibly pleased with himself and his knowledge of the Gaelic patronyms, "is rich and respectable."

"I felt my duty was elsewhere," she said stoutly.

She had never meant Walter to make her choose between Allegra and marriage to him, for she had thought that Walter had been sincerely attached to her. However, his reaction to her proposed guardianship had humiliated her and had, curiously, carried something of the undertone of her father's reaction. Yes, she had desired marriage to the very respectable Walter MacPhee. Yet she could not, would not abandon Allegra to the less-than-respectable upbringing that would be hers if the Camerons did not fully claim her as one of their own.

Elizabeth had never regretted her decision, but she would have a hard time concealing the fact that she had been deeply hurt by Walter's rejection, if His Grace were to ask whether she had been affected by the loss of the match.

His Grace did not ask. Instead, he remarked, "I perceive that your guardianship has something of the flavor of your decision to attend the summer meeting of the Royal Historical Society."

"Yes," she replied.

He smiled. "You are a determined young woman," he said, "and impetuous, I think. Ah, but that puts me in mind of something." He reached into his pocket and withdrew an object. He held it out in his palm. "Do you know anything about this, I wonder, Mistress Cameron?"

Elizabeth looked into His Grace's palm. She had expected to see her hairpin and had an explanation ready. What she saw instead was a broken half candle, its wick hanging long and forlorn, like the tail of a whipped dog. She figured this to be the candle she had lost the night before, when MacLaurin had hauled her into the passageway. From the chewed end of the wax, she guessed that the candle had been mangled by the passageway door closing upon it. The half His Grace held must have remained in the main hallway. The other half must still be in the passageway.

She had to swallow the too-ready words dancing on the tip of her tongue, which made her have to clear her throat. When she raised her eyes again to His Grace's, she worried that her hesitation had provoked his suspicion. Or, rather, it must have increased his suspicion, for he evidently had something on his mind to have shown her the candle in the first place.

"What should I be able to tell Your Grace about such a candle?" she replied. She regretted that her tone carried a shade too much defensive surprise.

"I do not know, my child," His Grace said, laying the pathetic thing next to his plate. "It reminded me of the candle you were carrying last night, when you and I left this very room together."

"There must be many such candles at the castle. In fact, I would venture to say that every candle here is identical to this one."

"That is no doubt true," His Grace acknowledged. "However, not all of them have the distinction of lying broken in the main hallway."

"I am not sure why Your Grace has asked me about this, then. The hallway is very long."

His Grace nodded. "I found it toward the end where lies your chamber."

"And so?"

"And so I thought to ask you how half a candle came to be lying in the hallway when I picked it up last night."

She tried a diversionary tactic. "That must have been when you took Lady Michael out for a walk in the garden but could not find it and so had to return."

His Grace did not bother to respond to that. His slight smile, just the merest lift of the corners of his mouth, was masterful. It suggested that her tactic was not only too crude for his taste but also not worthy of the intelligent woman he believed her to be.

She felt a flush crawl up her neck. She decided that the only way to counter such exquisite subtlety was by being, once again, bold. "What does Your Grace have in mind, I wonder? A broken candle is common enough and does not seem to be an item of interest or speculation."

"A broken candle," His Grace replied, "is an item of interest when it is out of place. Just as any common item—no matter how big or how small—becomes of interest when it is out of place."

He had found the hairpin, Elizabeth was sure of it, and had warned her of it. He had let her know that he was watching her. She was suddenly struck by the fact that he had learned more about her in the past five minutes than many of her fellow historians had learned about her in the past five years.

She did not look cravenly away but held his eyes. "As a historian, I applaud your insight. We historians look always for details that are not quite in place, for they are our keys into the past. With your acute sensibilities, you will be most welcome among us, Your Grace, I assure you."

"Very charmingly said, Mistress Cameron," His Grace replied without that note of warmth that would have made his praise real.

The subject, it seemed, was closed. Elizabeth felt as if she had just been subjected to a test whose objective was so obscure that she did not know whether she had passed it or not.

Thus, she was grateful that MacLaurin entered the banquet room then, providing distraction. He looked no less disreputable than he had the day before and seemed not to favor the practice of shaving in the morning. He also looked as if he had been tramping around the fields for several hours, which she was soon to discover that he had done. His appetite matched his mien, and by chance, the only place open at the banquet table just then was the one across from Elizabeth and next to His Grace.

MacLaurin took that seat with an air of open challenge, directed unmistakably at His Grace. His Grace's demeanor was one of contained dislike.

MacLaurin's greeting to Elizabeth was brief, and she returned it briefly. He turned focused eyes on her companion. "Devonshire." He pronounced the name like a foul disease. "Give you good day."

"Good day to you, MacLaurin," His Grace replied coolly. With a jaundiced eye he regarded MacLaurin's plate, which was piled high. "How I admire the Scottish early-morning appetite!" It was not a compliment.

MacLaurin began to eat. He flicked His Grace a glance. "I've been out in the fields for the past several hours, speaking with the overseer about his plans for increasing the Cairn stock of black cattle."

His Grace was politely interested. "Increasing Cairn stock? What a charming idea!"

MacLaurin laughed. "I'd call it progress."

His Grace's voice was level, but Elizabeth heard a note that caused her ears to prick up. "Some might call it ill-advised."

MacLaurin looked up from his plate. The focus of his gaze had sharpened to two hard blue points. "Ill-advised?" MacLaurin shook his head. "Only survival. That's the way of it for any operation, agricultural or otherwise."

"Indeed?" His Grace returned. "You propose, perhaps, that one must increase production or perish?"

"Right. Do or die." MacLaurin returned his attention to his food and continued to eat with obvious relish.

Elizabeth felt as if she could reach out and touch the arc of tension that stretched between the two men. The evening before, the tension had had an elastic quality. This morning it had turned brittle and seemed more dangerous.

"Does this mean," His Grace asked with a hint of sly mockery, "that you're taking an interest in your uncle's estate?"

"It means that I've always liked early-morning exercise, and I used the opportunity to brush up on my Gaelic, after so many years away." His smile was effective, but it was not the attractive one Elizabeth had seen on several occasions. "That's how we distinguish the insiders from the outsiders in the Highlands. By their Gaelic."

MacLaurin had been deliberately rude, and His Grace's very composed features betrayed a certain displeasure. Elizabeth thought that he might retaliate. Instead, His Grace turned to her and asked, "And your Gaelic, Mistress Cameron?"

"Passable," she told him, "and necessary for full membership in the Royal Historical Society."

His Grace's brows rose, signaling his admiration of her accomplishment. He stood. "I am finished here," he pronounced, evidently not referring to his meal, "and need to discuss one or two things—" he looked down at MacLaurin with glittering gray eyes "—with my host."

MacLaurin kept eating. The moment shook with challenge and animosity, threatening to splinter the fragile arc of tension into bristling shards.

In an attempt to smooth it over, Elizabeth said, "We are sure to see one another again in the library this morning, Your Grace."

"Until then, my child," His Grace replied, his gray eyes quite cold. He glanced again at MacLaurin then back at Elizabeth. "You will recall what I said earlier about common items, Mistress Cameron." His voice caused a chill to dance on her backbone. "They become interesting only when they are out of place."

His Grace turned his back and left her to interpret that remark. Surprised that His Grace had so quickly retreated, she said to MacLaurin, "I think you won that round. Or almost."

MacLaurin looked up at her. "I didn't even come close."

"Well, then you antagonized him to no purpose, I would say."

His blue eyes were alive. "Not to no purpose."

"You were the one who said that we cannot afford the slightest misstep," she argued, "and should not draw suspicious attention to our activities. Before you joined us, His Grace had more or less told me that he was keeping a close watch on me. His parting remark suggests that he is now going to keep a close watch on you, as well."

MacLaurin's expression was cynical. He had apparently not missed the point of His Grace's parting shot. "My vanity is hardly wounded by being called a 'common item.' However, I'd say that Devonshire is more out of place here than I am."

"Perhaps," she acknowledged. "Nevertheless, it would seem prudent to keep a lower profile just now."

MacLaurin was working his way through his breakfast. "Do I take it Devonshire produced your missing hairpin?"

"Nothing so direct!" she exclaimed, keeping her voice low. For the moment no one around them was interested in their conversation, and she wanted to keep it that way. She referred with her eyes to the mangled candle on the tablecloth. "He noted merely that he found this broken candle in the main hallway."

MacLaurin glanced at it then back at her.

"It's probably the candle I was holding when you pulled me into the passageway," she said, "and it got cut by the sliding door."

He grunted noncommittally. "What do you think Devonshire suspects as a result?"

For some peculiar reason, Elizabeth thought that His Grace suspected that her virtue stood in danger from MacLaurin, for she had interpreted His Grace's last remark as a warning of MacLaurin's unsavory reputation. She was intrigued and slightly embarrassed to think that His Grace could imagine the possibility that she might be the object of MacLaurin's desire. She reviewed her conversation with His Grace for any suggestion that he might have meant it ironically, but she decided, no, he had been surprisingly and again, intriguingly, serious about his warning.

Since she was not disposed to telling MacLaurin any of this, she answered, "Nothing—yet."

"Devonshire didn't indicate, then, that he thought that I was connected to the noise last night that came from your bedchamber?"

She shook her head. "I don't think he suspects that." She glanced over her shoulder. His Grace was deep in conversation with Lord Mure. "Just as I'm sure that he didn't think you sat down here for the pleasure of my company, but rather to annoy him! However, he was inquiring into my life in a way that I found...unusual."

"Devonshire's not known to be inquisitive," he remarked. "In fact, he's known to be just the opposite, very private and discreet." He appeared to give the matter his consideration. "What was he asking you about?"

She had been meaning to remind MacLaurin to find a way to retrieve his jacket, shoes and stockings from her bedchamber, before she was caught with them. However, at his question, the thought flew out of her head, and her earlier good mood was suddenly restored. She felt possessed by the spirit of the new woman who had qualified in MacLaurin's eyes to be Lieutenant Beverly's lover. Her smile was coy. "Oh, he wanted to know about Allegra. That, and other things."

MacLaurin cocked a quizzical brow at his companion. His response was held off by his lordship's announcement that the inaugural sitting of the Royal Historical Society would take place in the library tower in fifteen minutes.

Chapter Nine

MacLaurin pushed his empty plate away. During the meal his hunger had subsided, but his headache had not. "Allow me to escort you to the library, Mistress Cameron. We can continue this conversation along the way."

Elizabeth's cheerful smile irritated him. "There's really nothing more to say about His Grace's interest in my personal affairs," she replied breezily. "Besides, since we are fellow conspirators now, I don't think it a good idea to be seen together too much."

"Yet you just pointed out that no one will think I sat down here for the pleasure of your company. It would be only natural for me to escort you, since I am with you now and everyone else is headed in the same direction." He rose from his chair and moved behind hers. "And there's a matter I'd like to discuss with you."

Her teasing expression turned instantly sober. "In that case, I would hate to defer our discussion until after the opening meeting," she said, "which I am sure will last the better part of the morning."

Reluctantly amused by her swift change of mood, MacLaurin realized that her curiosity would always get the better of her. As he helped her from her chair, he watched the others head out of the banquet hall. His uncle was standing at the door, directing the group, urging everyone along.

"If we hang back a bit," he said, "we can be private without seeming to conspire."

"True, but how long is the walk to the library?"

He ushered her before him. "A good fifteen minutes. My uncle likes to call things close."

She accepted the lead. "I don't want to be late, so we can't hang back too much."

"We've got five minutes to spare," he assured her, "because I know a shortcut that can get us there in ten, if need be."

She responded over her shoulder, "What, another passageway?"

He stepped next to her. "I know them all." It was a provocative but boyish boast. "Don't you trust me to get you to the library on time?"

She favored him with an expression more complex and disturbing than mere provocation, then cut her eyes straight ahead again. "I do, because we won't hang back long enough to make use of the passageway necessary. What is it you wish to discuss?"

Her sneak-up sensuality stunned him—again. This time, in broad daylight. He had not been expecting it. His fireplace demons had warned him of traps and had given him the devil of a headache into the bargain. He respected the power of Castle Cairn enough to believe that Elizabeth Cameron might have transmuted overnight into an irresistible beauty. Thus, upon entering the banquet hall this morning, he had set his sights on her and was relieved to have judged her as ordinary as the day before. For some reason his headache refused to go away.

Now that he took another look at her, he noted that her dress was flattering to her figure, far more flattering than either of the dresses she had worn the day before. Or was this new perception a result of having been squeezed against her in a darkened passageway and of having seen her in a soft and uncorseted state of undress the night before?

Before he could puzzle through that question, he had to pass by his uncle, who was still standing at the door, directing traffic.

"Ye're joinin' us in the library, then, Ian Mac-Laurin?" Lord Mure demanded gruffly. His air was none too inviting.

"I'm looking forward to it, Uncle," he lied pleasantly.

"Mistress Elizabeth, is my puir excuse for a kinsman giving you any trouble?"

"Why, no," she said with a surprised innocence that impressed MacLaurin. Her smile was kind. "He's a perfect gentleman and has offered me escort to the library, so that I shall not get lost."

His uncle let them pass. He seemed inclined to accompany them, but he had to wait for the last straggler, Godfrey MacQuarie. MacLaurin was pleased when MacQuarie latched on to his uncle and launched into animated discussion of some fine historical point.

MacLaurin led Elizabeth out into a wide, shadowy hallway. A group was ahead of them. His uncle and MacQuarie were behind them. He placed her hand on his forearm, thereby bringing her closer to him without overstepping his bounds as an escort. For her ears alone, he said, "I want to review Devonshire's reasons for being here."

Which was true. Despite his strong and unexpected reaction to her just now, he still considered her a more reliable sounding board for his thoughts than his fireplace demons.

She frowned. "Do you think his reasons stem from something other than the duel with Lieutenant Beverly?"

"Perhaps, and we'd do well to figure it out. Now, what do you know about my uncle's plans to sell Cairn land to the MacPhersons?"

Her expressive eyes widened. "Why, nothing!" she exclaimed on a whisper.

"And no talk of any land sales five years ago, either?"

She shook her head. "Not a word. Is it true?"

"According to the Cairn overseer, who told me about it this morning."

She cocked a brow at him, her expression more challenging this time than sensually stunning. "And you had the nerve to tell His Grace that you were expanding your cattle stock?"

He smiled. "It didn't do any harm to remind him that this second sale was not yet completed."

Her expression became speculative. "What is it between you and His Grace? I thought one of you would draw a sword before the meal was done."

He dismissed the exchange as mere "saber rattling" and commented, "As far as what's between me and Devonshire, you should know as well as anyone."

"I should?"

"You're a historian. You're bound to know more than I do about the bad blood that runs between the MacPhersons and the MacLaurins."

Elizabeth's smile was wry. "I know only more distant history, and the bad blood between your two clans doesn't run more than a generation or two back. We in the Royal Historical Society think anything that has occurred within the last fifty years is too modern for our taste. It's in our charter, in fact.''

''Your charter?''

''The society was founded ten years ago, in the wake of the Act of Union, as a way to preserve Scottish history. The genealogies are kept up, of course, but little is actually written on clan history until it becomes, well, historical. It's quite logical.''

''And useful,'' MacLaurin said pointedly.

''How so?''

''If someone is conducting business in the present that he doesn't want his neighbors to know about, he is assured that it won't be recorded until long after the deed is done.''

A canny light dawned in her gray eyes, making them sparkle. ''Since His Grace is a patron of our society, it's not impossible that he suggested the fifty-year rule of silence. I wouldn't know if he is the author of the idea, because I'm not a charter member, but it would be easy enough for me to find out.''

MacLaurin had never underestimated Devonshire, but he was beginning to see just how worthy an opponent the man really was. ''We can, at least, conclude that the fifty-year rule of silence does not work against Devonshire's interests.''

''Whatever they may be....''

''They may well be concerned with land.''

Her brow was creased. ''How much is your uncle selling?''

''A lot, I reckon. Does that surprise you?''

''Yes,'' she said, then added judiciously, ''and no. It's been a difficult past few years for all the estates in the neighborhood, but I hadn't thought that your uncle was suffering particularly."

"Just look around," he recommended, "and you'll see the signs of decay everywhere."

Elizabeth Cameron was indulgent. "Your uncle has simply been more interested in the past than the present, and Castle Cairn is monstrously old and hard to keep up."

"I'm speaking of the stables and the fields."

Her gaze became speculative again. "I'll ask you what His Grace asked you—are you finally taking an interest in the estate that should have been yours?"

He smiled at her in a way that brought color into her cheeks, and he was pleased. "I'm trying to establish Devonshire's reasons for being here and am toying with the idea that he has come primarily to finalize the purchase of MacLaurin land."

She shook her head. "It doesn't make sense. He could have sent any one of his many minions to do his business, and the coincidence of the duel, the document and the boxes of books is simply too strong not to be a factor." She considered further. "Although I will say that family business provides a perfect excuse for him to be here." She looked up at him. "It's very disturbing to think of his lordship selling Cairn property!"

"You said that the past few years have been difficult for all the estates in the neighborhood. How widespread is the difficulty? Have Cameron lands been troubled, as well?"

"In a way," she admitted. "But now that I have a sense of your uncle's problems, I'm thinking that my father has done remarkably well. Given the repeatedly poor crops of grain and some of my father's atrocious farming decisions, the Camerons have managed to maintain our holdings, even to prosper. I can't explain it, really." She seemed troubled. "However, I don't have the full view of my father's finances, much less your uncle's, so I cannot really compare them."

MacLaurin listened to this, then concluded, "I agree with you that the coincidence of Devonshire's involvement at Lady Michael's is too great to dismiss. At the same time, we'll keep in mind that his dealings here may be even deeper than we first thought."

She nodded, and they devoted the rest of the walk through the jumble of hallways to discussion of less weighty topics. They crossed several courtyards before they entered the wing that led to the library tower and arrived at the steep spiral of steps. The group, which had thinned out during the journey, coalesced at the bottom of the stairwell into an animated mass that now included Devonshire.

Lord Mure led the way. He puffed up to the first landing, halted at the wide door studded with iron, and produced a heavy *trousseau* of keys. In a trice the massive door swung open on well-oiled hinges, and his lordship announced, "Here we are, then."

MacLaurin had only a shambling memory of the library from the days of his father, but his memory matched little of the visible wealth he now beheld. The rest of Castle Cairn might have been crumbling around his uncle's ears, but the library was a showpiece. The basic features of the room had remained the same over the years, of course. It was almost, but not quite, fully round, with either end flattened and the diameter measuring at least thirty feet. The back end through which they had entered was squared off to allow for the door, which was three feet wide.

From either side of the door the walls bowed in a perfect circle to the far front end opposite the entrance,
which was also squared. No door stood at the front,
however, only carved paneling a good five feet wide,
which rose gracefully from floor to fifteen-foot ceiling.
The bowed walls held in their gentle embrace three beautiful leaded windows on each side. The light they allowed in showed every surface in the room to be clean,
every strip of wood to be polished.

MacLaurin had rarely ventured to the library in his
father's day and then only to consult odd volumes concerning mechanical marvels and the manufacture of artillery. Yet he was quite sure that the shelves had not then
stretched from floor to ceiling, nor had they been filled
with as many leather-bound books. Neither did he recall
the gorgeous walnut balcony floating ten feet above the
floor encircling the entire room, the thick carpets underfoot or the four crystal chandeliers overhead.

For the occasion of the society meeting, several long
trestle tables had been shoved to either side and positioned under the windows, one empty and one spread
with a display of books. The center of the room was set
with about two dozen chairs in several rows, in front of
which was a small dais upon which sat a lectern, a table
and a magnificently ugly thronelike chair. As the group
filed in, they began to fill the rows of chairs.

Elizabeth Cameron walked straight to the front row,
where she began to chat with Godfrey MacQuarie.
MacLaurin sought a likely seat, then decided to take a
half-standing position against one of the long tables, so
that he could be closer to the displayed books, which he
figured to be those brought by Lady Michael. He leaned
against the end of the table and surveyed the situation.

Quite a few more society members had arrived this morning, bringing the total attendance to about twenty, meaning that most of the chairs were filled. Lady Michael, MacLaurin noted, had not yet made an appearance, and he guessed that the empty chair next to his uncle in the first row had been saved for her. Elizabeth Cameron sat on the other side of his uncle. Devonshire took a position directly behind her in the second row.

Before seating himself, Devonshire crossed glances with MacLaurin. The message MacLaurin read in the chilly depths of Devonshire's eyes was not difficult to interpret and confirmed a stray thought that had crossed MacLaurin's mind at breakfast. MacLaurin did not think that Elizabeth Cameron was in Devonshire's usual style, but he was sure that Devonshire had just declared her off-limits. MacLaurin also wondered why Devonshire was so obvious about his proprietary interest in a young woman of no extraordinary charms, and he was unable to tally Devonshire's methods or motives.

His uncle stepped to the dais, blustered a welcome, cracked a few jokes that were heartily received and proceeded to rattle off the membership roll and other official opening business. Wholly uninterested, MacLaurin let his eyes travel idly around the room, computing fairly accurately the fabulous sum his uncle had spent here. His gaze stopped next to the door where huddled a pile of large boxes. These were presumably the boxes that had held the books that were now spread out on the library table. Three boxes were stacked there. Only three. His gaze swept the room for sign of a fourth box, but he saw nothing. Curious. Even troublesome. He made a first, rapid count of the books on display and arrived at the round number of sixty.

Godfrey MacQuarie, the society's current chief, came forward and rambled on about MacLaurin knew not what. He eventually seated himself upon his throne and yielded the floor to the society's recording secretary, who was received with a warm round of applause.

To MacLaurin's surprise, Elizabeth Cameron stepped onto the dais to read the report of the society's final spring meeting in Edinburgh. She read with feeling, smiled, made jokes that were actually funny, and responded with aplomb to comments from the old historians, who obviously adored her. She confirmed her own place on the program and said that she would read her treatise on the day after the morrow. She was clearly in her element and at ease. MacLaurin could not deny that she had presence.

And a fine figure.

MacLaurin glanced at Devonshire. He was not looking at Mistress Cameron but was rather contemplating his hands composed upon one elegantly crossed knee. MacLaurin glanced back at Mistress Cameron and wondered if Devonshire had discovered that Bev had ruined her and now thought her ripe for plucking. Perhaps Devonshire saw in her the same thing that Bev had seen in her. Or that he himself saw in her.

Which was what, precisely?

Nothing. He wasn't interested in her. Not in *that* way. Definitely not.

MacLaurin readily admitted, however, that Devonshire's move to make her his private reserve was enough to fan his own noninterest. Standing in this library, begun by his father and made magnificent by his uncle, he came to a rich understanding that his intense dislike of Devonshire was, finally, one passion he shared with his father.

MacLaurin returned his attention to the not-so-ordinary ordinary young woman who was soliciting from the floor items of new business. She was smiling and laughing and carrying on. The veil of his headache descended, causing his temples to throb and his gaze to go fuzzy. He became aware of her shimmering outline only. Her aura seemed to be magically wreathed in scrolls of ivy and thistles.

He stood up straight. Elizabeth Cameron was standing in front of the carved paneling covering the flat portion of the far end of the room. He realized that the lacy loops of ivy and thistles encircling her came from the pattern in the paneling behind her. He realized further that it was a pattern he knew by heart. He was astounded. Until this moment he had thought that every paneled room in the castle had a different pattern to call its own and that the pattern of ivy and thistles in his bedchamber was unique to his room.

He knew that an odd corridor in a wing linking the east wing to the main wing came to a dead end at the place where it joined the library tower just on the other side of the paneled library wall. He had always thought that the corridor provided no access to the library from behind the paneled wall. He began to doubt now, however, that the end of the dead-end corridor ran flush against the other side of the paneled wall.

He was willing to bet half his recently made fortune that the panel carved with ivy and thistles would slide aside to reveal a room whose existence had been hidden from him all these years. He was willing to bet the other half of that fortune that he knew just where to look for the catches in this particular panel pattern.

His headache vanished.

Chapter Ten

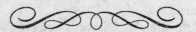

When the suggestions for items of new business began to subside, Elizabeth decided that she could now announce her mysterious letters and ask for help in interpreting them. She began, "I would like to take this opportunity to introduce what I predict will be an exciting research project—" but got no farther.

At that very moment Lady Michael swept into the room through the door at the back. Although only Elizabeth and Godfrey MacQuarie were actually directly facing her, her ladyship was still able to command everyone's attention. The fact that the assembled company turned as one to watch her ladyship's entrance was not due to the fact that Elizabeth broke off her speech. The sequence of events was rather the other way around: Elizabeth stopped speaking when she no longer held the attention of her audience. Even MacLaurin, who had been staring strangely at the paneling behind her only the second before, turned toward the back of the room.

Elizabeth studied Lady Michael for the first time in the bright light of day. She saw that her ladyship was a good ten years older than she was, but still radiated youthful energy. Her figure was well proportioned, and she carried herself with the air of a beautiful woman. In truth, she was more alluring than beautiful, and Elizabeth admired the way she cultivated that allure. She had dark hair arranged to ringleted perfection, dark eyes, a confident smile and a truly breathtaking dress of deep amethyst silk that was, paradoxically, both daring and entirely appropriate to the occasion.

Elizabeth watched in fascination as Lady Michael sized up the situation in a flash. Her dark eyes rested a fraction of a second on MacLaurin before they flicked, almost dismissively, across herself, then paused at His Grace. Her attention settled, politely, on her host, Lord Mure, who rose to escort his guest into the room.

Elizabeth might have felt diminished by Lady Michael's quick, slighting appraisal of her, but she was too engrossed in her ladyship's expert, understated performance to bother taking offense. Neither was she offended when her ladyship's entrance altered the course of the opening session and put Elizabeth's own moment on center stage at an end.

Lord Mure settled her ladyship in the empty seat next to him in the front row, and Godfrey MacQuarie welcomed her officially and in a way that suggested that he had become instantly infatuated. After some gushing, he recalled himself, cleared his throat, then said to Elizabeth, "I thank ye, Mistress Cameron, for reporting on the old business of our last meeting in Edinburgh and for completing the duty of announcing the new business at Castle Cairn."

Elizabeth had not completed her duty, but since no one seemed to notice, she decided that it would be impolite to put the society's chief in the wrong. So she nodded and stepped down from the dais and took her seat on the other side of Lord Mure. By the end of the afternoon session, Elizabeth was to be very glad that Lady Michael's entrance had prevented her from offering her letters to the scrutiny of the finest historical minds in all of Scotland.

Godfrey MacQuarie called for the first treatise. Patrick Grant stepped up to read "The Antique Scene," and his opening lines contained the following proposition: "The history of Scotland may be divided into the three ages of Barbarism, Civilization and Decadence, the last sadly encompassing the present and the future. That the word *decadence* is a synonym for Anglicization is well-known among those who speak the true Scots tongue."

Patrick Grant stopped abruptly and turned red. Then with a bow to Lady Michael, he commented, "Having said that, your ladyship, I mean to cast no adverse reflection upon the quality of the great English culture."

Lady Michael declared herself charmed by his characterization of the three phases of Scottish history.

Patrick Grant bowed again and felt compelled to add, "However, again and again, your ladyship, one observes that in the play of the historic forces, a great civilization imposed on an alien and lesser has compassed that alien's downfall."

Lady Michael was sure that this must be true.

"Thus are we, in the Royal Historical Society, committed to preserving the authentic Scottish civilization by recording its true history."

Lady Michael said that she had come to this morning's meeting expecting no less and begged him to continue with his evocation of "The Antique Scene."

Patrick Grant obliged her by reading on. He proceeded to tell a detailed, amply documented account of the history of the world as told through the history of Scotland. After the last sentence of "The Antique Scene" had been uttered, a spirited discussion ensued.

Douglas MacKinnon was up next with a history of Aberdeen, "The Silver City By the Sea," whose stout citizens were most famous for their incurably anti-Highland sentiments. MacKinnon's rather poetically phrased account of Aberdeen history was followed by an original poem. Written and delivered by Ganon Graham, it dealt with an obscure piece of Clan Graham history and comprised over one hundred verses, taking over half an hour to read with all the dramatic pauses and asides. The imagery was considered to be beautiful, the poem's mystery clever and open to interpretation. Half the audience believed that Tam had not killed his cousin. The other half believed he had.

Ganon Graham conceded that the deciding clue was hidden in verse seventy-four, and the morning's work continued with a researched genealogy of the principal Highland clans prepared by Brian Sinclair. This genealogy was enormously well received by the society fellows and was later described by MacLaurin to Elizabeth as "mind numbing." What His Grace and Lady Michael thought of it they did not reveal. However, when Brian Sinclair sat down and Godfrey MacQuarie declared the morning session to be at a close, both His Grace and Lady Michael rose rather quickly from their chairs. They complimented Brian Sinclair on his work, but neither lingered by his side to pursue the fine points, as did several of the society's keenest genealogists.

Lord Mure informed the assemblage that in the interests of facilitating ongoing discussions from the morning session and to give more time to the afternoon session, he had arranged for a midday dinner to be provided in the library itself. As he spoke, heavily laden trays were carried into the library and set upon the empty trestle table. Lord Mure invited his guests to fill their plates and to circulate as they saw fit. He asked only that they not bring their food in the vicinity of the display of new books on the table opposite, so as to avoid staining the bindings or the pages.

MacLaurin made his way through the milling crowd and managed to position himself next to Elizabeth as if by accident. By a nudge of his shoulder against her side he maneuvered her to a spot of relative privacy, out of immediate earshot.

Looking away from her, as if they were discussing a topic of little interest to him, he asked, "How many boxes of books did you say that Lady Michael was bringing?"

Her brow furrowed with worry. "Why do you ask?"

He glanced at her and recommended, "Show no interest. Affect boredom or displeasure in my company— ah, that's better. Now, I'm asking about the number of boxes only to remind myself what you told me yesterday."

Elizabeth seemed to accept that explanation. She replied, "Lady Michael was supposed to have brought four boxes."

"That's what I thought you said. Do you know how many books my uncle ordered? No," he said quickly, "don't look at the table and betray your interest in what's there."

She returned her eyes to his face. They narrowed suspiciously. "About eighty, give or take."

She looked ready to ask him why he was asking these specific questions. Since he did not wish to divulge that he had counted only sixty books on display—meaning that a good twenty books were not—he forestalled her line of questioning by saying, "Now, tell me whether you discovered if Devonshire was the one to have ordered the fifty-year rule of silence to be written into the society charter.''

His ploy worked. Her very lively eyes sparkled. "He did!" she said with barely suppressed excitement. "Before the opening of the meeting, I spoke with Godfrey MacQuarie about the original charter, and he was more than happy to describe how it came to be written the way it did.''

"Good work, Mistress Cameron."

She merely nodded in response, apparently less interested just then in his praise and far more interested in the puzzle that was Devonshire. "I think this *proves* that His Grace has something to hide, don't you?" She did not wait for his response. Somewhat abstractedly, she continued, "I don't trust him. Not for a minute. Why, from the moment I saw him last evening, I had an odd feeling about him. Then it came to me during one of the sessions this morning—out of the blue—that I had met him not only once when I was a girl, but more like two or three times." Again, she did not wait for his response to any of these remarks. Instead, she focused suddenly very clear eyes on him and said, "It is imperative that we retrieve the document at the end of the afternoon session.''

"It is?''

She looked surprised. "Of course it is. Do you doubt it?''

"Ah, but how do you propose that we retrieve it in full view of so many people?''

"Well, no one can peruse the volumes now, as you know, and I am guessing that his lordship will make time available at the end of the afternoon session for the first inspection of the books. I will make sure to be at the head of the line. If you come right behind me and shield me, more or less, from view, I can make a quick check of each volume as I go.''

He was already acquainted with her notions of workable schemes. He said, ''Content yourself with having discovered Devonshire's interest in the guidelines of the society's charter, and I'll consider that a good day's help from you.''

She cast him a very cool look over her shoulder as she moved away from him and toward the line forming around the table with the food.

MacLaurin eventually made his way to the food, as well. He chanced to find himself in line with a group whose center was Lady Michael, and she was expressing her great desire to bring ''the Highlands into fashion in London.'' MacLaurin was impressed to hear how readily her plan was met with approval, given that he could recall from his youth one of the men of the group swearing a solemn ''pox on all Sassenachs pollutin' the straths and braes of Alba.''

During a moment when the group was being re-formed, Lady Michael turned to him and said, low and privately, ''Ian, how lovely to see you here.''

MacLaurin bowed. ''Juliette.''

One of her brows lifted. ''And how surprising to see you here in Scotland, of all places.''

''I'm a Scot,'' he said with a rare allusion to his heritage, ''which gives me hope that I shall soon be in fashion in London.''

Her pretty brow arched. ''You already are, my dear! Your ingenious inventions are all the crack, and it's no wonder that King George has commissioned you so handsomely!''

He bowed again. "You flatter me, and I begin to understand how it is that you have charmed the Highlanders into submission."

"All but one," she said provocatively.

She did not press the point that several years before he had flirted on the edges of flirtation with her. Nor did she suggest that she had hinted him away when it became clear that he was too busy with his work to give a woman of her appetites the amount of attention she craved. Soon thereafter, he learned that she had taken up with Devonshire.

"The one being my uncle?" he ventured. It was not his style to be deliberately obtuse, but he wanted to turn the conversation. "I understand that you've performed a signal service for him, but I warn you—he's a confirmed bachelor!"

She laughed. "I know, and you're referring to the books, I suppose. I'll have you know that I didn't bring them to pique his interest in me, but rather because we share a love of literature."

"So great is your love that you hauled hundreds of miles a dozen heavy boxes?"

She smiled, dimpling. "No, only four. Are you surprised?"

"Relieved, rather. Rumor had it that you were bringing no less than twelve boxes, so when I saw three empty ones by the door earlier this morning, I was imagining the library soon to be swamped with nine more boxes." He kept his tone light and playful. "So where's the fourth box? Did you abandon it in Yorkshire?"

She shook her head, smiling still. "The fourth one's still in my bedchamber. I haven't yet removed the odd personal items I threw in at the last minute."

He found his opening. "Personal items?"

She paused, as if to register a subtle change in the atmosphere. "Does that interest you?"

"It might."

Her smile turned sultry. "You'll let me know...if you discover a desire to help me unpack my personal items before I hand the box of books over to your uncle?"

He knew that she just might be playing him off Devonshire, and he knew that Devonshire just might take great exception to any liaison he might attempt with her. He recalled the warning of his fireplace demons that the traps were everywhere.

Nevertheless, he met her speculative gaze with a cool one of his own and said, "I will."

Godfrey MacQuarie called out from the lectern on the dais that the afternoon session was about to begin.

With a mighty inviting note in her voice, she said, "Your uncle expects to see his fourth box of books tomorrow morning." Without a backward glance she sought her seat in the front row, next to his uncle and in front of Devonshire.

MacLaurin found the afternoon to be even more stultifying than had been the morning. He suffered through a history of Edinburgh and the biographies of some obscure chieftains. The history of whiskey making nearly engaged his attention, although he was glad that he had other things to occupy his mind. To relieve his boredom, he mentally played out the possible effects of getting involved with the alluring but demanding and possibly dangerous Juliette Michael in order to retrieve the document. No clear conclusion presented itself, but he knew that, one way or another, the issue would be decided before the coming night was over.

The long afternoon came to a close on his uncle's own history of Castle Cairn. MacLaurin could not have been less interested in the dates of the construction of various wings, the list of the building materials or a discussion of the size and variety of the courtyards. During the description of the Fleurise Garden, his thoughts drifted to Elizabeth Cameron, for this particular site had been the setting of his chance meeting with her the previous afternoon. He wondered, idly, what interest she could possibly be taking in this crushingly tedious treatise.

Chapter Eleven

MacLaurin would have been amazed to learn that the sound of the name Fleurise Garden had caused a jolt to Elizabeth's senses. She spared no thought for her meeting there with MacLaurin the day before. Instead, all her attention was riveted on the reference to such a garden in the heartbreaking letters written by the ardent lover. Until this moment she had assumed that the Fleurise Garden was not an actual place but rather a product of the ardent lover's poetic imagination.

By the time Lord Mure finished speaking, Elizabeth had realized what a stroke of luck it had been for Lady Michael's entrance to have prevented her offering the letters for public inspection. If she had stumbled upon a piece of very local history, she saw the need for discretion.

When it was her turn to respond to his lordship's treatise, she said with what detached professionalism her excitement would allow her, "Now, the name Fleurise Garden interests me. I, of course, know the word *fleurise* to be Scots for *blossom* and that it was borrowed from the French. Thus the name must be of recent origin, but I assume that the garden is quite historic. So, my question to you, your lordship, is, does the garden have a more ancient name, perhaps, a Gaelic one, as one would expect?''

"A very fine point, Mistress Elizabeth!" his lordship exclaimed. "As you guessed, the garden *does* have an older, more traditional appellation in Gaelic," and he proceeded to detail its history, as if this point were the aim of her question. "I called it the Fleurise Garden out of habit, I suppose, it being a nickname that—" here his lordship's gaze strayed to his nephew, then back to Elizabeth "—my brother favored, and he assumed the practice from our mother's usage. However, I do not recollect exactly if my mother or my grandmother was the first to call it by that name. Nevertheless, I used the nickname without thinking, and I should have been more historically accurate."

At this point Godfrey MacQuarie wondered if perhaps there had been a vogue at some point for renaming old castle gardens, and he inquired of the assembled body whether one of them knew of any other such Fleurise Gardens in Highland castles. Many garden names—from the Gaelic, French, English, Latin and Greek, and even the Persian "Parizade"—were called forth, but not another one among them duplicated the name of Castle Cairn's.

Elizabeth's head was spinning. She was dazzled by the possibility that the solution to the mystery of her letters might be within her grasp. She was eager to leave the library in order to reread those letters with an eye to discovering whether they could have been written by—or to—a former inhabitant of the MacLaurin family seat.

Godfrey MacQuarie was about to pronounce an end to the first day of the summer meeting when a new voice unexpectedly entered the fray.

Ian MacLaurin had not participated in the proceedings the entire day. Now, however, he sprang a fountain of questions for his uncle pertaining to the history of Castle Cairn. Elizabeth was puzzled by the questions, which were reasonable but not the kind she guessed either would interest him or whose answers he did not already know.

After more than half an hour of exhaustive discussion, Godfrey MacQuarie called a laughing, gratified halt to the discussion, clearly delighted with the day's finale. He bowed ceremoniously to Lady Michael and His Grace in the second row and expressed the hope that they were satisfied that the work of the Royal Historical Society was of the highest caliber. With a glance over her shoulder, Elizabeth confirmed that both of these exalted guests were still awake and seemingly alert.

Lord Mure rose next to say that, because of the last, most fruitful discussion, there was no longer any time to inspect the displayed books before supper. Elizabeth now understood MacLaurin's purpose in prolonging the discussion, which realization reminded her that this was the moment she had intended to retrieve the dratted document from one of the books on the trestle table. However, since she was now unable to do anything to accomplish that worthy goal, she set her sights on achieving a less worthy one.

While everyone was filing out of the library, Elizabeth fell into step next to MacLaurin.

"It won't work," she said to him in aggrieved undertones.

MacLaurin's glance nicely blended amusement and innocence.

She was not diverted. "You think I don't know what you're about?"

His blue gaze rested on her. His tone was provocative. "I wonder if you mean to explain yourself, Mistress Cameron."

"You deliberately foiled the perfectly good plan I proposed to you at midday."

"How did I do that?"

"By asking a load of questions just now that absorbed the time we would have otherwise spent looking at the books on display."

"Now, why would I have done that?"

"Because you wish to retrieve the document all by yourself, without any help from me."

He appeared to consider that. "So you think I, er, foiled your plan out of vainglory and not because I perceived it to be idiotic and most likely counterproductive. Is that right?"

"*Your* plan is at least as idiotic as any of mine!" she fired back on a whisper.

His smile was charming. "My plan?"

Her smile was superior. "You mean to break into the library tonight."

"That is correct, Mistress Cameron."

His ready honesty took the wind out of her sails, but she did not flounder for long. "I'm coming with you."

"I don't think so."

"You think wrong."

"I'll do the job quicker and easier without you."

"You need my help."

His expression was unmistakably skeptical.

Since she did not want to give him another opportunity to deny her, she dropped back a pace in order to strike up a conversation with the man behind her. Upon further reflection, she decided that MacLaurin's idea of breaking in to the library was not such a bad one after all, but she would certainly not give him the satisfaction of saying so.

The guests retired to their chambers to dress for supper. Elizabeth was so uninterested in the details of her evening's toilette that she dismissed Mary, who left clearly doubtful of Mistress Cameron's ability to dress her own hair, which was in considerable disrepair at the end of the day. Elizabeth chose her most serviceable dress to wear, one she thought would be the least cumbersome skulking around in darkened hallways and in the library at night. She actually chose it for its dull gray color, since it would blend perfectly into the darkness. She repinned her hair with more speed than expertise, then devoted the rest of the short time before supper to the real object of her interest.

She retrieved the packet of letters from the corner of her wardrobe, thereby uncovering MacLaurin's shoes and stockings, which were hidden beneath. She groaned when she remembered that she had meant to remind Mac-Laurin to fetch his things before supper, but in the press of the events of the day, she had forgotten it. She could do nothing about the problem now, so she took the packet and crossed from her wardrobe to her window. In the light of the dying day she scanned the letters until she came to the passage describing the Fleurise Garden.

On this second reading, she recognized the setting perfectly: the berry bushes at one end, roses climbing the wall at the other end, the well in the center set off by the curved benches, the flower beds marking the pathways. Upon first reading this morning, she had not been able to associate the Fleurise Garden with the pleasance of the day before because of the distinctly unblooming quality of the present garden. Upon this second reading, she felt the thrill of her discovery from head to toe and was absolutely certain now that the writer of these letters had had some association—some fairly recent association—with Castle Cairn. She decided to scan the MacLaurin genealogies for possibilities when she and MacLaurin broke in to the library tonight.

She put the letters back in the wardrobe and left her room, too excited, too confident even to bother with a candle. Once in the dark hallway she touched the locket nestled between her breasts. Through the material of her bodice she felt the jeweled case that protected the image of her mother. Comforted, she smiled to herself and decided that she rather enjoyed the spooky sensations that spirited up and down her spine as she encountered the eerily wisping shapes traveling the hallway with her.

She was delighted to meet her fellow historians at the top of the main staircase, just as she had the evening before. This time, however, she greeted them with no overpowering sense of relief. Instead, she was rather pleased when Donald Graham exclaimed in surprise, "Why, Mistress Cameron! I did not rightly perceive ye at first and thought ye were one of the remarkably distinct castle shadows! And here ye are brave enough to walk the hallways without even a wee candle to light yer way!"

She took that remark as a good omen.

She thought the course of the supper boded well, too. She was glad to have supper seating similar to that of the night before. More table leaves had been inserted and more places set to accommodate all the recently arrived guests, and this put her at an even greater remove not only from MacLaurin but also from His Grace. The place across the table from her that had been empty the night before was now occupied by Lady Michael, and she was glad of that, too. Lady Michael reigned supreme at her end of the table, thus leaving Elizabeth to her own thoughts and quiet conversation on either side of her. The atmosphere in the banquet hall was lively and convivial, the food copious.

When it came time to repair to the receiving hall for whiskey and port, Lord Mure put it to the men whether they would permit the two ladies present to be invited. This irregularity was heartily approved, so Lady Michael and Elizabeth went to the receiving hall along with everyone else. The talk ran merrily there, too, and evening stretched into night. As the guests excused themselves, one by one, pleading the need for a good night's rest before the rigors of the morrow's exercises, Elizabeth kept her eye on MacLaurin, with whom she had exchanged no private conversation since the end of the afternoon session.

At last she saw MacLaurin slip out of the room. She followed him, feeling fearless in the hallways that had frightened her only the night before. Although he pursued a tricky path, she kept up with him and even fancied that he did not know she was behind him.

She turned a corner where the future was particularly dim and walked straight into the solid body of a man—tall, firm and muscular.

"By—" she began.

"St. Angus," MacLaurin finished.

She might have known. "You didn't need to make me stub my toe," she complained, "just to let me know that you knew I was following you."

"If you had guessed that I knew you were following me, you would have avoided running into me."

She realized then that she was standing stock against him and that, on impact, he had grasped her forearms. She realized further that her preoccupations of the day must have obscured his effect on her, for now that she was standing next to him in the darkness, she became aware of the enchantment that seemed to unsettle the air and sharpen her senses when she was with him.

She took a step away from him. He dropped his hands. "We're on our way to the library, right?" she asked.

"Not yet."

"Not yet?"

"I didn't choose the most direct route," he informed her, "in case someone was following you."

"No one's following me."

"You don't know that."

"I'm sure that no one is—"

"Had you considered the possibility?" he interrupted.

She hadn't.

"Well, then," he said to her incriminating silence, "it's just as well that I took the precaution. Now, follow me."

"That's what I've been doing," she said confidently. However, her confidence ebbed when she felt him move away but did not know in which direction. A moment later his hand grabbed hers, and she was being pulled along behind him.

They traveled a dark corridor that seemed to slope downward. The air was wet. The experience was both wholly new and oddly familiar, and she began to think that being connected to him only through his touch and surrounded by darkness was completely normal.

"Before I forget," she said, "I must remind you to take back your coat and shoes and stockings from my room."

"I may do it tonight."

"Very well. That would be after we visit the library, then?"

"Yes. As it turns out, I may need to go to Lady Michael's room tonight, depending on what we find in the library."

"As it turns out?"

His response to that was a soft chuckle.

After a moment or two of silence, she said dryly, "You're right, it is far more entertaining for me to guess what you meant by that! Let me see. You asked me earlier in the day how many boxes of books Lady Michael brought with her, and I said four. So I must guess that you do not think that all four boxes are now in the library. Is that right?"

"Not a bad guess, Mistress Cameron."

"After five years in the historical society, I've developed the skill of inferring elaborate schemes from spare details. Recall how quickly I realized that your arrival at Castle Cairn had something to do with Lieutenant Beverly and his association with Allegra."

"Ah, but that was hardly guesswork on your part, was it?"

Her response to that was a soft chuckle.

She felt the quality of his grip on her hand alter subtly, as if he were weighing the import of her response. She did not let him dwell on the implications, but said briskly, "It is more to the point, sir, for you to tell me how many boxes of books, in your estimation, made it to the library."

"Three."

"And the fourth is still in Lady Michael's chamber?"

"It is."

She sighed and said, "Oh, dear."

They traveled on, still on a downward slope. From the clamminess of the air she guessed that they were underground. From the serpentine turns MacLaurin negotiated she would have said that they were in the intestines of the castle.

After a while she said, "Are there any creepy, crawly things down here?"

"Devonshire's still in the receiving room."

Elizabeth swallowed a laugh and said sternly, "Very amusing, sir! If we're to trade jests, I might point out that *you're* down here."

"Complaining?"

"Not at all." Her voice was excessively sweet. "There's no one I'd rather be here with than you."

"A high compliment, Mistress Cameron."

"Only you would recognize it as such, sir! But this is hardly to the point, and I won't be diverted from the discussion at hand. Now, the subject of the fourth box reminds me of the other question you asked me at midday. I assume you counted the books on the table. Exactly how many are there?"

"Sixty."

Something in the heaviness of his tone prompted her to ask with mischievous seriousness, "Are you sure?"

"I counted them no less than five times."

She smiled broadly in the darkness of their netherworld. "If you were bored, it's no more than you deserved," she chided him, "for holding out on me."

"Holding out on you?"

"You could have told me about the number of boxes and books at the midday break."

"I keep my own counsel."

"We're in this together now, you know," she objected.

He grunted.

She continued, "Well, if Lord Mure ordered eighty books in all, that leaves twenty books in the box in Lady

Michael's chamber. Although the odds are in our favor for finding the document in one of the books already in the library, I see what you mean about remaining open to the possibilty of going to Lady Michael's chamber tonight. Do you want me to employ the ruse we had in mind last night to draw her from her chamber?"

"I'm not quite sure."

Something in his voice prompted her to ask mischievously, "Do you mean to use that secret panel between our rooms again?"

"It's hardly the ideal passage," he acknowledged, "given the condition of the machinery. Nevertheless, my access to the main wing of the castle is easiest by way of your room. We'll see how it goes for us in the library, but I may have to ask you to leave your chamber window open in case I need to go in and out of it."

The man assumed much. "Sir!" she reproved him, just for the fun of it. "You mean to come and go freely in my chamber, just like that, without so much as a by-your-leave?"

"I'll check through the peepholes in the wall between our rooms to make sure I'm not catching you at a bad time," he said coolly and quoted back to her, "We're in this together now, you know."

She thought it wiser not to respond to that. Fortunately she did not have to reply because they had come to the bottom of a stairs.

He released her fingers and slid his hand up her forearm so that he could draw her in front of him. With one hand cupping her elbow, the other hand at the small of her back, he guided her up a narrow, treacherous flight of stairs.

"We're underneath the library tower," he explained, "and this stair leads directly to the tower courtyard. The door to the exterior is opposite another exterior door that will open onto the landing at the base of the interior stairs leading up to the library."

"Are those the stairs we took today to the main library door?"

He confirmed that this was so. "Let's hope we're not locked in down here, for we'll waste a deal of time retracing our steps."

"How reassuring to mention the possibility just now!"

"Don't worry," he said softly.

She could feel his breath on her neck, so closely did he follow behind her to keep her footing safe. Then he groped for her shoulder and halted her. The stairwell was too narrow for two people to stand side by side, so he had to slide his hands under her arms, as he had done in the passageway the night before, in order to find the latch for the door. He maneuvered with effort, bringing the front of his body in full and extended contact with the back of hers, before the door yielded with a creaking that made her wince.

She emerged from the bowels of the castle into the courtyard, with MacLaurin behind her. The flooding light of the nearly full moon was almost painful to her eyes. By contrast, the fresh air was sheer delight, and she gulped in a lungful. The contact of the air on her skin made her break a light sweat.

MacLaurin cocked his head in the direction she was to follow and led her halfway around the circular tower to the exterior door he had mentioned. This opened more easily but just as noisily, and they stepped into the landing at the base of the stairs that led to the library.

He ushered her before him. Hardly had she trod the first step when she heard a noise coming from the stairs above, perhaps in the library itself. She turned back to look at him.

He had heard the noise, too. He whispered, very low into her ear, "Let's wait outside until we know what's what."

They crept back outside. MacLaurin was unable to close the exterior door completely because the whine of the hinges would alert anyone in the stairwell—if some-one was, indeed, in the stairwell—to their presence out-side.

Their eyes locked when they heard a muted echoing that might have been the sound of the library door clos-ing. She looked up at him and admired, without embar-rassment, the way the lunatic moonlight chiseled his features and reversed his coloring, bluing his black hair and blackening his blue eyes. Those eyes assessed her frankly. They roamed her hair, her face, her dress. She was aware that the wet of the underground corridor had discomposed her hastily pinned coiffure. She felt damp tendrils misbehaving at her temples and heavy tresses falling about her shoulders.

They held their breath when steps could be faintly heard coming down the stairs. Those steps seemed to stop at the bottom of the landing and at the exterior door. Perhaps the person noticed that the door was ajar. Per-haps the onset of a whispering whine meant that the per-son was just now opening that door, wishing to investigate this odd circumstance.

MacLaurin shrugged and gave her a brief, almost apologetic smile, as if what he was about to do could not be helped. He pushed her gently so that her back was against the library tower wall. He put one hand on her shoulder, the other at her waist. Her back was pressed against the stones of the tower that held the warmth of the sun in them at night, and the heat sent a quiver up her spine. Then he bent his lips to hers and kissed her.

She was surprised by his tactic, by the softness of his lips, by the sweetness of his taste. She was also surprised by his growing ardor, because she knew he meant this kiss to be merely diversionary. Nevertheless, she lost herself in its pleasures and was brought to her senses only when a voice at her side enunciated, "Mistress Cameron." Then, after a moment and quite deliberately, "Mac-Laurin."

The voice was soft but stern, and unmistakably disapproving. The voice belonged to His Grace, the Duke of Devonshire.

Chapter Twelve

MacLaurin heard the far-off echo of the jeers of his fireplace demons. "The traps are everywhere!" they shrieked with delight, but at such a distance the voices were too dim to strike him as demonic.

MacLaurin had been aware of the traps all day, but at this moment he did not care. Nor could he, just then, think of any other way to account for his presence outside the library tower with Elizabeth Cameron than to be seen kissing her.

So he backed her against the tower wall and bent his head toward hers. He couldn't help it, really, that it would be such a pleasant diversion, and he was soon to discover that her kiss was more than pleasant. When he moved close enough to feel her breath against his chin, he experienced a moment of anticipatory intoxication, as if he had just uncorked a fresh bottle of the smoothest Scots whiskey and was breathing in the fumes that escaped.

He touched her lips with his. The taste of the whiskey itself was far better than the scent of the fumes. It was the kind of drink a man would sip with respect for its strength. The kind he could savor throughout the night.

The kind that would not make him drunk but that would make him always want just a little bit more.

He put one hand on her shoulder, the other at her waist. He pressed his lips to her lips, he pressed his body to her body. She was inexperienced, that much he could tell. Her innocence not only inflamed him with a desire to teach her the arts to which her body seemed best suited but also conflicted sharply with his assumption that she had been Bev's paramour.

Hardly had he time to recognize the contradiction before his thoughts were given a new direction when none other than Devonshire appeared on the scene. He did not immediately break the kiss upon Devonshire's quiet pronouncement of his name, which was spoken like a threat. He had no reason to obey Devonshire, and he had every reason to annoy him. If kissing Elizabeth Cameron annoyed the man, then kiss her he would.

It came to him then, precisely while he was kissing her, that Devonshire's taste in women was entirely different from Bev's. Now that he came to experience Elizabeth Cameron's physical charms, he remembered that while Bev's taste was for soft and sensual women, it also ran to flamboyant women who were stupid. Elizabeth Cameron surely qualified for soft and sensual, but her physical quality was of the sneak-up-and-stun variety that was far from obvious. And she was not stupid. Which made her much more Devonshire's type.

He wondered how he had missed the contrast. He would have begun to doubt that she had, indeed, been Bev's lover, except for the teasing remark she had made to him minutes before, when they had been traveling the underground passages. She had mentioned how quickly she had guessed that his arrival at Castle Cairn was involved with Bev and Allegra, and he had replied that it was hardly guesswork on her part. Now, what had been her response to that? Ah, yes, she had laughed softly.

Her kisses tasted like her laughter. Delicious.

"MacLaurin," Devonshire stated again. This time there was more than mere displeasure in his voice.

MacLaurin decided not to overplay his role of eager lover. He lifted his head and turned lazily toward Devonshire. He moved the hand at Elizabeth's shoulder across her back and drew her to him, tightening his hold on her waist. It was a protective gesture and a possessive one.

"Devonshire," he replied.

Devonshire's light eyes glittered luminous and cold in the moonlight. They flicked contemptuously from MacLaurin to the woman at his side. "I am returning to the main hall, Mistress Cameron," he said, politely enough, "if you would like my escort." His solicitous offer was a clear command.

MacLaurin did not allow Elizabeth to reply immediately. He said, "If you're returning, you must have been coming from the library just now."

Devonshire shifted his gaze back to MacLaurin. He paused the merest fraction of a second before saying, "Indeed. I have just come from the library. Your uncle gave me the keys—" he rattled these in his hand "—so that I could investigate one of the fascinating genealogical points that was raised during Brian Sinclair's paper but which was, unfortunately, not pursued in the rich discussion that followed."

It was equally likely that Devonshire had gone to the library to thumb through all the new books on display, possibly looking for Bev's document. Why—or if—Devonshire was interested in the document MacLaurin did not yet know, but he thought it wise to keep in mind the possibility.

"Did you find what you were looking for?" MacLaurin inquired.

Devonshire's expression made an interesting study. He never revealed his thoughts on his face, but MacLaurin would have said that Devonshire's slight smile did not bespeak a man satisfied with his trip to the library, whatever his purpose had been.

Devonshire's expression was at odds with what he said. "I found the precise genealogical point that interested me, yes."

Affecting an air of puzzlement, MacLaurin wanted to force Devonshire's hand. "But if you are on your way to the main hall, I do not understand this detour of yours into the tower courtyard."

Devonshire did not look at all pleased to be asked to account for his actions. He did not, however, hesitate to provide an explanation. "When I descended the stairs and crossed the landing, I noticed that the exterior door was ajar. Since your uncle is very particular about keeping his most valuable library locked, I thought I should step outside to make sure that it stood in no danger from unwanted intruders."

"At least you discovered that no one out here is interested in the library," MacLaurin said, then challenged, "but I wonder that you would notice that the exterior door was closed when you first passed by it. For one thing, the door is to the far side of the landing. For another, you carry no candle."

"I am very observant," Devonshire replied in a voice heavy with meaning, "and I enjoy particularly keen night vision." Then, to Mistress Cameron, he extended his hand. "Come, my child. There is a chill in the air. I shall escort you to your chambers." To MacLaurin he said, "Your uncle is looking for you, by the by. He is still in the receiving room."

For the sake of the situation, MacLaurin had no choice but to relinquish Mistress Cameron to Devonshire's care. Before he did so, however, he exchanged a glance with her that attempted to convey the message that he would be seeing her later in her room. He did not know, however, whether she, like he, understood that their trip to the library had not been a complete failure, after all. Her expressive face, turned up to him, glowed moon blue and reassured him, if nothing else, that she would be all right. Before she swept her lashes down and turned away from him and toward Devonshire, he thought he caught a trace of apprehension tinge her features.

In truth, Elizabeth was none too pleased to find herself in company with His Grace. She had more or less received the message contained in MacLaurin's parting expression, but she had not needed any prompting from him to guess that His Grace's mission to the library had not been successful. She had seen for herself that His Grace was not a man who had found what he was looking for.

None of these reflections was uppermost in her mind when His Grace linked her left arm firmly in his right and turned away from MacLaurin. Rather, she was concerned that the disheveled state of her hair gave His Grace reason to think the worst of her amorous interlude with MacLaurin, and she was struggling to overcome a sense of shame and guilt at having been "caught in the act." She had no reason, really, to feel either shame or guilt and could not understand why she did not simply feel embarrassed, but she did not.

She also feared, for some reason, that His Grace would subject her to an icy scold for her improper behavior. This fear soon proved unfounded. When His Grace led her back through the exterior door to the library tower landing, he said, quite pleasantly, "Your comments and questions in response to today's treatises were uniformly acute, Mistress Cameron."

A fear of a very different sort swept through her. Could he have reason to suspect why she was interested particularly in the history of the Fleurise Garden? She dismissed the possibility as a product of her fresh sense of guilt, gathered her wits and said, "Thank you, Your Grace. I found the various treatises very illuminating." She saw an opportunity to turn this uncomfortable encounter to her advantage and continued, "I particularly admired Brian Sinclair's discussion, which must have seized your attention as well, since you wished to return to the library tonight to track down a reference. Would you like to share the discovery you made just now with me, Your Grace?"

His Grace was leading her down the hallway that connected the library tower to the west wing. Its north wall was punctuated by a series of windows through which the moonlight streamed, thus making it less dark than the usual castle hallway.

"It was naught but a meticulous desire to verify the birthdate of a granduncle of mine, on my mother's side," he said without mentioning the name of that remote parent.

"Were you able to put your hands on Lord Mure's series of genealogies, then, with no difficulty, Your Grace?"

"No difficulty whatsoever," His Grace assured her. "Robbie informed me of the exact row and shelf upon which those tomes are arranged, and he gave me flints, of course, to light several candles so that I could read." He glanced down at her. "I took great care to extinguish the candles thoroughly before I left, in case you were worried that a careless amateur might cause harm to what you professionals hold so dear."

His Grace's possible carelessness had not worried her. Instead, she was trying to remember whether she had seen a light in the library windows after she and MacLaurin had spewed forth from the castle entrails. She recalled seeing no light, but neither had she looked for one. His Grace would have needed a light to search the genealogies. His Grace would have needed no light to thumb through the books on display in search of a hidden document.

"As a patron of our society," she said, "I am sure that you know how to treat valuable books." She searched for a way to extend the discussion. "Once you put your hands on the correct genealogy, did it take you long to find the date you were looking for?"

"Not very long at all," His Grace replied and turned the subject. "I was rather pleased to have determined the correct interpretation of Ganon Graham's poem, 'Tam o' the Wilds.' If I recall aright, I believe that you and I were of the same opinion that Tam was, indeed, his cousin's murderer."

She had to follow his conversational lead. "I have much experience with Mr. Graham's narrative methods," she replied, "and knew that the essential clue would be hidden at the story's most digressive point. So I cannot take as much credit as you for having detected Mr. Graham's ruse."

They spoke amiably of this and that, traveled a number of darkened hallways, which His Grace negotiated unerringly, and arrived at the entry hall, almost miraculously, from Elizabeth's point of view. The reptilian candelabra were still lit, and His Grace was able to lead her toward the main staircase without falling over any suits of armor. She looked admiringly at her companion. "How did you make it here and so easily, Your Grace?"

His Grace's expression was inscrutable. "I used to spend much time at Castle Cairn," he said, "when I was a young man."

She smiled. "You are not so very old, Your Grace."

His Grace acknowledged the compliment with a slight bow. "I should have said that I spent much time here when I was younger."

"When you were younger, Edmund?" a light, amused voice mocked from behind them.

Elizabeth turned to see Lady Michael emerge from the shadowy hallway adjacent to the main staircase. She was evidently coming from the receiving room, and she was carrying a lantern to light her way. Elizabeth was aware that a quiver of tension gently rippled the air. She curtsied politely. Lady Michael nodded graciously and remotely in response.

"My dear," His Grace greeted her. He extended his left arm to her ladyship. "May I escort you to your chamber, which, I believe, is just beyond Mistress Cameron's?"

Lady Michael accepted his arm. "You were escorting Mistress Cameron to her chamber?" she asked with a challenging inflection that pricked Elizabeth's ears.

"Why, yes," His Grace replied tranquilly.

The threesome proceeded to the main staircase and began to ascend.

"And the company of Mistress Cameron inspired your lamentation of lost youth?" her ladyship inquired archly.

His Grace's tone was silky. "Mistress Cameron assured me that I was not so old."

Lady Michael laughed gaily. "Why, you're old enough to be her father, my dear Edmund!"

His Grace paused just the right amount of time before he inquired, quite pleasantly, "Did you enjoy Robbie's whiskey tonight, Juliette? I find that the best Scots whiskey—and, indeed, Robbie stocks only the best—has a surreptitious quality. So easy to drink is it that one does not realize that one has drunk too much until . . . one has drunk too much."

Lady Michael hardly missed the point of that blunted barb. She did not back down but gave him some of his own back. Her voice was musical. "Oh, it is absolutely true that Robbie has only the best at Castle Cairn! Why, his food and drink are rivaled only by his guest list, and who would have thought that the intriguing Ian MacLaurin would be here? His presence was, apparently, most unexpected. Do you know why he has come, I wonder?"

His Grace referred the question to Elizabeth. "Indeed, I do not, but perhaps my companion knows, since she is rather better acquainted with him than I."

Elizabeth's heart lurched. She was hardly in position to disclaim knowing anything about MacLaurin, since she had just been caught kissing him. She also wondered whether His Grace suspected MacLaurin's reasons for being here or guessed that she and MacLaurin had intended to go to the library tonight—perhaps to find the very thing His Grace had been interested in finding.

"I understand that Lord Mure's nephew has come to attend the summer meeting of the Royal Historical Society," Elizabeth replied, but regretted the lack of conviction in her voice.

Lady Michael took no notice. "And why should he not?" she replied. She was determined to pursue her theme. "One is never too *young* to become interested in history."

They reached the top of the stairs and turned left. His Grace turned discussion down pathways that would not attract allusions to his age. For the rest of the journey they discussed such unexceptionable subjects as the beautiful summer weather and the haunted castle hallways. Holding her lantern high and peering into every corner, Lady Michael warmed to the last topic and declared herself mightily disappointed that she had not yet seen or heard anything spooky.

They arrived at Elizabeth's chamber door. His Grace released her arm, bowed and wished her an agreeable good-night. Lady Michael looked straight into Elizabeth's eyes and expressed the desire to become better acquainted with her. Elizabeth curtsied and murmured the appropriate replies. Then she withdrew her key, unlocked her door and entered her chamber.

Before she closed her door she heard His Grace say, "Juliette," but she could not hear the rest of his remark. She heard the hint of a caressing, seductive note in his voice and was pretty sure that she had stepped into a lover's quarrel. Perhaps she had precipitated it. Elizabeth was flattered that Lady Michael paid her the honor of considering her a rival for His Grace's affections.

Elizabeth was far more interested to discover whether His Grace stayed with Lady Michael, because that would mean that he would have access to the fourth box of books that was still in her chamber. So Elizabeth stood with her ear at her door, which she kept open the barest

crack. Within a few minutes she was surprised and relieved to hear His Grace's footsteps outside her door. He
was walking back down the hallway, and he did not seem
to be making an attempt to muffle his footsteps, although his step was never heavy. His footsteps did not
slow down as he passed her door.

So, His Grace had no access this night to the fourth
box of books. Perhaps he did not desire the books. Perhaps he did not desire Lady Michael. Elizabeth considered waiting for some sign from MacLaurin that together
they would lure Lady Michael out of her chamber,
whereupon MacLaurin could go through the books.
However, earlier in the evening she had been seized by a
sense of adventure and confidence, and she did not feel
like waiting around for a sign from MacLaurin.

She wanted to engage in her own reconnaissance mission. She decided to follow His Grace, just to make sure
that he was going to his chambers at the far end of the
main hallway and that he was not intending to return to
her end.

First, because her coiffure had already fallen, she un-
pinned her hair the rest of the way and let it fall freely
down her back. Then, leaving the key in the keyhole on
the inside of her room, she slipped out into the hallway.
She tiptoed down the hallway about fifty paces behind
His Grace. She kept to the edge, where the floorboards
creaked less, and had a hard time keeping up with him.
He seemed to be walking rather quickly. He seemed to be
in a hurry. Or miffed. Perhaps Lady Michael had rebuffed him?

He crossed in front of the landing at the top of the
main staircase. She paused and let him get farther ahead
of her. Then she slipped past the landing, which was
vaguely illuminated by the lights in the entry hallway be-

low, and continued to walk down the hallway, which was new territory for her.

Suddenly, with His Grace's footsteps still echoing faintly ahead of her, a ghostly apparition rose out of the darkness before her. She gasped. Her heart stopped beating. Her feet stopped moving.

When she recognized the man, she heaved a heavy sigh of relief. Twice before she had mistaken him for an otherworldly spirit. This third time she would not be so foolish.

She chided, on a whisper, "You always seem to appear out of nowhere to scramble my perceptions. How do you do it, Ian MacLaurin?"

The figure moved toward her. It did not appear to be walking, but rather to be floating. To her dawning horror, it did not become more substantial the closer it came.

It spoke. "Why do you call me by my son's name, young lady?"

Chapter Thirteen

Elizabeth's hand flew to her heart. She felt a spurt of relief to touch the small jeweled case lodged between her breasts. She hastily withdrew the chain from her bodice and grabbed her locket for comfort and protection. She did not know how this delicate object would protect her, and she felt only minimally comforted holding the image of her mother in miniature, but she did not know what else to do—was not even fully conscious, in fact, that she was doing it.

"Your son?" she breathed.

The spirit hovered closer. She clutched the locket harder.

"I have been troubled since his return," the spirit said. "Greatly troubled."

"H-h-have you?" she managed.

The wraith wavered away from her, like a drift of smoke. The trunk curled away first followed by the head and arms. "No rest," it sighed wearily. "No peace."

She had backed herself against the wall, mostly out of fear, not for support, but the wall was the only thing keeping her upright now that her knees had turned to soggy bread. The shadows in the hallway leaned at angles she had not seen before.

The wraith writhed back to face her. No longer surprised by the apparition but still surely terrified, she was able to register the arrangement of the gossamer tatters of its features. It was not precisely the face of Ian MacLaurin but close enough for her to know exactly whose ghost confronted her.

"I want rest," it stated. "I want peace, and I have none."

She whispered, "I'm sorry."

The spirit paid no heed to her sympathy. It floated away again. "Too many people. They must go away."

"Do you—do you feel this way every summer?"

It twisted toward her, its fluid parts forming the curve of a question mark. "Every summer?" it queried.

She felt its displeasure. She knew it was as absurd to reason with the wraith as it had been to sympathize. Nevertheless, she said, "But—but every summer the historical society has its meeting here hosted by Lord Mure."

Its displeasure grew. The wisping question mark wrung itself into a twist of translucence. "Lord Mure?" it echoed ominously.

She had apparently offended the spirit and quickly corrected herself. "Y-y-your brother, that is!"

"My brother is a wasteful fool," the spirit retorted in a condemning voice.

She did not take issue with the statement, although she did not know what it meant, if anything.

"Everything should have been different," the ghost said next. "Very different. But *he* ruined everything."

"Your brother?" she ventured, hoping to make any kind of sense out of this encounter.

Before her eyes, the spirit seemed to come undone, then to reform itself, latticing itself into a braid. "My brother has nothing to do with this!"

She quailed at its rage. She wondered why no one was coming to her rescue, then realized that the spirit's violence was a frail thing in physical terms, although its effect on her was enormous. She began to tremble uncontrollably.

The spirit whorled and whirled on her. "Who are you?" it demanded angrily.

Her grip on the locket tightened. "E-Elizabeth Cameron."

It regarded her with grim, exhausted eyes, those of a restless ghost. "Cameron?" it repeated meaningfully. If a spirit could be said to gasp, this one did. It drew itself in, puffed out like a bellows, then thinned to the point of disappearance. The next second it regained its misty existence and blew a cold mist upon her, causing her already trembling body to shiver.

"What are you doing here, Elizabeth Cameron?" it demanded.

"I came to attend his lordsh—your brother's meeting!"

"Did you come to torment me?"

"No!"

"Do you know who I am?"

"Yes!"

The gauzy outlines of the weird contortionist shook in contradiction. "You do not."

The voice was so hollow and so ominous that a greater alarm skittered up and down her already alarmed spine. She was nearly incoherent with fear. "You're—you're Gavin MacLaurin, the previous Lord Mure! Ian MacLaurin's father! Robert MacLaurin's brother!"

"I am much more than that to you, Elizabeth Cameron," it said. Then, without pausing for her response, it demanded, "What do you have in your hand?"

She felt the bite of the chain at the back of her neck, so fiercely was she gripping the locket. "Nothing," she lied. She knew the lie would do her no good but was unable to reveal the secret of her talisman, the only thing her crazed perceptions believed was keeping her from harm.

"You cannot tell me that something is nothing." It emitted an eerie sound, like a dead man laughing. "I know what nothing is."

To her horror the spirit glided closer. A wisp detached itself from the central column of the braid of its floating torso. The wisp shaped itself into an arm. The arm produced a hand, which evolved extended tendrils of fingers. Those tendrils streamed toward her, toward the hand she clutched at her breast. She strained away from its ghastly touch.

"Show me what is in your hand, Elizabeth Cameron."

"No, no," she breathed. "You can't have it."

"I don't want it," the ghost stated. "I want to see it."

"You can't see it," she said, not knowing why she should deny the ghost this request, only knowing that she must.

"You think I don't know what it is?" it demanded querulously.

Chills traveled her back. The hair rose at her nape and the backs of her legs. "H-h-how could you?" she returned.

"I know far more than you think," it replied, "and far more about you than you do yourself."

She was in no condition to solve riddles. She wished rather to appease the spirit. "You can't know anything about me," she contradicted, "because I've never been here before."

"I know that you have never been here before," the ghost intoned slowly, "because I have never before been so restless."

The ghostly tendril fingers curled forward to paw her. Her back was completely flattened against the wall. Her right hand was closed in a tight fist around her locket. Her left hand was flung flat against the wall. The ghostly hand was about to graze her skin. Her right hand jerked convulsively. The fingers of her left hand pressed themselves into the paneling.

Too many things happened at once for her to determine cause and effect. The chain at her neck broke. Her right hand opened and dropped the locket. A trapdoor on the floor not two feet in front of her opened. The spirit began to twirl and to funnel into the opened door. It was being sucked down in eddying circles by the pull of some stronger, nether force. Then the trapdoor sobbed shut.

Elizabeth did not wait to discover whether any part of the ghostly apparition remained above the floor to taunt her or touch her. She mobilized the limp fibers of her being, grabbed handfuls of her skirts and lifted them off her feet. Then, with utter darkness swallowing her flight, she ran back down the hallway without once stopping until she reached her chamber door.

She turned the handle, blessed herself for not having locked the door, and fell into her room. For no logical reason she turned the key she had left in the inside keyhole, knowing that nothing so trivial as a locked door could stop a ghost. She leaned against the door and closed her eyes. The back of her head pressed against the wood. Her blood was thumping, her nerves were snarled and her legs were still wobbling from her fright and her mad dash down a very long hallway.

Slowly, slowly she brought her swirling thoughts to order. She set about convincing herself that she had been imagining things. The shadows had played tricks with her eyes. The creaking of the old castle had played tricks with her ears. She lifted a hand to one temple and kneaded it. She put her hand to her breast, and her eyes shot open.

She was no longer wearing her locket. She must have yanked it convulsively from her neck in her fear. Yes, that was it. She had been so terrified by her own wild imaginings that she had torn it off. No, it was not the case that the ghost had touched her or taken it, because there *was* no ghost. She must have been startled into dropping the locket when the trapdoor opened, and the trapdoor must have opened when her fingers pushed some button hidden in the wall paneling. That was it.

As for those wild imaginings, she decided that it was the air of Castle Cairn that had disordered her senses. From the moment she had stepped into the shadow of the brooding facade, she had been too ready to set her fancy free during the daytime. Her dreamy daytime fancies had turned nightmarish.

All she had to do was go back down the corridor, retrieve her locket, and all would be restored to order. Right.

Wrong. She knew that no matter what her logical mind told her, she was not leaving her room again this night. She wanted to get into bed and pull the covers over her head and sleep. But would she ever be able to sleep after such a nerve-jangling experience?

She would have to try. She looked across her room to the window that she had not closed and whose curtains she had not drawn. She could not remember why she had not performed such routine tasks before leaving on her nocturnal misadventure, but she was glad that she had not. The moonlight flooding that end of her room was serene, and the gentle sounds of night wafting in on summer breezes were reassuring.

She crossed to the window. She latched the window in such a way to allow a drift of air to circulate, and she adjusted the curtains, keeping them open a slice so that a hard, bright knife of moonlight could cut through. She did not admit to herself that she thought the air and the moonlight would keep any ghosts at bay.

She found her bedside candle. Her fingers fumbled with the flint and trembled when she lit the taper. The pleasant glow of candlelight caused her nerves, tightly knotted, to loosen just a notch. She took her hairbrush from the dressing table and plopped down on the side of her bed. Her knees thanked her for being spared the necessity of holding her up any longer.

She placed her brush on the bed beside her and bent her head. She threw the heavy fall of her unbound hair over her head and began to struggle with the lacings at the back of her gown. She was so tired that when she succeeded in unfastening the bodice of her dress, she did not stand up to step out of it. Instead, still seated on the edge of the bed, she shimmied the skirts up and drew the entire garment over her head. She tossed the dress so that it billowed haphazardly across the chair at her dressing table. She sat for a moment, feeling the safe haven of her bed surround her, relaxed to be wearing only her chemise. Her snarled nerves unknotted themselves another notch.

She picked up her brush and began to bring her tangled hair into order. It was soothing to brush her long, thick hair, to stroke her scalp, then to extend the brush through the light brown mass as far as her arm could reach. She let her head roll with her brush strokes, this way and that, over and over, and as she did so, she felt the muscles of her neck unbunch. At one brush stroke, her hand inadvertently caught the loop of the bow holding up her drawstring bodice. As she extended her arm, the bow became untied and the drawstring sagged over her breasts. The cotton caught on one rosy tip, fluttering teasingly on the soft edge, but did not fall. Most, but not all, of one creamy white breast was exposed.

She shrugged, did not readjust her chemise, and kept brushing. Her nerves were relaxing and losing all flexibility. She was feeling like a sprung spring that could never recoil. She was limp now, not from fright but from relief to be on the bed, feeling safe, feeling protected. She put her hand to her throat, just to make sure that her locket had truly fallen off. She could not, at first, reconcile the locket's absence with her feeling of safety.

She had been twelve years old the day her father had given her that locket. He had said, "This is all I have to give you of your mother." He had smiled at her, somewhat sadly, and added, "You'd do well never to show it to anyone."

The twelve-year-old girl she had been had thought that her father had given her a magic locket, one that was powerful but finite. The moment she had slipped the locket around her neck and let the jeweled case slip between her developing breasts, she had felt very warm and safe. At the same time, given her father's warning, she had decided that her mother's image must be quantified, like a sack of flour. She had imagined that each sight of it represented a scoop and that if she was too greedy with looking at it, the sack would one day be empty. Over the years she had measured glimpses of her mother's image very sparingly.

It was irrational, this feeling of safety and protection now that her precious locket was gone. But it was no more irrational than any other emotion she had experienced during the course of this extraordinary night: in the bowels of the castle being drawn along by MacLaurin; out in the moonlight, in his arms, with his lips against hers; in company with His Grace and with Lady Michael and feeling as if she had stepped into the middle of a lover's quarrel or caused one; in the hallway speaking to a ghost that could not possibly exist.

In the space of the past hour or more, she had been optimistic, transported, apprehensive, embarrassed, emboldened and frightened out of her wits. Now, without her protective necklace she felt, paradoxically, protected.

No. That was not quite right. Now, without her protective necklace she felt free. Liberated. No longer burdened by her mother's watchful eye. No longer constrained by her care.

She kept brushing her hair. The feeling of freedom lasted. She sighed dreamily. She glanced lazily about her room, checking the odd corners for ghosts. She looked into the strange little alcove that served no purpose and went nowhere. She saw no shape there to frighten her. Her gaze drifted to her armoire, grazed over the fireplace, then across the paneling of the wall that ran in tandem with MacLaurin's bedchamber wall. It stopped at the section of the wall to the right of the fireplace that had moved the night before to allow MacLaurin's entry to her room.

Her gaze returned to the fireplace. She looked at her fireplace nymphs and began to listen. This morning she had thought she heard her nymphs sigh. Now, and to her surprise—but, then again, nothing would surprise her this night—she thought she heard them singing. Very faintly. High and far off. Very beautifully. A siren's song. The kind that caused ancient heroes to wreck their ships on ragged rocks.

She smiled to herself and let the music become a part of her, entering her ears and gliding like golden honey down her neck. Her brush strokes became longer and more languorous. She was relaxed but not really tired. She felt dreamy. Almost enchanted, but with a smooth curve of contentment.

Her eyes fluttered shut.

Her eyes fluttered open, lazily but with a new awareness.

She was not sure when she became aware of it or how she became aware of it, but she knew that she was being watched. She could feel someone's eyes on her. A man's eyes, and this man was no ghost. She remembered the way she had felt when the eyes of the ghost of Gavin MacLaurin had touched her—but, of course, there had been no ghost. Still. She was able to discern the contrast between a ghost's eyes and a living man's eyes upon her. She could feel it by the way this man's eyes increased her feeling of liberation. And something else again. Was it arousal?

The siren's music became sweeter. She caught the spell of the siren's song and held it within her. With the song inside her, she felt irresistible.

She knew who was watching her. He had told her that he would check through the peepholes in the wall between her room and his, but she could not remember why he had stated such an intention. She did not think it was to spy on her, to catch her while she was undressing. No, she did not think that spying on an unsuspecting woman would be in his style. But now that he was spying on her, she did not want him to stop. She wanted to keep his eyes on her, and she knew just how to do it. She needed only let the siren's song fill her. The song inside her and his eyes upon her felt delicious.

But not as delicious as his lips had felt on her lips when they had stood in the moonlight, when the warm night air had caressed her skin, making it pleasant for his touch, then more than pleasant. Earlier, when they had been in the underbelly of the castle, surrounded by damp and dark, connected by their hands, he had said something like "We're in this together now, you and I."

Yes, they were in it together. Most definitely.

She remembered awaking this morning a new woman. She had thought perhaps she was Fiona. Or Allegra's mother. Now she knew who she had become, and it was an extraordinary feeling. She was free. Free of her father's constraints, free of her mother's jealously protective eye, free of the taint of Fiona's mistake, free of her own limited ideas of who she was.

She was not a woman who was beautiful like Fiona or her mother, who had been a beauty. Neither was she obvious like Fiona. Elizabeth recalled how, when she had first met Lieutenant Beverly in company with Fiona, Fiona had gazed into Lieutenant Beverly's eyes and stated her desire with one long look that said, *Take me now.* Lieutenant Beverly had never once looked at Elizabeth, but he had tired of Fiona within the month.

She knew who she was. She was a fireplace nymph come to life in flesh and blood. She was not someone else. Not Fiona. Not Allegra's mother. She was herself, and she was wonderful. Walter MacPhee, rich and respectable, had refused to marry her. Well, he could eat his heart out.

So could the man watching her. She had only to brush her hair and let her chemise ride tantalizingly on the crests of her breasts, and she would lure the watching man to her shore.

She smiled. She did not want him to run aground just yet. She was enjoying the display, his attention and the effect of his attention on her. She liked the fact that he could not simply press a button and have the secret panel slide aside because he would rouse the entire castle with the hideous noise. She liked the fact that he had to remain on his side of the wall, a helpless spectator to the charms that she had always thought she had but had never been able to deploy to their fullest, most powerful effect. She was curious to test their limits. She always had been curious. Now her curiosity had a new dimension.

It was lovely, this power, this knowledge, this new curiosity. She put her brush down, wound the fall of shining hair around her hand, then began to braid it. Slowly. She twisted his gaze into her plait. She curled him into her hair. She did not readjust her chemise. It floated just over the top of one breast. She felt his hot gaze upon her, willing the chemise to fall, to expose her to him, to show that he had power over her and not the other way around. She was unconcerned. She knew that the chemise, however precariously caught at the veriest edge of her raised nipple, would not fall until she was ready to let it fall.

She sighed twice, deeply, letting her breasts rise and fall, but still the chemise held. She propped her hands behind her and leaned back, displaying herself, but not quite exposing herself. His gaze felt too good, too arousing to wish to stop just now. She was teasing him. A little unmercifully. But he deserved it. For mistaking her first for a castle retainer, then for Lieutenant Beverly's lover. For toying with her. For kissing her more to annoy His Grace than for pleasure. For handing her over to His Grace without a second thought.

When she felt that she had aroused him—and herself—enough, she leaned over to her bedside table. At the moment she blew out the candle, she let the chemise slip completely off one shoulder. The warmth she felt flash over her skin, the surge of warmth she felt in her blood from his gaze convinced her that her timing had been perfect.

Chapter Fourteen

MacLaurin watched Devonshire lead Elizabeth Cameron away from the library tower courtyard and felt relieved.

He chose to believe that the reason he had handed her over to a man he hated was that it would look suspicious if he did not. He certainly did not want to give Devonshire cause to think that he and Elizabeth Cameron wished to hang around the library tower a little longer in order to go into the library as Devonshire had done.

So he handed her over, and when she was standing next to Devonshire, MacLaurin realized that he had let her go because he had been afraid of her. He had kissed many women, but he had never kissed one like Elizabeth Cameron. He had never kissed one with the effect of Elizabeth Cameron. Because he had never kissed one on a moonlit night within the walls of Castle Cairn.

The moment she turned and walked away on Devonshire's arm, he felt the spell break and was glad of it. He realized only in retrospect that his fireplace demons had tricked him into thinking of her as a trap. It was only *thinking* her a trap that made her one. As long as he did not consider her one, she could not be one. He would not be trapped here, and she could not trap him here, as long as she was not a trap.

Or was he double-crossing himself in *not* thinking of her as a trap?

He ran his fingers through his hair. He tried to shake off the slightly sticky feeling of having traveled the castle innards and of having kissed an ordinary woman whose effect on him was out of the ordinary.

He resented being caught unawares. He resented the feelings he was feeling. He resented finding himself back at Castle Cairn. He searched for someone to blame for this return to his boyhood home and naturally began with Gabriel Beverly. He was here because of Bev's foolish duel, because of Bev's more foolish siring of an illegitimate child whose identity had to be protected.

He looked down at his hands and flexed his long, supple fingers. His hands were his life and his livelihood. He had risen quickly through army ranks for his skill in using and improving artillery. And when the Peace of Utrecht had been signed in '14, he had received ample funding from military men of rank and wealth to pursue his artillery improvements in peacetime.

He had skills for peacetime enterprises, too, and had become London's best and most expensive man of mechanical ingenuity, his locks and clocks and machines of all varieties much in demand. His recent commission from King George had been a windfall. If the Hanover wanted palace walls that moved for better access to his two German mistresses, MacLaurin could think of no easier assignment. But the fact remained that he would not still have his hands if it had not been for Bev. No, he could not blame Bev.

He would do better to blame Devonshire. That was easy enough. Devonshire was a rat—not that he had ever looked like one or had overtly acted like one. Nevertheless, MacLaurin felt a bone-deep dislike of the man that surely equaled the intensity of any emotion he had ever experienced.

As he stood in the library tower courtyard, bathing in the moonlight, MacLaurin suddenly realized that he had never learned exactly why his father had also hated Devonshire. Of course, Devonshire was dislikable on his own terms, and of course the MacPhersons had long been determined to see an end to the MacLaurin line. Yet, now that he came to think of it, he began to suspect that his father's hatred for Devonshire had been more than habit of clan animosity. He had hated him on a personal level.

MacLaurin could understand. He had not liked the look, fleeting but possessive, that Devonshire had cast upon Elizabeth Cameron when he extended his hand to her to lead her away. MacLaurin was sure now that Devonshire's interest in Elizabeth was more than fleeting. Devonshire had better taste in women than Bev—MacLaurin would grant him that.

Which observation led his thoughts in a new direction. As long as he felt it necessary to blame people for the profusion of unpleasant emotions weeding through his breast, he would do well to blame Elizabeth Cameron. Her warmth. Her intelligence. Her absolute ordinariness that was not at all ordinary. She was the kind of woman who clearly attracted Devonshire. But was she also the kind who had attracted Bev? He was beginning to doubt it—which also made him wonder at her motives in allowing him to think that she had been involved with Allegra's father.

He cursed a pox on all fathers, and before he could check the thought, he wondered whether Elizabeth

Cameron was the kind of woman of whom his own father would have approved.

At last he was getting somewhere. It was his father he needed to blame more than anyone else. His dour, passionless father who had wanted to constrain his only son to a dour, passionless marriage. He had refused the insipid lass his father had chosen as his bride and had taken up with all the wildest women around. He had also been disinherited and had left Castle Cairn in disgrace.

He should consider himself lucky. His head and his heart were not in farming, and he had made a life for himself in London. No matter that his uncle would never produce an heir, had less head for farming than any MacLaurin in many a generation and was selling off land to the MacPhersons. MacLaurin certainly didn't want to live out his life in this depressing, haunted wreck and couldn't imagine why anyone else would, either. All the better if his uncle ruined the place. His uncle—

Devonshire had said that his uncle wanted to speak to him, but he didn't necessarily believe it.

MacLaurin glanced up at the library tower. He would search the displayed books another time, there being no urgency for the task now that Devonshire had gone before him. Instead, he decided that even if his uncle did not necessarily want to speak to him, he wanted to speak to his uncle.

He made his way back to the receiving room. He came to the entrance just as Juliette Michael was leaving it, carrying only a dainty lantern for company. When she passed him, she did nothing more than arch her brows invitingly. It was a bold enough reminder that if he wanted to search the fourth box tonight, he could do so within the context of an amorous adventure. That aspect of his night's work had a great deal more appeal at the moment than it had when he had first considered Juliette's invitation during the midday break.

Somewhat to his surprise, the moment he stepped into the receiving room his uncle sat up straighter in his chair and said, "There ye are, lad, and here I was wanting to speak with ye."

"So Devonshire told me," MacLaurin replied. He nodded a brief acknowledgment of the two guests still remaining to sip whiskey, but they were so far gone in their cups that they did not seem to register his greeting. He noticed that one of them was snoring lightly. "Did you have something particular in mind, Uncle?"

His uncle invited him to sit in the wing chair next to his by the fireplace. Low embers mulled on the hearth, keeping the cavernous room dry. Between the two chairs stood a little table upon which were arrayed two glasses and one unstoppered bottle.

"Nay, then, Ian," his lordship said blurrily, "I was wanting to catch up on yer life, is all."

MacLaurin sat. "There's little to say."

"Not to hear Lady Michael tell of it!" His uncle chuckled. He owned a hard head, and despite the quantity of whiskey MacLaurin guessed his uncle had absorbed this evening, his speech was not seriously slurred. On the other hand, his burr was pronounced. "She says ye've been making quite a name for yerself in the highest circles."

"She's flattering you, Uncle. Trying to get herself into your good graces."

His uncle's glance was remarkably clear and ironic. "Do ye think, lad?"

"Why else would she bring you a load of heavy books?"

"Why not?" his uncle returned.

"That's what I'd like to know. She told me earlier that she brought them for you because you share a love of—what was it now?—literature?"

"Aye, that we do."

"She's not known for her love of literature."

His uncle smiled a little hazily, a little oddly. "I don't know about her love of literature, but her ladyship certainly knows some interesting bookshops in London. When I was last there, some months ago, I was invited to her home by His Grace. She and I got to discussing books and soon enough hit on subjects of interest to both of us."

MacLaurin reached over to the unstoppered bottle and splashed amber into his uncle's glass. "Juliette Michael has an interest in history?"

His uncle smiled another hazy, odd smile. "Well, not history! Not every book I buy is a history book."

"The others being literature, then?"

"In a manner of speaking. A man has to have other diversions in life besides history, ye know!"

"I know, and yet when I think of the diversions that seem to occupy Lady Michael's days, I just can't imagine her holding a book—historical or literary."

His uncle chuckled again. "Depends on the book, I suppose. But, if ye're wanting to know, Lady Michael agreed to transport my books only recently. I'm guessing she must have learned that His Grace was making the journey north to Edinburgh, and was hoping to cross paths with him in Scotland!" He lowered his voice confidentially, almost comically. "'Tis my understanding that she and His Grace have had a falling out. Well, her journey has worked well for her, given that His Grace came here himself and saved her the trip to Edinburgh to intercept him."

So that was it. It made sense. Juliette's motives were centered wholly on Devonshire. She knew nothing—and would care nothing—about the document in the book that was most likely in the box still in her chamber.

His uncle fixed a bleary eye on him. "Lady Michael tells me that ye've been making a name for yerself in London, in the highest circles."

"So you've said."

His uncle glared into his whiskey glass, as if trying to calculate how much he had drunk. "Are ye saying I'm repeating myself, lad?"

"I am."

"Then I shall risk yer further displeasure by asking ye again if ye've returned to Castle Cairn to make amends."

"And I shall repeat myself by saying again that I've no amends to make."

His uncle scowled. "Do I take it ye're no longer ruining the lassies, at least?"

"No longer?" MacLaurin echoed. "I never did. They were already ruined when I got to them."

"I can think of one ye ruined."

MacLaurin said without hesitation, "Elspeth Mac-Millan."

His uncle shook his head mournfully. "She was disgraced, puir lassie."

MacLaurin's gaze was steady on his uncle's face. "She surely was," he agreed pleasantly. "Did she ever marry?"

"No. Who would take her when you were done with her?"

"Thomas MacGillivray, I'm thinking."

His uncle's glance was sharp. "Thomas MacGillivray ended by marrying a woman from the north. Why would ye be thinking that he'd marry Elspeth MacMillan?"

"Because when I rode out to Elspeth's farm yesterday, I saw a ten-year-old lad going about his chores who looked remarkably like Thomas MacGillivray."

His uncle said nothing.

"Surely you noticed the resemblance," MacLaurin pursued, "between Elspeth's son and MacGillivray."

Still his uncle said nothing.

"Or, at least, noticed the remarkable lack of resemblance between Elspeth's son and me," MacLaurin continued.

His uncle was not going to concede the point, but MacLaurin was satisfied that it had been registered. The moment now seemed right to learn what he could learn, so he continued smoothly, "Now that that's out of the way, you can tell me about the relationship between Mistress Cameron and Devonshire."

"Relationship?" his uncle queried. "'Tis no relationship there to speak of. They met only yesterday evening when I introduced them."

"But she said earlier—well, never mind. Tell me instead how long Mistress Cameron has been a member of the Royal Historical Society."

"Five years now."

"Is she an active participant?"

His uncle managed to pull himself up in his chair enough to suggest a challenge. "Why do ye want to know, lad?"

MacLaurin replied easily, "Since I've just proven that I'm not the heartless seducer of my exaggerated reputation, you can answer my question with an easy conscience."

His uncle subsided in his chair. "'Tis the first time Mistress Elizabeth has attended the summer meeting here at Castle Cairn."

MacLaurin found that an interesting tidbit, but far from thrilling. "So why did she come now for the first time? Or, perhaps I should ask, why hasn't she come in the past?"

"Her father always forbade her our summer meetings."

MacLaurin smiled faintly, imagining Elizabeth Cameron being denied anything she was determined to do. "I see. Her father would be Joseph Cameron, no? Do you know what caused his change of heart this year?"

"He went on a business trip, and so he does not know she's here. She decided to come at the last minute."

MacLaurin betrayed his interest with a very meaningful "Oh?"

His uncle looked up and wagged a finger at him. "But she's a good lass, for all of that, and ye'll not be thinking that because she's come without her father's permission, she'll yield to yer artful ways, lad! Nay, then!" He dropped his hand so that his fingers curled around his glass. "Now, she offered me a perfectly good explanation for why she decided to come, but I can't quite rightly remember it."

MacLaurin pressed his uncle to remember.

"Well, now," the older man said, "I'm thinking it had something to do with historical documents. Aye, that was it, then. Historical documents."

"What kind of historical documents?"

His uncle said something about the documents containing "a surprise" then drifted off. When further prodding yielded nothing, MacLaurin fetched a retainer to help his uncle to bed. He made his way to his own chamber, mulling over the remarkable coincidence that neither he nor Devonshire nor Elizabeth Cameron were supposed to have come to the summer meeting of the Royal Historical Society.

MacLaurin had a fair idea of at least part of Devonshire's reasons for being here, but he could not quite guess at Elizabeth Cameron's. Was it disobedience, pure and simple, that motivated her? An opportunity to defy her father while his back was turned? MacLaurin considered the possibility, but he did not quite think backhanded disobedience fitted her patterns of behavior. He sensed that he was holding parts but not all the pieces of an intricate bit of machinery—and he was nothing if not good at assembling intricate machines.

When he arrived at his chamber, he had come to a decision. He would go to Juliette's chambers tonight and make pretty but otherwise unremarkable love to her. Then he would search through the fourth box of books, solving at least part of a suddenly larger puzzle. Slipping out of his jacket, he cast a glance at his open window and remembered that he had told Elizabeth that he might have to come through her window. That would, of course, necessitate telling Elizabeth that he didn't need her help drawing Juliette out of her chamber. Would Elizabeth be able to infer that he intended to remain with Juliette and seduce her?

Elizabeth would. Bad idea, then. He wouldn't go through Elizabeth's chamber at all, but would take the circuitous route through the castle from his wing to Juliette's chamber.

Wait. Had he told Elizabeth that he would come to her room later tonight to discuss their strategy? He couldn't remember, but he did remember thinking that he needed to check in with her. He could look through the peepholes. Ah, that was it. That way he could see if she was waiting up for him, or if she was already in bed asleep, in which case he would not have to bother her at all.

He crossed to the carved panel of the wall that ran next to Elizabeth's chamber. As he slid back the screen over one set of peepholes, his fireplace demons began to chatter unnecessarily. He told them to be quiet, then positioned his eyes at the convenient holes. He had a perfect view of the adjoining chamber's bed.

He was unprepared for what he saw. Light criss-crossed the chamber, a slice of moonlight from the window intersecting with the light from the bed-table candle. At the center of the intersection sat a woman brushing her hair on the bed. But, no, it wasn't a bed. It was a wave of white foam, and he was transfixed to see that the mermaid of his dreams was seated in the center of it, as if ready to rise from the sea.

Her breasts were visible, but not completely. He saw that she was wearing a chemise. He wondered groggily why a mermaid would be wearing a chemise but decided that he did not care about that question as much as the next. Would the mermaid rise from her seated position? Would she have legs, since she was now on land? If she had legs, that meant she would also have—

Her chemise shifted, as if the drawstring had been caught and was being pulled. The mermaid's head was moving back and forth, back and forth, with the strokes of her brush. At one moment her face was fully illuminated by the light of the candle. She opened her eyes. He was looking at Elizabeth Cameron.

He tried to look away, but was unable. He tried to shake himself, but it did no good. It was as if he had swum into a calm sea and encountered a bad undertow. Her chemise fell precariously. It slipped to the tip of one full, white breast. It hung there, tantalizing him, teasing him, tormenting him. He wanted it to fall.

The chatter of his fireplace demons—damn them—rose in intensity, but not in volume. No words were discernible, only a massive, indistinct, noisy throbbing, just below the threshold of his awareness. The throbbing was in his head, pounding at his temples. No, not at his temples, for God's sake. There was no throbbing there. He looked down at his body and saw where the throbbing was centered.

He looked back through the peepholes. Could he get into the adjoining chamber and make the chemise fall? He labored through a plan of the practicalities. He knew he could not use the secret panel. Juliette would have returned to her chamber by now, and she would hear the ungodly noise. No good.

Juliette. What was he supposed to be doing with Juliette tonight? He couldn't remember. No matter. He couldn't think of Juliette when he was watching Elizabeth brush her hair and beckon to him.

His window. He could go from his window to hers, as he had done the night before. He glanced down at himself again. No, he was in no condition to romp on a ledge fifteen feet above the ground. He didn't have enough control for that.

Raucous encouragements of "Do it! Do it!" penetrated the demonic burble filling his ears, his body, his chamber.

He told his fireplace demons to shut up. They obeyed him no better this time than at any other.

He focused on the scene in the adjoining bedchamber.

He wanted that chemise to fall.

He was hooked, completely hooked, and she was reeling him in.

She leaned over and blew out the candle. As she did so, he glimpsed a very soft and round expanse of flesh tipped with an inviting rose. The adjoining chamber went dark.

He broke out in a sweat.

It was going to be a very long night.

Chapter Fifteen

When Elizabeth awoke the next morning, the new woman inside her was ready, even eager, to throw back her covers and face her fate, which meant facing Mac-Laurin. Her old, familiar self preferred to hide under the covers the day long for daring such a display, for daring to think that such a display would be enticing to a man. Her new self was strong, but her old self was well entrenched. She was momentarily paralyzed.

Seeking comfort and counsel, her hand automatically went to touch the locket at her breast. She grasped nothing: no locket, no mother, no protection—and no constraint. Her internal stalemate was broken. She threw back the covers, went to the window and drew the curtains. She was dismayed to see how high the sun had already risen, but if she hurried, she might be able to retrieve the locket she had dropped at the other end of the hallway before anyone else saw it.

She had no desire to wait for Mary to help her with her toilette, and to save time she donned the dress she had worn the day before, which was lying across her dressing-table chair. She laced it rapidly, smoothed out the wrinkles, then turned attention to her hair. She unbraided and repinned it in her usual style, but the disordered mass defied the pins, leaving some curls to dangle around her ears. She slipped on shoes and stockings, unlocked her chamber door, relocked it out in the hallway and stashed the key in her skirt pocket. She made haste down the very long corridor.

The walk this morning was much less frightening than it had been the evening before, but her heart was pounding equally hard. She was afraid to find the locket, for if she did, she would have to put it on again, and she feared for the loss of her new freedom. She was afraid not to find the locket, for that would mean that Gavin MacLaurin's ghost—but, of course, there had been no ghost—or someone else had taken it. She felt a childish panic to think of someone else setting eyes on her mother's image, as if they might look at it too much and use it up.

Even in the daytime the hallway was spooky, with creaking boards and shifting shadows. This morning it seemed to stretch endlessly, for it took her half of forever to come to the landing of the main staircase. She tried to remember how much farther beyond that point she had traveled the night before, but she could only begin to guess at the precise spot where she had stopped. She kept her eyes on the floor, anxious to catch any glimpse of gold.

She saw none. She went a good way down the corridor and retraced her steps slowly to the landing of the main staircase. Fortunately she encountered none of her fellow historians during the search and did not need to explain her actions. After quite a while, she gave up looking for the locket and made her way downstairs.

As she approached the last corner before the entrance to the banquet hall, she heard a group of historians ahead of her, out of sight. She recognized the voices of Godfrey MacQuarie and Brian Sinclair, among others. She expelled a sigh of relief to think that she was neither too early nor too late for breakfast. She was about to turn the corner and join her friends when she thought she heard one of them say the name Cameron.

She was not sure what caused her to conceal her presence, but instead of revealing herself, she edged closer to the corner. She held her breath and listened.

"Aye, then, ye've the right of it, Godfrey," Sinclair was saying. "'Tis Katherine Cameron, and a rare beauty she was."

Elizabeth's stomach twisted. Bumps rose on her skin. They were speaking of her aunt, her father's sister. A woman who had died just before she was born.

"Puir Joseph!" This from MacQuarie. He clucked his tongue sympathetically. "Distraught he was to have lost her. To have lost the both of them!"

Sinclair agreed. "'Tis no easy thing for a man to bury a beloved sister, then to lose a staunch and true wife."

MacQuarie clucked sympathetically again. "And Joseph was left to raise the wee bairn alone."

Elizabeth knew that her aunt Katherine and her mother had died within a month of one another. She knew that her father had had a difficult time when she had been an infant. What she did not know was why these men would be raising such a topic now. She reasoned that the air of Castle Cairn had a way of stirring up old ghosts, but still a splinter of unease scratched at a corner of her mind.

Other voices entered the discussion, murmuring fondly and sadly.

"A rare Highland lassie was sweet Katherine."

"A pity she went before her time."

"And her with such a promising match on the horizon."

"Ah, but to see her image again like this, so beautiful . . . 'Tis enough to bring back all the fine memories."

Elizabeth's heart froze. Her hands turned to ice. She noted, with perfect detachment, that she was still able to breathe and that her feet could move. She commanded them to take one step forward, then another, until she was around the corner.

She was hardly able to compose her lips into a smile of greeting, so stiff were her facial muscles. She attempted a "Good morning, gentlemen," but it came out more as a croak.

None of the men seemed to notice. They were all smiles and good humor. "Well, and if it isn't Mistress Elizabeth herself!" Sinclair exclaimed jovially. "We were just speaking of ye, lass!"

Brian Sinclair did not make a habit of reducing her to a lass, so Elizabeth did not call him on it. At the moment, however, she was unable either to contest it or to make a joke of it.

"And of the dead," MacQuarie added in hushed tones, while he and the others bowed their heads respectfully.

"Were you?" Elizabeth managed.

"You'll never guess what we found upstairs in the hallway!" MacQuarie continued, holding up a thin gold chain suspending a tiny jeweled case.

Elizabeth stared wordlessly at the locket dangling from MacQuarie's hand.

"An old locket carrying a picture of your aunt," he carried on cheerfully. "And to think that it appeared this morning out of nowhere, like magic!"

With great effort she spoke the simple words, "It's mine."

"Yers?" Sinclair queried. "We hadn't guessed that, had we? Nay, then! When Godfrey saw it in a most forgotten corner of the hallway upstairs, we speculated that the pretty thing must have been lying there for years and years!"

As if from a great distance, Elizabeth asked, "Why did you think that?"

"Because Katherine Cameron was such a favorite at Castle Cairn in the old days! She spent ever so much time here with your father and your mother, Mary, and with Gavin—rest his soul—and with Robbie, too! Most of the rest of us came in and out, but not so often. Och, now, we were a happy group!"

Elizabeth lifted her hand toward the necklace, but MacQuarie was not yet ready to relinquish it. He asked with a frown of puzzlement, "But what was yer locket doing lying in the hallway at the other end from yer chamber, I'm wondering?"

The lie came easily, as if she had scripted it beforehand. "I got lost last night. I took a wrong turn at the head of the stairs. The clasp had been giving me problems for some weeks now, but I never bothered to get it fixed. I noticed only this morning that my locket had fallen off, and of course, I had no idea where to look first."

MacQuarie inspected the clasp. "Nay, then, 'tis secure. 'Twas one of the links that was faulty. Looks to have been broken." He shrugged and said, "'Tis the way of it with an old piece like this, and so fragile!"

Elizabeth's hand shook slightly as the locket was dropped into her palm. She closed her fingers around it and jerked her arm down at her side.

Sinclair nodded. "Makes more sense that the locket belongs to one of the living." He patted her on the back and essayed a mild jest. "Ye've not got the look of a Cameron, Mistress Elizabeth, but ye've the loyalty of one! 'Tis a fine thing to honor yer aunt by wearing her image."

Elizabeth was wrestling with a slippery beast that menaced her with the knowledge that the image she held was not of her aunt but of her *mother*. She seized at the possibility that her fellow historians were wrestling the same beast of confusion.

Her voice broke a little when she ventured, "There would be no mistaking my aunt for my mother, now, would there? After all these years..." She instantly regretted the question, since it would be very odd for her to think there might be no difference between her mother's image and her aunt's.

Fortunately, her query was seen in the light of a challenge. Sinclair cocked a brow and said archly, "Testing us, are ye, Mistress Elizabeth? We may be an odd lot of aging historians with our heads in our books, but there's not a man among us who would confuse the black hair and eyes of Mary MacDonald with the green eyes and red-gold curls of Katherine Cameron!"

Voices rose to tease Elizabeth for her naughty test and to extol Katherine Cameron's charms. Kind words were said over the soul of Mary MacDonald, as well. On these happy choruses the historians ushered Elizabeth into the banquet hall, sat down as a group and continued their reminiscences of auld lang syne.

Elizabeth could only pick at her food and listen with half an ear. She knew that she should be listening most intently, in hopes of gleaning information about Katherine Cameron's life and death, but her mind was racing to catch up with the swift unfolding of events.

Two nights she had slept at Castle Cairn. Two mornings she had awakened with the feeling that she was leaving an old self behind and becoming a new woman. She had not realized, until this moment, just how new a woman she would really become. So new that she had ceased being the child of the respectable Mary MacDonald Cameron and had become the daughter of a very different woman, one who had not been so respectable. It was difficult to believe.

Or was it?

The occasion called for honesty, and she admitted to herself that it was not so difficult to believe. No, it was no more difficult to believe that she was the product of an illicit union than it had been to realize the truth that Gabriel Beverly was Allegra's father. To know that she herself was a love child—be honest!—a *bastard* child, like Allegra, instantly resolved the ragged ends of her life. Knowledge of her birth made interpretable those disconnected events in which her neat historian's mind had previously discerned no pattern.

But another part of her had always known she was a child without a name, and it had not taken much for her to know it. Like bits of grit that bother oysters, she had sifted the tiniest clues here and there over the years, to produce this finished pearl of understanding today: her too-strict upbringing; her father's refusal to discuss anything of that painful period in his life when he had lost both a sister and a wife; the need to keep private the image in her locket; her peculiar difficulties in finding a respectable marriage partner; her desire to protect Allegra's good name at all costs; her hunger for the secret details of forgotten history; her passion for genealogy, which mapped the bloodlines of belonging; the feeling, ill defined but bred into her bones, that she did not quite belong.

Ye've not got the look of a Cameron, Brian Sinclair had told her. She had always known that, but she didn't favor the woman in the locket, either, and it had always troubled her that she did not, apparently, have the look of the MacDonalds. It came as a curious relief to know that the woman in the locket had been a Cameron, too. So, whose look did she have?

It was easy to reimagine her mother, for all she had to do was transfer a new name and a new history to a miniature image she had worn since she was twelve. But what of her father?

If she was not Mary MacDonald's daughter, then she was not Joseph Cameron's, either.

This realization was more difficult to assimilate. Joseph Cameron, for all his strict ways, had been her flesh-and-blood parent. He had given her his name and a home. He had cared for her. And he loved her. She was sure of it. To be unable to truly call him "father" was more than difficult. It was painful.

She felt as if she had been turned inside out, and in the turning, her most intimate secret had become known to herself. With her next breath came the question: how widely was her secret shared?

She cast a glance at her fellow historians. They were still eating and talking, seemingly oblivious to her preoccupation. They had known Katherine Cameron, but they-who-knew-bloodlines-so-well had never betrayed to her the slightest hint that she was the daughter of Katherine and not of Joseph. She was encouraged to think that Joseph Cameron had kept his sister's secret close all these years. She even had a remarkably good idea how he had done it, for the story he had circulated of her birth was not so very different than the story she herself had devised concerning Allegra's.

Elizabeth knew that Mary MacDonald was supposed to have suffered a difficult pregnancy and died from childbirth. Elizabeth knew that Katherine was supposed to have remained faithfully at her sister-in-law's side, tending her until she herself died of an unexpected and unexplained fever. Elizabeth now guessed that Mary MacDonald had been confined with a true illness while Katherine had increased. If both women had been shielded from the view of all but the most trusted servants, no one would have been the wiser about the exact date of Elizabeth's birth.

Elizabeth glanced down at the broken locket she had tucked under the lip of her plate. She felt naked not wearing it. Her old self thought the nakedness shameful and needful of covering. Her new self sensed the power of defiance in nakedness, but the feeling was too new to be experienced as anything more than a mild surge before Lord Mure was calling out the approaching start of the second day's meeting of the Royal Historical Society.

Chairs were pushed back from the table. People were rising to file out. Elizabeth rose with everyone else. Snatching her locket and slipping it into her skirt pocket where it chinked gently against her key, she was vaguely aware that someone had stepped up behind her.

During the breakfast hour she had paid no attention to the comings and goings in the banquet hall. She had not noticed whether MacLaurin was in the room. She had spared no thought for how she would behave when next she saw him, but she thought of that horrible, desirable moment now and braced herself.

She stood and turned and looked straight into the face of Lady Juliette Michael. She was at once relieved that she did not yet have to confront MacLaurin and alarmed by the cast of delicate calculation lurking in the shadow of the older woman's pleasant smile. Almost without realizing it, Elizabeth slid her hand into her pocket and grasped the broken locket.

"Shall we walk to the library together?" Lady Michael invited.

Elizabeth saw no way and, indeed, had no reason to decline. "That would be a pleasure, Lady Michael."

"Juliette, if you please, and I shall call you Elizabeth—" she paused "—so that we may dispense with the formalities in order to become better acquainted, as I mentioned to you last night."

"Yes, you did."

Juliette grasped Elizabeth's arm and linked it companionably through hers. She smiled a very lovely smile. "I hope, in fact, that we shall become good friends."

Could she take such a statement at face value? She suddenly remembered that MacLaurin had said something the night before about going to Lady Michael's room to search the fourth box of books. Perhaps MacLaurin had paid a late-night visit to Juliette's chamber. Perhaps he had missed Elizabeth's siren-song display. Perhaps she had deluded herself that MacLaurin would have been interested, had he seen it. Was Juliette now going to claim MacLaurin as her property and hint Elizabeth away?

Elizabeth decided to force the issue. "I hope so, too," she said. "When you arrived two nights ago, I had it in mind to help you unpack, since you arrived so late. But, precisely because it was so late, I thought it better not to bother you." She hoped her expression was entirely innocent. "Do you need any help now? I know that, in addition to bringing your own belongings, you carried a heavy load of boxes of books."

Juliette's expression was wry. "Those boxes!" she exclaimed lightly. "Everyone has been interested in them!"

They had left the banquet hall and were heading out into the corridor to follow the crowd to the library tower. Elizabeth had not seen any sign of MacLaurin, but she noted that His Grace was part of a group walking a short way ahead.

"Everyone?" Elizabeth queried.

Juliette laughed. "Well, not everyone, and mainly our host. But I'm through with the lot of them, because Robbie hauled away the last box this morning, thank goodness! But he came at an ungodly hour, and I'll not soon forgive him for that."

"The last box?"

Juliette sighed. "I made rapid work of unpacking the first three, but I didn't get to the fourth until last night." She glanced at her companion. "It was tedious work, all in all, and I could have used your help. I'm sorry I didn't ask when I left you at your chamber door last night."

Elizabeth interpreted that to mean that Juliette had spent the evening alone. But what of the night? She replied, "I'm sorry I didn't offer, but I confess that the idea didn't occur to me, given the circumstances."

"Because we were with Edmund?" Juliette's tone was artfully casual. "Well, if you had offered, I would have known just how to handle him." She squeezed Elizabeth's arm playfully. "I knew just how to handle him, anyway." She paused, again artfully. "If you know what I mean."

Elizabeth looked at Juliette Michael and saw a woman who far outstripped her for experience and allure. She thought of the locket in her pocket and of her newfound sense of defiance and freedom. She saw an opportunity to learn how to control that defiance and freedom, how to use it to good effect.

Elizabeth said slowly, "No, I don't know what you mean, and I wish you would tell me—as a friend."

The study of Juliette's expression figured as Elizabeth's first, tricky lesson in powerful womanhood. The older woman said, "I will tell you, then, my dear, that Edmund followed me here. He had not originally intended to come to Castle Cairn. He evidently changed his mind when he attended a soiree at my home in London on the eve of my departure last week and discovered that I was on my way north. It seems he wishes to make up to me his earlier . . . cruelty."

Juliette intimated, then, her desire to make His Grace suffer and her plan to accomplish that worthy end. Elizabeth listened and learned more, perhaps, than Juliette intended. She knew that she had just been firmly slapped, as if she were an overinquisitive girl playing at her mother's dressing table. Her attention, however, was not captured by the fact that both His Grace and MacLaurin had been declared off-limits. Rather she was more curious to learn how to compose such an expression that was both caressing and dismissive, seductive and commanding.

Chapter Sixteen

MacLaurin was up and out and diving into the bracing waters of a Highland burn before the sun was up. Refreshed but not relieved of the curse that Castle Cairn had put on him the night before, he returned to the stone monster to carry out his original mission.

He was in luck. After stopping in the kitchens to feed a hunger that could not be filled with food, he made his way to the library. The hour was early, and he guessed that most of the guests were still straggling down to breakfast. On the tower stair landing and to one side of the iron-studded door to the library, he saw an empty box. He stepped into the library and found his uncle fussing over the arrangement of the books on display, obviously making room for all the new volumes he had unpacked this morning.

MacLaurin crossed to the table and greeted his uncle, who turned briefly to greet him in return. Only a faint whiskey-hazed blear remained to shadow the older man's eyes.

"Finished with the last of them?" MacLaurin queried casually, nodding at the books.

"Aye," his uncle replied, "and I plan to make time for the formal presentation of my new acquisitions this morning before the sessions begin."

MacLaurin reached out and selected a book. He held it between his hands a moment and stroked the leather binding. "A fine piece of workmanship," he commented. "It must have cost you a pretty penny."

His uncle straightened and said curtly, "'Tis none of your business, Ian MacLaurin, how much my books cost."

MacLaurin opened the book in his hands, thumbed the uncut pages and shook it lightly by the spine before returning it to its place on the table.

"Indeed, it's not," he agreed amiably. He picked up another book and subjected it to the same treatment. "I'm impressed, rather, by the cumulative effect of so much beauty." He continued to pick up books here and there, trying to establish a system of searching that looked random. He had no way of distinguishing which books had been added to the display this morning.

"Are ye, now?" his uncle asked, frowning slightly as if trying to determine whether his nephew was speaking the truth.

MacLaurin smiled. "I can't keep my hands off them," he said, holding up the latest book he had chosen. He peered at the spine and read, "Rupert's *Factual History of Egypt and Abyssinia.*" He opened it, admired the frontispiece, thumbed its pages, found nothing and put it back.

"Rupert's a fine historian," his uncle informed him, "and he's a member of our society by correspondence."

MacLaurin had to find a way to continue his search without rousing his uncle's suspicions. He began to read aloud the titles engraved in gold on the leather spines as he picked them up and flipped their pages. After a half dozen books, he said, "You told me last night that not all the books you bought were history books."

His uncle's glance was sharp. "I did?" Then, with a trace of apprehension, he added, "What else did I tell you?"

"That Lady Michael knows the good bookstores in London."

An oddly satisfied look crossed his uncle's features before he schooled them to blandness. "Aye, that she does. Anything else?"

"Not much else on that subject." MacLaurin kept books passing through his hands. "I'd be interested to know which are the ones that were purchased at those good bookstores. I gather they're not the history books."

His uncle hesitated. Then he reached over, selected a book from the far side of the display and handed it to his nephew.

MacLaurin opened it to the title page and read, "*Oroonoko* by Aphra Behn. Published in the year of our Lord 1688."

"It's the fictional story of an enslaved African prince," his uncle said. "The other literary selections purchased from the same bookseller are on this side of the table, as well."

MacLaurin took mental note of his stopping place in the middle of the table before he turned his attention to the books at the far end. He handled a number of Behn volumes, which included several plays and collections of poetry. MacLaurin was not entirely convinced that these were the books from the shops Lady Michael had recommended. What was certain was that they held no loose document.

His uncle finished his fussing, then announced his intention to descend to the banquet hall to call everyone to the second day's session. His uncle quit the library, leaving the door open and MacLaurin alone with the entire contents of the four boxes spread out before him.

MacLaurin began at one end of the table and worked his way to the other end. He checked rapidly but thoroughly each book on the table. He even rechecked those several dozen volumes he had already handled. By the time he reached the last volume he was empty-handed and puzzled.

He began all over again, this time looking carefully in the pouches created by the sheaves of the books whose pages had not yet been cut, in case the document had gotten wedged. Unfortunately, he was not able to perform this painstaking procedure on more than three or four books before he heard the echo of animated voices drifting up through the library tower from the connecting hallway.

With a sinking feeling he realized he'd never be able to reexamine the rest of the books on the table in the next few minutes. "Eighty books," he murmured in disgust, "not twenty, not fifty, but eighty. My uncle had to order eighty."

He surveyed the table as a whole and felt hope stir. Eighty? Were, in fact, all eighty on display?

He swiftly counted the books once, twice, thrice, and arrived each time at seventy-four.

He whirled and stared at the wide swath of paneling that rose from floor to ceiling at the front end of the library. He reimagined the secret room that must lie hidden behind that panel. His hopes rose. He had a strong intuition that his uncle had come early to the library to store those six books in his hiding place. Those six books that were not history books. Those six books that were not, he would guess, especially literary. But what kind of books were they? And why should they be hidden? More to the point: was it possible that Bev's document had been stuffed into one of those books and that his uncle did not yet know it?

If his uncle made a practice of using that secret room, then the sliding mechanism of the panel would be in good working order. He might just have time to slip in and out of the chamber before—

There was no time. The group was in the stairwell and fast approaching. He would do well simply to take up his position at the edge of the table and bide his time until he could return tonight. In the meantime, he would resign himself to the tedium of the day's proceedings. At least he would be content with the knowledge that if he couldn't get to the final six books, no one else could, either.

Devonshire arrived in the first group, was the very first one to cross the threshold, and upon entering, cut his gaze immediately to the trestle table. MacLaurin was mighty interested and mighty satisfied to see Devonshire's expression of surprised displeasure when he saw who stood there.

MacLaurin smiled pleasantly, causing a wave of suppressed irritation to ripple Devonshire's expression. MacLaurin folded his arms across his chest and leaned against the table. Devonshire flicked him with a flinty glance and made his way to the rows of chairs. MacLaurin's smile turned into a grin, for he was sure of it now: Devonshire wanted the same thing he did.

Toward the end of the procession Elizabeth Cameron entered on the arm of none other than Juliette Michael. His grin faded. Elizabeth glanced at the table, then glanced away. He could not see her expression, and that was just as well, because he wanted to have as little to do with her as possible. Juliette's expression was, on the other hand, entirely readable. He was sure to hear how he had stood her up the night before.

Before everyone sat down, his uncle invited them to come forward to behold the complete collection of his latest acquisitions. He encouraged his guests to browse for a quarter hour before the society was called to session.

MacLaurin stepped aside to allow access to his end of the table and kept his eye negligently on the browsers for any chance paper that might fall from one of the books. At the same time he was able to note that Devonshire made a point of not approaching the table. Instead, he was engaged in what looked to be a rather interesting tête-à-tête with Juliette.

Just as MacLaurin was returning his attention to the people milling around the display table, he felt an accursed wave of awareness ruffling the hairs on his neck. He knew that she was standing next to him before he actually saw her. Sure enough, he looked down at his side to see Elizabeth affecting great interest in the books before her.

She did not look up at him. Instead, with her head bent as if she were intently reading, she whispered, "Well?"

He replied in an undertone, "Well, what?"

Still without looking up, she whispered, "Did you have any success?"

"That might depend on what you mean by success," he answered.

She looked up then, startled, and he stared back at her. She looked no different than she had the day before, but after last night it was impossible not to see her differently. It was impossible not to *feel* differently about her, and this new feeling carried the punch of a cannonball of desire. He knew that his potent desire for her had been induced by the mischievous night air of Castle Cairn, but knowing such did not diminish her impact on him even now, in broad daylight, staring up at him wide-eyed, surprised and suspicious. Knowing such did, however, give him the strength to withstand the impact.

He stood there before her and renewed his resolve not to succumb to the lure of his boyhood home. Castle Cairn may have taught him everything he needed to know about ingenious mechanisms, but it had also been determined to quench his love of life, to kill the spirit of invention that made him live. It had been bad enough when his father was alive to spread his miasma throughout the very castle air, sucking MacLaurin in so that it had taken extraordinary effort on his part to get expelled. Now, with his father's restless ghost haunting the premises, the air was even more deadly, and he had never before encountered such a powerful trap as Elizabeth Cameron. The clever spirits of Castle Cairn might have brought her here to catch him, once and for all, but he was determined not to get caught.

"I think you know what I mean," she said. "What I want is a straight answer."

He gave it to her, straight. "I shall let you know if I need your help."

She favored him with an assessing glance that robbed him of breath. Then she moved away.

His breath came back, and he was satisfied. Tonight he would retrieve the document, and tomorrow he would be quit of this depressing wreck and never come back. Before he left, he'd find a way to let Elizabeth Cameron

know, of course, that he had the document safe. And
he'd be sure to let Devonshire know that he'd won.

Deciding to put Allegra's well-being before her own,
Elizabeth had steeled herself for the encounter with
MacLaurin. She had imagined a variety of scenarios. If
MacLaurin had not seen her outrageous display—and she
had no reason to be entirely sure that he had—he would
treat her exactly as he had the day before, that is, with
trifling enticement—to which she was, admittedly, not
immune. If he had seen it, he might intimate either that
he scorned her attempt to attract him or that he was willing to take advantage of what she had been freely offering him.

But she had not expected him to throw up a high wall,
keeping her out, and that was exactly what he did when
he dismissed her with the words *I shall let you know if I
need your help.* He had tried to dismiss her with those
very words in the Fleurise Garden.

She was insulted and confused, even a little humiliated, if only in her own eyes, for thinking that she might
have caught his attention the night before and held it.

She took her seat in the front row next to Lord Mure
and settled in to the morning's session. She could hardly
listen to the various treatises, for her mental energies were
harnessed to a team of disturbing new questions that were
galloping out of her control. Since she had come to Castle Cairn, the equilibrium she had so carefully main-
tained all these years had been stripped from her
emotional center, just as her locket had been ripped from
her neck.

Her locket. She slipped her hand into her pocket. She
smoothed her thumb across the flat underside of the tiny
case, then harped it across the jeweled ridges of the front.

Instead of feeling the weight and urgency of disturbing questions, she felt that nakedness again, that lightening of the burden of history, that glorious sense of starting afresh.

She thought of her mother. Then she thought of Juliette Michael and decided that she was greedy to claim both men. She thought of MacLaurin's rude dismissal and decided that she would not allow him to dismiss her so easily. The morning passed. The midday break came and went. The afternoon plodded interminably but finally came to its trudging end. Many people remained in the library, milling about, extending discussions. One by one they left. Elizabeth was determined to stay.

So, too, was MacLaurin, for he kept his position at the end of the display table. She made her way to the table and, beginning with the very first book at his end of the table, she began to pick them up, one by one, and look through each one carefully.

She had made her way through a half dozen books when MacLaurin demanded in low, curt tones, "What do you think you are doing, Mistress Cameron?"

Without looking up, she replied, "I think you know what I am doing." She put one book down and picked up the next.

"I do, and that is what troubles me."

She glanced at him briefly, without interest. "Oh?" She returned her attention to the book in her hand.

"You are being obvious. Anyone with an interest in the books similar to ours will guess what you are about."

She was unimpressed by his censure. She took a step away from him, moving down the table. "What is obvious, sir," she said to the book in her hand, "is that you have not recovered the document."

"How do you know?"

"Because you would have left the library by now," she replied, "and quite possibly have left Castle Cairn. And speaking of being obvious, since you were the first one in the library this morning, anyone with an interest in the books similar to ours, as you have put it, would have guessed you had come to check the books from the fourth box. So I conclude—either the document is not here, or your search was insufficient."

She took yet another step away from him, and he had to close the distance between them if he wished to continue speaking to her without raising his voice. She felt his hesitation, but then he moved from the corner of the table and followed her progress down the table.

"Will you know which conclusion is correct by the time you reach the end of the table?" he asked.

"I already know that the document is not here."

"So why are you risking this obvious action?"

"Because you, sir, are not willing simply to tell me what you did or did not find. This is my way of verifying my guess that the document isn't here. My further guess is that you know where it is."

"What makes you guess that?"

She paused and smiled at him, without warmth. "Because, if you didn't know where it is, you would have left the library by now. So I'm guessing that it's here somewhere."

"You've a talent for answering your own questions, it seems." He did not mean it as a compliment.

She did not take it as one. "Ah, but my real question is, why aren't you owning up to what you know?" Her gaze was direct. "I thought we were in this together."

"You've attempted to hoodwink me with that position from the beginning."

"Hoodwink you?"

"When it comes to not owning up," he said, "you've kept back your fair share of information."

"I have?"

"I wonder if, for instance, you mean to tell me why you have come to Castle Cairn?"

She wrinkled her brow. "To attend the summer meeting of the Royal Historical Society, of course."

"But why now, for the first time," he pressed, "and against your father's wishes?"

She mentally replayed the chain of events that led from receiving a mysterious packet of old letters to discovering the real name of her mother. What had begun as a brave bit of disobedience had ended as nothing less than the search for her identity. Did she wish to tell Mac-Laurin that? Did she dare?

At her silence, she saw an expression of satisfaction settle across his face. She took the offensive. "You haven't quite owned up to your motives for being here, either."

"You know why I've come."

"Yes, of course, but you have not explained exactly why you are performing this heroic favor for Lieutenant Beverly—and so much against your wishes, I would say! Is it that he saved your life?"

He answered readily, "Bev saved something more important than my life."

"More important?"

"My hands."

She looked down at his long fingers, which he flexed. She looked up at him, a question in her eyes.

"We were on a campaign in the Spanish Netherlands. I was charging a cannon. I had carelessly scooped several pounds of powder into my bare hands while holding a lit cannon match between my teeth. The match began to sputter, showering sparks downward. Bev was standing nearby and happened to witness my folly. In that instant he picked up a bucket of water and doused the shooting sparks before they hit the powder. He saved a good many of my fingers, if not all of them.''

He continued, ''It's one thing for a man to lose his life on the field of battle, and I could have died all those years ago with few regrets. It's another thing for a man to have to live with no means of surviving on his own. I make my living with my hands. I would not have wanted to live without them.''

He had answered her question honestly. She was forced to answer his just as honestly. She was forestalled when an all-too-familiar voice said behind her, ''Everyone has left the library now, Mistress Cameron. May I escort you downstairs?''

Chapter Seventeen

Elizabeth turned to His Grace. They had played this scene before, but this time she was almost glad to see him. She also knew just what to do.

"No, thank you, Your Grace," she said politely. "I'm not through here yet."

"Not through?" His Grace inquired, raising a quizzical brow.

His tone and his expression chilled her, but she kept her course. "I wish to become acquainted with every single new book that Lord Mure has acquired, Your Grace. Since I am only halfway through my examination, I cannot ask you to wait for me, and in any case, Your Grace, MacLaurin has agreed to keep me company."

His Grace's fine gray eyes focused on her momentarily with a glimmer that might have been admiration but, then again, might not. What he permitted himself to reveal on his face was an expression of only mild surprise. She did not know whether his surprise stemmed from the statement of her intention to search the books, her refusal of his escort or her expressed association with MacLaurin. She did guess, however, that His Grace would neither insist she accompany him nor risk being rebuffed twice, and he did not prove her wrong.

"Very well, Mistress Cameron," His Grace said with a bow. He turned smartly on his heel and left her, without acknowledging MacLaurin's existence.

Elizabeth turned back to the table and to her search through the books. She registered His Grace's exit by the ever-dimming sound of his steps retreating across the polished parquet and down the tower stairs. Even after the echo of his footsteps had disappeared, she felt the room quivering with his presence. Or was the quivering emanating from MacLaurin?

MacLaurin said sardonically, "And what was that all about, if you would be so good to tell me, for once, what *your* motives are? You might as well have told Devonshire that you were looking for the document."

"Then I might well have been telling him nothing that he did not already know," she said, "and I have discovered that with His Grace, it is better to be bold."

"Bold?"

She knew it, then, from the tone of his voice and the light that blazed in his blue eyes. He had seen her last night through the peepholes when she had been bold.

"Yes, bold," she repeated, and the very sound of it emboldened her further. "In any case, we don't know His Grace's motives for being here, do we? As recently as yesterday you thought he may have come merely to effect the transfer of land from the MacLaurins to the MacPhersons. For all *I* know, he followed Juliette Michael here in order to win her back."

"You have that backward," MacLaurin said. "My uncle told me last night that Juliette agreed to transport the books only after she discovered that Devonshire was traveling north. If I believe my uncle's tale, it was only a coincidence that Devonshire happened to stop here and thus save Juliette the trip to Edinburgh. And you told me yesterday that the various coincidences were too strong for Devonshire *not* to have come here for the document.''

Elizabeth considered that. ''Then the best we can say is that we don't know whether His Grace has only one motive for being here.''

''So might we all have more than one motive,'' MacLaurin said, ''which brings us back to where we were before Devonshire's interruption.''

Elizabeth merely arched a brow and picked up the next book on the table.

''Yes, Mistress Cameron, I want to know *your* motive for choosing to come to Castle Cairn now, for the first time, and in apparent defiance of your father.''

The words *defiance* and *father* bolstered her boldness. She was racing through the books now. When she opened the last one she said, ''I'm finished and—'' she thumbed it rapidly ''—as expected, I found nothing.'' She put the book down. ''I will be happy to tell you, sir, why I chose to come here when you decide to tell me where you think the document really is.''

He did not look prepared to tell her that, and thus they had arrived at an impasse. MacLaurin made no move to leave the library, and Elizabeth was determined not to leave him in the library alone. They stood staring at one another long enough for her to realize that she no longer cared about the document. Neither made a move until a voice called out their names.

Elizabeth looked away from MacLaurin's blue blaze to see Lord Mure's arrival at the library door.

''His Grace told me that several people had lingered in the library and that the door was still open!'' his lordship said jovially. ''Come along, now,'' he cajoled. ''I'm wanting to lock up!''

Elizabeth crossed to the library door with MacLaurin close behind her, and his lordship locked up. The three returned to the main wing of the castle engaged in a conversation whose burden was carried primarily by Lord Mure, seemingly oblivious to the storm cloud that hung between Elizabeth and MacLaurin.

MacLaurin left them at the first opportunity. To Elizabeth's great satisfaction, Lord Mure told his nephew that he expected to see him in the banquet hall for supper in half an hour and that he had better dress for the occasion. This meant, to Elizabeth, that MacLaurin would have no time to return to the library on his own before supper. She guessed, in fact, that he did not intend to return until the night was far advanced.

When supper was over and the guests were repairing to the receiving room, Elizabeth had her plan in place. She sought out Lord Mure and explained to him that she was anxious about delivering her treatise before the society tomorrow morning. She said that she needed the keys to the library so that she could check several of her dates about which she was not quite certain. Lord Mure reassured her that her scholarship had always been impeccable and tried to dissuade her from such labor. However, her smile was so pleading, as if she were wretched with nerves, that he relented and handed her the keys.

She thanked him with a convincing rush of relief. "I'm embarrassed to be checking my facts so late, so don't tell anyone where I've gone, I beg you!"

His lordship replied, "I won't. But don't spend too long there, my dear, and tire yerself. Ye passed the day in the library and will spend the next there as well, so return to us soon. Ye're fixing to overwork yerself."

She made her way to the library tower staircase without making one false turn and without encountering one menacing ghost. She decided that her inner fierceness must have radiated a shield around her and kept them away, because she had actually been daring one to confront her. She had not even lit the candle she carried, in hopes of encountering one and facing it down.

She mounted the stairs, opened the wide door on its well-oiled hinges and left the keys in the lock. She paused and shivered with the thrill of what she hoped to discover. She went straight to the cabinet of drawers near the display table of books. Fortunately, the light from the full moon was flooding through the tower windows and was strong enough that she did not need to light her candle to read.

She placed her candle and flint atop the cabinet, then bent until she found the drawer marked Genealogies and opened it. She withdrew a thick stack of note cards and began to read the indications of the exact placement of the individual volumes on the bookshelves, which were numbered by section and row. She began with the first card, whose heading read MacDonald of Glengarry, noted the numbers, proceeded to MacDonald of Keppoch, then MacDougal, MacDuff, MacGillivray, and so on, until she found the names without the Mac, beginning with Brodie and ending with Urquhart. Judging by the ascending numbers, the genealogies were arranged in alphabetical order.

She put the cards back in the drawer, then took her candle and flint from the top of the cabinet. She moved toward the closest section of floor-to-ceiling shelves and began to find the numbers of the sections in the moonlit glint of the various brass plaques. She needed only find the correct section and begin at the beginning of the row until she came to the volumes she wanted. Would she begin first with MacLaurin to look for names likely to be associated with her mysterious letters? Or would she begin with Cameron to see if the name Katherine Cameron filled the line above her own name and birthdate? She wondered whether anyone had dared supply the name of her father.

She squinted hard in the dark and identified the proper number of the row she wanted. She was glad that it was waist-high and handy and that she did not have to climb the corkscrew stairs to the balcony above her. Unfortunately, the moonlight did not reach far enough into these shadows to be able to read without the aid of her candle. She had wanted to avoid lighting it, and when she tried to light it now, her hands were trembling.

At last she succeeded, and with heart beating and palms sweating she raised her candle to read the spines of the fat, old genealogies and read—yes!—MacDonald. Her eyes skipped to MacGillivray, became greedy and ran to MacKinnon, then MacKintosh, MacLachlan, MacLean, MacLennan. Her eyes and heart stopped at MacLeod. She had missed MacLaurin. She reversed her review and again saw no MacLaurin. She looked past the Macs, in the next row down. The volumes began with Brodie, Bruce, Buchanan and were followed by Campbell and Clelland. No Cameron. She quickly scanned the second row, which ended as it should with Urquhart.

Elizabeth clung to a hope that the volumes had been misshelved. She looked at each volume in turn, not rushing herself this time, looking for any book out of order. Then she looked in the rows above the genealogies, below them and on either side. Nothing. No MacLaurin. And no Cameron.

She considered the possibility that the MacLaurin volume might have a place of honor somewhere else in the library, but she did not want to return to the cabinet of book cards to check its precise location. Instead, she was more interested to discover why the Cameron volume was missing. She wondered whether Brian Sinclair had ordered that clan volumes with entries for bastard children be removed from the open shelves in order to protect the people involved, if they were still alive.

In order to test her theory, she decided to see whether the volume MacMillan was on the shelf. She was somewhat surprised to find it just where it was supposed to be. She opened to the last pages of entries and quickly found the name Elspeth MacMillan, to which no marriage line was attached. She was even more surprised to read the name of Elspeth's son entered directly under hers: "Hugh, born January 21, 1711, called MacMillan." She looked to the right of Elspeth's name and was downright shocked to read the name of the father entered as Thomas MacGillivray.

She closed the volume and put it back, having learned more than she bargained for. She had discovered not only that bastard children received their proper entries but also that MacLaurin had been wrongly accused of fathering Elspeth's child. Then she realized, with a wry twist of humor, that there would be no volumes on the shelves if all that had something to hide were removed.

She knew that each family had a scribe who was responsible for coming to Castle Cairn to keep the genealogies current. She knew that the society took no interest in events of the past fifty years. She knew that a volume could be absent for many reasons. Still, she could not rid herself of the notion that its absence had something to do with her.

She took a step back, stared at the neat, mysteriously incomplete set of genealogies and wondered where the Cameron was and why it was missing. So deeply engrossed was she in frustrated musings on these questions that she was not aware that someone else had entered the library until he was almost at her side.

She felt his presence like a breeze grazing over her skin, warming her, disturbing her. She turned toward him. He remained a step outside the small glow of her candle. She guessed that he would not step into the circle of her light, so she blew the candle out. She would be dressed in shadows as dark as his own.

Standing before him, hardly able to see him, she assimilated the unexpected truth that he was not the father of a bastard child. It struck her odd, even tantalizing, to realize that he was, if not quite virtuous, then at least respectable. It was equally odd, equally tantalizing, to think that he had not been far off when he had mistaken her for the mother of a bastard child. She knew now that she was not at all respectable; and the night before, when she had brushed her hair and let her chemise fall, she had finished with being virtuous.

"Well, well," he said softly.

"Surprised to see me here?" she asked.

"Uncle told everyone that you had retired to your chambers to give a last look at your treatise."

"And you believed him?"

He did not respond.

She smiled. "You must have believed him enough," she said with satisfaction, "to have come here on your own, imagining me to be out of your way."

"Find what you were looking for?"

"No," she said, "but I found other things, equally worthy of my interest. But don't let me stop you. You've come for a purpose. Please proceed with your business.''

He was silent. She had spent enough time with him in the dark to understand the quality of his silence. She had goaded him, and he was resisting her, just as he had resisted her when she had approached him this morning. This time his resistance felt more flexible, more resilient. Less repellent. More attractive. Stronger. More challenging.

"Sure, now, Mistress Cameron," he said, "I'll be pleased to proceed with my business when you tell me yours. I'm more familiar with the library than you, perhaps, and I know the stacks well enough to know we're standing in front of the genealogies. What did you find there that was worthy of your interest?"

He took one step toward her, then another, so that he was standing right before her. The moonlight streaming in the windows pooled far behind him, giving a shimmering glow to his outline. She could feel his breath on her hair. She raised her face to him. She felt his eyes upon her. They had stripped her down to her chemise.

She was glad that the locket was in her pocket and not around her neck where it would delicately restrain her words. "I found, among other things, the entry for Elspeth MacMillan."

She could feel more than see his smile. "Surprised?"

"At least as much as you might be if you checked the entry under Allegra MacDonald and read the name of her mother."

His head bent closer to hers. "I might be less surprised than you think by the name of the mother."

Two desires coursed through her, one to find the Clan Cameron genealogy, the other to kiss him. Both were strong, unable to cancel the other, so they merged, and their merging made her crafty. "Let's look together for the name of Allegra's mother in the Cameron genealogy."

"And then you'll tell me why you've come to Castle Cairn and to the library this night?"

"Yes," she breathed, "and you'll tell me where you think the document is hidden."

"All right, then," he said. He touched his lips to hers, sealing their bargain with a kiss. But in the kiss, he let her feel his continuing resistance, as if denying the possibility that her kiss would affect him. "Open the Cameron volume."

"I can't," she said.

"Why not?"

"Because it isn't here."

"Where is it?"

"Maybe the same place as the document," she suggested provocatively.

He placed his hands on her shoulders, drew her against him and kissed her fully. Her arms went around his neck, and she kept tenuous hold on the candle and flint in her hands. She kissed him back, yielding to his demand and her desire.

"You've told me nothing so far," he said.

"But the truth," she whispered.

"You think I'll fall for such a ploy?"

She loved playing the temptress. "You did last night."

His embrace became more impassioned. He put his lips to her neck. His hand went to the breast she had previously bared to his view. She surrendered herself to the luxurious pleasures of his scent, of his kiss, of his touch, of his desire. She was in a garden, surrounded by roses, breathing enchanted air and drinking from an enchanted well. So this was the Fleurise Garden. She licked the drops of moisture that lingered on her loved one's lips and was sure that she had never tasted anything so refreshing, so seductive.

He broke the kiss long enough to ask, his voice low and rough, "You think I don't know why you're here?"

Her lips curved against his in a smile. "Tell me."

He never had a chance, for once again, Lord Mure's voice could be heard calling to her from the library door, "Mistress Elizabeth! Are ye there, Mistress Elizabeth?"

Chapter Eighteen

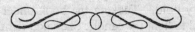

Elizabeth turned and saw a wave of lantern light splash across the threshold. Standing deep in the shadows, she knew that they could not yet be seen.

She raised on tiptoe and whispered into MacLaurin's ear, "I'm not going to let you remain behind in the library without me."

"I know," he returned, just as softly. She tried to move away, but he did not release her. Instead, he asked, "What's the subject of your treatise?"

"The subject of my— ? Why on earth do you ask?"

"Because you might not wish to be caught in front of the genealogies," he replied.

She saw his point.

"Mistress Elizabeth?" his lordship called out again.

She broke the embrace with MacLaurin, then groped for his hand. She pulled him away from the genealogies, walked around the semicircle of book stacks until she could delay no longer in replying. She fumbled with the flint and said, "Over here, your lordship!" In an aside to MacLaurin, she asked, "What section are we at now?"

"Farming," he whispered back.

Under her breath she moaned, "Oh, dear." She reached out and withdrew a book at random.

"How do you plan to get yourself out of this one, Mistress Cameron?" he asked.

Although his question was barely audible, she felt the air crackle with challenge. "I plan to be bold, sir," she returned softly and in a way that invited him to kiss her again. "Very bold." Tucking the book under her arm, she managed to light the candle. She said brightly, "I was checking my facts for tomorrow, as you know, your lordship, and MacLaurin was so good to assist me."

The lantern light swam closer. At her comment, his lordship paused, then inquired, "Ye again, Ian MacLaurin?"

"Always," MacLaurin replied, stepping into the pool of Elizabeth's candlelight.

"The library was completely dark when I entered just now," his lordship remarked, "and I was worried that something untoward had happened to ye, Mistress Elizabeth."

"The moment before you arrived I had inadvertently blown out the candle," she replied in soothing tones. "We were so absorbed in trying to relight it that we did not immediately answer you, I'm afraid."

The explanation was weak, but his lordship did not take issue with it. At least, not in words. He had come close enough now that she could see worry and skepticism ruffling his brow. He chose, however, to stay with the explanation at hand.

"I'm glad I came to fetch ye, then," his lordship said, "since ye're determined to overtax yerself with work. Seemingly, I need to keep ye and my nephew—" here his voice twisted "—from ruining yer eyesight."

"You're considerate, Uncle."

"Well, 'twas His Grace who noticed Mistress Elizabeth's prolonged absence," his lordship admitted, "and expressed his concern that she be looked after."

His Grace was unusually solicitous today, Elizabeth thought. "You needn't have worried, however," she said pleasantly. She began to walk toward her host and prodded MacLaurin to move toward him, too, with a determined poke in his back. "You see that I am well attended by your nephew, and I have found just the book I was looking for."

She held it up to him and noticed with dismay that the volume was entitled *Farming at Dunachton*. It was not a book that would inspire her interest, nor could it be used as a reference in her treatise on the morrow.

Fortunately his lordship was not interested in the book. He said merely, "Well, come along, then. If ye're needing to use it, I invite ye to take it out of the library. For the night only!" He gestured for them to follow him out of the library. "'Tis not the usual practice, ye'll be knowing, but under the circumstances, I can easily permit it."

The three fell into step and crossed to the library door.

"What, precisely, are those circumstances?" MacLaurin asked, and Elizabeth could have kicked him.

His uncle did not seem to care much for the tone of that question, either. "The circumstances, Ian MacLaurin, are that I had no wish to absent myself from my other guests who are needing my attention, but neither did I wish to leave Mistress Elizabeth to fall prey to a wrong turn and spend the night wandering the hallways, lost!"

"She's safe with me, Uncle, and would never get lost."

His lordship favored his nephew with a glance that did not suggest he thought Mistress Elizabeth was safe with him. He confined himself to replying, "She won't get lost now, in any case, because His Grace was kind enough to come with me to the library, and he's remained at the bottom of the stairs in the tower." To Elizabeth he continued, "His Grace has agreed to escort ye to yer chambers, if ye are ready to retire, so that I can return to my guests in the receiving room."

Elizabeth merely nodded. When they arrived at the tower stair landing, Elizabeth let his lordship know that she had left the keys in the door. He closed it, clipped the keys at his waist and ushered her and his nephew down the stairs, calling out unnecessarily, "We're here, then, Yer Grace. Mistress Elizabeth has found the book she was looking for."

Holding her book in one hand and her candle in the other, she descended the last step, whereupon His Grace materialized at her side. His Grace looked up at the man following her, and evinced no surprise, as his lordship had done, to perceive Ian MacLaurin. His Grace's smile was sly and, oddly, retaliatory. Elizabeth had no time to consider the meaning of that smile, for she was devising ways to shake herself of His Grace's company. She was coming to the inescapable conclusion that there was none.

The four of them walked from the library tower to the hallway that connected to the main building, Elizabeth and His Grace ahead, MacLaurin and Lord Mure behind. Over his shoulder His Grace said to his host, "You see, then, Robbie, that I was right. Mistress Cameron is too zealous with her work. I think you should post a watch outside the library door the night long to prevent her from returning and ruining her health."

Elizabeth was, at once, enraged by his obvious and high-handed manipulation and pleased that His Grace was also putting MacLaurin on notice that the library would be well guarded this night.

His lordship chuckled, as if at a good joke. "Aye, then, ye've the right of it, Yer Grace!" He invented a plan, on the spot, for posting a round-the-clock watch.

Elizabeth did not think it mattered whether Lord Mure intended to carry through on this plan, for she reckoned that His Grace would. Soon enough, they arrived at an intersection of hallways. His Grace paused long enough for Elizabeth to say good-night to her host but not long enough for her to exchange any conversation with MacLaurin.

His Grace led her away in silence.

Feeling more uncomfortable by the moment, she said at last, "You are too good, Your Grace."

"Not at all."

She was determined not to let him get the better of her. "But this is the second, no, the third time that Your Grace has led me from one point to another."

"The third time, my child? This afternoon, as I recall, you would not accompany me."

Was he now punishing her for her disobedience? "Ah, but you alerted his lordship to the necessity of locking the library and, thus, indirectly were you responsible for drawing me from my work. Then, of course, last night you escorted me from the receiving room to my bedchamber, just like tonight."

"Yes," His Grace replied and left it at that.

They walked on. She cast wildly about for a safe topic of discussion. When she thought she had finally hit on one, she cleared her throat and opened her mouth to speak.

She was prevented from saying anything when His Grace reached down and lifted her hand that held the

book. He raised the book to the candlelight and looked
at the title. Then he looked at her, saying nothing.

He did not need to, for his telling glance said it all. He
dropped her hand. She dropped her eyes. They walked
on, the silence becoming more uncomfortable and more
condemnatory with every step.

At her chamber door His Grace bowed deeply and
said, "Good night, Mistress Cameron."

Never would she have thought that so few words could
contain so much information, namely that it would be
most unwise of her to attempt to leave her room again
this night. His Grace had come with a small but efficient
retinue. She had a fair idea that His Grace intended to put
them to work not only outside the library but also outside her chamber door.

She curtsied and put her hand in her pocket for her key.
Her fingers brushed the locket. She withdrew the key,
looked him straight in the eye and returned bravely,
"Good night, Your Grace."

She entered her chamber and locked the door behind
her, trying to find an explanation for His Grace's baf-
fling behavior. She considered the possibility that he
might desire her, but he had never once, by word or deed,
suggested anything improper. It was an absurd idea,
anyway, that he might desire her, and it was distasteful,
as well. Nevertheless, it did seem that he was determined
to keep her away from MacLaurin, as if MacLaurin were
his rival.

She crossed her chamber and set her candle down on
her bedside table. Puzzling over the matter, she drew the
pins from her hair and tossed them atop her dressing table. She unlaced her dress, pulled it over her head and
cast off her petticoats. When she had stripped to her

chemise, her ear was caught by a faint sound, and she turned toward her fireplace.

She caught the strains of a high, sweet melody and remembered that she had promised MacLaurin that she would be bold. She scanned the paneled wall between her chamber and MacLaurin's. She saw nothing, of course, but more importantly she felt nothing. Yet. So she turned back the covers of her bed, picked up her brush and sat amid the sheets to wait.

She was in no hurry, and she had plenty to do in the meantime. She brushed her hair and let the song of the sea nymphs fill her. When her hair was shining and her body was full of honey, she untied the drawstring of her chemise and arranged it around her shoulders for best effect. She was playing a game. She had to play it so that MacLaurin would remain in his room this night. Although they both knew that the library would be guarded, MacLaurin might still be able to get in and retrieve the document without her.

Or maybe this was a test, to see who was stronger. That was it, then, a test of wills between her and MacLaurin. He deserved everything that she could test him with, tempt him with, because he had not been playing fair. He was withholding information and resisting her, as if she were somehow his . . . his what?

The word *nemesis* came to mind. Odd. Laughable. *Insulting.* She did not aspire to be his nemesis. Her chemise rode the tips of her breasts. She knew that *she* was not playing fair now, but no matter. The wall panel between them could not be moved without making the great shout of the rusted mechanism arouse whatever retainer His Grace had decided to plant outside her chamber door for the night. She knew it, and MacLaurin knew it, too.

She propped her arms behind her, leaned back, closed her eyes and dipped one shoulder so that her chemise slid off that side. She felt immeasurably better. Better to be bold. It worked with His Grace. It would work for MacLaurin—only differently, of course, with more sensual effect. She liked the freedom of her breasts exposed to his view. The feel of his eyes upon her was comforting and caressing.

She let her head fall back. She closed her eyes. She imagined him kissing her, and that simple exercise proved so easy and arousing that she was sure that he was looking at her now through the peepholes. She had kissed him in the library. She had kissed him the night before in the library tower courtyard. She had felt his body molded against hers, in almost every conceivable position, in the various passageways they had traveled together. Why, even within the first few minutes of meeting him, he had swept her into his arms and held her against him.

This, *this,* then, was why she had come to Castle Cairn. He had asked her why she had defied her father, and she willed him the answer: *For this.* She had been prompted to come, of course, by the receipt of the mysterious packet of love letters, and thinking about those letters, she realized how appropriate was their content.

She had come to Castle Cairn to shed the ways of a narrow-minded historian who lived only through others' lives. She had come to Castle Cairn to be free of the strict and respectable ways she had been taught as Joseph Cameron's daughter. She had come to experience the passion that she had inherited as Katherine Cameron's daughter. She had come to Castle Cairn to discover the delights of the Fleurise Garden.

She had promised to be bold. Before she extinguished the candle, she pulled one side of her chemise onto her shoulder and stood, so that the light could shine through the thin material and outline her entire body. When she blew the candle out, a wave of sensation passed through her. Because the sensation was as disturbing as it was arousing, she wondered whether she had just wakened something more powerful than her own desire and his.

MacLaurin had known the night was doomed from the moment he had come upon Elizabeth in the library. He had, foolishly, not expected to find her there. After finding her there, he had not meant to kiss her. After kissing her, he had not meant to provoke her. After provoking her, he had tried not to understand what she meant by being bold, but really there was no way to avoid understanding *that*. Still, he had not been ready to resign himself to his fate until his uncle, guided by the invisible hand of Devonshire, had arrived on the scene. At that moment MacLaurin had had a pretty good idea how the rest of the evening would unfold.

So far, he had been right. His uncle had led him to the receiving room where he had wasted a deal of time speaking of nothing at all. Then his uncle had accompanied him all the way to his chamber. At his chamber door his uncle had bidden him good-night in such a suspicious way that MacLaurin was sure that Devonshire was calling the shots in the castle tonight.

MacLaurin entered his chamber, trying to decide how best to reverse the tide of the night's events. He needed no candle, since he had left his window and curtains open, and moonlight flooded across his floorboards. He stripped off his suit coat, momentarily distracted by the thought of the jacket he had left in Elizabeth's room. Shaking off the implications of that thought, he went to his armoire, opened it and reached for a hanger. He was startled by what he touched. He snatched his hand away, with the flesh crawling from the tips of his fingers to his shoulder.

He steadied his nerves and peered into his armoire. He knew what he had touched, and it was not some scaly beast. Rather, he was looking at the soft folds of a generous length of MacLaurin plaid. The quiet forest green of the tartan was muted to brown in the shadows, and he needed no extra light to trace the thin threads of red and yellow crisscrossing the green. He immediately suspected Barrow of this devilry. He thought it better to leave the plaid there for now. He could get rid of it in the morning.

He turned to confront his fireplace devils. They were yammering quietly, not bothering him, really. He demanded, "Well, what do you have to say for yourselves?"

They continued to mutter incoherently.

"Surely you're pleased," he said, walking toward them.

He would have expected them to shriek with malicious glee at his reaction to the MacLaurin plaid, but their mutterings remained indistinct. Feeling testy, he wanted to draw them out. He wanted a target for his frustration, so he chose a subject sure to rouse their interest.

"Daring me to look?" he dared them in turn.

No answer. They were preoccupied. They were ignoring him.

"Think I'm not strong enough to step into the trap and not get caught?" he asked carelessly.

Still their chattering did not engage a counterchallenge. Perverse creatures that they were, he decided that their very lack of response was a new and ingenious way of challenging him.

He knew what he was doing and knew he shouldn't. Yet, just as he couldn't help kissing her or provoking her, he couldn't stop himself from walking to the paneled wall, pushing back the screen over the peepholes and looking at her.

What he saw was all that he had imagined. She was sitting, as if bathing in moonglow, on the shores of a white linen ocean. Only part of her beautiful body was available to him, and he wanted reassurance that she was not a mermaid but a true woman. He wanted her to stand and show him her legs. He begged her to stand. He *willed* her to stand.

She stood.

He surged with desire. The mermaid of his dreams had legs. Shapely calves. Even shapelier thighs.

Only then did he become aware that the chattering of his fireplace demons had risen to a maniacal and restless pitch he had heard only once before. Ten years ago he had heard such a noise on the night his father's cold anger had robbed the castle of air, and the next day, in order to breathe, he had left this depressing wreck and had not returned.

Until now.

She blew out the light, her beauty swallowed by the dark.

It was difficult to think when his body wanted to be on the other side of the wall, when he wanted to see her and to feel her and to wrap her shapely legs around him. He had a hazy but firm notion that he shouldn't try to operate the secret panel. He thought of the window and was crazed enough to think he could make it to her window by way of the outside ledge. The worst he would have to encounter would be his father's ghost.

That was it, then. His father's ghost was whirling, swirling, twirling throughout the castle. He could feel its presence now, just as his fireplace demons could feel it. He wanted to put his father's ghost to rest. He wanted to be free of the passion-sucking force that his father had had in life and that his ghost had in death. Suddenly an idea for dispelling that ghost blossomed in his desire-drenched brain, and it was so simple, so appealing, so *right* that he wondered why it had not occurred to him years ago. Then the reason came to him: never before had opportunity intersected with inclination.

He would have to be strong. He would have to keep breathing against the suffocating power of his father's ghost. He would have to ignore the passion pounding in his blood from Elizabeth's temptation. He would have to make it through the night.

Chapter Nineteen

What a difference a day could make.

As a historian, Elizabeth had been used to identifying changes as they occurred over the months and years to alter the fate of a people or a nation. She was aware, of course, that battles could be won or lost in the heat of five decisive minutes, and that clan chiefs could die on the instant, thus turning the tide of history. However, she had never before realized that an individual's entire identity could be unmade and remade overnight.

She realized it now, while she dressed for the day. She chose to wear her special dress of pretty mauve silk just so that she could display her sash of vivid red-and-black Cameron tartan. The moment she draped the fine wool over her shoulder and affixed the ends to her hip, she renounced Joseph Cameron as her father and became her mother's daughter. She reached automatically for the locket to arrange at her neckline, but of course it was no longer there. She felt proud and defiant and fueled with determination to become her father's daughter, as well, but first she would have to discover his name.

Mary came to assist Elizabeth and was surprised to discover, once again, that her mistress needed no help. Elizabeth allowed Mary to fiddle with her hair but did not linger over the primping. She hurried Mary along, then gathered up the pages of the treatise she was to read this morning, remembering to take with her the useless book on farming to return to the library. Then she left Mary behind to make her bed and tidy the room.

Elizabeth entered the banquet hall and looked around until she found Brian Sinclair. Happy to find him alone, she went to the table and sat next to him.

"Mr. Sinclair, good morning," she said pleasantly. "I'm very excited about the work we have before us today."

"Oh, indeed, Mistress Cameron," the society genealogist readily assented. "Fascinating topics! This morning we're to hear Graham's treatise on the Clan MacBean, Murray's on witchcraft and, why, I'm thinking that *ye'll* be speaking, too, no doubt on yer continuing study of the Clan Cameron."

"Yes," she said, "I've been working on the complete clan history some years now, as you know, and I was thinking to fill in some of the odd gaps in my account while I was here, with Castle Cairn's excellent library at my disposal. However, yesterday afternoon I was looking for the Clan Cameron genealogy and could not find it on the shelves." She furrowed her brow lightly, and her voice took on a puzzled tone. "Do you think any one of us could be using it just now?"

Sinclair had to give that weighty matter some thought. "Nay, then, Mistress Cameron, there's not one among us who is researching anything to do with the Camerons— excepting yerself."

She assumed an air of concern. "It couldn't be lost then, could it?"

Sinclair was plainly horrified. "Lost?" he gasped. "A clan genealogy—an *entire* genealogy—*lost?*"

"Is it possible?" she asked, as innocently as she could.

"Nay, 'tis what's most *im*possible, Mistress Elizabeth!"

"You relieve my mind," she said. "But, then, could it be misshelved and sitting out of order in some other part of the library?"

Sinclair shook his head. "Robbie's a demon when it comes to the order of his library. So, I'm thinking that ye need to try again, Mistress Cameron, to make sure that ye did not overlook the volume. Unless—" A light dawned in his glaucous old eyes.

"Unless?" Elizabeth prompted eagerly.

He shook his head again, this time with a kindly old man's smile. "'Tis not what I can tell ye!"

She had never before used feminine wiles on her fellow historians—indeed, had never had reason to—but she did not hesitate to deploy her newfound feminine powers now. She gave Brian Sinclair a teasing smile designed to melt the man's reluctance. "What can't you tell me, sir?"

To her surprise and pleasure, she saw Brian Sinclair blush. "Well, Mistress Cameron, I cannot tell ye what I cannot tell ye!"

She went so far as to bat her eyes and to nudge him playfully. "Then just give me a hint!"

Sinclair's blush deepened. "'Tis to say that Robbie has a special— Nay, then, but his collection would have naught to do with the Cameron genealogy!"

She turned on the charm of her smile full force. "His lordship's collection?" she echoed. She was not sure how she was doing what she was doing. She was only glad it seemed to work.

Sinclair looked at her, mouth slightly agape. "He's known to have a collection of books."

"Of course he's known for that!"

"A private collection," he said and looked quickly away.

When he looked back at her, she batted her eyes again and was amazed to discover that such a ploy could be effective.

Sinclair said, as if in spite of himself, "A collection that he has built, here and there, quite apart from the history books that he buys. Or, rather, I should say that he has built it along with the history books that he buys."

Still she said nothing, merely continued to gaze at him.

"But I've not seen a one of them, and never do I wish it!"

She raised her brows.

"And now I've told ye what I cannot tell ye!"

She had tortured the poor, flustered man as much as she dared, and she thought she had gotten the gist, more or less. She was not sure what to make of the apparently embarrassing nature of his lordship's private collection of books. More importantly, she was not sure whether the missing Cameron genealogy had anything to do with it.

She turned the topic, and Sinclair was visibly relieved. The empty seats around them filled, the breakfast hour came and went, and then it was time to begin the day.

When she arrived at the library she went first to the stacks to return the volume on farming. Then she crossed to the trestle table where the new acquisitions were laid out and performed the most ordinary of tasks: she counted the number of books on display and arrived at the number seventy-four.

Well, well. So this, then, was the piece of information that MacLaurin was holding back from her: knowledge that six books remained unsearched. She guessed that MacLaurin had an idea where those six books might be found, and that his idea focused on the library. She looked around her and surveyed the floor-to-ceiling shelves, the rows and rows of books. Could Lord Mure have chosen to "hide" his private collection in plain sight but in a little-used section of his general collection?

Although she had no clear answer to that important question, when Godfrey MacQuarie called the meeting to order she was able to take her place in the front row feeling very satisfied with herself. Robert MacDuff was up first with a report on "The Most Ancient and Most Noble Order of the Thistle." He concluded by discussing the origin of the motto *Nemo Me Impune Lacessit* or No One Provokes Me With Impunity, which, to the delight of his audience, he rendered in plain Scots as: Wha Daur Meddle Wi' Me? Donald Graham came next with his treatise on the illustrious MacBeans, that being the clan of his mother.

Then it was Elizabeth's turn. She stepped up to the dais, put her pages in front of her on the lectern and turned to Godfrey MacQuarie to thank him, as was the custom. She looked out over her audience. She felt more than bold, she felt brazen to be standing in front of the assembled group, wearing the tartan of her mother's clan. When she made eye contact with MacLaurin, perched on the edge of the display table, she felt frankly exposed. She was also more nervous than she had expected to be and could not understand it, for she had spoken before the group many times and had never felt so jittery. Could her nerves be rattled by the presence of Lady Michael and His Grace and MacLaurin?

She composed herself and began with a disclaimer. "As most of you know, I have been working for some time on the history of the Clan Cameron. Last year I came across an odd reference to an event in the life of one of my ancestors, and the reference piqued my interest enough to compel me to investigate further. Since then I have tried to piece together the story of Margery Cameron, who lived over two hundred years ago, but I am far from finished. What I have to share with you today is an incomplete picture.''

Elizabeth framed her story by reminding her audience of the well-known fact that the Camerons and the MacDonalds had been bitter enemies for generations until the year 1510, when the chief of the Camerons and the chief of the MacDonalds had declared a truce. The reason for the truce was generally known to have been that each of the chiefs had fallen in love with a woman of the rival clan, thus leading to the reconciliation.

What Elizabeth had to tell them today was Margery Cameron's direct role in creating the conditions that led to this important clan truce. Elizabeth described how she had come across a part of Margery's journal where Margery detailed the plan that she and a young Beatrice MacDonald had concocted. Margery wrote that she and Beatrice had each agreed to hide in the bedchamber of the opposing clan chief. Since both chiefs were unmarried, it would be necessary for each chief to marry into the rival clan, come morning, or lose their honor. From all that Elizabeth had been able to discover, Margery and Beatrice had carried out their plan and had effectively tricked the clans into laying down their arms. Elizabeth noted that both marriages seemed to have been successful ones, thus making the truce lasting.

When Elizabeth came to the end of her treatise, she produced the fragments of the journal written by Margery Cameron. Godfrey MacQuarie accepted them and officially declared them part of the valuable society papers. Discussion was lively, for her fellow historians liked nothing better than discovering a new interpretation of a well-known event. Speculation rose whether Beatrice MacDonald had left a similar journal, and suggestions for places Elizabeth could look for supporting documentation of this charming scheme were generously offered.

She was pleased to answer the questions that came her way, for this was always the part of delivering a treatise that she liked best. When it came to Lord Mure's turn to ask his question, she was smiling with relief that the event was over and happiness that it had been a success.

His lordship asked, "Now, tell us, Mistress Elizabeth, are these pages from Margery Cameron's journal the rare historical documents that you said you'd surprise us with here?"

Elizabeth's smile froze. Her stomach dropped. She had forgotten that she had mentioned anything about it to his lordship. Put on the spot like this, she could not remember exactly what she had told him about those documents. Had she said that she had come across letters? Had she mentioned that they had been sent to her by the mail, out of the blue? She had initially guessed that one of her fellow historians had sent her the letters and had absentmindedly forgotten to add a note, but now she did not wish those letters to become public.

"Yes," she said, her voice too bright, "these pages from Margery's journal are exactly what I spoke to you about when I arrived."

His lordship persisted. "But I recall you telling me something about having discovered Margery Cameron's journal some months ago already, and I had a feeling that you had come across documentation of another sort. You made these other documents sound like a secret!"

"Oh, no," she said a little feebly, "I must have found extra pages of Margery's journal. That's it, yes. I found extra pages of the journal very recently."

She felt MacLaurin's eyes upon her. She felt her smile go awry. She felt that her lie had been transparent to everyone present.

Ganon Graham asked, "And what does yer father think of such a ruse by one of his clanswomen?"

She was rattled and echoed blankly, "My father?" She was so startled that she almost blurted out that she did not know who her father was. Then she recovered her senses. Ganon Graham was referring to Joseph Cameron, of course, and he was making a little joke. He was teasing her.

"My father thinks Margery was a wise and courageous woman," she said. Another lie. Joseph Cameron would have deplored Margery's tactics had he known about them, which he did not.

She could finally step down from the dais and was glad. She hardly heard the next treatise on witchcraft, so preoccupied was she with recalling her conversation with his lordship concerning the mysterious letters. By the time Godfrey MacQuarie declared an end to the morning session, she had decided that she had revealed nothing to him and that her lie could not have been apparent. Her nerves settled down.

Everyone rose to move their legs and to partake of the repast that Lord Mure had, once again, brought to the library. With all her good sense restored, Elizabeth intended to take MacLaurin aside and let him know that he was not going to get to look at the six books alone—wherever they were. However, when she looked around for him at the display table, he was not there or anywhere else in the library.

During the midday break Brian Sinclair approached her to peruse the genealogies with her, but since she did not want to alert anyone to her interest in those volumes, she told Sinclair that she had already located the missing book. Yet another lie. Fortunately, Brian Sinclair merely smiled in his abstracted way, and she was encouraged to think that he would no longer concern himself with the Clan Cameron volume.

The afternoon session resumed, and MacLaurin did not return to the library. Elizabeth was puzzled but not disturbed. If those six books were somewhere in the library, MacLaurin certainly could not get to them if he wasn't here. She imagined that he was avoiding her, rebuffing her as he had done the morning before. However, she did not think that was the case, at least, not judging from the way he had riveted his attention on her during the delivery of her treatise. She felt that he had undressed her several times, and perhaps it was his mental undressing of her that had made her so nervous. She realized now that she had not been nervous exactly. She had rather been distracted. MacLaurin was responding to her challenge of the night before, and she had been aware of his responsiveness.

The afternoon came to a close, still with no sign of MacLaurin. Supper was served, as usual, in the banquet hall. MacLaurin was there, but did not come within ten feet of her. Yet she was aware of him, of his challenge, of his responsiveness. After supper, in the receiving room, her awareness of him was so acute that she felt she had to retire early, unable to remain in the same room with him without touching him or expiring.

She pleaded tiredness and excused herself early. His Grace was at her side on the moment, ready to escort her to her chamber. He explained that it had become his custom.

"Your custom, Your Grace?" she repeated warily as they left the room together.

"Do you recall, my child," His Grace replied, "that the evening we arrived at Castle Cairn we discussed the dangers of daughterly disobedience and a too-keen curiosity?"

"Yes, Your Grace."

"And do you recall the advice I gave you then?"

She tried to remember. The answer came to her with stunning force. "You said, Your Grace, that such traits could contribute to a questionable reputation."

"Very good, my child. Let me add now that a young lady can never be too careful with her reputation."

Had His Grace read her thoughts and discovered the disreputable turn they had taken? Whatever the case, it took little effort on her part to read his thoughts. His Grace was telling her that he was placing guards outside her door again tonight. He was letting her know that his guards would keep careful watch over her reputation.

The moment she entered her room she felt as if she were a prisoner. Caged. Her emotions were stirred. So were her nerves. Perhaps the ghosts were restless again tonight, stirring up trouble and her nerves. She was restless tonight, too, as if ready to jump out of her skin.

Skin. She wanted MacLaurin's skin next to hers. The panel couldn't be used, of course, so she walked to her window and threw it open. She looked out and up at the bleached oatcake of a moon. Let him come through the window.

She began to pace.

She did not know how many times she had crossed from the door to the window, but at one of those crossings she stopped to look at her fireplace nymphs. She waited for the feeling to come over her. The different kind of restlessness, one that was not jittery and jumpy but a sweet and honeyed restlessness. A wanting. Not an empty wanting, but a very full wanting.

The feeling came. Quietly. Softly. Completely. It was the desire to be desirable. The desire to dare. The desire to be bold.

She sighed deeply, then stretched and let the beautiful siren's song fill her and overflow. This was not a night to hold anything back.

Chapter Twenty

MacLaurin knew what he wanted and how he was going to get it, and his desires and plans tonight had nothing to do with retrieving Bev's document. He felt confident and was capable of biding his time. Although the hour was not late, he saw Elizabeth leave the receiving room in company with Devonshire. He hated seeing her on that man's arm, but he knew that her early exit would only hasten his own pleasure.

When Devonshire returned alone to the receiving room, MacLaurin decided it was time to leave. He had been avoiding Juliette Michael all day long. He saw that she was not about to let him get away without being punished, a little, for having stood her up the night before.

"Have you been enjoying yourself at Castle Cairn, Ian?" she asked, catching up with him in the darkened hallway.

Not yet, he thought. "Sure, now, Juliette. What could be better than spending the day listening to treatises?"

"Spending the night talking about love," she said.

She was bold, but not in the way he had grown to prefer. He stopped. He could scarcely see her. Better to let her down gently. "My boyhood home is hardly the place to inspire in me fond feelings."

"Then back in London—?" she said, her voice heavy with suggestion.

London. At the moment he couldn't remember why he had been in such a hellish hurry to return to London. At the moment all he wanted was to return to his chamber. "Devonshire is pining for you, Juliette. Put him out of his misery."

He left her standing there and strode down the hallway into the darkness. The ghosts—and one in particular—tried to cow him and corner him, but the heat generated by the thrum of his blood seemed to vaporize them before they appeared. He strode with a sure step, knowing that the closer he came to his chamber, the closer he would come to penetrating castle secrets and laying old ghosts to rest. And if his plan didn't work, then at least he'd still be a very happy man.

He entered his chamber. His fireplace demons were chattering. He told them to shut up. They settled down, somewhat. He liked that. He stripped off his jacket and tossed it across his bed. He shed his lace cravat and dropped it on the floor. He kicked off his shoes and rolled down his stockings, all the while walking toward the panel and the peephole screen. He didn't miss a step.

He shoved open the screen. He loosed his shirt from his breeches. She was there, where he had expected her, and she was perfect. How had he ever thought her ordinary? He didn't know, for there was nothing ordinary about what she was doing, for him, for herself, for them. She was teasing him, provoking him, peeling off her layers and loving it. He had glimpsed her playful nature that very first afternoon in the Fleurise Garden. He remembered how she had thrust herself into the thick of his mission, and he had told her not to push him. From that moment on, it seemed, she had pushed him one moment and pulled him the next.

She was reeling him in, and he wasn't even fighting it. Let her unpin her hair and unlace her dress. Let her slip off her petticoats and drop the shoulder of her chemise. Let her brush her hair and sway before the candlelight, so that he had a perfect view of the outline of her shapely legs and the curve of her hips. Let her stand there and tempt him for as long as she liked. For as long as she could stand it.

But let her not stop there. Let her also cast the chemise aside. Let her also look straight at him and invite him in. Let her be bold. Let her move beyond bold. Let her show him what she dared.

He dared her to dare. He dared her to be bold. She had teased and taunted him this far. Let her not stop now, when she was so close to beaching him. He would happily wreck his ship on her shore. All she had to do was drop her chemise, look at him, and *beg*. She dropped her chemise. She was bathed only in moonlight. She looked at him. Her eyes were gorgeous. But she didn't beg. She *demanded*. Fair enough. The part about begging was a quibble.

He shoved closed the peephole screen. He touched his right hand to a twig of wooden ivy. He touched his left hand to a wooden thistle. He turned the knobs. The wall panel slid back noiselessly.

He stepped into her chamber.

The wall panel slid back in place behind him. He took professional pride that it hadn't made a sound and had produced only a whisper of air in the sliding. He took several steps toward her while she groped for a dressing gown at the end of her bed. When he was a foot away from her, she managed to tie several ribbons around her thighs and waist. However, she had not gotten very far, and one beautifully formed breast was exposed. It hardly mattered, since the material was nearly transparent anyway.

Her eyes were wide. "You're not a ghost?"

He shook his head slowly. "Do I look like one?"

"No," she said, "you look like you did when you caught me in your arms and saved me from the candelabra."

"And what did I look like then?"

"Very different from when I first saw you and thought you were a knight in armor come back to life. You didn't come to rescue me this time, either, did you?"

She didn't explain herself. He didn't ask.

"No."

"How did you get in here?"

"Through the secret panel."

She was still bewildered. "It made no noise."

"Not a sound," he agreed.

"But...but..."

"You thought you could risk all without incurring risk?" he asked. He put his hand out and grasped the edge of the dressing gown, drawing her toward him. They were not yet touching fully, but her scent was all around him. "Without reaping reward?"

Her expression improbably blended dismay and desire. "I thought you would come through the window."

"A clumsy way to enter a woman's room."

"How did you do it?" she asked, nodding at the paneled wall.

"I remembered seeing a large crock of oil in the barn the other day. While everyone was far off in the library,

I spent the afternoon greasing the mechanism. I reset it, too, since it seemed to have fallen off track.''

"And now?" she wanted to know.

She was muddleheaded. She was a temptress. The combination was irresistible. "And now," he said, pulling her silk-veiled nakedness next to him, "you're going to tell me why you came to Castle Cairn."

He liked the look of pride and defiance that came next over her expressive face. "Where do you want me to start?"

"With an explanation of the rare historical documents that you brought with you as a surprise."

"You didn't believe me when I told your uncle that I had found more pages of Margery Cameron's journal?"

He shook his head again, this time very, very slowly.

"I'm not sure where to start—" she said and got no further.

He heard a faint clicking, whirring noise behind him and put a finger to her lips, silencing her. It seemed to come from inside the wall he had just stepped through. The noise could not have been audible outside the room, but it was remarkable to him for being one he had never heard in the castle before, and it captured his complete attention.

He turned at the moment the clicking, whirring noise stopped and a faint creaking began, quiet and prolonged. It came from the far corner of the chamber, from the odd alcove, and sounded like the brittle crack of fragile old bones. The hairs rose on his nape before his mind grasped the significance of the sound. He looked down at her and saw that she, too, was looking in the direction of the darkened alcove. She transferred her gaze to him. He read her desire for him in the luminous depths of her eyes. He read there, too, her curiosity, and it deepened her evident desire. She was dearer to him then than she had ever been.

Here was a secret passage, unknown to him all these years, suddenly opening up to him. His desire to explore it was the equal of his desire for her. He wanted to explore it, but he didn't want to lose her. He decided to have both and knew he had no time to waste, for he had no idea how many seconds the passage would remain open.

He released her, saying urgently, "Get your candle and light it. I'll go to the door and keep it open—if need be and if possible."

He hurried to the alcove and saw a new darkness pull away from the room to reveal an inked-out space that suggested a darkway behind a doorway. She joined him a few moments later, with the candle lit and held high. The light glowed through the doorway and illuminated the darkway enough to show that it was very narrow.

He looked at her.

She looked at him.

He nodded and stepped through the door. He turned back, saw her lovely, fearful, desirous expression and extended his hand to her. She laid hers in it and stepped through the doorway to join him. Two heartbeats later the panel moaned shut.

Her hand convulsed in his. They were wedged into what must have been the narrowest passageway in Castle Cairn, and all they had for company was each other and the glow of her candle.

"You're afraid," he said. He kept his voice very low, since he did not know whether the sound carried outside the passageway.

She whispered back, "A little. What just happened?"

"I'm not sure. When I reset the gears of the panel this afternoon, I must have unknowingly tripped the mechanism for this door. I never knew this passage was here."

"Where does it lead?"

"We'll find out."

He moved forward, ahead of her, and the passage was hardly wider than the width of his shoulders. He held tight to her hand and drew her along behind him. She was holding the candle as high as she could to illuminate his way, but that was impractical. It was difficult, given the narrowness of the passage and the lowness of the ceiling, for her to pass him the candle, but eventually they managed to transfer it. In one hand he held her hand. In the other he held the candle.

"The passage is well ventilated, at least," he said.

"How do you know?"

"If it weren't, the candle would be sputtering. Then, too, the air isn't stale, although the passage might not have been used in decades, even centuries. Are you having trouble breathing?"

"No trouble," she said.

They traveled a way. They came to a step up, then another step up. It was a stairs. A full flight. He had no idea where this passage would end, but he knew where they were going, for he mentally mapped every twist and turn to keep their location clear in his mind.

The stairs ended, but not the passageway.

She began to speak. "I'm not Joseph Cameron's daughter," she said to his back. Her voice was musical, sad, defiant and confessional.

His spine thrilled to the unexpectedness of this disclosure. He kept his reaction minimal, however, so that he would not discourage her. He grunted inarticulately, to signal that he had heard her.

"I'm his niece," she continued. "My mother was Joseph Cameron's sister. I don't know who my father is. That's why I came."

He squeezed her hand for reassurance. He was traveling an unknown passageway with a woman who was turning his life inside out, and she was telling him that she wasn't who he thought she was. He didn't know where they were going, any more than he knew what she would say next. He knew only that at the end of all this he would either make love to her or die. Maybe both. He welcomed the danger. He would accept the death.

"I came to Castle Cairn to find out who my father is," she said. "I didn't know why I came before I came." She laughed softly. "I know that sounds absurd. Nevertheless, when I arrived here the other day, I was still Joseph Cameron's daughter. It was only after your father's ghost tried to grasp my locket and it fell off that I discovered the truth."

He stopped abruptly. She stumbled against him, and her lush curves were pressed against his backside. "You saw my father's ghost?"

"Oh, yes, and he looks remarkably like you, I think. But as I was saying, I didn't truly know why I had come until yesterday."

She had seen his father's ghost. Any lingering doubts he had about this night's plan were dispelled. His desire increased, if that was possible, and he could have unleashed all his passion for her here in the passage, if he could have figured a way to turn around. On second thought, this wasn't yet the time or place. A curse bubbled to his lips. It came in Gaelic, for emphasis.

He hurried their step.

She continued, "I went to the library last night to read the latest entries in the Cameron volume."

He was beginning to understand. "Ah, the genealogies."

"Yes, the genealogies. I know that even...illegitimate children are properly registered with the names of the natural parents, because I saw the entry for Elspeth MacMillan's son."

He smiled. "But you didn't find the entry for your own birth."

"No," she said, "because I couldn't find the Cameron volume."

"I never paid much attention to that section of the library," he said, "so I couldn't say where it might be."

"Well, the MacLaurin volume wasn't there, either, in case you're interested." She sighed. "I don't know if their absences are significant or not."

"Are any other volumes missing?"

"Perhaps," she said, "but I had no reason to look for any others so particularly."

"What drew your interest to the MacLaurin genealogy?"

Her soft chuckle was like a caress. "A historian's fantasy, I suppose!" she said. "Last week—or was it a million years ago?—I received a packet of historical documents in the mail, you see—and, no, they were *not* pages from Margery Cameron's journal."

"Does this happen often?"

"Does what happen often?"

"That you receive documents in the mail?"

"No, it's never happened to me before," she said, "but I suppose that my fellow historians might receive such mailings from time to time."

"And the nature of the documents?"

"One half of a correspondence of old love letters from a man to a woman that hint at tragedy. Very affecting!"

"Is their story significant?"

"Not beyond the fact that I was so intrigued by the first few letters I read that I decided to come to the meeting. I thought I could reconstruct the story with the help of my fellow historians and your uncle's library."

"And your interest in the MacLaurin genealogy?"

"I believe the letters were written by someone intimately connected to Castle Cairn."

"Did you discover that much by consulting your fellow historians?"

"No, after arriving here, I decided to keep the letters private."

"So who sent this packet of letters to you?"

"I don't know."

"You don't *know?*"

"Well, how was I to know? There was no note attached, and I couldn't read the frank. I imagined at first that one of my fellow historians had sent them to me and absentmindedly forgotten to attach an explanatory note, but then I decided that wasn't likely, either. In any case, it didn't matter to me much who sent them, because I was more interested to discover the story involved behind the—"

"You didn't think your *first* task," he interrupted, "was to discover who sent them to you?"

"No, why?"

Muddleheaded. Definitely muddleheaded. "Because it seems important to know who sent them to you."

"The crucial point here," she defended herself, "is that the letters piqued my curiosity enough to attend the summer meeting against my father's wishes."

"The crucial point seems rather to be the remarkable number of coincidences that have brought you and me together, not to mention Devonshire."

"I'm way ahead of you on that," she said airily. "I've already considered the possibility that the letters had something to do with Lieutenant Beverly's document."

"And what is your considered opinion?"

"The letters I received were written well before the lieutenant's time."

"You sound confident."

"I am. In addition to which, neither Lieutenant Beverly nor my cousin Fiona have any relationship to Castle Cairn, and I'm convinced that the letters concern events that happened here. So now I've confessed to you *my* motives for coming," she said and poked him provocatively in the back. "Now it's your turn to tell me where you think Lieutenant Beverly's document is."

They had followed a tortuous series of turns that ran parallel to hallways whose intersections he knew well. For the last one hundred feet or so, he guessed that they had been traveling a pocket within the odd corridor that linked the east wing to the library tower. He also guessed that they were coming to what he had previously thought was the dead end of that corridor, at the place where it butted against the library tower.

Sure enough, another step or two and they arrived at the end of the passage, which was blocked by a wall of wood. It didn't get any better than this. If his guesses were right, they stood at a back entrance to the secret room that lay behind the paneled wall at the front end of the library.

He said over his shoulder, "I think that Bev's document is in a book in the room on the other side of this door."

Chapter Twenty-One

Elizabeth caught her breath, dazzled by the blue glint of desire and discovery he threw her over his shoulder. She recovered enough to look beyond him to see what she could of the wall in front of them.

"Are you sure it's a door?" she asked apprehensively.

"I'm sure, but what I don't know is how to open it." He moved the candle up and around the seams formed by the three sides of the walls. "I've never encountered a door like this one in the castle, and the catches aren't in the usual places. In fact, I don't see any catches at all."

While he examined the walls, she tried to control the panic that fluttered through her. She did not like the confines of this very narrow passage and hated to think that they might be blocked. Since it was nearly impossible to turn around, she imagined the horrible possibility of retracing their steps backward to her bedchamber. She wondered whether he would be able to open the door at that end, which might well be built along the lines of the one in front of them now—if that blank panel staring at them was, in fact, a door.

This closed end of the passage did not feel as well ventilated as the rest, and although she did not think they were in danger of running out of air, the stuffiness did nothing to allay her panic. She was glad of the fact that she was wearing only a light wrap, so that she was not suffocating in a tightly laced dress and muffled in volumes of petticoats.

"Any luck yet?" she asked.

"Not yet," he admitted but added that he'd do better if he had both hands free. He suggested that she slip her arms around his waist and hold the candle for him.

She pressed herself to his back and slipped both arms around him at his waist. She positioned her hands, and he placed the candle so that she could grasp it. Upon contact of her front to his back, her panic stepped out of the way of the desire that rushed forward and flooded her.

She was fully aware that her light wrap hardly covered her nakedness, and she knew that her nakedness had eased her confession about her uncertain parentage. It was as if, in daring to strip to the skin in front of him, she had nothing left to hide. Then, too, she was able to say anything to him when they were in one of these passageways. And if they never got out of here—

"Ahh," he said at last, with such satisfaction that a quiver ran through her.

The door jumped aside with a slight bounce, and fresh air drifted over them. He grasped her hands holding the candle and drew her out of the passageway and into a small room.

"You found the catches, then," she remarked.

"There were no catches, only a pattern of wood on the left side that made me think the door opening operated like a puzzle," he said, "and it does." He ran the candlelight along the right side of the door in order to examine the hinges. "Springs," he commented with interest. "I've never thought of using springs on such a large item."

"Do you use springs on smaller items?" she asked, curious.

"On boxes and secret drawers," he replied with a detached professional air. He tested the give of the hinges by moving the door back and forth. He remarked that it didn't seem to be hooked to a timing gear, but rather would be closed manually. "We'll leave it open for now." He nodded. "I like it."

"I'm just glad we're out of there," she said with another quiver, this one of relief at their narrow escape. "But where are we?"

"The library tower," he said.

He raised the candle to illuminate what he could of the room. The space was small, not more than twelve feet by twelve, and not quite square because the side walls bowed, apparently with the curve of the tower. Most of the available wall space was covered with floor-to-ceiling shelves, but not all of it. In the center of the room was a table, upon which stood an unlit branch of candles. The room had no windows, therefore concealing its existence from the outside. However, a diagonal column of moonlight angled through an opening that looked to have been created by the removal of several thick blocks of stone. Those removable blocks were stacked on the floor below the opening.

"My best guess," he said, "is that we're in a room hidden behind the carved panel in front of which the dais stands. I would think that the wall opposite us aligns with the main library wall."

"You've never been here before?"

"Never."

Elizabeth looked around, amazed. "This is where your uncle keeps his private collection of books, isn't it?"

MacLaurin looked surprised. "It's generally known that he keeps a private collection?"

"I'm not sure how generally it's known. However, Brian Sinclair intimated the existence of the collection this morning when I asked him if he knew what had happened to the Cameron genealogy."

"Does he know?"

She shook her head. "He was horrified by the suggestion that it was lost, doubted that it could have been misshelved and knew that it was not currently in use." Her heart was beating so rapidly that she had to put her hand on her breast to calm herself. "I have a good notion that it's in here."

"Along with the book holding Bev's document, I warrant."

She slanted him a glance and said wryly, "Not to mention the other five that didn't make it to the display table in the library on the other side of that wall."

"You counted them?"

"It didn't occur to me to count them until this morning. You must have done so yesterday, and I'm guessing that we both came up with the number seventy-four." She drew a breath and looked around again. "Where should we begin?"

"With the six new books in Uncle's collection."

"Unfortunately, I don't know the titles."

"Then we'll have to begin at the beginning."

She suggested that they make a complete circle of the room. "Checking every book as we go, until we have what we want. If you light the candles on the table, we'll have an easier time of it, but we'll still need the single candle as we proceed around the room."

When he went to the table to do as she bade, she stepped to her right. About three feet of wall spanned the section from the door to the beginning of the book-shelves. From the bit of moonlight in the room, she could tell that a dozen framed pictures filled this part of the wall, but she could not see the pictures clearly. As the candles were lit one by one on the table behind her, she was shocked and fascinated to behold the scenes that came to life before her very wide eyes.

She was witnessing a wall writhing with couples en-gaged in various and inventive stages of sexual congress. Some of the couples were half-dressed. Some were com-pletely naked. Some were not entirely human, but either part beast or all beast. All were built for sexual pleasure. None showed modesty. Their expressions and their po-sitions were unapologetic. Unashamed. Healthy. The combined effect was too much to take in at once, so she slowed her eye to consider the individual pictures.

One scene depicted a bacchanalian orgy spread out across an idyllic landscape with couples behind bushes, in trees, under outcroppings of rocks and right out in the open. Another scene portrayed a more modern cavalier whispering fond words into the ear of his ladylove. From the expression on his ladylove's face, not to mention the position of her body, she was being moved from reluc-tance to acquiescence. The moment was a delicate one, and her expression perfectly captured the moment of transition from denial to desire. Elizabeth could see that in the very next moment the ladylove would turn to her cavalier and surrender herself to him.

When MacLaurin stepped up behind her, the light from his candle brought into vivid relief the details of the rich and varied amorous encounters. His presence be-hind her also dramatically altered the quality of the air.

With explicit displays before her, and his heat behind her, she was lapped with a desire whose waves had been growing within her since the sea nymphs had made her their ally three nights ago. Her skin felt damp and sticky.

"Leda and the Swan," she said weakly, referring to the graphic depiction of the beautiful Greek queen's exquisite ravishing by Zeus in animal form.

He leaned into her, peering over her shoulder at the picture below it. Against her neck he said, "I've never tried that, but I'm mighty inspired to now."

At the glorious feel of his lips on her neck, she closed her eyes. "Shouldn't we move on?" Her voice was shaky, her knees watery. "Because if we don't..."

"If we don't," he said, turning her head gently so that he could kiss her lips, "we never will. True enough."

She made the mistake of lifting her lids and was seduced by the attractive devil dancing deep in his eyes. She had moved far past the acquiescence the cavalier inspired in his ladylove.

"If we don't move on..." she repeated.

"Right," he said, releasing her with obvious reluctance.

They walked the few feet toward the shelves. He placed the candle upon a slight extension of the shelf that was designed for the purpose of holding a candle for reading light. Then he reached up and unshelved the first book. Before opening it, he said, "I had hoped to discover castle secrets tonight, but this exceeds my expectations."

He opened the book, examined it for Bev's document, found nothing, then turned back to the frontispiece. "I've tried that," he said, pointing to the entwined couple, "and recommend it highly."

Elizabeth gasped for breath. "I think I have a fair idea

now of the nature of your uncle's private collection. The mere mention of it miserably embarrassed poor Brian Sinclair, and I can see why. It's . . . it's extraordinary.''

He reshelved the book. ''It makes me feel better about him, I can tell you. I had always wondered about this part of Uncle's life and am glad to know that it exists, if only on pages in books and pictures on walls.''

''The pictures are more . . . effective than I would have thought,'' she admitted, ''and I can only wonder what it's like to read the books.''

''Why read about it?'' he asked and placed his hands on her shoulders and drew her against him. He slid his hands inside the folds of her dressing gown, down her breasts to the flat of her stomach.

When his hands moved farther down, she stopped them. ''We've looked at one book only and have hundreds to go. If we stop now, we shall never get what we want here.''

''We shall get half of it,'' he argued, nuzzling her neck, ''the important half.''

''No, really,'' she protested.

''Really,'' he murmured as he slid his hands back up to caress her breasts, his rough hands more stimulating than the feel of the smooth silk.

Only by sheer strength of will was she able to step back from him. She put up a hand to brush her hair from her face and steadied herself against the bookshelf. ''Let's separate. You start at the other end. I shall continue here. We shall meet in the middle.''

''Meet in the middle,'' he repeated doubtfully, then with considerable interest.

She shoved him gently toward the opposite corner of the room.

"The quicker we work," she said, "the sooner we shall meet—"

"In the middle," he finished as he walked away.

Feeling less distracted with the distance between them but certainly no less desirous, Elizabeth drew a deep breath, adjusted her dressing gown and began to search the books. She decided not to read any passages and refrained from looking at too many pictures.

Book after erotic book passed through her hands, and then without quite realizing it at first, she drew a thick volume from the shelf and discovered that she was holding one of the missing genealogies.

"Here it is!" she cried softly.

"The document?" came the quick response.

"No, the MacLaurin volume," she said, looking down at the pages to which the volume automatically opened.

For no apparent reason her heart twisted and her breathing became more rapid, although not from sensual stimulation of MacLaurin's approach. What she felt was more like fear, and her hands were suddenly trembling.

"I'll put this down near the good light so that I can read it better," she said, walking toward the table in the center.

MacLaurin was looking at her, a question in his eyes and on his lips. "Why do you need to look at it now? Bev's document couldn't be there, because that book is not one of the ones Juliette Michael transported here. Why don't you put it aside and look at it later?"

She spread the volume out on the table. She wiped her suddenly sweating palms on the silk covering her thighs. "Of course you're right. Bev's document isn't here... couldn't be here, but," she said, aware of the wavering in her voice but unable to control it, "the volume opened to other loose documents inserted among the bound pages. I think I'll take a moment to read through a few of them."

MacLaurin regarded her a moment, then turned back to his labor at the shelves opposite her.

She had, indeed, opened the volume to a small sheaf of folded documents filed at the last completed page of the genealogy. The last entry, she noted, was Mac-Laurin's own date of birth, and she saw that he was three years her senior. She surmised, then, that the documents were a quarter century old, more or less. She untied the bundle and unfolded the first one.

She saw that it was a letter—a love letter that looked to be written in a woman's hand. She began reading and, with an odd, elated leap of her heart, she realized that she had stumbled across the other half of the ardent lover's correspondence that she had mysteriously received in the mail.

The fit seemed perfect—or almost. The letters began with the same interest and growing ardor. They contained some of the same phrasing, some of the same references, even made an allusion to the evil one, the ardent lover's rival. However, this lady's prose did not develop quite the same pitch of passion to which her ardent lover's letters rose. Over the course of several letters the lady remained diffident. She was playful. She teased her ardent lover, just a little, with her interest in the evil one. The next letters continued to hold her ardent lover off, yet managed to keep him on the edge, as if she were almost—but not quite—ready to yield to him. To give him all. To meet him in the Fleurise Garden.

One letter was signed. Elizabeth's hand froze, and her blood ran cold when she read the woman's name.

The little room echoed with agony. She realized dimly that it was from the sound of her voice moaning, "Oh, no."

She looked up. She must have been wearing her stricken feelings on her face, for when MacLaurin turned to her, he frowned with concern.

She cast the letter from her, as if it were a poisonous beast. With shaking hands she wrapped her dressing gown more tightly around her, then crossed her arms in front of her breasts, shielding them belatedly from his view. She swallowed hard and looked away from his beautiful blue eyes. She could not look at him when she said, with despairing coldness, "Your father and my mother might have been lovers."

Chapter Twenty-Two

Elizabeth forced herself to continue. "Your father might be my father," she said. The hideous implications of that statement shot through her in pins of pain and shame.

She glanced at him and saw that his expression was arrested at shocked understanding. His words dropped like shards of ice. "What makes you think that they were lovers, that my father could be your father?"

She spread her hands to indicate the unfolded pile of letters on the table and the remaining letters still folded in the MacLaurin volume. "What I have before me."

He took a step toward the table and the evidence.

She recoiled. "No, don't come any closer."

He stopped, halted by her words and her tone. His eyes narrowed, and his body seemed to turn to stone. "What, exactly, do you have before you?"

Under his hard gaze she explained that she had been reading love letters from a woman to a man; that these letters seemed to match the ones she had just told him about, the ones she had received in the mail; that these letters had evidently been written to a MacLaurin man.

She pointed at the last opened letter in her pile. "She signed her name. It's Katherine."

"Is the letter written to Gavin MacLaurin?"

She shook her head. "No, she doesn't address him by name, but the letters are inserted here, at the last page. They must have been written to a MacLaurin man of my mother's generation."

"They could have been written to my uncle."

She shook her head sadly. "No, I know from the other half of the correspondence that the man to whom these letters are written was a widower with a young son. A toddler." She paused and said, "You are three years older than I am."

"Katherine is a common enough name," he said. "How do you know that the woman writing the letters was Katherine Cameron?"

"I don't," she admitted. She put her hand to her forehead. "One of my fellow historians... I don't remember which one... mentioned that my mother was a frequent visitor to Castle Cairn. In the old days." It was difficult to recall that conversation, with her temples throbbing so unbearably. "What did he tell me? That my mother and your father made part of a happy group?" She shook her head. "I don't know. I wasn't listening carefully, because my thoughts were elsewhere. At the time I was concentrating on the fact that my mother was not Mary MacDonald, after all, but Katherine Cameron."

He cut his eyes away from her, but not before she saw cold anger flash in them, killing the devil of desire that made them dance. His voice was harsh. "So you think the letters were written by your mother?"

"I don't want to think it, but I do think it."

He spoke very slowly, still looking away from her. "And you think that she and my father were lovers."

"I don't know. I'm not sure. I haven't reached that part yet. I can't read on."

"You must."

The tone of his voice jerked her head up, as if it were on a string. "I'd rather read the brutal fact in the Cameron genealogy under my name."

"I don't want to waste time looking for a volume that might not be here when you can read what is before you."

"I *can't.*"

"You *must,* or I shall read them."

He took another step toward her.

She did not want him near her. "No!" She quickly unfolded the next letter and began to read, hoping against hope to find some indication that Katherine had held off her ardent lover—Gavin MacLaurin! That she had not entered the Fleurise Garden with him. That she had not borne his child. That she and Ian MacLaurin were not...

It was difficult to read when her hands were trembling, with her eyes so dry they were parched. It was difficult to make sense of the words scrawled on the page, with the blood at her temples churning with chips of ice and clots of hot shame. It was difficult to breathe, with MacLaurin's cold anger squeezing the small space of good air, leaving room only for evil castle spirits.

She wished that she was fully dressed. She wished that MacLaurin would do something other than stand there and stare at her. When he began to pace, she wished he would stop. When he stopped pacing, she wished he would leave the room, but she was glad he didn't abandon her to the isolated agony of this research. Then he was behind her, at the bookcase. That was better. At least they weren't facing one another. With him behind her, out of her line of vision, she felt better.

MacLaurin did not share her relief, for he had touched her, kissed her and wanted her like a lover. The actual act did not seem to matter as much as the desire and the feelings. The actual act would not have increased his sense of betrayal or his fury to find himself caught in a hateful web of his father's making.

Was this, then, the castle secret whose penetration he had welcomed not more than an hour ago? He was filled with disgust to think he had imagined a very different solution to the secret. He was bitter that a boyish eagerness to make love to Elizabeth Cameron had broken through his cynicism. He had even felt happy. *Happy?* He wanted to spit. Vile, absurd, *betraying* emotion! His happiness had turned foul, and its putrid remains had closed the crust of his cynicism and thickened it. He knew the process well.

Just like old times? Not even close. He remembered old times at Castle Cairn. No previous grief, shame, constraint or powerless rage had felt like this!

He looked at Elizabeth. Her head was bent over the letters. Her whole body was trembling. Her lips were moving silently as she read the words her mother had written to his father. He wished he could direct some of his rage at her, but he could not. He needed a physical outlet and began to pace. No, he could not be angry with her, for she was as much a victim of past lies and secrets as he. She had tempted him in a way no other woman had tempted him, and she had done so unwittingly. Deeply. Purely.

Better not to think about her, especially if he could not muster ugly thoughts. Better to rail against her, rage against her! Why was she taking so long with those letters? Why didn't she have the answer to her parentage *now,* this instant? Was she deliberately trying to torture him?

Perhaps she had been right, that it would be simpler to read the name of her father in the entry for her birth in the Cameron volume. He stopped pacing and decided to look for the Cameron volume.

He walked around the table and went to the bookcase behind Elizabeth, to look first in the vicinity of the space vacated by the MacLaurin genealogy. Next to that empty space he withdrew an old book and discovered not the Cameron genealogy but the MacLaurin accounts. While he had it in his hands, he decided to get an idea of the amount his uncle's obsession for erotic literature was costing the estate in terms of land. While his uncle diddled away MacLaurin land, the Clan MacPherson was increasing its influence. He hoped that whatever his uncle was charging Devonshire per acre, it was a lot.

He began flipping through the pages, looking for the most recent financial statements. He came to the section detailing castle expenses under his father's stewardship. He wasn't surprised to find so little money devoted to improvements in the farmlands or maintenance of cattle. He was surprised, however, to come across several pages of meticulously recorded travel expenses. The cold boil of his rage did not quite subside, but it seemed to lift momentarily, as if held in abeyance.

"I'm coming to the last letter," she whispered into the fraught silence of this secret annex.

He grabbed the candle from the ledge where he had set it earlier to provide reading light. He moved toward the center table, bringing the volume of MacLaurin accounts with him.

"What have you discovered?" he asked.

"Nothing," she said, her voice wavering between hope and doubt. Then, again, "Nothing."

When he came near the table she felt his proximity to be repellent, as if the positive poles of two magnets had approached one another. She turned her head away from him. She was relieved to feel him take a step away from her.

"You mean nothing to prove or disprove they were lovers?"

"That's right," she said, fixing her eyes on a darkened corner of the room.

"Which tips the balance a bit toward thinking that they were not lovers, in fact," he said. "Don't you think?"

She dared to look back at him. She did not want to raise false hopes. "I'm not sure," she said, then glanced away again, "but even in her last letter, my mother was holding off your father."

"I'm glad to hear it," he said, "and I'm not surprised. He was a dry old stick, my father, and I wouldn't have thought much of your mother's taste to learn she actually succumbed to him."

"Oh, no," she protested, "to judge by his warm and beautiful letters, your father was a passionate man. I'm amazed my mother wasn't madly in love with him." Feeling the horror of the situation wash over her afresh, she covered her face with her hands and cried in distress, "What have I said?"

MacLaurin's voice cut through her distress. "What month were you born?"

She dropped her hands to look at him. This time she could tolerate holding his gaze steadily. "May," she said, then amended, "No, it must have been April."

MacLaurin was evidently puzzled. "You don't know?"

She shrugged and explained, "I've always celebrated my birthday in May, but Katherine Cameron died in April. I was reputed to have been a late baby, and an exceptionally big one—no doubt accounting for the difficulties Mary MacDonald had in 'delivering' me. However, now that you ask, I think at the date of my supposed birth I must have been already a month old."

To judge from the look on MacLaurin's face, she had told him something important. "April, May, it doesn't matter," he said with a faint smile. "The point is that you were born in the late spring, right? Could there be any more than this one-month discrepancy, earlier or later?"

She affirmed cautiously, "I...I don't think so. It seems impossible to think that I could have been born *before* Katherine Cameron's death, and there would be no reason to date my birth after Mary MacDonald's. Is it important?"

He took a step toward her, saying with soft reassurance, "No, don't turn away from me." He stopped and extended to her the MacLaurin ledger. "Here, take this. Look at the hand of the writing on these pages. Does it match the hand that wrote the love letters you received?"

She accepted the ledger, making sure not to touch him. She studied the scrawling script, identified characteristic loops and said, "Yes, it matches." She dared to look up at him. "It's your father's handwriting, isn't it?"

"Yes."

"And the significance?"

"Look closely at the dates and at the locations next to the entries."

She scanned the first columns. "Here's Dumfries, Carlisle, Leeds, then Nottingham. He's evidently traveling south in the summer." She turned the page. "Ah, yes, then he stays in London several months at the end of the season before returning north—'' She broke off and returned to the beginning of his travels. "What year is this?" She paged back to the beginning of the calendar year.

"The year before you were born," MacLaurin replied. "I turned two years old that February."

Elizabeth caught her breath and returned her attention to the ledger. "He left Castle Cairn in June that year, according to these accounts, and did not return until the following June."

"I remember the day my father returned from London," MacLaurin said. "I was already three at the time. He had been gone a long, long time, but I had no notion until now that he was absent for a year."

"If he was gone from one June to the next, and I was born in April or May..." She trailed off when she stopped to count out months on her fingers.

"I was so looking forward to his return," MacLaurin said. "I can remember his horse approaching the courtyard. I can remember running to greet him. I can remember the look on his face when he swung down from his horse. I thought I must have done something terribly naughty to have received such a stern look from him. From that day until the day I left ten years ago, he made my life hell."

Relief began waving through her, outrunning her conscious thoughts, making her weak with happiness that verged on giddiness. Still, she needed to spell out the pieces in words. "Yes, before he left, your father was in love with my mother and was a passionate man capable of writing beautiful letters. By the time he returned, she had died giving birth to another man's child, and he had become harsh and bitter."

"But why did he leave, I wonder, if he was so in love with her and wished to win her?"

She closed the ledger and put it down on the table next to the pile of letters Gavin MacLaurin had received from Katherine Cameron. "I don't know," she said, trying not to laugh, but bubbles of merriment were floating up her throat. "And I don't care." She essayed a joke. "Maybe the evil one sent him away!"

"Thank God for the evil one," MacLaurin said.

"Oh, that means, that means—"

"That means I never have to call you 'sister.'"

She covered her face with her hands again, this time in an effort to assimilate the absurd relief that threatened to steal her reason. When she removed her hands, MacLaurin was standing in front of her, gazing down at her in a very unbrotherly way.

When he placed his hands on her shoulders, she flinched in delayed reaction, but he gentled her by running his hands down her arms and entwining her fingers in his. The gesture was, at once, affectionate and arousing.

"Do you think, do you *truly* think there's no chance that we're . . . we're . . ." It was easier to say now that the horrible possibility had receded. "Brother and sister?"

He took her hands and put them behind her back, holding on to her so that he was standing flush against her. He bent to touch her neck with his lips. "You don't look like any MacLaurin woman I've ever seen."

Her relief continued to course through her in waves. "You're right! I don't! Why didn't I think of that to begin with?"

"Indeed, why didn't you?" he agreed. "It was cruel of you to have thrown me into such a crucible these past minutes.'' He nuzzled her dressing gown off one shoulder so that he could kiss her where he wanted to.

When he found the flower at the tip of her breast and nipped it with his teeth, she sighed and turned halfheartedly away from him. ''MacLaurin, you're sure now, aren't you? We have to be *sure.*''

His lips and teeth found her other breast. ''If my father had experienced the passion he desired,'' he said, ''he would not have denied me mine all these years.''

He released her hands so that he could part her dressing gown. The ribbons gave way at his touch, and he slipped his hands under the silk, around her shoulders, and brought her nakedness next to him. His hands traveled down her back and grasped her buttocks.

''If you need further evidence,'' he said, kissing her neck, her ear, her eye, the corner of her mouth, ''of the logical sort, you might consider the fact that my father never once made an effort to see you. If you were his daughter, the product of his loving union with your mother, he might have claimed you somehow, if only as a good friend's child.''

''Oh, yes,'' she said, lifting her arms around his shoulders and clasping her hands behind his neck. She thought vaguely that if Gavin MacLaurin was her father, his ghost would not have treated her so cruelly, but she hardly cared to think of a ghost when she was holding a very alive man in her arms.

Her playful nature had surfaced in full force. She kissed him back, temptingly, teasingly, at his temple, at his cheek. ''Does this mean, sir, that we're not going to make an effort to find the Cameron volume anytime soon and discover the name of my father?''

He conveyed to her, emphatically, his complete uninterest in the Cameron volume and expressed a similar uninterest in finding the book hiding Bev's bedeviled document.

He adjusted his hold of her so that he was leaning her back over the table, where it seemed they would end up soon enough. One hand held her around her waist. The other hand came to her throat. He began to trail one finger down between her breasts, to her navel, to the juncture of her thighs, which he had spread around him.

"This means, mistress," he said very low into her ear, which he tickled with his tongue, "that you're going to get what you've been asking for for the past three nights."

Chapter Twenty-Three

"No more delays," he said. "No more impediments."

She could not deny that she had been asking for just this. The waves of relief had transformed themselves into waves of desire, and the desire had pooled into purest lust. She couldn't imagine thinking of anything else, doing anything else, being anywhere else except in his arms, kissing him, giving herself to him.

He found the cocoon of her desire and seemed to want to prod from it a beautiful butterfly. Soon her desire was spreading its wings, spreading through her veins as inevitably as spilled wine along the threads of a linen tablecloth. She pulled him down on the table so that it creaked and groaned under their weight and caused the branch of candle, along the candlestick, to rattle. She felt happy and abandoned and never more ready to be ruined.

She was put in mind of one last point, a minor detail. She managed, between kisses, to say, "I never had an affair with Lieutenant Beverly."

He propped his elbows on the table on either side of her and cupped her head with his hands. He smiled down at her, satisfied and superior. ''I ceased giving Bev that much credit a couple of days ago.''

The slight pause in the vigors of their embrace allowed them to perceive an ominous creaking and cranking coming from within the wall that ran contiguous to the library. MacLaurin heard it first. He turned toward the wall at the same time that he drew himself to his feet and pulled her up with him. He twitched her disheveled dressing gown around her shoulders.

When the noise in the wall increased to a grinding, suggesting that the gears had been put in motion, they regarded one another for the space of a heartbeat and poised themselves for flight.

MacLaurin swore violently under his breath and said, ''The panel. It's going to open.''

Elizabeth had to pull herself together, literally and figuratively. MacLaurin, ever quick, restored the two volumes to their places on the shelves, then blew out the candles. He took her hand to draw her to the secret passage, but Elizabeth had enough of her wits about her to grab the candle they had brought with them, to leave behind no sign of their presence.

They could begin to see the panel drawing back. They could hear the voices on the other side, but faintly, threading through the grind of the gears.

MacLaurin shoved her into the passage before him and followed her, drawing the spring-hinged door to a sure closed click behind him. They were in utter darkness in the narrow passage. Although the situation was terrifying to Elizabeth, she knew that the perils of the passageway paled in comparison to the consequences of being caught, naked, in MacLaurin's arms. In one hand she gripped the unlit candle in her hands, squeezing the poor thing in her jumping fear. In the other hand she clutched the folds of her dressing gown that were tumbling around her.

MacLaurin's hand found its way to her mouth and covered it. He was telling her not to speak. Then he put his hands on her shoulders and moved her gently forward by locking the fronts of his legs with the backs of hers. They walked together in a kind of sliding motion that would create the fewest reverberations.

MacLaurin was not sure they had gotten away without being seen; and even if they had not been seen, it was possible that the dissipating smoke from the extinguished candles would provide a clue to their presence. He didn't know if his uncle knew of this passageway, but he did know that his uncle was too rotund to use it. Nevertheless, MacLaurin wanted to get as far and quickly away from the secret door as possible, in the event his uncle should open it and try to see who was escaping.

After many long minutes of careful movement he guessed they were nearing the end of the corridor that led directly to the library. Still exercising caution, he breathed into her ear to ask, "Are you all right?"

"My initial terror has receded into normal fear, if that's what you mean," she replied, keeping her voice equally low.

He was satisfied that she was all right. "That's what I mean."

"Do you think we were seen?"

"No, but it's always a possibility. My guess is that they were more intent on looking at the books than in looking for evidence that someone had been there before them."

"There were two voices, weren't there," she said more as a statement than a question.

He figured that she knew as well as he did who his uncle was treating to the pleasures of the secret annex.

"I suppose Lieutenant Beverly's document is lost to us, then," she said.

"Perhaps, but that doesn't mean we won't try again to recover it. However, at the moment I don't give a damn." He pressed his front to her back. "If you see what I mean."

"Oh, I do," she said in a provocative voice that did nothing to lessen his acute discomfort.

She moved ahead of him then, abandoning the effort at cautious movement, and he let her go. If he couldn't have her now, beneath him, around him, he would do better to have some space apart from her.

They walked on. After a while she commented, "Do you have any idea how many encounters we've had in these infernal passageways?"

"No," he said, "but if this one weren't so narrow, we could make this an encounter to remember."

He felt the darkness pulse, no, *throb,* around him.

"MacLaurin," she said on a plaintive note, "are you absolutely sure that we're not—?"

"I'm sure, absolutely," he said, "and I've never been so glad to disclaim kinship with anyone in my life."

Her little trembling moan of agreement nearly undid him. Considering every test of willpower and patience that he had met in the past several days, hours and minutes, he had done well. But he was coming to the end of his endurance.

They turned several more corners, and he caught her just before she fell down the flight of stairs they had mounted coming in the other direction.

At the bottom of the stairs she said meditatively, "Do you think that the difficulties we've had, um, getting together are a sign that we *shouldn't,* um, get together?"

His answer was unequivocal. "If you think that I won't ravish you the moment we get out of here, I shall have to reconsider my opinion of the ventilation in this passage, for clearly no air has been getting to your brain."

Elizabeth seemed to consider his statement, then said in the most outrageously demure voice possible, "Well, I see your point, but I don't think you've put the matter as poetically as your father would have phrased it—that is, in his better days, before my mother spurned his love."

"You, Mistress Whoever-you-are," he said between his teeth, "are asking for it. *Again.*"

"I am," she admitted. "Shamelessly."

Fortunately, they had arrived back at the beginning of the passage. Unfortunately, they were in the complete dark, he had no idea how to get out, and when he turned to the wall that led to the alcove in her room, it did not have quite the angle he thought it should have. It was almost as if a second wall had slid into place. If his physical condition had not been so extreme, he would have taken great interest in figuring out this new problem. As it was, however, he had had enough of castle secrets. If he couldn't get them out of the passage and into her bedchamber, then the crazy logic of the situation told him he could get them into—

His bedchamber, which, by his mental map of the relationship of the alcove and the passageway to the two chambers, had to lie straight ahead.

He put his hands around her so that he could feel the wall ahead of her and hoped he would not explode with the contact. Hanging desperately on to his self-control, he felt the wall ahead of him for catches. Finding none, he refined his finger search for the minute puzzle of wood, similar to the one he had found at the other end of this passageway on the door to the secret annex.

A few seconds later a door sprang open and they tumbled together into his bedchamber, which was bright with moonlight. He would admire the craftsmanship of this spring-hinged door much later. He similarly deferred consideration of the fact that if his armoire had been placed several feet over, it would have blocked the door.

He was back where he had started, this time with Elizabeth. The sense of coming full circle and finding himself enriched made him feel very happy.

He drew her roughly into his arms, shoved the dressing gown from her shoulders where it fell in a silken puddle, discarded his own clothing, all the while kissing her and touching her everywhere at once. At the same time, he was able to get them across the room and to throw back the cover of the bed upon which they fell in an entwined heap.

After a moment of lusty tussling, MacLaurin became aware of distracting breathing and murmuring that did not emanate from the bed. He paused in his pleasurable labors and lifted himself to his knees. He looked to his fireplace demons and commanded, "Close your eyes and go to sleep."

For the first time ever, they obeyed.

He was awed. He was elated. He was exultant. "It works," he said, almost disbelieving.

He looked at his ladylove, lying beside him and looking up at him partly mystified, partly amused, wholly desirous. Never before had he seen such a beguiling sea nymph. Never before had he held one in his arms, and his desire for her swelled to mythic proportions.

He lowered himself next to her. "I'm not usually the man who cares to take his pleasure first, Mistress Elizabeth..."

He paused to kiss her.

"But I'm thinking that after all we've just been through..."

He shifted her body to fit with his.

"We shall have to dispense with further preliminaries..."

He accommodated her treasures to his truly heroic desire.

"And I shall set about making you mine."

His eager sweetness was meant to minimize her inevitable pain, but it could not last, and spilled out into a vigorous urgency when he finally made her his.

Elizabeth luxuriated in a drowsy garden, full of berry bushes and climbing roses and a charming well. She had sipped its enchanting water and let it dribble down her mouth, down her body until it dampened her thighs. She had kissed its intoxicating drops from MacLaurin's mouth. Together they had flirted with a thousand tendrils, all responsiveness, swaying along the crests of the flower beds, thick with growth from the moist earth below.

She slept and dreamt and took his hand. She led him into the frame hung on the library's secret annex and continued their frolic amid a luscious landscape of rolling meadows and shade trees and bushes, lots of bushy bushes. MacLaurin was chasing a butterfly. No, he was letting it go. He had searched its hidden cocoon, teased the poor budding beast until it begged for mercy. Until it flapped its wings and flew away from him, laughing and beckoning him to follow.

MacLaurin, the butterfly-freer, had more than made up for his first, selfish, very endearing possession. Not that she had had anything to complain about. But if he wanted to make it up to her, he was most welcome to try. He tried. He succeeded. She had returned the favor by taking him into that very beautiful landscape of privacy and daylight.

Her eyes opened to blinding daylight. Her immediate landscape was a froth of beaten egg white linens, faintly musky, and an unaccustomed perspective on male muscle and sinew.

She shifted. She groaned. She was startled awake by the gentle slap of a broad hand on the curve of her hips.

She turned to look at him over her shoulder and ran an assessing eye down his graceful length.

He drew the sheet around him to his chin and piped, "No, kind sir, don't look at me like that!"

"As if I could do anything more," she sighed gustily, "at this moment, with your beautiful body, sweet mistress."

He dropped the sheet. "Such a relief."

She leaned back against the pillows. The quip that hovered on her tongue flew right off its tip when she spied the curious faces carved into the stone fireplace. She recalled an odd moment after arriving in this chamber.

"Last night you told someone or something to close its eyes and go to sleep. What was that all about?"

"My fireplace demons," he said. "Nosy creatures."

Elizabeth thought of her fireplace nymphs and had no difficulty understanding what he meant. "I suppose they would be, given the variety of exploits they must have witnessed over the years on this bed."

"They've encouraged some of my worst impulses," he told her, "but none of them have been played out on this bed." His smile was boyish and satisfied. "I'll have you know that you are the first woman I have entertained in my chamber."

Elizabeth was skeptical. "Even with that very convenient secret panel at your disposal?"

"There was never a woman on the other side who inspired my desire to use it, which was perhaps why it got so rusty since I was a lad."

She was still skeptical, but also flattered. "You said something like 'It works.' What did you mean?"

He touched a finger to her nose and said, "You, my voracious Elizabeth, are fishing for compliments, and it does not become you. I was surprised that my fireplace demons closed their eyes and went to sleep, for that was the first time they ever obeyed me."

"Voracious?"

"Yes, to my complete satisfaction."

"What did I do to fish for compliments?"

He smiled mysteriously and shook his head. "I have yet to see whether my entire plan will work so well as my mastery of the fireplace demons, and I shall let you know if it does. In fact, you will be the first to know!"

She saw that she would get no more out of him in this mood, so she did not try. Besides, it was far past the dawn, and she would need to get back to her room if she was to unmake her bed and mess it up before Mary arrived to attend to her.

She moved her sated body to the edge of the bed and found her silk wrapper. She slipped into it, drew her unbound hair from the collar and flipped the untidy mass down her back. Thinking ahead to the day that stretched before them, she asked idly, "So, what don't you like about His Grace?"

MacLaurin had rolled over on his side and had propped his head on his hand to watch her. "What's to like about him?" he returned.

"He's terribly high in the instep," she said, "and rather cold, I think, but not otherwise objectionable."

"I find him completely objectionable."

"Well, if your uncle chooses to sell him MacLaurin land—and I agree with you that it is unsettling!—it is not His Grace's fault, after all. He may not even be eager to buy the land, rather to do your uncle a favor."

"Hah," was MacLaurin's response to that.

"What is it, then, that makes His Grace so objectionable to you?"

MacLaurin shrugged. "When I returned to London after the wars on the Continent, I began to notice that he had a genius for getting in my way. Never a lot. Never quite openly. But he was always *there,* somehow, just at the edge of my line of vision."

"Can you give an example?"

He smiled wryly. "No. I could never be sure that Devonshire was the one to block a business deal or keep me from a gentleman's club or any other sort of annoyance, but I always suspected him."

"Might you not be imagining things?"

"Possibly. But here he is now, most unexpectedly, bedeviling my attempt to retrieve Bev's document, even if we can't be sure what he's doing here or why."

She considered that but arrived at no conclusion. "He's a strange man. Did he never marry?"

"Lord, yes, to a woman who conveniently died some fifteen years ago after producing the requisite heir. That was well before my time in town, so I know nothing about it, except to have caught wind of the story that his grief at his wife's passing was remarkably brief."

"And the heir?"

He paused to search a memory. "A youth who is sporting mad, I think, and spends all his time in the country. That is to say, far away from his father who is, undoubtedly, a parent of the most indifferent sort."

She tried to imagine His Grace displaying paternal affection and failed. Nothing in that part of his life, however, helped her decipher his reasons for being here now, so she abandoned interest in the topic and repeated her need to get back to her room before the sun rose any higher.

MacLaurin escorted her to the wall and showed her the ingenious knobs of ivy and thistle. When the panel slid soundlessly aside, he gestured her into her room with a solemn, ceremonious flourish.

She stepped across the threshold grandly. Before the panel closed, separating her from MacLaurin, she remarked, with a glance around the convenient opening, "I commend one of your forebears for this truly excellent invention!"

Chapter Twenty-Four

It was impossible for Elizabeth not to feel radiantly happy. Soon enough, she realized that she would be wise not to act radiantly happy.

Once inside her room, she disordered her bed to make it look as if she had slept in it, then dressed herself before Mary's knock was heard at the door. Mary complimented her mistress for looking so well rested. Elizabeth grinned a little too broadly, drawing a curious stare from Mary, then quickly softened that grin to a pleasant smile.

On her way to the banquet hall Elizabeth began to hum a Highland melody, meaning to suppress it before anyone could hear her. She mistimed herself and her approach to the main staircase, and her chipper, chirping mood caught the ear of some of her fellow historians. They could not help but comment on her happiness as they escorted her to breakfast.

She hastily rigged an argument. "I suppose I'm happy because I don't have to read my treatise today. Yesterday, I'm afraid, I was all nerves."

"Och, now, ye've never been nervous to speak to us before, Mistress Cameron!" came the reply.

"That's because the castle library is so grand, and I was overwhelmed."

"What, now? The library in Edinburgh is far grander than Robbie's, though his is a beauty! What's this with ye today, Mistress Cameron?"

Having tripped in the rigging of her own argument, she fell back on an innocent smile of gentle confusion. She decided that she would do best by saying least and reflected that intense pleasure must dull the senses. She was looking forward to becoming ever duller. Still, her wits had not yet grown piteously useless, and she realized that she had better act a little sharper if she wanted to escape notice.

It was just as well that she had gathered her wandering wits before appearing in the banquet hall. The first person she saw was Juliette Michael and she, poor dear, did not look as if her senses had been at all dulled from a night of pleasure. In fact, she looked quite the opposite, all spiky irritation, like a cat whose fur had been rubbed the wrong way. Or rubbed not at all.

Elizabeth kept her demeanor as demure as her expression. She thought it prudent to give her ladyship a wide berth today and thus placed herself at the other end of the table. Within a minute she realized her mistake. In choosing to sit far away from her ladyship, she had jumped, it seemed, from the frying pan into the proverbial fire.

"Well, my child, did you rest well last night?" His Grace inquired at her side.

She had not seen him approach or sit down, yet there he was next to her. She was tempted to flaunt her happiness. She was equally tempted to affect grogginess and say that the snoring of His Grace's guard outside her door had kept her awake the night long. She chose the middle ground.

"Yes, I rested very well last night," she said truthfully, but kept her voice free of innuendo. "I'm glad that I retired early."

"Yes," His Grace agreed, "you had an eventful day yesterday."

"There is nothing to restore one's spirits like a good night's sleep. And you, Your Grace?"

His Grace's fine brows rose. "I, Mistress Cameron?"

He might as well have said that she was impertinent, that a commoner—and an unmarried young woman!—did not ask a peer of the realm if he had slept well. She had always been bold with His Grace. Her happiness made her bolder.

"Yes, Your Grace," she said, looking at him directly, "I wonder whether you retired early like I did and slept well, or whether you found diversions last night beyond the receiving room."

The expression that came into his eyes made her wonder whether she had been too bold. However, since she perceived that it would be unstrategic to back down, she continued to meet his eyes with a level gaze.

At that moment she felt a stirring of awareness that MacLaurin had entered the room behind her, but she did not turn to look at him. Instead, she noted that His Grace's eyes left her face to follow MacLaurin's progress around the room and to the seat on the other side of the table and down several places.

She felt as if His Grace were daring her to look at MacLaurin and acknowledge him. She accepted the challenge by glancing at MacLaurin and nodding her head in greeting. When she looked back at His Grace, she was pleased that her cheeks had not flushed, nor did her eyes flinch from His Grace's scrutiny. Happiness, it seemed, might make her stupid, but it also did wonders for the steadiness of her nerves.

"I passed a very pleasant evening, Mistress Cameron." His Grace relented to answer her question. "With Robbie. He is such an entertaining host, and his residence is so full of interesting features." He betrayed no more hint of hidden meaning than had she. "After a most fascinating discussion with Robbie, I retired in a very agreeable frame of mind."

Elizabeth could only guess at what he thought of Lord Mure's collection of erotic books, but she did not think that they, in particular, had put him in an especially agreeable frame of mind. Still, his tone was of such bland evenness that she was not quite sure whether he had—or had not—retrieved Bev's document.

"But I do not care to discuss the previous day," he said, "when I have the new day and more interesting treatises ahead of me."

"You plan to attend the day's meeting, then, Your Grace?"

He assured her that he was looking forward to the day's discoveries.

She wondered whether his continued presence meant that he hadn't yet retrieved the document.

"I shall be departing on the morrow, alas, since it is the last day of the summer meeting."

Elizabeth thought it just as likely that he had retrieved the document and decided to remain, so that his departure would not arouse suspicion. She said with bland politeness, "The week does pass quickly, with five full days of meetings, and one day of relaxation on either end."

"Do you leave on the morrow as well, Mistress Cameron?"

"I hadn't planned on it, Your Grace," she hedged.

"But the meeting is drawing to a close. Do you have reason to wish to stay on?"

"No, Your Grace, I wish only to enjoy the usual sociability of the last evening."

"But you have already enjoyed quite a few sociable evenings this past week, have you not, Mistress Cameron? If you find on the morrow that you have had enough, perhaps you will allow me to escort you to your home," he said, "since it has become my custom to see you safely to your quarters."

He was determined to unnerve her. Elizabeth was determined not to be unnerved. She avoided responding to his offer by saying playfully, "Is your excessively kind regard for my well-being prompted by your knowledge that I have come to Castle Cairn without my father's permission?"

His Grace smiled with spine-chilling gentleness. "Something like that, Mistress Cameron."

Her overall happiness shielded her from being truly disturbed by this disturbing conversation with His Grace. She was too happy to think that she would have to leave Castle Cairn with His Grace before she was ready. She was too happy to worry about what would happen beyond this night when she would tempt MacLaurin and he would push a knob of ivy and pull a knob of thistle to move a magic panel.

She decided that the purpose of this bracing encounter with His Grace had been to give her the inner stuffings to make it through the day without melting at a mere glance from MacLaurin. Indeed, she was rather proud of herself that she could encounter him in such a friendly fashion in front of everyone and talk with him as if he were merely a part of the delightful group. She listened to the treatises and asked questions that lacked her usual sharpness but had quite a lot of feeling.

The day passed, not speedily but not ploddingly, either. Dinner was not an ordeal; nor was the following hour in the receiving room excruciating. MacLaurin stepped into her orbit and stepped out of it as easily as any other guest. She was pleased, all in all, that by the time she was ready to retire, neither of them had given their lovely, lascivious secret away.

When His Grace escorted her to her room and, once again, intimated that her door would be watched, she thanked him with what gravity she could muster. Once inside her chamber, however, she gave in to the ridiculous smile that had tugged at the corners of her mouth all day.

She hastily discarded her hairpins and was beginning to unlace her dress when the horrible thought assailed her that perhaps MacLaurin had had enough of her and would no longer be tempted by her displays. After all, they had made no assignation for this evening. Nor had they exchanged any words of love. She had worked up a gust of worry, but before she had even pulled the dress over her head, the secret panel opened. In walked MacLaurin, wearing only breeches and shirt.

She fell into an uncharacteristic flutter. "But... but... but—!" was all she could manage when her love walked through the opening, which closed behind him.

He waved away her stuttering with the simple words, "It's my turn to do the tempting."

He walked up to her, critically surveyed her, then remarked that his tempting would go better if she was wearing less clothing. He began to correct that fault, and he was pleased by the sound of her laughter when she surrendered to his ministrations.

She asked, "Does your undressing of me count as part of the tempting, or not?"

"You tell me," he replied. "Now show me those letters."

She could not immediately respond to his request because he decided to kiss her, lingeringly. He also decided to rid her of most of her underclothes, leaving only her chemise. When he broke the kiss, and she looked up at him, her expression was dazed.

"What letters?" she asked, befuddled.

Muddleheaded. Definitely muddleheaded. He liked that his kisses rendered her senseless. "My father's letters."

Her expression cleared, but not the stars from her eyes. She took him to her armoire and withdrew a packet of letters from its depths.

They strolled to the window together and, in the light of the moon, he began to read the passionate enticements and entreaties written by Gavin MacLaurin to the beautiful Katherine Cameron.

He stumbled, startled, over various turns of phrase. It was difficult to believe that the man who had seemed determined to kill his son's passion had written them. He looked up and quoted skeptically, "'The honeyed seal of soft affections'?"

"It's a very beautiful image," she told him.

"It may well be," he acknowledged, shuffling through the gracefully yellowed pages in his hand. "However, if it took him these ten letters to work up to 'love's first snowdrop, virgin kiss,' it's no wonder that your mother tired of him and sought satisfaction elsewhere."

"We don't know that she tired of him," she replied, trying to push him away, "but we do know now that you're not romantic."

He reaffirmed his grip on her. "Is that what you like?" he asked and quoted, " 'To share these pledges of future bliss, these dearest ties of young connections'?"

"It's very appealing to hear pretty words," she said primly.

"I'd rather get the job done," he replied.

She turned her face away from him. "You, sir, are crude."

"I, mistress, am effective. My father, apparently, was not."

"He was wildly in love."

"Love," he repeated dismissively, thinking that words without action was no love at all.

"You deny the possibility?" she asked, resisting him.

He slid the letters back in the packet, and when he kissed her, he let the packet fall to the floor. "I can't change the past." Realizing that he could not be holding her like this if his father had put action behind his words, he added, "Nor do I want to."

Her resistance increased. "You could learn a lesson from your father."

He laughed. "I'd rather lay his ghost to rest, and speaking of getting the job done," he said, drawing her toward the alcove, "we have work to do."

She cried in dismay, "Oh, no, not the passageway again!"

"Shh!" He hushed her and cocked his head toward the door to the main hallway. "I've no doubt that Devonshire posted guards again," he said with a sly wink. "And, yes, the passageway again. I worked on the mechanism this morning and have it rigged to my specifications."

He tapped on the alcove wall, and the wall slid back. "In you go," he said. "I'm right behind you."

"No candle?"

"Not necessary."

"You're sure?"

"It's not as if we can get lost, you know. There's only one way to go."

As they traveled the corridor, MacLaurin was feeling very frisky. Despite the constraints of the narrow confines, his hands were able to find the most unlikely places on her body.

"Mmm."

"Stop that."

"Stop what?"

"Putting your hands—oh! You're being naughty."

"I'm not doing anything. It must be the evil castle spirits."

"*Naughty,* I said, not evil."

"Is there a distinction?"

The farther they went, the friskier he felt.

"I thought the passage was better ventilated," she said at one moment. "I don't recall it being this hot last night."

"It was this hot last night. Believe me."

At last they arrived and entered the annex. This evening the removable blocks had been restored to their places in the wall, thus blocking all air and the moonlight. MacLaurin palmed his way around the room to the wall and felt for the iron rings with which he could pull the blocks free. He found them soon enough, and the little room glowed with secret blue life.

Elizabeth walked toward the table in the center of the room. "And the job that needs to be done?"

"We shall finish what we started last night."

She slanted him a seductive glance. It took all his willpower to pat her on the rump and say, "You had got as far as the MacLaurin volumes over there, and I was through the first several shelves over here. We shall meet in the middle."

He liked the look of puzzlement and disappointment that flashed across her expressive face. She went to her side of the room and he went to his, whereupon he found the place where he had left off the night before and began the tedious task of checking every book thereafter for Bev's document.

He had no idea how long they spent, but when they met in the middle of the room she was, apparently, as empty-handed as he.

"No document?"

She shook her head. "No document."

"I'm not surprised."

"His Grace got it last night, you know," she said.

He shrugged. "Did he?"

She nodded. "I'd say so, given the conversation I had with him this morning. Did you come across the Cameron genealogy, by any chance?"

"No."

"Neither did I." She sighed. "Well, then, are we ready to go?"

"Now we shall finish what we started last night."

She paused. "You already said that." Then, with a seductive glance, "Did you think I'd fall twice into the same trap?"

"We began two activities last night, as you'll recall. This is the second."

"This?" she queried.

"My way of tempting you," he said. He took her in his arms. "Making you wait."

"What, no flowery phrases?"

"You know what I think of flowery phrases."

"A small expression of romance or...or chivalry wouldn't hurt, I think."

He whispered in her ear what he wanted them to do.

Her eyes widened adorably. "That's hardly a romantic expression!" she said loftily, but ruined her superior effect by denying that they would be able to maintain their bodies in such a position.

"My chivalric duty is clear," he said. "I'll bear your weight."

The sound she emitted hovered between a laugh and a groan of desire. She said weakly, "I still don't think it can be done."

He ignored that feeble protest, for the stain of his desire was spreading rapidly. He wanted to be surrounded by her liquid pansy velvet now, feeding his passion and hers. He wanted to fill with his life and breath the air of this secret library annex whose records bore testimony to his father's inaction twenty-five years before and whose erotic collection compensated for his uncle's incapacity now.

He did not want to waste words that he neither knew nor thought she needed. He pushed her gently against the back of the bookcase. "Remember that I'm good at tricky puzzles."

Chapter Twenty-Five

After spending the rest of the night with him in her bed, Elizabeth kissed MacLaurin goodbye before he disappeared through the secret panel to his chamber. Feeling lazy, she returned to her bed to doze, but instead fell back asleep. She was awakened only when Mary knocked and offered to help with her mistress's morning toilette.

Stretching luxuriously and yawning happily, Elizabeth was pleased to accept help this morning. She was unconcerned when Mary eyed with suspicion the truly chaotic state of her bed linens and realized that her mistress had slept naked. Nor did Elizabeth care that Mary saw the packet of love letters on the floor by the window where she and MacLaurin had left them the night before. What could Mary—or anyone else—prove, after all, since guards had been posted in the hallways outside her door, monitoring her movements, and no one could know that MacLaurin had free and secret access to her chamber?

Elizabeth swung her legs off the side of the bed and slipped into her dressing gown. She unhurriedly picked up the packet and tossed it atop her dressing table at which she plopped down and began to bring her tangled curls to order.

Mary's head disappeared into the armoire and reappeared to suggest several dresses that Elizabeth might consider wearing for the day. Elizabeth made her choice, Mary withdrew the garment in question and the dressing and the coiffing proceeded with no incident.

When Elizabeth was ready, she crossed the room, leaving Mary behind to straighten up. The moment she opened the door to the hallway, mischievous castle spirits must have rushed in, for two things happened at once, and their intersection proved to be a disaster.

Mary was standing by the opened armoire and holding up a distinctive cobalt blue wool jacket, shoes and stockings. She was fully visible from the hallway and she was saying, "What am I to do with these odd items, Mistress Cameron? I'm thinking that they couldn't belong to ye, for these are surely a man's clothes."

Too late Elizabeth realized her grievous mistake. She had not returned the clothing to MacLaurin the evening before when she had had a chance, and she had not remembered to replace the packet in front of their hiding place in the corner of the armoire.

Before she could formulate even the feeblest lie to account for why a man's clothing would be stuffed into the corner of her armoire, she noticed that His Grace stood outside her opened bedchamber door. From the too-bland expression on his face, she could tell that he had seen and heard all.

Her only hope for finessing the situation was to ignore it completely. Sailing out of the room, she told Mary that she would speak with her later, then closed the door behind her. She smiled as if she had nothing in the world to hide. "Good morning, Your Grace. How thoughtful of you to escort me both to my chamber in the evening and from it in the morning."

His Grace did not immediately reply. He merely turned and began to walk down the hallway beside her.

His cool silence unnerved her, so she filled the void by saying, "That is, if you *are* escorting me to breakfast." She immediately regretted her compulsion to speak.

He let the pause stretch before he said, "Yes, Mistress Cameron, I am escorting you to breakfast. What else would I be doing at your chamber door at such an hour?"

She bit her tongue against the answer. *Calling off the watch you posted outside my room.* Stating the matter outright would not improve her position. Stating anything outright would not improve her position, so she said nothing.

They walked together down the hallway. With each echoing footstep she felt the flaky edges of her happiness crumble away. With each passing minute she became ever more aware of an impending doom, inexplicable but very real.

His Grace said, "I will be leaving early this afternoon, and I will expect you to be ready to depart with me."

She opened her mouth to respond but was not permitted to speak.

His Grace continued calmly and authoritatively, "You will wish to attend, of course, the final morning session in the library. That is to be expected. However, you have no reason to stay beyond the midday dinner."

She tried to match his calm. "I told you yesterday, Your Grace, that I had not decided whether I would leave today or tomorrow. I believe I told you that I was inclined to stay until the morrow."

Looking straight ahead, His Grace said simply, "Perhaps you are aware that your friend, Ian MacLaurin, is engaged to be married."

She was not aware of that, of course. Her stomach lurched, her blood roiled and her skin crawled. She was unable to summon the bravado to say carelessly, curiously, "Why do you tell me this, Your Grace?" Neither could she afford the luxury of exposing her feelings, which were suddenly raw. She had been stunned but had to keep standing, as if nothing had happened.

They arrived at the head of the main staircase. His Grace bowed slightly, indicating that she precede him. When he was a step behind her, he said, "I shall meet you in the entry hall below this afternoon. Shall we say at two o'clock?"

She was both enraged and hurt that His Grace had nothing more to say on the subject of MacLaurin's marriage. She desperately wanted more information but couldn't bring herself to ask. She had the passing thought that His Grace was lying, but could conceive of no reason why he would be gratuitously cruel. That meant, then, that he was being purposely cruel.

The question she sifted from her pain was, "Why do you insist that I leave with you, Your Grace?"

"I do not insist, Mistress Cameron," His Grace replied with an inflection of surprise. "I offer my services, imagining that you have no further business at Castle Cairn."

"However, if you are continuing on your way to Edinburgh, as you mentioned when you first arrived, Your Grace, I must tell you that the Cameron property is out of your way."

"I know where the Cameron property is, my child," he said, "and I've a desire to make it on my way. It has been some time since I have paid a visit to Joseph Cameron." He favored her with an assessing glance that was neither fully condemnatory nor fully complimentary. "I would like to discuss with him why such a charming young lady as yourself is not yet married. I shall prompt him to arrange a marriage for you without further delay."

She nearly gasped. His Grace must know that she had ruined herself with MacLaurin, making her wholly ineligible. Or was his cruelty—strange thought!—rather a kindness, in that His Grace was attempting to have her save face and preserve her reputation with a respectable marriage? But why should he bother?

She said, a little weak and forlorn, "The topic of marriage seems to be on your mind, Your Grace."

His Grace nodded and turned the subject, and they proceeded to the banquet hall, speaking of this and that. Afterward Elizabeth had no recollection what topics His Grace had introduced, how she had responded or even if she had responded. She ate her breakfast, aware only of great pain. She clung to the hope that His Grace was inventing the story of MacLaurin's engagement, that for some incomprehensible reason he was bedeviling MacLaurin's life at Castle Cairn, just as MacLaurin said he bedeviled it in London. But that meant, then, that His Grace was affecting *her* life, too. She was anxious to see MacLaurin as soon as possible, to ask him about his forthcoming marriage.

Or could she ask him such a thing?

It didn't matter, because MacLaurin didn't come to breakfast. Nor was he in the library for the morning session. She nearly swooned with the thought that he had already left Castle Cairn and was on his way to London. Why, indeed, should he remain, since His Grace had retrieved the document and he had gotten what he wanted from her? He would wish, no doubt, to return to his love in London.

But did he have another love? How *could* he have another love?

Her encounter with Juliette Michael seemed to confirm the worst. At the end of the morning session, when Godfrey MacQuarie declared the meeting officially closed and pronounced it an extraordinary success, Elizabeth tried to maintain her best face while she said her goodbyes. She even managed a smile when she encountered Juliette Michael.

Her ladyship was all that was gracious and asked Elizabeth, by the by, whether she had seen MacLaurin this morning.

Elizabeth tested the waters by saying, "No, I haven't. Perhaps he is already on his way to London to prepare for his forthcoming wedding."

Lady Michael's brows rose with interest, but she said with just enough distance to show she was unaffected, "Oh, is he going to marry that pretty little daughter of the earl? I hadn't heard. There's been such a string of women over the years that I didn't know if one would ever catch him."

Elizabeth didn't know how that conversation ended. She knew only that she wanted to get to the safe haven of her chamber as quickly as possible. Once there, she did not think that the hour of departure would come soon enough, for the pain of remaining in this stone monster grew by the moment. To give herself something to do, she emptied the armoire of her dresses and stuffed all her belongings into her baggage.

Her agony was renewed and intensified when her eyes fell on MacLaurin's jacket, shoes and stockings, folded in a neat pile on the floor beside the armoire. Of course he had some woman—a pretty little daughter of an earl— waiting for him in London! Had she been so enchanted by the spell of Castle Cairn that she thought that *she* could have held his interest for more than a day or two? She who had no name, no lineage, no charms? It was not as if she hadn't known from the moment he set eyes on her what he thought of her!

She had let her fancy roam free. She had exposed herself and humiliated herself.

There came a knock at her door. Young Jonathan had come to carry her baggage to the front courtyard. She followed him out of her chamber door and down the interminable hallway filled with evil spirits who leered at her in her shame. She followed him to the wide stone staircase and began to descend.

At the half-story landing she crossed paths with MacLaurin, who was bounding up the stairs two by two. Her heart lurched. She halted. Jonathan descended. The weak light from the vertical row of three small stained-glass windows obscured the fine points of MacLaurin's expression, but she could see that he was smiling. It was his most charming smile, she noted, that transformed his not-quite-handsome features into an irresistible arrangement. It was a smile, she thought, that told her exactly how much she was missing. Her heart twisted.

"You're still here," she said, not knowing what else to say.

His smile curved up and lit his lively blue eyes. "Yes, I'm still here."

"You weren't in the library. I thought you had left."

His bright smile might have shaded into mild puzzlement. "You did? I was with the overseer all morning."

"Oh!" she said, then covered what she perceived to be an awkward moment with the information that his jacket and shoes and stockings were in her room by the door. "I didn't want to leave without returning them to you."

A small frown might have settled between his dark brows. "You're leaving?"

She glanced down into the vast hallway below and saw His Grace standing there, speaking with Lord Mure. At that moment His Grace looked up and nodded to her, minimally, graciously. She looked back at MacLaurin and remembered standing in his embrace the night before at the moment he had dismissed the word *love*. He had denied its possibility—at least in the context of holding her in his arms.

"His Grace has offered to escort me home," she said.

He looked down into the entry hall. His Grace nodded a second time, less graciously. He looked back at her. "I'm not sure what to say."

She wished she could ask him about his engagement. She wished she could lash out at him. But she could not, for he seemed very dear to her, even honorable in his own way, for he had never wooed her with false, whispered words but had taken her with frank, passing passion. If she had not been so in love with him, if she had felt less pain, if the evil castle spirits had not been let loose, if His Grace had not walked to the foot of the stairs to wait for her, she might have seen that MacLaurin's doubt lay not in disavowal, but rather in surprise and confusion.

Taking the true lover's part of making no demands, she said quickly, "You needn't say anything! I'd rather you not say anything you did not...not truly wish to say! I know how you feel about such things as flowery phrases." Here she flushed miserably, then struggled with the final words, "Let me now say goodbye and God-speed."

She continued down the stairs. She knew that Mac-Laurin had not moved from the half landing or taken his eyes off her back. She was grateful to accept the hand His Grace extended to her when she trod the last two steps. As much as she distrusted His Grace, she was happy for the comfort of the clasp of his hand that steadied her, reassured her and would whisk her away to safety and oblivion.

She took the last step and stood before His Grace. She dared to look up at him. His fine gray eyes were focused on her, very cool, very pleased. "You are ready to depart, my child?"

She was glad that he offered her no sympathy and no censure. She found that his cool demeanor reinforced her dignity. She was not going to crumple and cry or otherwise betray herself.

"Yes, Your Grace," she said.

Lord Mure joined them, and as a threesome they crossed the vast entry hall. For the first time in six days she left the confines of the castle, crossing under the carved portal and out into the bright light of the courtyard, where two carriages were waiting. She felt the stabbing pain of sunlight in her eyes and the beginnings of disenchantment, as if she were waking to a heavy head after a long night of drinking whiskey.

His Grace was in command. When he was informed that her carriage had been loaded with her baggage, he ordered that it be sent ahead without her. "You will travel with me, my child, in my carriage, back to the Cameron estate."

"Thank you, Your Grace," she said. Although his decision was irksome for its high-handedness, she was surprised to find that she actually welcomed His Grace's company and thought he might relieve some of the misery of the return trip.

When His Grace's magnificent carriage was brought around, he spoke briefly to his coachman, who brought the well-trained postilions to order, and the carriage steps were lowered.

All the while, Lord Mure was chatting amiably. He filled any possible uncomfortable silence by commenting on the fineness of the weather, on the excellence of the meeting, on the happiness of having received His Grace at Castle Cairn, on his wishes for a safe and pleasant journey.

When Elizabeth began to mount the steps, Lord Mure's desultory discourse took a fateful turn. "Why, seeing ye depart, Mistress Cameron, reminds me of yer arrival! I recall that hardly a week ago ye told me that ye had come across some rare historical documents that promised to be so fascinating that you decided to come to our summer meeting without yer father's approval!"

Elizabeth paused and turned toward her host. "Why, yes, I did," she said, "but I also told you during the meeting that what I had found were more pages from Margery Cameron's diary."

Lord Mure shook his head and wagged a playfully disapproving finger. "Nay, then, Mistress Cameron, I think ye're trying to put one over on me! I'm recalling clearly now that ye told me on the evening of yer arrival that the historical documents appeared to be one half of an exchange of letters. Ye said that they weren't signed, nor even dated, thus inspiring yer curiosity—and yer disobedience!"

"Mistress Cameron's curiosity?" His Grace inquired pleasantly.

A strange feeling passed over her when Lord Mure continued, "And I'm thinking now that ye made the story up to appease my misgivings!"

She lied calmly, "I did, and you've caught me at it."

Lord Mure sighed and said, "Well, then, I'm relieved that His Grace is returning ye right and proper to Cameron lands, and I'm hoping he'll tell the story to yer father so his disapproval is not misdirected at me, lass! I can imagine my old friend Joseph on his way here now, coming to demand satisfaction from me for having lured ye to the meeting that he's always forbidden ye!"

"You can imagine him on his way now, your lordship?" she returned, climbing into the carriage and sitting down. The strange feeling refused to leave her. "Now there's a thought!"

Chapter Twenty-Six

MacLaurin stood on the half landing. He was watching Elizabeth descend and letting her words *Goodbye and Godspeed* echo in his ears.

If he was not mistaken, she had just brushed him off. He was not so set up in conceit that he thought it impossible that a woman would love him and leave him. Still, he deemed it unlikely that Elizabeth wanted to end her relationship with him, but not because he thought himself so lovable. Rather, he had a high opinion of Elizabeth's honor and integrity. She had given herself to him fully and passionately, and he knew that she would not do so lightly, for she had never given herself to a man before.

He had been transformed by loving her, and he refused to believe that she had remained unaffected and unattached to him. He had felt the difference come over himself. He had seen the difference come over her. He knew that his unleashed passion had wrought changes in the castle air. Why, he had even subdued his fireplace demons!

Nevertheless, as he watched her descend the last two steps of the massive stone staircase, he could not help but wonder whether his belief in the return of her affection might not be just another illusion produced by the tricky spirits of Castle Cairn. A cold shiver touched his shoulder and spread through his very warm blood, and a change in the air made it suddenly more difficult for him to breathe. The old restlessness began to swirl around him, making him want to escape this depressing wreck.

But no. He resisted the restless chill, and he reasoned that nothing in this brief exchange with Elizabeth rang true. For one, why would she think that he had already left Castle Cairn? For another, why would she leave in company with Devonshire? What was she hiding now? From what he knew of her, it made no sense that she would smile at him tremulously, beseech him with her eyes, then wish him goodbye and Godspeed.

For all that he admired her qualities, he found her honor and integrity damnably inconvenient at such a moment. Her calm dignity was damnably incomprehensible. Her straight back and proud carriage were damnably—

She took the last step and accepted the hand that Devonshire extended to her. She turned toward Devonshire and lifted her eyes to him, so that they stood profile to profile from MacLaurin's point of view. In the mysterious light of the vast entry hall MacLaurin saw the outlines of their profiles only. The differences between the two faces had faded into the shadows surrounding them, while the angles of the noses and the juts of the chins were enhanced and in perfect symmetry.

So that was it, then. Her straight back and her proud carriage were damnably *familiar.* So was her profile, for he was looking at the model from which hers had been cut.

The disparate pieces of an intricate puzzle fell into place, and he beheld the mainspring of the mechanism of forces that had been working against him all week. All his life.

But did she know it?

It took him but a moment to answer his own question: of course she didn't. He had known from the moment he laid eyes on her that she was muddleheaded. His affection for her collided with his hatred for Devonshire and left him immobile at the moment she walked out of the castle on Devonshire's arm.

Devonshire. Always Devonshire. Now Devonshire's *daughter?*

What was he going to do about this unwelcome and wholly unpleasant discovery? The answer came to him as clearly as if it were his own voice whispering in his ear. "Get as far away from Castle Cairn as possible, if you want to live."

Just then, before exiting the entry hall, Devonshire turned to look over his shoulder and flicked him a glance of triumph. He was leaving with the document, with Elizabeth, with his secret safe.

Devonshire had made a mistake.

So what was MacLaurin going to *do* about it?

He frowned in concentration. He had seen unfold before him the solution to a variety of mysteries, but one eluded him. He had thought that the expression and exercise of his passion would be enough to give him the breathing room he needed here if he was to stay, but apparently it was not. Or perhaps the voice in his ear was right, and he was not destined to stay. Did he even want to stay?

In his mind's eye he traveled back through the narrow passages with Elizabeth, felt the four walls around them, felt her around him. His passion for her had been wonderful, but perhaps not wonderful enough. She had wanted something from him, but he could not think what it might be. It had not seemed important at the time, but it seemed important now. It reminded him, curiously, of the part of his father that he had never known. What was it, then?

"Flowery phrases," he murmured aloud.

The cold wisp at his shoulder took vague shape, and MacLaurin turned to look at the ghost of his father as it hovered beside him, then began to drift away from him. He had never been afraid of the castle ghosts, and he wasn't afraid of this one.

"Where are you going?" MacLaurin demanded.

The wraith curled back toward him, then curled away, the double movement conveying an insult that the question was not worth answering.

"We have unfinished business," MacLaurin said.

The ghost laughed a laugh that was so dry it was almost a cough. "The business was finished," it said, "long ago."

The misty wisp drifted up the stairs. MacLaurin followed.

"You chilled my shoulder just now and robbed me of air, didn't you?" MacLaurin accused. "You whispered in my ear just now for me to leave, didn't you?"

"If you want to live," the ghost threatened in return, floating upward faster.

MacLaurin took the stairs three by three. Even though he was coming closer to the ghost, the chill was leaving him, and his breathing was becoming ever deeper. "I shall live, all right," he said. "Here, or anywhere else I choose. It's the ghost of Gavin MacLaurin that doesn't want to be put to rest."

At the top landing of the stairs, the wraith writhed back toward him. "Rest? How can I ever rest?"

"When I've sought for you the satisfaction you crave."

"You are not capable."

"So you've had me think all these years."

"You have no idea what is required of you."

"I know that marrying the woman you chose for me ten years ago would have accomplished nothing more than condemning me to your life of misery."

The ghost's ethereal presence thinned to the point of disappearance. It spoke in accents of death. "You know nothing."

"I know that Elizabeth Cameron is Katherine Cameron's daughter. I know who her father is, as well."

The ghost seemed to draw together what little substantial existence it had. It puffed, with effort, "I won her with words."

MacLaurin said baldly, brutally, "He won her with action."

It quivered. If it had been capable of an emotion, its quiver would have been produced by equal parts anger and sorrow. "She never loved him and wouldn't have him in the end, even after she betrayed me."

"You left her," MacLaurin argued, "when she needed you most."

"He was too strong for me."

"You should have *fought* for her!"

A voice behind MacLaurin nearly caused him to jump. "To whom are ye speaking, Master Ian?"

MacLaurin whirled and saw Barrow ascending the stairs, his stiff gait eloquent of age.

Barrow continued, unperturbed, "The late lordship, perhaps?"

MacLaurin turned back around and saw that his father's ghost had evaporated.

"He's an edgy one at the best of times," Barrow added, taking the last steps so that he stood next to MacLaurin. "But he'll settle down again, now that his old friend has left."

"Old friend?"

Barrow's expression was unreadable. "Are ye planning to run away again, then, Master Ian?"

"I'd considered it," he said.

"And yer conclusion?"

MacLaurin thought about the decades of his father's misspent love. He thought about the years of his own misspent passions. He thought about a noble young woman driving off in the company of an ignoble duke and decided that, start to finish, she had caused him an uncommon amount of trouble. Still, it was impossible to think of her without being inspired by the courage that her curiosity continuously demanded of her and by her passion that he was sure she would never misspend. He knew what he had to do, and in order to do it, he knew that he would have to fight every habit of thought and action he had cultivated over the past ten years and more.

He didn't want to do it.

He had no other choice.

He clapped a hand on Barrow's shoulder and said, "I'm planning to leave the castle for a bit, but not to run away again." He held up a hand and said, "Oh, yes! I admit it! I ran away ten years ago, not knowing what else to do." He smiled. "By the way, thanks for the plaid."

When His Grace was settled on the seat opposite her, he gave the signal, and his fine equipage moved forward. Elizabeth flipped up the glass of the carriage window and watched the stone beast recede.

With the carriage wheels crunching the fine gravel beneath, she felt the spell of Castle Cairn wear off, realizing with renewed pain that her brief, giddy, enraptured world of secret passageways and secret passions had ceased to be. She was being released—expelled, more like—from the fantasy her fancy had woven over the past few days. It was as if the stage had gone dark and was empty, and the curtain had fallen.

The carriage turned the corner, and a thicket of trees in the alley obscured the stone monster from her view. She found herself suddenly and unpleasantly returned to a world where existence was utterly ordinary, where sea nymphs did not fill her body with siren's songs, where high passion did not throb in the air, where a vital young man was not driven to touch her and take her as if his life depended on it.

The play was over, and she was returning home. She was hardly the same as she had left, for she was doubly disgraced now, without her virtue and without a true name. She was returning empty-handed as well, for she had not found the document that would safeguard Allegra's future. She hardly cared anymore what His Grace would want with such a thing.

She looked out the window and saw fields in bad heart. MacLaurin lands. Their state matched her mood. She thought that Lord Mure might as well be selling off his acres, if he was not interested, or able, to farm them himself.

She transferred her gaze to His Grace, who was watching her silently. She nodded out the window, at the fields. "Do you plan to improve the yield of the Cairn fields, Your Grace?"

His Grace paused at length before answering. His words were harsh, his tone was not. "Your question is impertinent, my child."

"It is something that you state the case frankly," she remarked, looking out again at the sad, untended fields, "instead of leaving me to infer it."

"Your impertinence continues." This time his voice held a hint of reprimand.

She looked at His Grace again. She supposed that she should have felt more chastened, but she did not. "I ask, Your Grace, because I live in the Grampians and because I know that you are buying some of his lordship's land. Naturally, I am interested to know how the transaction will affect the general economy of the area." She drew a breath. "Or will you say that it is none of my business?"

"I shall say so, indeed, and I shall ask how you know that I am involved in such a transaction."

She had revealed too much. Again, she did not care. "The overseer told MacLaurin. MacLaurin told me. So, you see, as a resident of the neighborhood, I am interested."

His Grace said, "Of course I plan improvements. It is a pity to see such fine land lie fallow and the MacLaurin estate sink financially. The MacPherson clan has always been interested to see this corner of the Highlands survive and thrive."

She had a stray thought about the years of poor crops and about her father's—no, she corrected herself, her uncle's!—repeatedly poor farming decisions. She wondered idly if the MacPhersons had not bailed him out on an occasion or two—that is, if His Grace's account of the philanthropic impulses of the Clan MacPherson was true.

Looking at His Grace now, however, she did not think he often suffered from philanthropic impulses. In fact, looking at him now, with the curtain rung down on her absurd fantasies and her senses cleared of the spell of Castle Cairn, she saw him as a powerful man who would stop at nothing to accomplish his ends, whatever they may be. She recognized that kind of unchecked power as the source of evil.

Her heart began to beat irregularly. Evil? Why had that word come to mind? She suddenly realized that the curtain on the stage had not dropped, but had rather been pulled aside to reveal a new reality. She recalled her mother's letters to Gavin MacLaurin, teasing him with her attraction to the charm and power of his rival, the evil one. She looked at the man across from her and was aware—as she had been aware from the moment she had met him—of his charm and power. This new reality was frightening, concerned her vitally and was composed of facts that could be verified in no library.

She swallowed hard. "As the most illustrious member of the Clan MacPherson, Your Grace," she said, "although not, of course, the chief, I wonder if you have helped set the policy for this neighborly assistance?"

"Of course I have not," he replied. "As you have just pointed out, I am not the chief."

"But Lord Mure told me that you had come to Scotland to execute some family business, I believe, in Edinburgh. That business must pertain to the sale of MacLaurin land, no?"

The pleasant mask of his expression had not changed, but she could see that he was displeased. "I am a co-signer of the transfer documents, yes. I hardly need stress my position in the world to you, Mistress Cameron" He paused and added, "Although having repeatedly stressed it seems to have had little effect on you."

She crossed the line from being merely bold to becoming foolhardy. "You didn't recognize me when we were introduced, did you, Your Grace?"

"How could I have recognized you, Mistress Cameron?"

"When I was introduced to you, I recalled that you had made one visit to Cameron lands and that I was presented to you then. I was about ten years old at the time. Do you remember the occasion, Your Grace?"

"Perhaps. I am surprised, however, that you do, my child."

"Why should I not have remembered? I was certainly old enough to retain the memory of it."

"I do not recall that I was introduced to you by name."

"Should that make a difference in my memory of the occasion, Your Grace? It came to me, at some point during the last several days, that I had seen you on more than just that one occasion. My first memory was very hazy. Perhaps I was only five. You might have put me on your knee. My other memory was clearer, but in another sense more distant. I must have been fifteen at the time. You made your visit to my—my—"

Here she faltered. She was suddenly embarrassed to pronounce the word *father* when she was looking into a pair of eyes so similar to her own.

She did not have the look of a Cameron. She did not have the look of a MacLaurin. She did not have the look of a MacPherson, either, or of a member of any other Highland clan. Did she—horrible, dangerous, enticing thought—have the look of an English Havinghurst?

"My father," she continued, trying to gain control over her flush, "without asking to see me. From an upstairs window I caught a glimpse of you on horseback, leaving the house. I asked who you were, and I was told that His Grace, the Duke of Devonshire had come.''

His Grace remained cool. "What makes you think that I was the one to have come on those three separate, imperfectly remembered occasions, my child?''

She lowered her eyes, and when she raised them again she was sure. Her knowledge spread through her as startling, happy and heartbreaking. It caught at her throat and squeezed her heart. She resisted it, too. She slipped her hand into her pocket to grasp the locket. She wondered under what circumstances she had been conceived but decided that it didn't truly matter. She had formed too much of herself alone to ever be fully his. However, she was enough of his daughter to play her part to the end.

"Because I suspect that your philanthropic impulses, Your Grace, have led you to contribute to the general well-being of the Cameron estate," she said, "for the past twenty-four years.''

His Grace's eyes glittered with admiration of her acumen and with anger at being touched at such close range. "Joseph Cameron has a wretched head for finances," he said, "and perhaps I should mention that a streak of gross impracticality runs in the Cameron clan. Which brings me to an important point—''

Before he could state that point, the carriage came to a heaving halt. Elizabeth's heart twisted to hear the sounds of a familiar voice calling anxiously, "Yer Grace! Yer Grace!''

Chapter Twenty-Seven

His Grace commented tranquilly, "Now all the accounts will be brought to order." Reaching forward to unlatch the carriage door, he commanded, smooth as silk, "Before I greet Joseph Cameron, I shall ask you, my child, to put into my safekeeping the documents that prompted your ill-advised trip to Castle Cairn."

She was more her father's daughter than she cared to admit. With matching smoothness she replied, "What documents?"

His Grace's voice was cold. It seemed he had finished with the games of hide-and-seek he had played the week long. "I am referring to the documents that were apparently sent to you some days ago from London."

She was surprised, because she knew that she had never specified to Lord Mure how she had come across these documents. She didn't waste further time in denial. Instead, she said the first things that came to mind. "First of all, how do you know that they were sent to me? Second of all, how do you know that they came from London?"

She was about to demand further, *And why would you care about love letters that Gavin MacLaurin wrote to Katherine Cameron?* when she stopped, mouth open.

The answers to her questions had come to her in a blinding flash.

She and MacLaurin had been following a false trail. The document they had been seeking did not concern Allegra's birth and had nothing to do with Lieutenant Beverly's indiscretions. The document they had been seeking concerned her own birth and the very private affairs of His Grace, the Duke of Devonshire.

No wonder, then, that His Grace had been willing to fight a duel with Lieutenant Beverly. No wonder that he had come so unexpectedly to Castle Cairn. No wonder that he had seemed to have been a step ahead of them at every moment.

She could not help it; she looked straight at His Grace's jacket, and His Grace noted the line of her gaze. She imagined that he carried the document safe in an inside breast pocket. But what, exactly, was the nature of that document? Could it be, perhaps, a letter written by Gavin MacLaurin to Katherine Cameron? One that formed a part of the collection that had been sent to her from London—the most incriminating one that alluded to Katherine's pregnancy and cursed the name of the father?

His Grace did not answer her questions, nor did he press her just then to give him what he wanted. Instead, he turned the latch at the very moment the carriage door was opened from the outside, and she was looking into the flushed and very harassed face of Joseph Cameron.

Joseph Cameron looked from His Grace to Elizabeth, then back to His Grace. He must have felt something of the delicate tension in the air, for his harassed flush became apologetic. "Yer Grace found her!" he expostulated, then recovered himself. "That is to say, good day to Yer Grace! I see that Yer Grace means to escort my wayward daughter to her home.''

"Yes, Joseph, I have found her," His Grace replied calmly as he descended from the carriage. He turned and extended his hand imperiously to help Elizabeth descend.

"Elizabeth!" Cameron uttered darkly, glowering at her.

She accepted His Grace's hand and stepped down into the summer sun and onto the hard-packed dirt of the road. She looked with new eyes upon the man with red-gold hair, green eyes and ruddy skin who had given her a name and a home. Her feelings were complicated, even contradictory.

"Hello, Father," she greeted him, for the sake of form.

"Ye've a deal of explaining to do, my girl!" Cameron reprimanded, but he was not interested to hear those explanations yet. He turned immediately to His Grace and launched into self-justifications that would have been disturbing and mysterious to Elizabeth if she had not already solved the central mystery.

"I returned from Glasgow only this morning, and I rode over here the moment I learned she had left for Castle Cairn!" Here Cameron gestured toward the sweating horse whose reins had been put in the hands of one of His Grace's postilions. "I have never given her my permission, Your Grace, to attend the summer meetings. 'Twas forbidden, in fact!"

His Grace remained unperturbed. "So I was told when I met her, and thus I was aware from the beginning that you had no hand in her decision to attend the meeting. I do not blame you."

"I've kept her away from Castle Cairn all these years," Cameron continued, obviously determined to clear himself of any wrongdoing. "I tried my best to keep her from attending the Royal Historical Society meetings altogether, but she wouldn't hear of it, and in the end, I saw no harm in her pursuit of the old history. In fact, it seemed to make her happy!"

"I am glad to hear it," His Grace soothed, "and, of course, there is little harm in one's interest in ancient history." He slanted a glance at Elizabeth. "She has an aptitude for library work."

"Ah, 'twas the Castle Cairn library I thought most—" Cameron broke off, and Elizabeth surmised that he would have completed his thought with the word *dangerous*. It must have dawned on him then that his protests and exculpations were strangely revealing. "I mean to say that she's been pursuing her unbecoming practices for too long, and I've always held the opinion that a week's study of history is unladylike!"

"You need say no more, Joseph," His Grace said. "I have become acquainted with Mistress Cameron over the past week, and I must say that she is a determined young lady."

Cameron looked at Elizabeth, his expression a hapless composition of worry and fear and exasperation and affection. It was plain that he had never understood his adopted daughter very well. "Yer Grace calls it determination, then?" he replied. "I call it a disgrace when a lass won't obey her—her—"

"Father," His Grace supplied. "You are quite right, Joseph, and you have been a fine parent. However, I became aware during the course of the week that I had been remiss in not paying you a visit in what must be almost ten years now. I learned, for instance, that in the meantime Mistress Cameron has been named guardian to a young girl whose name is, I believe, Allegra."

Cameron heaved a heavy sigh. "If Yer Grace thought that she put up a fight to join the Royal Historical Society, Yer Grace should know that—"

His Grace held up his hand. "We have agreed that Mistress Cameron is a determined young lady who knows what she wants and who follows through to achieve her ends at all costs."

Those words produced a chill that shivered down Elizabeth's spine. She shied from the implications. How ruthless could she be? How ruthless could His Grace be?

"If I've a reprimand to make, Joseph," His Grace said at his silkiest, "it's that this determined young lady is not yet married."

Cameron scowled and grumbled and cast a baleful look at Elizabeth. "Well, now, there has been a respectable prospect or two...." he said.

"Walter MacPhee," His Grace replied. "Yes, I know all about that failed alliance and, again, I regret not having helped guide your hand through the delicate business. Now, however, I think it imperative that, without further delay, Elizabeth be put in the care of a man who will protect her and establish her place in the world. You will not live forever, Joseph Cameron."

Cameron's baleful expression became perplexed, as if he wondered what sense Elizabeth could be making of this extremely peculiar discussion.

Elizabeth was making more sense of it than Joseph Cameron could have guessed. Of a sudden, she realized that she had been had. His Grace was manipulating her at will, and he had tricked her into leaving Castle Cairn with him. She guessed that MacLaurin was not engaged to be married to anyone in London, while she was being returned to the Cameron estate to be married off to the first eligible man of His Grace's choosing.

No daughter of the Duke of Devonshire would ever be allied to a MacLaurin man. Not that Ian MacLaurin had ever intended to marry her, of course—and not that he would ever consider it now, anyway, since she had left him standing on the half landing of the staircase to depart in company of his father's rival.

She could perceive now the web that had been woven around her and in which she had been caught. Had such a web been woven around her mother, so that her only course of escape was disgrace and death? It was an unpleasant notion. Nevertheless, she knew that His Grace would stop at nothing to keep her from MacLaurin, just as it seemed he had stopped at nothing to keep Katherine from Gavin. In fact, he had just told her as much.

Cameron's ruddy skin darkened several shades. He, too, seemed to have inferred something unpleasant from His Grace's statement. He repeated, "Imperative? Without further delay?"

His Grace smiled gently. "I hope you know, Joseph, that I am not one to exaggerate. However, on occasion, I will emphasize for effect. You see, the neighborhood is, perhaps, not as secure as it has been in the past ten years."

"Past ten years?" Cameron echoed, frowning mightily. "That was about the time that Ian MacLaurin ran off."

His Grace's gentle smile acquired a blade-sharp edge. "Was it, indeed? Well, now, he has returned. I am happy to say that the MacLaurin wolves, although always a hungry breed, are still easily scared off. So, you see, I do not exaggerate. I emphasize, only, as a precaution. I daresay Ian MacLaurin is returning to London, as we speak."

At that moment the bloodthirsty cry of *"Craig Tuirc!"* rent the peace of the summer afternoon as a horse and rider crested the slight rise to the side of the road.

Elizabeth hardly had time to register the significance of the MacLaurin battle slogan before the rider dismounted, sword in hand, with a swirl of green-and-brown plaid belted into a kilt. The remaining folds of his tartan were draped over his left shoulder under which he wore a white shirt. The man looked strong and wild and ready for battle, with black hair flying untamed around his shoulders.

It took a moment for Elizabeth to realize that she was looking not at some Highland man of yore, but at Ian MacLaurin. His Grace must have realized it sooner, for he moved swiftly back into the carriage. Swerving her head to watch him, Elizabeth saw with horror that His Grace reached up to unclasp some latches on the interior ceiling of the carriage, pulled down a hidden compartment and withdrew a sheathed sword.

When Devonshire reemerged from the carriage, armed, MacLaurin was hardly disappointed. He raised his sword and challenged, "It's a long and old score we have to settle, Devonshire."

"It is, my lad?" Devonshire replied, sliding his sword from its jeweled scabbard. "I am not aware that there's anything between us or that it could be very old."

"I shall be glad to refresh your memory," MacLaurin returned, "if you care to take off your jacket and meet me on my terms."

"Your terms?" Devonshire taunted lightly, flexing his wrist. "I shall refresh your memory first, my lad, by reminding you that the tender flesh of a friend of yours ate the tip of my steel as recently as last week."

"I know you rate your skill with a sword high, Devonshire," MacLaurin stated, "but I've yet to see you prove it."

Devonshire was not yet ready to engage. "Ah, my fire-breathing youth, you are foolhardy."

"You, Devonshire, are a coward, a liar and a rogue."

The older man's aristocratic features froze a moment in disbelief at the brash, unbearable insult. Then he slipped out of his jacket and handed it to Joseph Cameron, who accepted it with one hand and an expression of bewildered horror. Cameron's gaze drifted to Elizabeth. He favored her with an accusatory look, as if he had decided that this extraordinary scene must be all her fault.

His Grace tucked up the ruffles at his wrists. "You, MacLaurin," he replied with truly magnificent scorn, "are a disinherited Scot and a common locksmith."

"An uncommon one, if you please," MacLaurin replied, taking no offense. "As for my inheritance—or lack thereof—I can assure you that I shall stop you before another acre of MacLaurin land is lost to the MacPhersons. You will not sign those papers in Edinburgh."

MacLaurin lifted his sword in formal salute. Devonshire's sword answered swiftly. On a quiet summer's afternoon nothing could be heard save the measured clash and scrape of steel. Nothing could be seen beyond the flashes of liquid sunlight caught in brandishing metal. It was hard fighting in the first minutes. Devonshire's arm benefited from experience and expertise and the habit of hatred. MacLaurin unleashed on his opponent a lifetime's frustration fueled by a fresh desire to avenge his father's restless ghost and to fight for the woman he loved.

Elizabeth moved toward Joseph Cameron, who automatically put his free arm around her shoulder for support and comfort. She clutched her hands together prayerfully, completely at the mercy of the emotions colliding in her breast. She saw MacLaurin as her knight come to life, not in armor, of course, but in familiar kilts. When he raised his sword to meet his opponent's, she saw his loyalty and virtue, his strength and purpose. She knew that he was destined to rescue her, just as she had imagined he would when she had first seen him stride across the entry hall at Castle Cairn. However, in rescuing her, he would forever negate the possibility of their love by slaying the man who had given her life. Or perhaps—more horrible thought—he was destined to be slain himself in the effort.

Devonshire took the early offensive. He was determined to taunt. "Is that what you want, then?" he said, wielding his sword so that it rang harshly against MacLaurin's. "To save your pitiful estate after decades of wretched management?"

"No, I want Elizabeth."

Devonshire pressed his attack, as if he meant to make short work of an unworthy opponent. "You cannot have her. You will have to kill me first."

"I shall not put myself in such a difficult position with my future wife," MacLaurin said, fending off a vigorous attack, "by killing you, Devonshire. You'll not have that satisfaction."

Devonshire's fine brows quirked. Sweat beaded on his brow. "So you know."

"You'd be surprised at what I know."

"But what good is all that knowledge?" Devonshire wondered, swinging with speed and accuracy. "I am as likely to kill you, my lad, and send you to an early grave with all that knowledge."

"You'd better kill me soon, then," MacLaurin said, fending off yet another skillful blow, "because I claim that you used Katherine Cameron to destroy my father."

Devonshire's sure step faltered, but he quickly regained his footing. "No!" His denial was vehement, and his breath came more heavily now with his exertions.

"You're saying that you didn't destroy my father? That you haven't been wanting to wipe the MacLaurins off the map for the past quarter century?" As MacLaurin pressed in word, he also pressed in deed. "You and my father were friends in the old days."

"When I came to the Grampians in the summers, as a youth, we were friends, yes."

"And then rivals. For Katherine Cameron."

Devonshire gritted his teeth, against the force of his opponent's sword, against the emotion that was figured on his face. "I didn't use her," he grated.

"Ah?" It was MacLaurin's turn to taunt. "An honest emotion, Devonshire? Did you love her?"

"She couldn't make up her mind," Devonshire said. "I aided her decision."

"By sending my father away?"

"He left, the fool," Devonshire said. He was beginning to pant. "I arranged for urgent MacLaurin business to be conducted in London. He had no choice, because the estate was at stake. He thought she would wait for him."

"Leaving the field for you?"

"He...Gavin...thought I had left for London, as well," Devonshire admitted.

"Then you forced Katherine to your will."

"No!" Again, Devonshire's denial was vehement. "She chose!" he insisted. "She *chose!*"

"And you refused to marry her?" MacLaurin's blade took on a life of its own. "I called you a rogue," he grated. "I was too kind!"

The words that Devonshire uttered were startling. "She wouldn't...have me...in the end. She...wanted... Gavin."

MacLaurin struggled to grasp the implications. Devonshire had asked Katherine to marry him, and although she was pregnant with his child, she had refused him.

"You've kept quite a secret," MacLaurin observed easily. He had a second wind, given to him by his youth and his righteousness.

"The only thing...I hate...more than losing," Devonshire ground out, "is having my loss...made public."

MacLaurin perceived, then, the weight and curse of pride, pure and marrow deep. It was Devonshire's self-loving pride that Katherine must have recognized too late, and in refusing him, she had dealt a blow to that pride from which he had never recovered. MacLaurin was satisfied that his father's rival had suffered. He was satisfied that Devonshire had loved Katherine Cameron but not with the warmth and depth with which his father had loved her.

MacLaurin found his opening and the precise spot he had been aiming for since the opening salute. He lunged forward, and Devonshire's sword clattered to the ground. The older man staggered back with a hand clapped to his right arm.

MacLaurin did not wipe his wet blade, but planted it red streaked into the ground between his widespread feet. He looked down where Devonshire had fallen to a crouch. "I had no purpose to kill you before Elizabeth's eyes. However, I am assured that you won't be using that arm to sign any papers for a long time.''

Devonshire rose to his feet, swayed slightly, then steadied himself. ''Is this how you think to win her, then, by besting me?''

''No,'' MacLaurin said, ''I think to win her with words. I intend to cultivate what I've inherited of my father's gifts, after all.''

Chapter Twenty-Eight

Elizabeth turned wide eyes toward Joseph Cameron. "Is it true," she asked bluntly, "that my mother refused him?"

Cameron heaved his shoulders as if releasing himself from an old and heavy weight. "She wouldn't have him," he said, "and there was naught I could say nor do to change her mind. She was determined to wait for Gavin's return and to beg his forgiveness."

"But she chose, no?" she asked tremulously.

Joseph Cameron's eyes were sad. "It seems she made her choice of her own free will, then realized she had made a mistake. But she was not willing to make another one by marrying the wrong man. In the end, of course, in the end..."

In the end her mother had lost both her love and her life, and Joseph Cameron had been there, steadfast and stalwart, to pick up the pieces after Katherine's death and Elizabeth's birth. She looked into his eyes and understood the burden that he had carried all these years. It was a burden that had not been, had never been, the fact of Elizabeth's existence, but the burden of a proud and active clansman who had never been able to properly or publicly mourn his loss.

Her mother might have made a mistake, but Joseph Cameron had never made Elizabeth feel like one. She saw in her harassed, over-protective, often irascible uncle a man who had done his best, and she knew, from the rush of love she felt for him, that his best had far surpassed "good enough." She was happy to share the burden of unhappy history with him. She was happy to realize that he would always, in some sense, be her father. She was happy to confirm with a kiss on his cheek and a tear in her eye that she would always, in a true sense, be his daughter.

Joseph Cameron kissed her back and squeezed her once. Then, without explanation, he handed her His Grace's jacket and pushed her gently in the wounded man's direction.

She glanced at His Grace and saw a man whose pride had been momentarily stripped from him, but not his dignity. He had refused the solicitous help offered him by his coachman and was leaning against the door to the carriage. She moved toward him, and his gray eyes came to focus on her. He was still holding his arm, where the stain of red had spread to a stop on his white shirt. He had recovered his breath and his composure. She could not judge whether he meant to be difficult or not. Even in defeat he looked formidable.

She bent to retrieve his discarded sword, slid it into its opulent scabbard and propped the sheathed weapon against the side of the carriage. Then she moved in front of him and touched the hand he had clamped over his forearm to remove it. He resisted her touch. She drew a breath and gently but forcefully removed his hand to inspect the wound. The blood was still fresh, but it was starting to clot, and she could see that the slit was clean.

"Does it hurt?" she asked, daring to look into gray eyes.

"The tendon is cut," he replied without emotion, "and it will heal with little trouble and much time."

"Then let me help you into your jacket, Your Grace," she said, "and I shall seat you in the carriage."

His eyes narrowed before a shadow of pleasure crossed his grim features. "I shall accept help with the jacket, Mistress Cameron," he replied, "but I assure you that I am capable of seating myself."

So saying, he pushed himself away from the carriage, which was holding him up. He permitted Elizabeth to slip his wounded arm into one sleeve, then winced with the effort to slip his left arm into the other sleeve without unduly wrenching his right.

She pulled the beautifully cut jacket over his shoulder and smoothed the lapels. In performing these tender ministrations her hand passed over a thin bulge with squared edges. It was no doubt a folded letter lodged in an inside pocket of his jacket. She thoughtfully patted the document he carried over his heart, then removed her hand. Some secrets he should be allowed to preserve. She was not going to ask him to show the letter to her. Nor was she even going to mention it.

Instead she said, "I would like to see you again, Your Grace." She swallowed hard. "Preferably before another five or ten years pass."

He nodded graciously. "I should like that, too, Mistress Cameron." He glanced over her shoulder, referring with his eyes to the man who stood behind her and whose sword had not yet been wiped of his blood. "Do you mean to see me alone, or do you mean to see me in company with him?"

Her heart leapt at the possibilities embedded in the very frame of the question. "With MacLaurin, Your Grace."

"You sound determined, Mistress Cameron."

"I am," she said, adding audaciously, "I seem to have inherited the quality from both sides."

The man who had loved unwisely and not quite well enough replied with a piece of parental advice. "Then you must be doubly careful with that determination. And remember that if you marry where I do not like, you may receive no further inheritance from me."

He acknowledged her in the very act of denying her, but it was acknowledgment just the same. She suppressed a smile, and her voice was admirably sober. "Yes, you have said that a streak of gross impracticality runs in the Cameron clan."

His Grace looked down at his right sleeve and the minute stain of rust that had seeped through the gray silk. "As well as a faulty taste in men."

He did not want her sympathy. She would give him none. She smiled. "Speaking of defects of the Clan Cameron, would you happen to know, Your Grace, where our genealogy is?"

"Curious, Mistress Cameron?"

"My besetting sin," she replied, "along with my determination, my impracticality and my wretched taste for MacLaurin men."

He answered her, "I must suppose that it is in the Castle Cairn library, on the shelves where sit the other genealogies."

"Oh, did you put it back there, then?"

His expression was unreadable, but she thought she caught a twinkle in his eye. "Do you ask, perhaps, because you looked on the shelves and did not find it?"

"Yes, three evenings ago I searched the genealogies and found neither the MacLaurin nor the Cameron volume."

"Well, then, they may well be shelved in another area of the library."

"Ah, but when I looked in that other area," she said, giving the word *other* suggestive overtones, "I did not find it there, either. However, I did come across the MacLaurin volume."

His Grace appraised her coolly. "What do you know of that other area, Mistress Cameron?"

"As much as you do, Your Grace."

"If you know so much about it, then I can tell you that two nights ago I transferred the Cameron volume from the library annex to the main room." He paused. "I arrived there just after you and MacLaurin had left."

"I figured as much, for when we returned last night—" She broke off and regarded him with surprise. "How did you know we were there?"

"From the drifts of smoke that rose from the extinguished candles. You must have left only moments before Robbie and I arrived."

"Yes, but how did you know it was *us?*"

His Grace's eyes glittered wickedly. "I didn't, until now that you have just admitted it. Tell me, is there a back entrance to the annex?"

She knew there would be no repairing her mistake. "You will have to ask MacLaurin, Your Grace."

His eyes glittered with a different force when he said sternly, "You will permit me to mention, Mistress Cameron, that the library annex is a most unsuitable place for a young lady to visit with a young man."

For a response, she blushed and lowered her eyes.

"Most unsuitable," he repeated with audible displeasure, and flicked another glance over her shoulder at MacLaurin.

He was about to say something further, possibly on the subject of young ladies and young men, when his attention, and everyone else's, was diverted by the appearance of yet another player on the scene.

A carriage had clattered to a halt behind His Grace's, and out stepped a magnificently dressed man, the likes of whom Elizabeth had never seen. He was neither young nor old. He wore a long purple cloak, rose lined, which hung from his shoulders and which fell carelessly back from his dress, revealing a full-skirted coat of purple satin laced with gold, a waistcoat of flowered silk and faultless small clothes. His *tenue* was completed by a sprinkling of jewels on his cravat and breast, and a three-cornered hat that was set upon his powdered wig. In his hand he carried a long, beribboned cane.

Elizabeth was both disconcerted and suspicious. For no conscious reason she stepped in front of the scabbard that she had leaned against the carriage, so that it was hidden by her skirts. In the same movement she had placed herself next to His Grace in such a stance that anyone looking casually upon them would not be able to see the spot of blood that stained his sleeve. She noted with interest that MacLaurin had taken similar precautions, for when she looked up and over at him, she saw that he had sheathed his sword in the scabbard that hung from his saddle.

The middle-aged exquisite minced forward with all the elegance of one descending a fashionable London thoroughfare. He looked about him with exaggerated admiration and wonder. "Ah, the rare beauty of the Scottish countryside," he commented soulfully. "It quite takes my breath away, just as it did take my breath away those many years ago when I last visited." He bowed. "Give you good day, Edmund."

His Grace bowed slightly and said one word. "Rupert."

The exquisite looked about him again, his gaze moving lazily from His Grace to Elizabeth to Joseph Cameron. He started visibly when his eye fell upon the fourth member of the set. "Why, MacLaurin!" he squeaked. "I hardly recognized you! My, my, but you are looking so...rustic."

MacLaurin's face did not move a muscle. He said, "Warenne," and left it at that.

The hairs on Elizabeth's nape rose in alarm. One word in her brain was attached to the name Rupert Warenne. Unscrupulous was the man who had set into motion an extraordinary chain of events when he staked a sensitive document in a card game where he was losing by twenty thousand pounds. His very presence suggested to Elizabeth that he had not foreseen the strange turn those events would take and had come to Scotland to repair what he could of a brilliant plan gone awry.

"And you are looking so fierce, if I may say," Rupert Warenne continued, inspecting MacLaurin with interest, "just as one would imagine a clansman. Are you carrying—what is it called, now?—a claymore, perhaps? Such a charming weapon." He appeared to reconsider his opinion. "But a bit clumsy, perhaps."

MacLaurin did not dignify those remarks with a reply.

Warenne was not waiting for one, either. He continued. "But I could not expect all my Highland fantasies to come true, just like that." Here he waved his beribboned cane as if it were a magic wand. "And yet, as I stand here among such a very... unusual assortment of people, I cannot help but think that dark doings are afoot, truly worthy of Highland dash and daring. Or am I too late?"

"Too late for what, Rupert?" His Grace inquired with silky charm. "From the direction that you have been traveling, I surmise that you have lately come from Castle Cairn. Surely you learned there that you have arrived too late, indeed, for the summer meeting of the Royal Historical Society. It ended this morning."

Elizabeth forbore to look at His Grace when he made this speech, fearing that her concern for his well-being would be too evident in her expression. She was glad to hear that his voice was controlled. She only hoped that he would have the strength to make it through this strenuous occasion without exhausting himself.

"I learned that, of course," Warenne said, his smile indulgent, "from Juliette Michael. She was inclined to think that you, Edmund, were preoccupied this week, apparently lost in the fascinations of the past! But, of course, I do not refer to the fact that I arrived too late for the meeting of the Royal Historical Society, which is not, I fear, at all in my style of entertainment.

"Having said that, however, I do confess to my share of interest in history and in the lengths one will go—shall we say?—to conceal its most telling secrets. Oh, yes! Let me say, rather, that I wondered at first whether I was too late for... a duel, but since no one lies prostrate upon the ground, I must suppose that I have interrupted the promising beginnings to one."

MacLaurin moved away from his horse and toward the newcomer. "Why would you imagine that, Warenne?"

Warenne's response was oblique. "Did you know that I met your father—dear me, it must have been some twenty-five years ago now—when he traveled to London?''

"I've known you these past six years, Warenne, and you never mentioned it before."

"But seeing you in your very charming kilts reminded me of it, as well as the fact that a little more than twenty-four years ago I made my last trip to these parts." Warenne smiled. "After I had met your father."

Joseph Cameron had been eyeing Rupert Warenne suspiciously. At that, he stepped forward and said, "I met you then, Mr. Warenne, if you'll remember."

"How could I forget?" Warenne wondered, amazed afresh by all his startling recollections. "You are Joseph Cameron, brother to the very beautiful Katherine Cameron, are you not?" His eyes went misty. "I recall meeting her then, as well. Very briefly, one beautiful April afternoon. Perhaps you were not even aware of our meeting, Mr. Cameron." He sighed. "Such a memorable young woman. And in the fullness of impending motherhood."

Joseph Cameron was no fool. He said bluntly, "You were remembering my wife who was carrying our child at the time."

"Was I?" Warenne paused to reflect. He waved his cane again, coming back to his senses. "Ah, but no, I don't think I misremembered the woman, her name or her condition. I have, sir, an excellent memory."

"Memory is a fickle jade, sir," Cameron said. "My wife gave birth to my daughter, Elizabeth, twenty-four years ago."

Warenne rolled lively eyes now in Elizabeth's direction. "Mistress Cameron?" he inquired. He bowed deeply and doffed his hat with a flourish. "Mistress Elizabeth Cameron?"

"Yes, I am Elizabeth Cameron," she said evenly.

"You are a member of the Royal Historical Society, are you not?" Warenne asked.

"I am."

"I have heard of you and your skill with old records and documents, Mistress Cameron," Warenne said. "Why, I even corresponded with you recently. I sent you some papers."

"Did you?" Elizabeth replied.

She had guessed by now that Warenne's game was blackmail. She also guessed that he must be gambling on the possibility that she desired, as much as he did, to profit from her secret heritage. He must have sent her the less revelatory letters that Gavin wrote Katherine in hopes that she would be interested to unravel the mystery. Or perhaps he had sent them to her as a safeguard, knowing her to be a historian who would be likely to preserve the letters until he might need them again.

"Why, yes, mistress."

"I do not recall receiving any documents in the mail."

"Perhaps you did not realize they came from me," Warenne said pleasantly, "and that is why I have come to Scotland." He bowed. "To repair that omission, and to introduce myself to you."

She was pleasantly apologetic in return. "There is no omission to repair, sir. I fear you have come on a useless errand. I know of no documents."

Warenne's crafty eyes narrowed, as if trying to gauge the truth of her denial. "I sent them several weeks ago, I believe. Are you sure you received nothing?"

Elizabeth appeared to give the matter some thought. Then she widened her eyes and said, "Oh, but I did receive a packet! I'm afraid that I didn't look at it carefully when I first received it, for I was busy with chores, and it looked to be filled with old papers that I would want to read at my leisure. I was sorry that I negligently left them on the kitchen worktable, for they fell to the floor, and sometime later when I went looking for them to read them over carefully, I learned that Catrina, the serving girl, had swept them into the fire. *Those* must be the documents you are referring to!''

Warenne looked mighty surprised and displeased by this news. He also did not look willing to swallow the lie whole. His gaze shifted pointedly from Elizabeth's face to His Grace's, and his recognition of their family resemblance could be read plainly in his expression. He was not yet defeated.

''It's a pity,'' Warenne said lightly. He was apparently a man who could cut his losses, for he looked next at MacLaurin, hoping to seek advantage in that quarter. ''Yet—and yet!—it is a strange composition I have stumbled upon here!'' He gazed about him with every evidence of deep appreciation. ''As delightful as this turning in the road may be, I cannot think that this is a friendly encounter, my dear Ian, between you and Edmund. There has never been any love lost between you, I think, and so it would please me enormously to learn what business has brought you to this precise spot and this precise time!''

MacLaurin knew how to play this one. ''I owe you no explanation, Warenne. In any case, the nature of our business here is private.''

Warenne smiled in anticipation. ''Private, dear boy?''

''Very private,'' MacLaurin acknowledged. ''Between me, Devonshire and Gabriel Beverly.''

Warenne's smile evaporated. ''Beverly?'' he repeated with a flash of irritation.

"You are quite right that a duel was in the offing this afternoon," MacLaurin said, "at least in my mind! I came to avenge Bev's defeat last week at Devonshire's hands. However, since Devonshire's head is cooler than mine, he was able to explain to me just now how Bev had cheated him, and he was able to do so without spilling any more blood—namely mine!"

Warenne seemed to be assimilating with difficulty the fact that the marplot, Beverly, would foil him from beginning to end. "So you came to Scotland to avenge Bev's defeat and were persuaded from your errand?"

MacLaurin had closed ranks with the Camerons. "I came a very long way for nothing, Warenne." He had no intention of exposing Devonshire to any form of disgrace. "And so have you."

Recognizing his own defeat, Warenne turned away with an angry swish of rose-lined purple satin and climbed into his carriage. He commanded the driver to turn back around. As the dust from the churning carriage wheels clouded upward, His Grace collapsed in Elizabeth's arms.

Chapter Twenty-Nine

Elizabeth struggled with his weight and was immediately assisted by both Cameron and MacLaurin.

She was worried. His Grace's face was ashen, and the rust spot on his upper right sleeve was spreading. The wound must have opened with the strain of concealing his condition for so long. She did not want to jolt his arm unnecessarily, so while Cameron opened the carriage door and MacLaurin momentarily bore his full weight, she ripped the jacket sleeve from its shoulder seam and stripped it off his arm. With the length of gray silk she bound the wound to stanch the blood.

"Unnecessarily dramatic, my child," His Grace managed. "You have ruined a perfectly good suit."

"You can afford another one," she replied and commanded, "Don't speak."

His Grace was in no condition to disobey her, for his arm had begun to ache unbearably. He sighed and closed his eyes against the inevitable jars and jolts of being maneuvered into his carriage by three people.

When the patient was in a half-seated position and as comfortable as he was going to be, MacLaurin helped Elizabeth out of the carriage, then climbed out after her. "Joseph, you stay here with Devonshire," MacLaurin said, holding the carriage door open. "I shall tell the driver to move on out. Do you know of a local surgeon?"

Cameron confirmed that he did.

"I shall sort out what needs to be done with your horse and Elizabeth's carriage," MacLaurin said to Cameron, clearly in command of the situation, "and bring her back to you in time."

Cameron looked at Devonshire who looked at MacLaurin. "In time?" Devonshire queried. His voice was weak, but his meaning was strong.

"This afternoon," MacLaurin confirmed. "We've one or two things to establish between us."

Devonshire did not immediately reply. At last he said, "Yes," and with that one syllable he righted decades of wrongs.

"You'll be returning to London?" MacLaurin asked him.

"Eventually," Devonshire confirmed. His voice was now weary.

"Do you need for me to return to London, as well, to ensure that Warenne is properly chained, if not muzzled?"

This polite offer brought the life back to Devonshire's face. "You need do nothing further for me, my lad," he said with a cold, alert light in his eyes. "As for my dear friend Rupert..." His voice trailed off, but not for lack of strength.

Indeed, the gears of his internal mechanism seemed to have reengaged, and his voice had regained its ring of authority when Devonshire continued, "As for Rupert, I admire his cunning, and I must say that I understand what must be his current frustration. He held in his possession the key to a vast fortune. To have been foiled by that idiot puppy Beverly—I beg your pardon, Mac-Laurin, if he is truly a friend of yours—"

MacLaurin bowed, ironically.

"—was an error, surely, but not a fatal one, I think. However, to have waited a quarter century only to find, in the end, that his timing was off by not more than a quarter hour...ah, that must be galling." He smiled. "Positively galling."

MacLaurin was much struck by this. "Had he arrived fifteen minutes earlier, he would now be a very happy man."

Devonshire's smile was wintry. "However, as it stands," he said with complete satisfaction, "Rupert is not only unhappy, but decidedly impoverished. His finances have sunk in the past two quarters to a new low, which is why, no doubt, he thought to cash in the financial insurance policy of Gavin's letters now. I think he meant to live off my continually well-managed funds, perhaps for the rest of his life." He closed his eyes, breathed in deeply and twitched a little at the pain in his arm. "Poor Rupert. He will soon be utterly ruined."

"He will?" Elizabeth asked, apprehensive of the note in His Grace's voice.

Her rich and ruthless father opened his eyes and regarded her. "You must understand, my child, that Rupert Warenne is one of my oldest cronies. I certainly know enough about his life to destroy him, just as he has lived all these years with his knowledge of my life." He smiled indulgently. "He would expect me to exact retribution. In fact, I am sure he would be offended if I did not."

Joseph Cameron chimed in at this point and said, "I'd like to know how he came by Gavin's letters to Katherine."

His Grace said in his customarily silky tones, "I am sure you would not." He closed his eyes again and drew another deep breath. It seemed that his one desire at the moment was to enjoy the contemplation of Rupert Warenne's ruin.

MacLaurin closed the carriage door, nodded a goodbye to Joseph Cameron and directed the coachman to depart. Then he took Elizabeth's hand in his. He crossed the road with her, passed by his horse and waded into the meadow beyond the rise that sloped down into a hidden valley.

"You've really no choice, you know," she said, finding herself knee-deep in heather.

"I know."

"Well, you needn't sound so glum about it."

"It's a sorrowful moment, lass, when a man's stiff tongue is put to the test," he replied. He cleared his throat, then broke out in verse. "An' we'll gang nae mair a-rovin', / A-rovin' in the nicht, / An' we'll gang nae mair a-rovin', / Let the mune shine e'er sae bricht."

"That's *awful*, MacLaurin!"

He turned bright blue dancing eyes on her. "What's this, lass? You told me now that I have no choice. You wanted flowery phrases and that's what I'm trying to provide you."

"No, I meant that you have no choice about *marrying* me."

He waved that triviality away. "Of course I had no choice about that. That was decided some time ago, I'm thinking, that we shall be marrying."

"No, I mean—" she tried again "—that there's no getting around the fact that I am that man's *daughter*. Do you realize it?"

"I do realize it, lass, and am proud to say that I twigged to the solution before you did. Had it been the other way around, you would not have left with him, and I would not have been able to rescue you."

"I mean," she said with determination, "that he's . . . he's a monster! Think of what I must be like, at least in part!"

Again MacLaurin's response was an airy wave of his free hand. "That's why I'm perfectly resigned to marryin' you, lass. Do you think I'm daft enough to refuse to marry the monster's daughter—especially after she's told me I have no choice?"

"MacLaurin, be *serious!*"

"I am perfectly serious, my monstrous Elizabeth, but you keep interrupting me with irrelevancies."

Elizabeth gave up.

MacLaurin thought deeply a moment, then declaimed to the sloping hillside, "Frae bank t' bank, frae wood t' wood I rin, / Owrehailit with my feeble fantasie; / Like til a leaf that fallis frae a tree, / Or til a reed owreblawn with the win'." He looked down at her, his expression comically compounded of distaste and hope. "Was it not too bad?"

She shook her head. "Worse than the first."

"Ah, well! How am I to woo you with words, if you're proof against all my fine verse?"

She laughed. "Flowery phrases, I think I said, not wretched verse. But you hardly need to woo me with words after what you just did to save me."

"Well, that simplifies the matter, surely."

"Or woo me at all," she added.

"But you see, lass, my intention is to woo you, one way or the other."

She was surprised. "In broad daylight?"

He smiled down at her, and she began to have an inkling that daylight might offer some new delights in her experience of him. She could not help but notice that he cut an uncommonly fine figure in his plaid.

Nevertheless, she was still partially awed, still partially appalled by her discoveries of the past hour, so she could not help but press the issue. "Even knowing whose daughter I am?"

He continued to smile down at her when he said, "I suppose I shall have to thank my future father-in-law some day for not having left the field open to my ineffective father. However, the evil one and I have not progressed enough in our relationship for such a discussion, nor are we likely to arrive there anytime soon."

She heard the relish in his voice and drew an unflattering inference. "No doubt you're inclined to marry me in order to annoy His Grace."

He stopped and drew her into his arms. "I'm sure I could find ways to annoy the man without going to such drastic lengths as leg-shackling myself." He kissed her. "In fact, I'm near certain that *not* marrying you would annoy him more." His embrace became more intimate. "But I'll confess, lass, that I loved you before I knew whose daughter you are."

She could imagine a more flowery phrase, but certainly not a more effective one. He released her and took her hand again. She was content to follow behind him on the path he created.

"By the way," she asked, "where are we going?"

"To a wee loch."

Elizabeth scrambled behind him over some ancient rocks and descended the winding, mossy trail until she glimpsed a blue hem of a hidden loch below her. The sun above, the water below, the rocks all around felt infinitely familiar to her and, at the same time, utterly new. She was no longer content to follow along behind him. She stopped, and because she was still holding his hand, she tugged on his arm and drew him to a halt, as well.

He turned and looked at her, a mild question in his beautiful MacLaurin eyes.

"It's just not that simple," she said.

He registered her comment, then cocked his head. "You mean to be difficult, I see."

She shook her head. "No," she said. "You've put on a plaid, and suddenly all is well. It's not that simple."

"I'm trying my old self on for size," he said. "Do you blame me?"

"Well, no," she conceded. "But I do know that when you arrived here last week, you had no intention of staying."

"True enough."

"You were anxious to return to London, to your work," she said, "and to your diversions."

"My diversions were paltry."

She had to smile. "But your work wasn't, according to what I heard."

He frowned a little. "True, but I was glad to learn a new trick or two from the castle, and I'm thinking of making the east wing into my workshop."

"Will it serve?"

"The roof is good."

"I mean, will you be satisfied?"

"That remains to be seen, lass. You might have something to do with my satisfaction, when all is said, and it occurs to me as well that you'll be more than satisfied with the library."

She smiled again, wryly. "I shall! But I don't think you fancy yourself a farmer."

"Neither does my uncle," he replied, "and I've the better head for it."

"But you don't *like* the castle," she protested.

"I didn't like the castle air," he corrected, "but it's clear now, and I can breathe freely."

"What do you mean?"

He shook his head in mock disgust. "I said you'd be the first to know if my plan worked," he said, "and it does, but I was fixing to tell you so down there, *afterward.*"

"Afterward—?" she echoed, then broke off, blushing at his meaning. In some confusion, she said, "But I want to know *now.*"

He drew her into his arms again and took the length of tartan from his shoulder to wrap it around her, binding them together in soft green and brown. "The Mac-Laurin plaid becomes you," he remarked. He kissed her nose. "Now, in finding my own true love," he explained, "I was able to tame my fireplace demons, and in besting my father's rival, I was able to lay my father's ghost to rest. It's what I had to do, if I was ever able to live at Castle Cairn."

Elizabeth imagined that the slumbering stone monster had slept off its enchantment to become again, or perhaps for the first time, an ordinary building. The thought made her sad, but she could not truly sustain the sadness while she stood in his embrace. "But if your fireplace demons are tamed," she said, raising her eyes to meet his, "I'm afraid my fireplace nymphs might be, as well."

He blinked. "Your fireplace nymphs, lass?"

"They would sing to me, you see. . . ." she said, with a slight, mischievous smile of seduction.

He saw. His embrace became more purposeful, and she realized that they would get no farther down the slope.

He dropped his teasing manner. His expression irresistibly blended awe and boyish desire. "I tamed my fireplace demons by drawing them inside of me," he said, putting his lips to her neck. "They are not gone, my delicious and desirous Elizabeth, daughter of a true monster. They are rather at my mercy." His hands were already under her skirts, and his fingers were running rapidly up her thighs.

"You've made me realize that I had underestimated the power of my plan, the *whole* plan," he said. When his fingers reached their goal, he groaned into her neck and began to lay her down, with his plaid for ground cover. "But now that I've a grander vision of it, I'd say that your fireplace nymphs have been spirited inside of you."

Elizabeth luxuriated against him and decided that it must be true. She reached for the clasp of the belt holding the folds of his kilt around his waist. "I've always wanted to know what's under these things."

"Curious?"

"Very."

"I'm bursting with flowery phrases."

"Save them. For afterward."

He smiled. "What's your fancy for now, lass?"

She smiled in return. "It's free."

* * * * *

Harlequin® Historical

WOMEN OF THE WEST

Exciting stories of the old West and the women whose dreams
and passions shaped a new land!

Join Harlequin Historicals every month as we bring you
these unforgettable tales.

Don't miss any of our **Women of the West!**

OFFICIAL RULES
PRIZE SURPRISE SWEEPSTAKES 3448
NO PURCHASE OR OBLIGATION NECESSARY

Three Harlequin Reader Service 1995 shipments will contain respectively, coupons for entry into three different prize drawings, one for a Panasonic 31" wide-screen TV, another for a 5-piece Wedgwood china service for eight and the third for a Sharp ViewCam camcorder. To enter any drawing using an Entry Coupon, simply complete and mail according to directions.

There is no obligation to continue using the Reader Service to enter and be eligible for any prize drawing. You may also enter any drawing by hand printing the words "Prize Surprise," your name and address on a 3"x5" card and the name of the prize you wish that entry to be considered for (i.e., Panasonic wide-screen TV, Wedgwood china or Sharp ViewCam). Send your 3"x5" entries via first-class mail (limit: one per envelope) to: Prize Surprise Sweepstakes 3448, c/o the prize you wish that entry to be considered for, P.O. Box 1315, Buffalo, NY 14269-1315, USA or P.O. Box 610, Fort Erie, Ontario L2A 5X3, Canada.

To be eligible for the Panasonic wide-screen TV, entries must be received by 6/30/95; for the Wedgwood china, 8/30/95; and for the Sharp ViewCam, 10/30/95.

Winners will be determined in random drawings conducted under the supervision of D.L. Blair, Inc., an independent judging organization whose decisions are final, from among all eligible entries received for that drawing. Approximate prize values are as follows: Panasonic wide-screen TV ($1,800); Wedgwood china ($840) and Sharp ViewCam ($2,000). Sweepstakes open to residents of the U.S. (except Puerto Rico) and Canada, 18 years of age or older. Employees and immediate family members of Harlequin Enterprises, Ltd., D.L. Blair, Inc., their affiliates, subsidiaries and all other agencies, entities and persons connected with the use, marketing or conduct of this sweepstakes are not eligible. Odds of winning a prize are dependent upon the number of eligible entries received for that drawing. Prize drawing and winner notification for each drawing will occur no later than 15 days after deadline for entry eligibility for that drawing. Limit: one prize to an individual, family or organization. All applicable laws and regulations apply. Sweepstakes offer void wherever prohibited by law. Any litigation within the province of Quebec respecting the conduct and awarding of the prizes in this sweepstakes must be submitted to the Regies des loteries et Courses du Quebec. In order to win a prize, residents of Canada will be required to correctly answer a time-limited arithmetical skill-testing question. Value of prizes are in U.S. currency.

Winners will be obligated to sign and return an Affidavit of Eligibility within 30 days of notification. In the event of noncompliance within this time period, prize may not be awarded. If any prize or prize notification is returned as undeliverable, that prize will not be awarded. By acceptance of a prize, winner consents to use of his/her name, photograph or other likeness for purposes of advertising, trade and promotion on behalf of Harlequin Enterprises, Ltd., without further compensation, unless prohibited by law.

For the names of prizewinners (available after 12/31/95), send a self-addressed, stamped envelope to: Prize Surprise Sweepstakes 3448 Winners, P.O. Box 4200, Blair, NE 68009.

RPZ KAL